WILD
HORIZON

JAN RUTH

WHITE HORIZON
Copyright Jan Ruth

SECOND EDITION 2013.
(original edition 2012.)

Published by Celtic Connections.

This is a work of fiction. While the locations in this book are a mixture of real and imagined, the characters are totally fictitious. Any resemblance to persons living or dead, is coincidental.

Acknowledgements:

My son; for his patience with all matters technical.
John Hudspith Editing Services:
For super sharp crossing and dotting.
J. D. Smith Design: for beautiful insides and outs.

FOR DAVID

Contents

CHAPTER ONE

Victoria told herself she wasn't remotely interested in Daniel and Tina's wedding. Even so, she found herself drawn to the article in the local press with a slightly cynical smile. The smile was down to an old blurry photograph of the happy couple, speeding across the local school field on a motorbike, and just out of shot, an enraged headmaster.

The Welsh Coast Weekly made their subsequent life story sound like a low budget film. There was mention of some kind of controversial inheritance, how it had sealed their fate to return to their home town after some twenty years, to be married in the local church. Given their Bonnie and Clyde style status at school, Victoria had always imagined they would get hitched somewhere like Las Vegas, or John o' Groats. Oh, and his proposal was the result of a *drunken pact!* Great basis for a marriage! But who was she to judge. She'd married Max, and a fine upstanding pillar of society he'd turned out to be.

She shivered involuntarily at the thought of Max. How weird that the sensation of fear in her gut was physically almost the same as sexual anticipation. The idea of that, the sudden connection of it, both frightened and revolted Victoria, but she expertly pushed it to one side and crossed to the French windows to stare at the delicately frosted garden. The ancient trees and the stark vision of Aphrodite holding out her hands to catch the winter sun, filled her with calm. After all, the statue represented the goddess of love, despite the frozen tendrils of ivy clutching her stone heart.

Victoria made some strong coffee and took the cup and the paper into the conservatory, where she smoothed out page five onto the glass table. This time she went through the story more carefully, looking for confirmation between every line that all that wild behaviour had got them absolutely nowhere. Why did she feel the need to know that? To reaffirm to herself that her life was so much better? Not surprisingly, it didn't work. She didn't succeed in feeling any kind of relief or superiority. Eventually, the paper went into the log maker in the formal sitting room and Victoria felt a certain measure of satisfaction in crushing all the words, ready for burning.

But then, when the wedding day came around the weekend before Christmas, it wasn't just curiosity which led Victoria away from the shops in Conwy and into the grounds of St. Mary's Parish Church. It was bordering on dusk, and the orange glow of a December sky streaked across Snowdonia. Bitterly cold, but romantic, for a winter wedding, and Victoria felt an uncomfortable weight of emotion settle in her chest. What was it; hope, envy, or regret? Probably just a weird middle-aged nostalgia for the years already gone.

She was not alone. There were many hundreds of people, waving frantically as they recognised faces from the past, some with more enthusiasm than others. Victoria stood away from the melee, telling herself she'd stay for a glimpse of the bride and groom, just long enough to see how they'd aged, what they were wearing, all the usual sort of thing, after which she could go home and forget all about it. At that moment Linda Williams caught her eye, and they became swept along with the massive congregation. The ushers had mostly given up trying to segregate bride or groom relations, and settled for keeping the crowd orderly. Inside, there was a buzz of anticipation, as if it were a theatre production.

The 12th century church didn't disappoint as a venue. It was beautifully atmospheric from a spiritual point of view, and maybe even from the point of view of a staunch atheist. The fusion of brand new Christmas decorations and wedding flowers, together with the gravitas of the dark ancient wood, stained glass windows and stone floors was, to Victoria at least, perfect.

Someone lit the huge candles on the pulpit, and the scene was set.

It was the same church in which she and Max had said their vows.

Forsaking all others...

Victoria studied the order of service, then turned and smiled at Linda, hoping it disguised her melting pot of feelings. They were both squashed in the middle of a row, but close enough to the front to witness any flaws, faltering or false claims. Surrounded by old school faces, it reminded Victoria of standing in morning assembly and Linda was just as talkative, just as likely to be chastised, but Victoria found she rather enjoyed the running commentary; mostly about everyone's love affairs.

'Do you think Danny's still as hot as he used to be?' Linda said, removing her shoes and rubbing her feet. 'Talked to Tina loads, but I haven't seen Dan in ages. I used to really fancy him, do you remember?'

'You and half the school. Just remember he's forty now. And the way Dan and Tina were he's probably fat, bald with a collapsed lung and a gasping liver.'

Linda shot her a little frown. 'You could be right. Well at least he's solvent.'

Victoria knew this from the newspaper article. Daniel had apparently purchased Crafnant Hall; a dilapidated hotel situated several miles down the valley, surrounded by mountains and woods and a boating lake. It was isolated, and no one had made much of a success of it, being crippled eventually with loans, mortgages and all the on-going repairs. For the previous two years it had been reduced to something of a white elephant, a local landmark with sad, haunted problems.

'To be honest, I can't believe Dan and Tina are both still together,' Victoria prompted.

'They agreed that if they were still unattached by the time they hit forty, they'd marry each other and settle for what they've got.'

'Which is?' Victoria said, still not knowing if she found the idea funny or sad, certainly not romantic, but not unexpected.

'About twenty-four years of on-off love-hate.'

They both laughed a little and Victoria said, 'Bit sad though isn't it?'

Linda, newly separated, shrugged and put her shoes back on.

Their attention was taken by the vicar, holding up his hands for quiet. There was a lot of loud expectant shuffling and throat clearing, mobiles silenced, children hushed.

'P'nawn da! Good afternoon and welcome everybody,' he said, astonished or mildly embarrassed it was hard to say, at the crowds. 'Goodness; what a popular couple! I'm afraid we're running awfully late now. Does anyone have *any* idea where the bride and groom might be?'

Much laughter, groans and general hubbub at this, even some obscenities were shouted, but then the church doors swung open and on cue the groom and best man fell into the aisle. There was a collective intake of breath. Both men made their way to the front, Daniel nodding with recognition at some faces, obviously not too happy about a few of them and clearly bewildered at the volume of people.

Linda had a good look and nudged Victoria.

'He's not fat or bald. *Love* the hat.'

'Yes, love the hat,' she said carefully. Some of the congregation were laughing. The groom was not traditionally attired. A dirty white shirt, torn denims covered in plaster with some pliers in the back pocket and a pair of building site style boots. The only touch of glamour, was a glittery white pork pie hat.

'Sorry, sorry,' the best man said breathlessly to the vicar, 'Been in an accident. Both here now.' He looked awfully young, and his face was bone white, to the extent that he might keel over, or be sick.

'That's Troy. *Their* son,' Linda whispered with a nod, 'Dan and Tina's.'

The vicar did his best not to stare. Eventually he dragged his eyes away and nodded at the organist. The wedding march began and the atmosphere became charged. When nothing happened, the organist started again. After much longer than anyone else might have dared leave it, Tina made an entrance. Something of a Marilyn Monroe lookalike, she could play the slightly vamp bride to good effect. She even had the same white blonde hair and ice blue eyes. The procession was slightly spoiled by her entourage. Her father, shuffling and grey in a suit that hung off his lanky frame, was in much poorer condition and his progress was only made possible because Tina was more or less holding him up.

'Has he had a stroke?' Victoria whispered.

Linda shook her head and made a gesture of knocking back drinks, *'Alcoholic.'*

Following behind were Tina's two sisters, in matching black and white. It was quite clever really, in that the larger of the two wore a black jacket and a white skirt, and the older, thinner sister had the same outfit only in reverse. Both wore matching hats and shoes with dark pink accessories.

Someone shouted, 'Come in for milking have you love?'

Tina came to a regal halt at the front of the church and turned to look at her groom. There was a moment of spectacular quiet as she took in his dusty appearance. Daniel only got one heartfelt 'sorry' in before everyone's attention was taken by the best man falling face first into the eight-foot Christmas tree by the pulpit.

It went down as if it had been felled by an axe, the top of which landed just short of a magnificent candelabra, festooned with huge flickering candles and artistically placed festive blooms. The girth of it though was huge and ungainly, and about two hundred silver and white baubles scattered everywhere, mostly under the pews.

The best man, seemingly unhurt but still very pale, climbed out of the foliage holding his bloodied nose. He staggered to his seat, managing to resist someone's suggestion of forcing his head back, before Daniel's mother - miraculously keeping the blood away from her linen suit and white fur stole - made the correct diagnosis and forced his head down, then stuffed his nose full of tissues.

Several male guests came to the rescue of the tree. Within minutes it was upright and back on its stand. Linda said the instructions sounded like someone trying to reverse a transit van into a small space. During this interlude, Tina took the opportunity to start a spat with Daniel, mostly concerning his attire, and the monochrome Maids of Honour also told Daniel exactly what they thought of him. The vicar, anxious to get on before the congregation became ugly, clapped his hands together for quiet, and somehow the service began.

It was mostly traditional, and the singing was loud and enthusiastic, with one especially strong lead male vocal, something which cheered the vicar, but put a shadow of fear on Daniel's face. When it came to that part of the service where the vicar asked if anyone knew of any lawful impediment etc.; there was another tense silence, broken by a single voice, 'Yeah! She's up the duff!'

Daniel spun round and scanned the congregation; but the vicar, keeping his eyes on the Welsh gold nestling in the spine of his open bible, remained stoic and continued regardless.

'Who said that?' Victoria whispered.

'Barney Rubble we used to call him, remember? Big lad with some kind of death wish? Got Dan in a headlock once in double science and set fire to his tie with a Bunsen burner. He had the strength of two men, even then.'

Victoria remembered. Voice of an angel, spawned by the devil, that's what everyone said. All those years ago, and yet some memories never went away. She looked across the cold church, and her eyes lingered on Tina and Daniel. He kept glancing apologetically at his bride but Tina was clearly still miffed about the builder's outfit. The young man with the nosebleed looked to have recovered enough to dispense with his fistful of tissues, but no one knew what to do with them.

On the same pew was a girl holding a Chihuahua. Victoria instantly recognised her from the back pages of Alright! magazine. Bluebell Woods. Small time model and singer, big time drug addict.

Linda followed her gaze. '*His* daughter.'

The service ended with a Christmas carol, and the atmosphere lightened. There was a crush to get out of the church, and someone showered the happy couple with rice. Linda reckoned it was leftover egg fried, rather than proper good luck rice. In the graveyard, Tina finally let rip about the photographs, and Daniel's missing wedding suit.

Daniel looked cold, and slightly desperate. 'What if I stand at the back?'

Tina looked up at the sky and practically snarled.

'No? Look, I can't do anything about it now! An oak beam and a load of plaster fell on me; look at my leg if you don't believe me. If I'd stopped to get the suit I would have been over an hour late! Why can't we do the pictures another day?'

'What? The wedding's *now, Daniel.* And what about all

the *relatives?*'

'What about them? You'll only end up cutting them all out anyway!'

Everyone watched as Tina tore all the heads off a lot of dark pink roses and flung them in Daniel's direction, then marched past the waiting photographer and into the wedding car. It pulled away and there was a sudden, almost tangible sense of disappointment.

'And they said it wouldn't last,' Linda said, stubbing her cigarette on the bottom of her shoe. The photographer was hijacked by Tina's sisters. It looked like they were on a glamour shoot, draping themselves unattractively over ivy covered pillars and ancient tombstones. There was another man with a camera, but he looked more like press, running after Bluebell, shouting at her to turn around but Daniel shoved him backwards into some recycling bins. He should have left it at that, but Daniel couldn't help himself, grabbed the front of the guy's jacket and almost managed to shove him head first into a wheelie bin, before Daniel's mother intervened.

'Daniel, *stop it!*'

Presently, Daniel and his mother, the best man and Bluebell squeezed into a white Porsche, and the guests began to run to their cars as the first flakes of watery snow began to fall. Barney Rubble had an old bashed up BMW. It had endured a bad respray and the rear windows were blacked out. It backfired then roared after Daniel's car in a haze of oily smoke, followed by the local paparazzi on a motorbike.

End of act one.

Victoria pulled her fur coat round her and pulled on a matching hat. *She could go now.*

'I should go,' she said, although Max wouldn't miss her, he was at a charity dinner and *they* went on forever.

'You can't go now! We've got full invites,' Linda said, waving a white card.

'I haven't,' Victoria said. 'I haven't been formally invited.'

'Small technicality. My invite says Mrs Linda Williams and Mr Michael Williams. Thing is, *Mr Michael Williams* is not available. He was big friends with Dan, remember? Seems no one is good enough for him now.'

'I'm sorry about Mike.'

'Yes, well... me too... so, you coming with me? I could do with a good meal and a night out. Be a shame to waste it.'

'I'm not really dressed for it,' she said.

'Neither is Daniel!'

They travelled to the hotel in Victoria's car. Well it was Max's car really, the silver Lexus. Victoria hated it. It was too big and ostentatious, and a nightmare to park. Max fretted about its welfare more than their children's. Victoria preferred her little sports car but her daughter had borrowed it, yet again.

Linda slid into the dark leather interior of the car.

'Wow, recession not hit Max?'

'No, he knows how to play the game.'

It wasn't the only game Max knew how to play, but that could wait. *He* could wait.

Outwardly, everything in Victoria's life was pretty good, but her comfortable life was flawed, so flawed. She stole a quick sideways look at Linda, and felt nostalgic for something she'd lost along the way, something honest and ordinary. And it made no sense that Linda actually only lived a couple of miles away, and yet only a wave across the supermarket car park had passed between them for years, separated by their social strata. Did that make her a snob like her mother? Is that how people saw her?

The wedding reception was at Coast, the most prestigious venue in Llandudno. Like most of the buildings along the curved seafront it was Victorian and finished in a pastel shade the colour of vanilla ice cream. Fairy lights swung furiously in the keen sea breeze and a few couples were bent double along the promenade.

The mothers were on meet and greet duty. They learnt that Daniel had gone to get showered and changed. Tina wasn't mentioned. Daniel's mother, polite and impassive, made a little smile and a nod of recognition at Victoria and handed out flutes of champagne. Tina's mother, already over-emotional and overdressed in something floaty with a lot of feathers and a large hat; was a lot more theatrical and flung her arms round both Victoria and Linda. Everything was late, thanks to the church service, and everyone was waved along into the dining room. Victoria found herself between Linda, and Tina's cousin Bethan.

'Sorry, I know I should be a man,' Victoria said to Bethan's blank face. 'You were expecting Mike?'

'Don't talk to me about that idiot.'

The bride and groom eventually made a subdued appearance to a discreet show of applause and there was a tangible atmosphere of relief.

'At last,' Bethan grumbled. 'I'm starving.'

Daniel looked more the part in a dark grey suit, a wilting pink rose in his lapel. The shellfish starters arrived but Victoria was allergic to them so she slipped off to the powder room. It was opulent but not showy, nice touches of flowers and hand lotion, but when she looked at herself in the huge backlit mirrors Victoria was suddenly filled with sadness. She didn't belong to this wedding. She didn't really feel as if she belonged to anyone, or anywhere.

Her appearance would never suggest there was anything wrong. She'd always been slender, classic styles always looked good on her and Max was generous with her clothing allowance. She had wardrobes bursting with bespoke pieces, although the wool trousers she'd chosen for shopping were too warm now. Her hair was still dark, not needing any help yet. She looked pale though, her complexion like parchment, and her hazel eyes dull.

Victoria looked exactly what she was - the well-off idle wife of an accountant. Idle, because both their children were at university and Max would never let her work. They even had a cleaner and a gardener. She did dinner that was all; and then formal dinner parties for her husband's friends and business associates. Yet she was so tired; why was that when she never did anything productive? Her days were filled with shopping, lunching, horse-riding and the gym, and idle chatter. They had ski holidays, sun holidays, golf holidays (mostly Max) and city break holidays.

She took a deep breath and reapplied her neutral lipstick. Her hands shook ever so slightly; although they were beautifully French manicured and bore the gifts of twenty-two years of marriage to Max. She needed to get a grip on these negative thoughts. She'd recently taken to the internet in a big way, searching for... what exactly?

Victoria took her seat again. Someone had eaten her starter. The main course was butterflied chicken in an artful tower with the obligatory jus, crispy potatoes and honey-roasted vegetables. It tasted quite nice and she ate most of it. Then they had a meringue concoction, the speeches, thanks, and cake cutting; all the usual traditional expectations. The best man did quite a funny speech about Tina and Daniel, during which Bluebell fed the Chihuahua leftover chicken. Daniel's mother, Marian, did her best to keep Tina's father focused and seated. Throughout all of this, Daniel was sober and articulate, quietly contemplative of the growing swell of alcohol fuelled relatives.

They moved onto the next stage. Another delay while Dan and Tina made up for the missing photographs. On their return, Tina had changed into a black dress. She still turned heads; she had that ability to wear almost anything. Although with her tiny waist, big bust and wide mouth, Tina tended to make everything look slightly tarty, a fact which never worked against her but ensured she had constant male attention. She was quite different to her sisters, soft-hearted and pretty, a real life Cinderella.

The DJ played their songs by U2, One, and Beautiful Day. Daniel and Tina did that strange sort of 'shuffling together at a wedding' dance, because they wanted to hang on to each other; and as they kissed, everyone clapped, and the party commenced.

'Looks like he's forgiven,' Linda said, and passed a white wine spritzer to Victoria.

'They haven't changed. They know how to work each other.'

The music gradually moved up a gear and Linda and Victoria found a table. Tina's sisters were in full flow in their killer heels and fake tans, fake designer handbags weighed down with charms and trinkets. Their fake nails were studded with fake diamonds. Everything was fake; even one of the crowd had breast implants, and they were coveted and drooled over. The men and women all had the same hard faces, with black hair and soft, flabby bodies decorated with tattoos.

Victoria hated all that; their misguided belief that it made them better, more attractive, more envied. But who was she to judge? There were vast areas of her life which were just as false. They were just more cunningly disguised. She bought Linda another glass of wine and checked her phone again. No messages.

Could she go now? Would it be rude? Would anyone notice, or care?

The older generation were struggling to hear what anyone said by then, or were already fast asleep, slumped in a chair. Tina's father was a mess, loud and staggering about. Tina's mother was crying. Marian took it upon herself to try and restore a sense of decency, although even she was almost defeated by the sheer complacency and tardiness of her daughter in-law's family, and had to resort to Daniel manhandling the old man into a cab.

Daniel seemed used to it, knew the right words and knew the right way to get hold of him. On watching this painful grappling, Marian was close to tears herself; clearly not understanding why *his* family - the silly fake women and their useless men - thought it was funny to see a once dignified man in his seventies behave like a desperate tramp. His grandchildren, dressed like miniature adults, captured it all on their mobile phones.

'He's not been that bad before,' Victoria heard Daniel say, on his return.

'Get used to it,' his mother snapped. 'They'll all be on your doorstep with their *problems.*'

'No. I married Tina, not her bloody family.'

'Oh no, Daniel, let's be absolutely clear. You have inherited *all of them!*'

The remainder of their conversation was lost, suddenly drowned out by deafening drum rolls and electric guitars then someone tapping a microphone and making some kind of introduction, but Victoria could still see their faces; Marian angry and tearful, Daniel calm and resigned.

On stage, the DJ had gone and a band was tuning up. Everyone recognised the introduction to the Snow Patrol track, Chasing Cars; and there was a smattering of applause as most of the guests recognised Daniel's daughter. Close up, she looked like a miserable blonde version of Amy Winehouse with the same kind of skinny, tortured body.

'This is for my dad,' Bluebell uttered, no smile. 'This is for Tina, and my dad.'

Then Bluebell began to sing and everything changed. She had a massive, powerful voice. When it left her mouth it was as if the voice didn't really belong in there, like it was a demon fighting to get out. She didn't move much, all the expression was channelled through her face and her hands. Victoria felt her spine tingle. She glanced round the room and everyone was spellbound. Everything lifted to a different plane. The drunken chaos fell away, mouths fell open.

Four and half minutes, which connected everyone in the room.

Four and half minutes of understanding what the whole day was about. The lyrics could have been written for Daniel and Tina. The applause, the stamping and shouting was deafening. There followed a strange suspension of time until there was a reconnection with the harshness of the real world as the stage was plunged into darkness, and some bland recorded music filtered through the speakers. Victoria felt oddly cheated; she'd wanted more, much more.

Linda looked at her and mouthed, 'Wow.'

Everyone was talking about Bluebell Woods and heading for the bar again, but Victoria looked at the empty stage in the dimmed light. Daniel had his arms folded around his daughter. After a moment she struggled out of his grasp and looked at the floor, and Victoria looked away.

Seconds later, Daniel was at the bar with Tina and saying hello to everyone, and asking Linda where Mike was. He nodded at Victoria but he didn't remember her, not really. Hugs and kisses were exchanged, Tina's ring admired, more promises to be better at keeping in touch.

'Everyone says that don't they?' Tina said, slightly slurring her words, 'But we've no excuse now, I'm back and I need all the friends I can get since it looks as though I'll be trapped in the back of beyond. Dan said there were *bears.*'

'It's not the back of beyond, it's the Snowdonia National Park,' Daniel said patiently, then looked at Linda and Victoria. 'Tina thinks a few fields and some trees make a wilderness. The bloody A55 is only a couple of miles away. The bears were a joke, love.'

It wasn't quite true, the part about the isolation. Linda raised her brows at Victoria but they all laughed about the bears, and then they got on to the wedding ceremony, and why Daniel had been late. Every so often he was interrupted by Tina's larger sister Mandy, trying to get to the bar for more bottles of Magners.

Daniel looked more relaxed than he had all day. A glass of champagne in his hand, his tie was in his pocket and the white hat back on his head, keeping some control over his dark hair, spiked up slightly with the addition of some gel. Tina leant against him, one arm around his waist, happy to let him do all the talking. Listening to Daniel and watching them both was like going back twenty-five years.

There were always together, him and Tina, always in some sort of trouble, most of it funny or it seemed so at the time. She remembered him driving some panicking stray sheep through the school corridors, everyone hysterical with laughter, skidding on the resultant mess underfoot, and he'd been suspended for a while after that. Then of course there was the cider, sex and smoking, and bunking off. Considering the more insidious pitfalls of present day school life, it all seemed small fry now, but at the time most of the school had admired Daniel's nerve and couldn't wait to see what he did next. Then Tina had an abortion when she was fifteen and it was suddenly all serious.

But Daniel always rescued her, he always played the big man to her beautiful vulnerable clown. Later, Victoria heard that Tina had ended up in a movie themed bar and Daniel was on a Whimpey construction site.

And she'd stupidly thought they'd blown it, everyone did.

Victoria had gone to university and married Max.

To love, cherish and *obey...*

Daniel might have left school with nothing, but somewhere along the way he'd acquired a PhD in life. It showed in his face, in his manner, in his laughing dark eyes, aged now, with not unattractive crinkles. Feature by feature, Daniel wasn't classically good looking, but he'd always had a streetwise sexuality, a vitality which drew people to him. At school, in the confusion of teenage angst, Victoria could never decide if she actually liked him or not. He'd asked her out once, when Tina was in hospital having her tonsils out. Caught off guard and horrified by the implications, Victoria had turned him down.

'Why not?' he'd asked, all surprised.

'Because you're Tina's boyfriend.'

Victoria had watched him shrug and walk away. She remembered feeling deflated that he didn't seem bothered. He never asked her again.

'...and then the whole bloody lot fell on me,' he was saying, pulling up his trouser leg to reveal an untidy bandage... 'massive oak beams they are. I knew I should have used acrow props.'

'Did someone say alcopops?' Mandy said, 'get us a drink Danny boy,' and nudged him with her bulk, but Daniel ignored her. He was squinting at Victoria. 'I remember you now.'

'She was Vick the stick,' Mandy butted in, weighing her up out of the corner of her eye as she lifted another bottle to her lips, '*vapour* rub.'

'Your mum and dad had all those posh flower shops,' Daniel said.

'Florists.'

He nodded slowly, sipped his champagne.

Tina said, 'So, you married now? Got kids?'

Victoria told them a bit about Emily and Richard, both at university. Married to Max.

'What does he do?' Tina said, 'What does your Max do?'

'He's a partner in a firm of accountants.'

'Dan needs an accountant, don't you Dan?'

'Might do.'

'Max is having a fiftieth birthday party in a few weeks, why don't you come?' she said rashly, knowing full well that

Max would never take on Daniel Woods as a client. There was a good chance he wouldn't even let him in the house. As soon as the words were out of her mouth, Victoria regretted it, but Tina's face lit up, and anyway, what the hell, she just wanted them to be there.

'Oh we'd love to, wouldn't we Dan?'

'Might do.'

*

Victoria and Linda didn't leave till almost midnight. Inside, the hardened party goers had progressed through songs from the eighties onto a form of Irish dancing. Even Daniel and Tina had made their escape to the honeymoon suite. Outside, it was snowing hard and there was a careful scramble to get out of the car park. Barney Rubble was just sitting in his, going nowhere, lighting matches and throwing them into the snow. Bluebell was in the passenger seat, with the window rolled down, smoke curling into the cold air.

They reached Linda's semi on the edge of the council estate. In the dark Victoria could make out a neat square with pots of shrubs and a Ford Fiesta. Next door had a full size trampoline in the front garden and four vehicles bumped up on the pavement. The front of the house was covered in a pulsing medley of Christmas lights, and there was an inflatable Santa and two reindeer lashed to the chimney, struggling to stay anchored in the wind. A huge dog looked to be tied up outside, and another smaller one inside, yapping and leaping under the net curtain at the smeared windows. Inside, looked busy and noisy.

'Looks like a party,' Victoria said, glancing nervously at the Lexus.

'Party night every bloody night. Come in for a nightcap?'

'Okay. Make it a small one though or I'll be over the limit.'

They talked about the wedding and then they got on to Mike. He was living with a seventeen year old Polish girl above his garage down on the Morfa Road.

'I mean, what I don't get, is what does *she* see in him? A bloody middle-aged mechanic?'

'Escape?'

Linda, quite drunk by then, was intent on telling Victoria the whole unabridged version of her marriage breakdown. Victoria didn't mind, in a way it was good to fill her head with someone else's problems. She poured herself a large glass of wine and resigned herself to calling a taxi. She didn't fancy getting the Lexus up the mountain pass to Capelulo in the snow anyway. Linda said it would be fine, on her driveway.

The taxi came straightaway, the driver grumbling about the lack of fares because of the weather, but stopped before the steep incline at the bottom of the private road, the wheels starting to spin. Victoria watched it turn around and fade into the night, its headlights picking up the swirling snow. She began to tramp up towards the drive, glad of her wool trousers and boots again.

Victoria's home was The Old School House. Built in 1892 it was a grade II listed building and one of its best features were the carefully restored stone mullioned windows to the front facade. Other than the security lights, and the old street lamps studded along the drive, it was in total darkness. It was private, its seclusion further accentuated by all the ancient oaks and firs. Then there were tall hedges of holly and six foot spiked iron railings surrounding the whole property. Max was keen on privacy and security.

Everything was enveloped in soft thick snow, muffling her footsteps. It was profoundly quiet; she could only hear her white breath, panting by the time she reached the front door. She stamped her boots free of snow, and turned her key in the lock.

'Max? You in?'

She heard him and her stomach tightened. For an anxious second, she wished she was still in Linda's cosy sitting room.

'Why are you in the dark? Max?'

He was in the kitchen. Max, tall and distinguished, good looking and popular. She threw her bag onto one of the chairs and shrugged off her fur coat. He studied her with his hard, baby-blue eyes, a nerve twitching in his face.

'Where the hell have you been?'

'Old school friend's wedding.'

She picked up a beaker and went across to the sink but he grabbed her wrist, crushing her grip, and pushed his face close to hers. She winced and dropped the glass and it splintered on the granite work surface, cutting her hand.

'Where's my car?'

'It's perfectly safe.'

'Where?'

When she didn't reply he slammed his fist against the cupboard above her head. 'I asked you *where*, Victoria?'

A beat passed. 'Porth -Y- Felin Road.'

He put his hand round her throat and pushed her back hard against the kitchen units, and she could taste his anger. He spat the words at her.

'You, left my car, on the *council estate?*'

'Max let go of me you're scaring me.'

'You left, a *sixty thousand pound car,* on the *fucking council estate?*'

She felt her resolve buckle then, her body suddenly limp. 'Please...'

He pushed her, pushed her away from him. Victoria crossed to the sink and ran her hand under the tap, watching the blood gushing down the plughole. And she wanted to cry, she wanted to hurt him, she wanted to run, she wanted to scream, she wanted to kill him. She wanted to do all of that, but Victoria knew she never would. Instead, she looked for the dustpan and brush, and swept up the glass.

Max was her husband. In *sickness*, and in health.

Till death do us part.

CHAPTER TWO

The honeymoon suite was pretty special. Apart from a few incidents he'd rather forget and the throbbing gash on his shin, the whole day had been pretty special. His *wife* was pretty special.

They were lying on top of the messed up bed, wrapped in white towels and feeling mellow. They'd made love in a lazy, almost asleep way, enjoyed a bath in the sumptuous spa and poured themselves a final glass of bubbly. Daniel was staring at the ceiling, his mind still buzzing. He couldn't wait to show Tina the hotel.

She hadn't seen it for about six months because she'd been living at their Manchester flat, still working in the city as a restaurant manager. Daniel had been living in a caravan on site during the week and only going back home at the weekends. The last time Tina had seen it, it was a jumble of unattractive extensions from the fifties, sixties and seventies. In the end, Daniel had demolished it all but the original Victorian house, stripped it all back and restored it to a white shell.

The house was Welsh slate, slightly gothic with high ceilings and an amazingly tall roofline. The frustrating aspect of it was that it had its back to the lake. With sympathetic consideration from a local architect, Daniel felt he had finally uncovered its real potential. The house now boasted a full height, glass and wood beam extension overlooking the lake. On the ground floor, the glass doors could be peeled back in sections, giving access to a huge decked area over the water. From any direction, but mostly from the approach along the single track lane by the lake, it was incredibly imposing and exactly the image he'd strived for.

It had been tough since October, the dark days, the cold, and the loneliness when the rest of the team had gone home. The whole project had been, either slow with not much progress; sometimes due to the incredibly difficult access up from the main road, then suddenly exciting or scary as another stage was realised.

Daniel had project managed many times before, but this was different. This was *his* money and *his* dream. On paper he was a millionaire, no *they* were millionaires. The best thing about it was he'd done it all without borrowing any money. Not bad for a lad who started on the building sites, and a waitress with attitude. They'd both learnt from the ground up.

It had all been worth it, this was when his life finally came together.

From this day, it was all good.

It would be good for all of them. A chance to put mistakes right. Troy needed a sense of direction. Bluebell needed a shot of just about everything that was normal; and that meant getting her away from her silly soap star mother and all the hangers-on. She'd already scuttled back to London for Christmas but Daniel was hoping he'd done enough to prevent the rot setting in again. Most importantly Tina deserved a sense of security for once. *He* deserved a sense of security as well. They'd been through just about everything life could throw at them and yet here they were, properly married and all grown up now.

Proper responsible adults.

'Who was the idiot that shouted she's up the duff? Tee?'

'I dunno,' Tina mumbled into her pillow. 'An idiot? We know loads.'

Daniel laughed, picked up her hand and told her about the lake, the mountains, the wild ponies; she nodded and smiled, eyes closing. Tina had tried to delay getting married till Easter, but Daniel wanted to catch the season and be up and running by then. He'd been getting tired as well, commuting backwards and forwards down the motorway, and they'd both lived separate lives for long enough. So he'd got his own way with a Christmas wedding.

He'd had to up the ante on the living quarters. Rushing this morning to get the bedroom finished was when the accident had happened. Troy had nearly passed out, but it was lucky he was there and lifted the beam off his leg. It was still incredibly painful, maybe he'd see what there was to put on it. He found nothing medical in the bathroom. It looked like a department in Harrods. Tina's stuff was everywhere, some of it on the floor. When he went to scoop up a big bag of cosmetics and lotions, her contraceptive pills fell out. He couldn't help looking at the foil strip. Day 18 had been dutifully consumed, and all the ones before it. Course she wasn't pregnant, he'd *know*. She'd had an awful time with Troy from day one and there was no way she was going through that again, she'd said so, more than once.

Annoyed with himself, Daniel got into bed, pulled the duvet over them both. Jumping to conclusions and listening to hearsay had to stop.

'Tee, you awake? I love you, wife.'

But she was fast asleep.

*

It was Monday before they checked out of Coast. They didn't have a honeymoon planned. It would have been nice to jet off somewhere hot before the real work started but in truth he couldn't afford the time or any more expense. The cost of the wedding combined with the approach of Christmas, and the investment in the hotel, was staggering.

They'd made it last, the honeymoon suite, the spa and the fine dining. Then when Daniel had gone to reception to pay the bill, he discovered his mother had paid for their suite and all the trimmings. He sent her a huge bouquet of flowers.

Tina pushed their cases into the Porsche and they set off for the hotel. The sea was crashing over the promenade, a huge restless grey void with angry white foam at its crest. When Tina shivered and sunk into her coat, Daniel caught hold of her hand. She was such a city girl, and not for the first time he felt suddenly anxious about it all, this massive life change he'd committed them both to.

But when the guests started arriving and the place got established, she'd grow and flourish in all those social roles she was so good at. She was going to be such a fantastic host, his wife. She was flirty and fun. Everyone loved her.

'Can't wait to show you,' he said. 'You won't recognise it.'

She smiled at this, catching his enthusiasm at last. 'I should hope not. I've hardly seen you for six months.'

'There's loads to think about. I need your input now.'

'Oh yeah? I might have other plans, like Christmas shopping.'

'Don't you have to obey me now, wife?'

'Dan, did you not listen to a word that vicar said? I made him leave that bit out, it's so old fashioned,' she said, the tiniest sting in her voice. 'No one says that any more, Dan.'

'I'll carry on doing as I'm told, shall I? What about the love and honour bit, or is that dead in the water as well?'

'Don't be stupid. I'll always love you.'

After forty minutes, Daniel turned off the valley road, the old hotel sign, still collapsed in the hedge and pointing to an old water butt. He needed to do something about that. A steep single-track lane led them up through the fringes of Gwydyr forest. The snow had remained on the higher ground, catching the tops of the fir trees and winter sunlight flickered through the branches.

'Close your eyes,' he said, as they neared the start of the lake.

He wanted to watch her reaction. It was a sparkling winter morning, still early. The mass of Cefn Cyfarwydd rising to the right, was lit with silver waterfalls, and cast a deep shadow over the ancient trees along its flanks. The water was shivering in the pale light, reflecting the broken clouds and the moody sky.

At the head of the lake, the best part of a mile away, rising out of the brown reeds was what Daniel hoped was something just as raw and honest. A piece of architecture both ancient and brand new, yet fitting as beautifully into the landscape as if it had every right to be there.

'Can I open my eyes yet?' Tina said, 'It makes me feel weird.'

He steered her out of the car and faced her the right way, feeling ridiculously apprehensive. 'Okay. I hope you love it as much as I do.'

She blinked and stared. Then she whipped round to face him.

'Oh my God, Daniel... what did you do?'

'I told you it was different.'

She got back into the car, left him standing there.

'Come on! Drive.'

He drove. As they followed the edge of the water, he kept glancing at her for some sort of reaction, but she didn't take her eyes from the lake and the approaching buildings. He parked the car round the back of the hotel, where there was still an untidy collection of vehicles and skips, two caravans and a load of building materials.

Still nervous, he took her by the hand through the massive oak doors, into the hall and reception area. No one saw or heard them. He needed to do something about that. Inside, a sweeping staircase led to six bedrooms and then another short stairway to three small attic rooms, one of which he hoped Bluebell might use. They could hear drilling and hammering above, a radio and someone whistling, Troy's voice singing along. It smelt new, of sawn wood and paint.

'Only us!' Daniel shouted, and the hammering stopped.

'Dad? There's a problem.'

'So, sort it out. You're the assistant manager.'

There was a short silence. 'Yeah? Oh okay, cool.'

'He won't sort it,' Daniel said to Tina, and she actually smiled.

He led her through the reception area with its stripped floors and leather sofas, and the huge black glass chandelier, and let her admire it all for a moment; before pushing back the oak and glass doors to reveal the new extension. There was a small bar and some experimental furniture, still on loan. Daniel had kept it all simple, modern lines with real materials, big beams of aged wood and white walls.

Tina gasped when she walked into the room. The light and the height of the vaulted ceiling were amazing enough; but then there was the view. Daniel let her walk alone towards the window, allowing the scenery to do the talking.

It was like being part of the water, the mountains, the trees and the sky. It was like walking into a dream. The sunrises, the sunsets and the changes in the seasons would be captured there forever.

It was a while before she turned to face him.

'Dan,' she whispered, 'what have you *done?*'

It wasn't quite the reaction he was hoping for, and he shrugged. 'You tell me.'

'It's just... I just, I can't think of the right words.'

He showed her how the doors folded back onto the huge

deck. In the summer they could have parties, concerts, weddings. They stood in the cold air; looking down into the dark water and watching the trout dart through the reeds.

'I want to call it The Bears' Retreat, what do you think?'

'I think that's pretty stupid, Dan.'

'See those woods over there, that's where the bears live.'

'Funny.'

'Well, serious now. I've gone with our first choice, The Lakeside.'

'Uh huh... I like that more.'

He showed her the little stainless steel kitchen and she trailed her hand across the gleaming surfaces. 'You do remember that neither of us can cook,' she said.

'I know that. We're gonna need some staff.'

'Staff? God, Dan it's all a bit, I mean it's all a bit overwhelming.'

'Sure it is, but only cos it's all new and different,' he said, putting an arm across her shoulders. They'd been through all this before, many times, the planning, the ideas. He wanted to keep everything restrained, easily manageable. 'After Christmas we need to interview, advertise. Troy's done an amazing website, come and look.'

Daniel sat at the new chair at the new desk in reception and started tapping away at the computer. Tina looked at the website with wide-eyed concentration. 'Troy's done this?'

'Yeah, well with his girlfriend. Look at the hotel diary.'

'There's a booking. Dan, there's a booking for Easter!'

'At last some enthusiasm!'

She gave him a strange look then, pushed past him, and climbed the stairs. Presently he heard her talking to Troy, her heels clattering on the bare floorboards as she wandered from room to room. Eventually she shouted down. 'Dan, which is our room?'

'You interested?'

'Yes! Come here and stop being an idiot.'

Their personal space was his favourite part of the build. It was only small, but it formed part of the new extension overlooking the lake with a small balcony. Separate from the rest of the guest bedrooms, it was accessed through what would have been a tiny box-room in the original house. Door-less now, it created a small private vestibule.

He let her open the new door.

Built right up to the roof with skylights, there was a lot of glass but because of its elevation, their rooms were completely private, nudging the tops of the fir trees. She went from the balcony to the little kitchen, the bathroom and then the bedroom. She went to look through the window.

'Not big but I don't reckon we'll be in here much. Need a bit more furniture and stuff, you can do that, get what you want...' he said, trailing to a halt. Tina was ominously quiet, but when she turned around she was all choked, with tears in her eyes and mascara running down her cheeks.

'I can't believe you've done all this. I think it's all amazing.'

'You sure?' he said, a bit puzzled by all the emotion. It wasn't like Tina to be quite so effusive. 'I need you with me on this, Tee. Say now if there's something not right.'

He wondered at the wisdom of this. He couldn't exactly change anything now, but she shook her head, hunted in her bag for a tissue.

'I love it *all*,' she said, wiping under her eyes.

'Come here, Mrs Woods. Let me give you a bear hug.'

'Will you shut up about the bears? I know they're not real, Dan.'

Daniel caught her in his arms and breathed a silent sigh of relief. The tears were for the right reasons. You could never be sure with Tina and tears. It was no good just asking. She put her hands round his face, an action which always got to him and he put his mouth on hers. They fit together so well, sort of dovetailed. She kissed him back in such a way that he found himself dropping the lock on the door.

Then she lay back on the bed, he went to her, pulled her boots off, and kept going till she was in her underwear. After a few minutes, they heard a knock and Troy's voice, 'Dad? You in there?'

'He's just coming,' Tina said, giggling as Daniel put his hand over her mouth. After a second Troy said, 'Oh I get it. Okay. Cool.'

Tina started to shake with laughter and Daniel gave up, the mood gone.

'No wonder our kids are messed up.'

'Troy's okay. Anyway it's only sex, Dan.'

'If I said that to you, you'd cut off my man parts with a blunt knife.'

'That's right and don't you ever forget it.'

'Stop being a tease, Mrs Woods,' he said, grinning as she pulled the duvet around herself. It had no cover yet and the pillows were at the bottom of the bed. His mobile started to ring.

'Sorry baby,' Tina said, leaning across to kiss his face. 'I've been in a strange mood, I know.'

'It's okay.'

Daniel answered his phone, his eyes still on hers for a moment, then he had to get up and stand by the window because the signal was poor. It was about the alcohol license and a pub management course. He could see a cluster of ponies down by the edge of the water, browsing through the limited greenery. To the right, above the vista of the water, the lower slopes of the mighty Carneddau were touched by a million sun strokes, just for a second, and then they were gone.

'Sorry, what were those dates?'

Daniel finished the call, scribbled the dates down and started to tell Tina. 'You need to keep those days free, Tee? It's important.'

But when he looked down at her, she was fast asleep.

He covered her, even managed to shunt a pillow under her head and she didn't stir.

Daniel went to find Troy. He was moon dancing with a trowel in one hand and not surprisingly, making a bad job of plastering over a chimney breast in room two.

'Don't disturb your mum, she's shattered.'

Troy gave him a goofy grin, his mother's blue eyes, wild blonde hair, denims hanging halfway down his backside, and a daft pink knitted hat. 'Yeah *okay*, Dad, I get it, you old folks still need your fun.'

'I mean it. Keep the noise down,' Daniel said, unplugging the radio. 'What's this problem anyway? You've got too much water in that mix. Look at the bloody mess!'

'There's more than one problem now. Number one; take a look at the papers.'

Daniel picked up the national trash first. There was a big close-up of Mandy pursing her lips at the lens and hitching up her skirt, another of The Crafnant Hotel about five years ago and one of himself covered in plaster.

The headline said, 'Bob the Builder has White Wedding; and gets a White Elephant!'

The text was predictable, all about Bluebell's drug problem and her stupid mother, Mia. At the end of the piece it said, 'According to local source, the hotel renovation is funded by a controversial inheritance.' There was a small shot of Barney Rubble looking especially thug-like, accompanied by the caption, 'guest.'

Great! He needed to get some good publicity off the back of the bad. He needed a press party, some fancy food and champagne, something classy. Tina would be good at that.

The local rag had breaking news on the front page about some flower beds being vandalised in Llandudno; but *they'd* made page five.

'Local Lad Brings Jobs to the Area. In a brave move,

Daniel Woods has taken on the *doomed* Crafnant Hotel.'

Great! He'd get every unemployed dishwasher within fifty miles knocking on the door.

And what was with the *doomed?*

Tina appeared and hung her head over his shoulder. 'Why are the press so horrible?'

'Well if you hadn't blabbed all over Facebook we might have had a more normal wedding and then all this crap wouldn't be happening now!'

'Dan? That's not very fair.'

'No, I'm sorry. I'm on it. Don't worry we'll turn it round before we open.'

He watched her shrug her coat on, and reapply lipstick.

'What are you doing?'

'I promised Linda we'd go to Chester, Christmas shopping. I've got nothing to wear; all our things are still at the flat. Can I take the car?'

'I thought you were tired.'

'Christmas won't get done by itself.'

'Neither will everything here!'

'Dan. I can't plaster walls. I can't tile floors. I can't wire light fittings.'

'I know that! There's loads of other stuff, oh look just forget it, all right?'

She snatched up her keys and he heard her heels tap down the stairs. He went back into their room, crossed to the window, and watched his white Porsche zip along the lake road until it was swallowed by the forest.

*

It had been dark for several hours before Daniel realised what time it was. He'd been sanding floorboards for four hours. Troy had long since packed up and gone home, although he wasn't far away. Home for Troy at the moment was one of the caravans, where he was in loved-up bliss with his girlfriend, saving all their money to go backpacking in India to save the elephants. The other caravan was occupied by Tony and Tristan, also in loved-up bliss, supposedly in control of security.

Daniel took a shower in their room; the water pressure was a bit low. He needed to do something about that. Tina's stuff was everywhere, but at least she'd unpacked their cases, and he felt a bit better when he saw that she had lined up all her lotions and potions. He took the top off her bottle of Coco Channel and inhaled the heady perfume. When he glanced at the clock and saw it was nearly eight, a rise of panic made him grab his phone. Six missed calls! Shit... barely a signal. He went to the window and called her mobile. Nothing... voice mail. He left his phone outside on the balcony, the cold air filtering into the room.

While he was getting dressed, it came to him that this was the same sort of feeling he'd had when she'd cheated on him the first time. *There was something he didn't know.* Not that he was blameless in that department but they were married now, past all that. They'd been married for three days, he should feel great, and she should be here with him. He started to pull his clothes back on, angry and fed up. Then when his phone rang, he had one leg in his denims and nearly fell over a load of boxes trying to get to it.

'Dan? It's Linda.'

'Linda. What's happened?'

'Tina's at mine. We had a bit of an accident but it's okay, don't panic.'

Daniel started to panic. 'What accident? Tina?'

'She's all right just shaken up. Dan? You might want to come and pick her up. Number seven, just down from Tina's parents.'

'Yeah okay... pick her up.'

'Dan, she's *okay* so don't drive like a lunatic, all right?'

Daniel took the old Land Rover they used for collecting building materials, and drove like a lunatic, scaffolding and tarpaulin bouncing about in the back. It was pitch black down the lakeside road. He needed to do something about that. Forty minutes later he was hammering on Linda's door. Tina was curled up on Linda's sofa. She'd been crying and her hands wouldn't stop shaking. She stood up when he came to her.

'Dan I'm *so sorry.*'

'It's all right, it's all right, come here.'

It was an age before she'd let go of him. Linda said something about needing to go to work, so Daniel began to collect all the bags of shopping strewn at Tina's feet; then when he was in the hall, struggling with the front door, Linda came to him.

'I'm so impressed you haven't even asked where your car is.'

'Where is it?'

It was on its way to the nearest Porsche garage, fifty miles away, not unexpected. Linda passed him a business card with the details.

'So, what happened?'

'I'm not sure. One minute we were driving along; then as we entered the Conwy tunnel near the Morfa, we veered into the wall. It was all over in seconds. She wasn't doing more than thirty, I swear. She wouldn't go and get checked out but I honestly don't think she even bumped her head or anything.'

'Are you okay?'

'I'm fine, other than a touch of dented pride.'

'How do you mean?'

'I got Mike to come with the pick-up, and he dropped us here.'

Daniel wordlessly threw all the bags of shopping into the

Land Rover and Linda followed with more bags. 'How does Tina seem to you?' Daniel said, nodding at next door, 'Does that dog never stop barking?'

'No,' Linda said tiredly.

Tina appeared at the door, hugged Linda briefly then climbed into the dirty passenger seat of the Land Rover. On the drive home she stared ahead.

'Well, that was an expensive afternoon,' Daniel said.

At home, Tina was tired, weepy and distracted, dropping things. He ran her a bath, and made her get into bed. 'Right, wife, you're going to do as I say. You're going to obey me *or else*.'

'Wow... I'm *loving* that, Dan.'

'Yeah? So domination is back on? You're going to stay there and rest until I say you can come out.

*

It was well after midnight before Daniel lay down but sleep was elusive; his mind was on overtime, making mental lists of stuff to do. Crockery... square or round? Fix the water pressure. Lighting was a big one; down the lakeside road, deck lights, and something under the water? Security, health and safety certificate, food hygiene course, press party and advertising. What kind of food? Furniture, blinds for the windows, bedding and towels, everything white, yeah. Music system, what kind? Indie rock and a bit of classical. Live music, a harpist?... Bluebell. Need to check what she's doing. Problems? Troy didn't tell him what the other one was! Christ I'm starving; did I have any dinner? Can't remember. Tina's accident... yeah, worried about Tina...

'Dan? I know you're not asleep.'

'So do I.'

He rubbed his eyes and turned to face her. 'My head's all

34

over the place.'

'Dan, you're going to make yourself ill. Let's just have Christmas and chill out.'

She folded her body round his and kissed his hair. She smelt gorgeous, she felt gorgeous. He wanted her so much, but she wouldn't respond.

Christmas! He hadn't got her anything.

He needed to do something about that.

CHAPTER THREE

Christmas Day, Linda was woken by something frantically bumping the window. When she thought about it, it sounded like a giant balloon, which was fairly unlikely. Driven mostly by irritation, she finally got up to look. It was next door's inflatable Santa, caught up somehow on the bird feeders attached to the window. Feeling mutinous, she went downstairs, shivering in the dark, and pulled out the toolbox from under the stairs. Selecting a suitably sharp instrument - she wasn't entirely sure she knew what it was for - she went back upstairs, shoved the window open and murdered Santa. She stabbed him over and over, with more force than was necessary, until he swung all shrivelled and deflated. It felt good, the stabbing. Ho ho ho! Then she cut it free, and the dog saw her, hanging out of the window. It jumped up from a brief moment of repose, looked her in the eye and immediately began barking.

'You next!' she yelled at it.

Then she got back into bed and cried with frustration. The parties, the dog and the trampoline were getting to her. The trampoline was the worst. Last night, no, the early hours of the morning it must have been, she looked out of the window and there were dozens of kids and teenagers jumping up and down on it. When they caught sight of her, they gave her two fingers and turned up the music.

Linda looked at the clock. Almost time to get up and go to work. She'd had four hours of sleep. She reasoned though that it was easier to go to work than spend most of the day by herself, and everyone was so grateful that you'd turned in. Her clients were always grateful, well most of them. The majority were nice old people, but there was a small hardcore of not nice; not nice at all.

'Make sure you wipe my bottom hard, there's a good girl.'

Home caring was the job no one wanted to do, and it wasn't that well paid, although she'd get double time for Christmas Day. Some aspects of it made Linda thoroughly depressed and frightened of the future, more so now that she was alone. A big chunk of her work was just okay, and a small percentage of it was even uplifting. She used to find some of it quite funny and liked to tell Mike about her day, but Mike wasn't interested in her day any more, and it was getting more difficult to see the humour in anything.

Even Mr and Mrs Owens, the sex freaks were getting on her nerves; at it like rabbits even when she hammered on the door, and shouted up the stairs. They always claimed they were stone deaf. They loved being caught out, like some weird pensioner's fantasy. One of her clients had got slightly more interesting though, or disturbing, depending on your point of view.

Barbara Jones, Barney Rubble's mother. Not that he ever went near her. She had advanced arthritis and other age related symptoms, and on the face of it her life was pretty miserable. Linda usually took her shopping, then if she had time, and if she could bear it, engaged her in conversation. Two days previously the visit was especially trying; it being close to Christmas, even the disabled bays were full and they had to wait for an electric scooter. All was well until Barbara spotted Daniel's mother by the cereals.

'Hey you, bitch!'

Marian paled, and walked away.

'That's right, you walk away. You're lucky you can! How's that thieving, bastard son of yours?'

Linda said, 'Barbara what's got into you?'

'Take me home. I'm done here.'

*

Somehow, Linda got through eight calls. She'd left the house while it was still dark, and returned around four, just as it was going dark again. Miraculously, she managed to get a couple of hours sleep, probably because she was so exhausted; then she showered and poured herself a glass of wine to try and get in the mood for going out.

It wasn't proper going out, it was only going down the road to Tina's parents but Tina had insisted she join them, and it had to be better than staying in all alone. Linda's daughter-in-law had tried to get her to meet up in London but Linda had no money for something that extravagant, the trains were slow and unpredictable, and her son's friends would be horrified to find they were expected to party with a miserable, recently dumped forty year old. Her other son was in Australia and had no idea what his father had done, and that was how Linda was happy to leave it for the time being.

Frustratingly, Mike had been a brilliant father to their sons. Sad that all the morals and principles he'd instilled in them, had now been blown apart by his own shortcomings. Mike Williams. She was so ashamed of him. He'd made her feel so cheap and worthless, hiding away with a girl younger than his own offspring. It might have made her feel a bit better if he'd run away with someone rich and fabulous. And yet, if he turned up now and begged forgiveness, Linda reckoned he was still in with a chance. Just.

Hanging on the wardrobe door was her new top from Monsoon. It was rich and fabulous. Tina had bought it for her when they were in Chester. It had been a strange afternoon, and Linda had thought about it a lot. At first Tina had seemed okay, and Linda had enjoyed having her friend back. She hadn't changed much even though Mr and Mrs Woods were obviously pretty well off; but Tina was still unpretentious, warm and kind-hearted. They both were.

After lunch the day had gone haphazardly downhill.

Linda dried her shoulder length hair; it was mousy and needed cutting and highlighting. She pulled on jeans and boots, then the rich and fabulous top. She drained her wine, found her handbag, and told herself she'd feel fine once she got there. Like she used to tell the children when they were small, and didn't want to go to school.

Daniel's truck was there. No sign of the Porsche.

Tina opened the door, gave Linda a hug and took her coat.

The house was loud and chaotic; jammed full of neighbours and Tina's relatives, and there were a lot of them. Abba was in full throttle and Linda was drawn into the vortex.

'Where's Dan?' she shouted to Tina.

'He's digging a hole for Shane. Dad tried, but he couldn't get the spade deep enough. Drinks are in the kitchen, help yourself.'

Linda went to the little kitchen. The units were the old ones out of Dan and Tina's flat. There were bottles filling every surface, and balanced across the borrowed crate of glasses from the supermarket was a crumpled box; containing some kind of solar powered garden ornament.

Solar Cross, a fitting memorial. No running costs, casts a warm glow as night falls for up to 8 hours. Meerkat Magic! Order the cross and get a standing meerkat free; will enhance any garden.

Inside the box, on a bed of cheap satin, lay the white solar cross.

When Linda looked through the window, she could see Daniel digging in the garden, and the scene was illuminated by the light of a lamp on a long cable hanging over the washing line. He stopped for a moment to wipe his brow on his jacket sleeve, and then dragged a dog-sized sack into the hole. He started to fill it in. There was no sign of the complimentary meerkat.

When Daniel eventually came inside, he looked cold and fed up.

Linda said. 'Is there room for another dog in that hole?'

'Next door still giving you trouble?' Daniel said, washing his hands in the sink. 'I went to the garage for some beers and fell over a bloody Alsatian with rigor mortis,' he said, hunting for a towel. 'Thinking about it, its legs were pretty much like that when it was alive.'

Linda couldn't help smiling, but because she was tired and missing Mike, she was close to tears as well. Daniel flipped the pull on a can of lager.

'So, how's Christmas been so far?' he said, his eyes on hers.

'Rubbish... you?'

'It started with the traditional argument. Troy and Elle were meant to be having lunch with us at Mum's but they have their own, weird idea's about celebrating things; like marching over the hills to the druid's circle with tin cooking pots and bottles of beer.'

'It has a certain appeal.'

'Not for me, I had to eat two dinners to appease my mother.'

She laughed and prodded his flat stomach. 'Any news on the car?'

'It needs a new nearside wing, a headlamp and a wheel.'

'Ouch.'

'Yep... could buy another car with the cost of that little lot. Serves me right for being a flash idiot and wanting a Porsche,' he said, then frowned. 'Lin, does Tina seem okay to you?'

'Yeah, course.'

'You would tell me if there was anything to worry about?'

She was saved from answering by Tina herself barging in to the kitchen. 'There you are! Mum wants us to eat some of the buffet.' They were steered into the sitting room.

The buffet was huge, like an advertisement for a supermarket. The extended table was filled with sandwiches and sausage rolls. Red and green tinsel snaked around the dishes of crisps and the platter of leftover turkey. There was a big grey lump of stuffing in a cereal bowl. In the centre, was a brightly coloured trifle covered in hundreds and thousands, and a Christmas cake with three kings sinking into the centre.

It was futile claiming a lack of appetite.

Tina's mother took any refusal to consume as the ultimate insult. Daniel said it was a form of force feeding; like they did to geese in France, to make pate. Linda wondered if the bad relationship with the older, skinny sister had its roots in food consumption. Julie was stick thin and lived on cigarettes and HRT. Tina said Daniel was scared of her.

As a last resort, plates were made up and cling filmed so that they could be taken home for supper. Before long, Linda had a plate in each hand, but it saved her from dancing. She needed to feel light-hearted or drunk to dance. Tina tried to get Daniel to dance but he must have felt the same way and held the bridge of his nose. 'Tee, I've had enough now. Can we go?'

She sloped off with a pout and casually grabbed hold of someone else's husband. Linda wished she had Tina's nerve sometimes, although she'd never pull it off. Tina looked to be on usual form. Daniel was unfazed by anything she did, but he was no fool, and he knew her better than anyone. They were so right for each other.

Linda glanced at Daniel, sat on the floor with his back against the sofa staring at the carpet and lost in thought, resigned to another half an hour of Abba's greatest hits. He was an attractive guy. He was funny and smart, industrious; they were all the attributes you would expect in someone when they hit forty. Not so long ago, Linda used to think Mike was all those things.

The downside of Mike was that he could be easily led by Polish teenagers.

The downside of Daniel was that he could be violent and impulsive.

Some days Linda felt violent and impulsive; and she had to *stop* fancying all her friend's husbands and partners. Once they twigged, she'd be ostracised forever.

Mandy sashayed across, her mouth full. She kicked Daniel's foot. There was a plate of untouched food across his legs, and it wobbled dangerously.

'Hey, Danny boy, now that we're family any chance of a job in that swanky place of yours?'

'No.'

'You not eating that?'

'No.'

At midnight, when Tina's mother announced Shane's funeral, with the imminent placing of the solar cross, lots of people went outside. Daniel announced he was *going home*, and shot Tina a mutinous look. She was another half an hour saying goodbye.

Suddenly tired, it had been a hell of a long day, Linda begged a lift.

When they pulled up outside her house, next door was in darkness, but when the dog saw them and sprang to life, Linda couldn't help a wail of frustration. 'I'm just tired,' she said, trying to open the door, but it was awkward and she had no strength.

'Dan, can't we do something?' Tina said. 'She shouldn't have to put up with this.'

'What do you want me to do? Bury it?' he said, then relented and peered at the house. 'Are you sure there's no one in?'

'I can assure you, we'd all know,' Linda said, wiping her eyes. Daniel looked at them both and sighed, then got out of the vehicle and slammed the door. Linda could just make out his shadowy figure in the garden, with a paper plate of sausage rolls, and she wanted to laugh and cry at the same time. The dog was apoplectic with rage; whining, snarling and growling, leaping on its hind legs at the end of its tether, then sniffing the sausage scented air, not knowing what to make of it all. Tina wound the window down.

'Dan, be careful it might bite!'

'You don't say?' he hissed at her, before turning back to the dog. He threw it a sausage roll and it was devoured. The animal hunkered down expectantly and there was a small submissive wag of its tail. Daniel inched closer, paying out the sausage rolls, then a slice of turkey.

Linda practically stopped breathing as he unclipped it from the rope, but the dog just seemed overjoyed to be free and leapt about like a puppy. It was quite a cute dog really; it looked mostly like a white Husky with maybe twenty percent of something else, something that barked a lot. When Daniel put his fingers round its collar it followed him back to the Land Rover and sprang easily into the back.

Tina clapped her hands.

'Dan! Fix the trampoline.'

'What?'

'Fix the trampoline. *Go on!*'

In less than two minutes, he'd found some sort of wrench in the glove box and pulled off five big springs and a metal rod from beneath the trampoline, which he then flung in the back of the vehicle. For good measure, he scored through part of the surface with a Stanley knife. Linda scrambled out of the cab and Daniel hugged her tight and kissed her hair.

'Merry Christmas, love, sleep well. Mike's such a prat.'

She just nodded, not wanting to let go of him. 'I know. Thanks, Dan.'

She waved at Tina, and Tina stuck her thumbs up and grinned.

Linda watched the Land Rover disappear down the road with the dog hanging out of the back, and hugged herself with a smile.

It was so quiet, so beautifully quiet.

Ho ho ho.

*

Christmas was got through and New Year came and went. Tina texted her about the dog. Daniel had given it to Tony and Tristan to train for security. They'd called it Bear, and it ran through the woods chasing squirrels in the snow, and slept in a bunk bed in the caravan. The woman next door had shouted across the hedge to Linda more than once, asking if she'd seen it.

'We've had to tell the kids it's gone to heaven,' the woman said, suspiciously.

It has, Linda thought.

The trampoline had collapsed during a mass jump up and down, and Linda had hidden behind her curtains and watched its slow, beautiful demise to a pile of torn rubber and metal poles. She wondered if Mike would have dealt with next door the way Daniel had; probably not. He'd have called the police, documented and dated it all on a sheet of paper, and tried to record the dog barking for environmental health. It would have gone on for months.

Socially it all went a bit quiet after Christmas, but Linda figured Dan and Tina were busy with the hotel. Victoria called about Max's fiftieth birthday party, and asked for Tina's mobile number. She seemed keen to re-associate herself with them all, and Linda had to admit, she was curious about Victoria's life.

'Will there be any rich single men?' Linda said hopefully.

'Why do they need to be rich?'

'I can give up work, that's one reason.'

'You're lucky having a job, a sense of purpose.'

'Well I'd happily surrender to being looked after.'

'We've had a history of women who fought for the right to work.'

'Huh. What the fuck for?' Linda said, then realised how bitter she was sounding. 'Look, I'd love to come to the party.'

Tina called her a few minutes after Victoria's call. 'You going to this party? Dan doesn't want to go. He's sick of driving and not having a drink.'

Linda offered them a room for the night, with the idea they could all get a taxi to and from, and then, rather rashly booked herself an appointment at the hairdressers to get her highlights done.

Just in case.

*

Max was fifty on the last Saturday in January. No one had ever met Victoria's husband, or been in her house but Linda imagined both would be opulent. She deliberated over a birthday present. What could someone like Linda possibly buy someone like Max? In the end, Tina said she had it covered with two bottles of vintage champagne in a posh box.

When they arrived at Linda's house, it was obvious Tina and Daniel had had a massive row. They weren't even on civil speaking terms. Daniel looked tired and moody and Tina had swollen eyes, just about concealed with make-up. Fortunately it was just a short journey. The taxi dropped them on Victoria's drive and for a moment they all stared at the house. Tina said something about there being no balloons on the door, but no one laughed.

'Wow, what a place,' Linda said, looking around at the spacious drive. 'No neighbours.'

'I'd love some neighbours,' Tina said.

'Is that a fact?' Daniel said. 'Well why don't you just piss off and find some?'

'I might just do that! Someone to talk to other than your drug addict daughter and those two poofs in a caravan.'

Daniel, about to retaliate in a big way, suddenly swallowed his reply although his mouth didn't quite shut, because Victoria came to the door. She looked like she'd stepped off a magazine cover in a stunning, Grecian style white dress. Her dark hair was caught up in a clever, artful creation with long tendrils escaping round her fragile face. She looked ten years younger than either Tina or Linda, but Linda reasoned she'd had no stress in her life.

They followed their host down the hall, with its creaking floorboards, eastern rugs and tapestries, past rooms of antiques and original paintings; although Daniel was more intent on looking at Victoria's rear view, rather than admiring the furnishings. The dress had a deep cowl neckline and fell from her shoulders in a waterfall of fine, silky fabric almost to the base of her spine. It clung to her tiny waist, and floated around her long legs.

Tina poked Daniel in the back. 'Stop *leering* at her. God you're so obvious.'

'And you never are?'

'You can't take your eyes off her!'

'Yeah well, she looks different out of school uniform.'

They were led to a huge modern kitchen, full of blonde wood and glass, which was something of a surprise after all the Georgian sideboards and books. Just beyond this, was a conservatory the size of Linda's entire house with a full-size fountain in the centre. Eva Cassidy warbled discreetly in the background.

They were introduced to Max. He looked like George Clooney and Linda fell in love with him instantly. There were a lot of cocktails and fine wines on offer, all explained by Max in great detail, and Daniel listened patiently, then asked for a can of lager. Victoria overheard the exchange and smiled expansively at Daniel, held the eye contact just a bit too long.

Daniel said, 'Is she coming on to me already?'

'No Dan, it's all in your head,' Tina said.

The guests were mostly local business people, all loaded and a bit snooty. The conversation was about holidays to places Linda had never even heard of, tax returns, private schooling, what luxury car to go for next and did anyone know of a lightweight hunter for sale, something forward going with plenty of bone?

Linda found two chairs in a corner by a lot of black bamboo and vines. Tina said the fountain noise made her want to pee all the time and the plants must be plastic, no one had the time to fiddle with all that greenery and keep it alive. Linda discovered all the vegetation was real, even the grape vine and the orchids, but all the time she was poking the soil and talking, Tina wasn't really interested. Her husband was having a better time.

Daniel looked to be involved in several conversations, but his eyes kept straying to Victoria. Their host was so polished, she moved expertly between the little clusters of guests, chatting, topping up drinks. When she got round to Daniel, she leaned in a lot closer to speak to him and put her hand on his arm. After a cosy little chat, she introduced him to someone else, and he was off again, talking away, not missing them in the least. Victoria smiled, excused herself politely and moved on.

All the men in the room were mesmerised by her.

'If you were a bloke, would you fancy her?' Tina said sulkily.

'I fancy her anyway,' Linda said, and they both laughed till they nearly cried.

Food was served.

Victoria's daughter, Emily, helped her mother in the kitchen. From the look of things Victoria had made *everything*, which depressed Linda and Tina further. It was all a bit nouvelle cuisine and looked very sophisticated. They overheard Emily say to someone that she was studying English literature, archaeology and Italian architecture, at Oxford University.

Tina listened to the list of subjects with faint disbelief. 'Are your boys clever?'

'I'm proud of them, they're decent people.'

'That's not the same thing.'

'No, but it's more important.'

'You need another drink; you're talking too much sense.'

Daniel made his way over to them with a plate. 'Have you tried this food? It's just brilliant.'

Tina wouldn't speak to him, and walked away. Daniel just shrugged, 'I give up with her.'

'You don't mean that.'

'You know what? I think I do.'

Linda felt awkward. What was she meant to do now? Presently, Victoria and Emily did the rounds with champagne flutes and cake, in preparation for a toast. They did the usual birthday stuff and Max thanked everyone for coming etc. etc., then he got on to how wonderful his wife was for arranging it all. When he put a hand on Victoria's bare back, was it Linda's imagination, or did Victoria flinch ever so slightly, and move beyond his reach?

Relationships just weren't worth the heartache. Yet, she longed for someone to look after her, cherish her; and she longed to love and cherish back, there was no denying all that lost emotion, it went deeper than sex. Love couldn't be short-changed, no matter how it was dressed up.

Max opened some of his presents. Aged wine, a Rolex watch, golf clubs, a weekend on someone's yacht, theatre tickets to the opera. When he saw the glow in the dark meerkat, his face was remarkably expressionless.

'Oh *God*! Don't tell Dan,' Tina said.

Eventually Max made his way round to them and topped up Linda's drink.

'Do you want another can of lager, Daniel?'

'No thanks,' he said, indicating his wine glass.

'So, Victoria tells me you're a builder, but you want to be an hotelier, is that right?'

'Not quite. You see I'm already an hotelier.'

'Really? What's this little project you've taken on?'

'The hotel? It's going well thank you, bookings coming in.'

'Really?'

'Yes really.'

Victoria joined them, a slightly wobbly Tina in tow and a man she introduced as Charlie.

Out of the corner of her eye, Linda could see Victoria gesticulating, '*divorced*'. He was quite dashing in a public schoolboy way, with his floppy blonde hair and trendy waistcoat. Expensive watch; out of my league, Linda thought, but when she looked up Victoria caught her eye.

'Have you tried the mead pate? It's *quite* rich, but not sickly.'

'Not yet...'

'I think you should *try it*. Charlie's a GP. Same field as you, Linda.'

'What field would that be?' Charlie said.

'Lin's a... a nurse,' Tina said, slurring her words, her overfull glass of red wine inclining towards Victoria's white, silk dress. Victoria moved tactfully away.

'Oh, what kind?' Charlie said; his green eyes on Linda. 'Medical or surgical?'

'Oh er...just a general one.'

Tina picked the right moment to swoon. At first Linda thought she'd done it to get her out of a fix, but she went down with no thought for her own safety. Charlie sprang manfully into action and caught her before she hit her head on the fountain, then lowered her carefully to the floor. The whole room of guests turned, looked, and watched as Charlie laid her flat and called her name. When there was no response, he carefully put her in a recovery position.

'Keep an eye on her,' he said to Linda. 'I'll get my bag from the car.'

'How much has she had to drink?' Daniel said, fuming. 'She's out *cold!*'

Linda tugged Tina's dress back round to where it should be, but it still didn't cover her knickers or bra very well and there was the equivalent of half a bottle of merlot staining the Welsh slate floor.

Charlie returned at a run and knelt on the floor by Tina. He shone a light under her eyelids, then as he began to take her blood pressure, Tina came to life and blinked at the stars through the glass roof.

'Where am I?' she whispered tearfully. 'Why am I all wet? Have I *wet myself?*'

'Tina? Take your time, you fainted,' Charlie said, reading the dial on the meter, 'BP's low.' He took the strap off Tina's arm and helped her to sit up. When it became obvious there was no need for further medical intervention, the room gradually tittered back into life. Victoria's daily help swept up the glass and got a mop and bucket for the floor and sloshed some disinfectant in it. Daniel watched from a discreet distance, holding the bridge of his nose.

Max watched the scene with a supercilious smile.

'I'll call you a cab, shall I?' he said to Daniel, and Linda decided she'd suddenly gone off him. He was nothing like George Clooney. Charlie and Linda helped Tina into the sitting room, where she perched on a Queen Anne chair with a glass of water. When the taxi came, Daniel practically frogmarched his wife into the back seat. Linda went round the room collecting their coats and handbags and apologising to Victoria, although she wasn't quite sure what for.

Charlie followed her to the front door, and his Armani fragrance came with him.

'Your friend isn't drunk,' he said quietly.

'I know.'

He scribbled a mobile number down. 'Make sure she contacts her doctor. Will you ring me? Let me know how she is?'

Linda nodded.

'I'd like to talk you again.'

Would that be for medical interest, or more personal reasons?

At home, all the lights were on in the lounge and she could see a football match on the television. Linda didn't remember leaving it like that; she was always turning things off. The reason became more apparent when they all fell over the bags in the hall. Mike appeared at the lounge door, cup of tea in hand and a slice of cake. He gave Daniel and Tina barely a nod of recognition.

'I've come home,' he said to Linda, as if it all needed explaining.

Daniel touched her elbow and said, 'Do you want us to

clear off?'

'No. No don't go.'

'So, we'll have an argument upstairs, and you can have one down here?'

'Something like that.'

There was an awkward moment then as Daniel and a tear-stained Tina, her dress soaked with red wine, made their way up the stairs with an overnight bag. Linda went into the lounge and closed the door behind her. Mike had turned the television sound down, but the score was flashed every few seconds, and now and again there was a muted roar from the crowd. Strangely it didn't annoy her, it was part of Mike. Part of what she'd wanted back. Maybe it was the Mr Kipling that did it. Did anyone eat cake if they were gripped with remorse?

She should have been angry, but it just wasn't there. All the clever bits of conversation she'd had in her head wouldn't come out of her mouth. Was that because she didn't care anymore or was it because she was just relieved to fall back into the groove because it was easier? Or was it because she'd met a man who'd knelt on the floor with her and looked at her with some honesty?

'Lin, I want to come back, can we talk?' he said.

She nodded, that was a good idea; maybe she'd remember what she wanted to say.

'Has her visa run out? Plonker, was it?'

'Armenka. I'll sleep in the spare room till we've talked.'

'Dan and Tina are in the spare room.'

'The box room… I'll go in there, yeah?'

'It's full of boxes, the boys' stuff.'

'The sofa then…'

Her phone bleeped with a text. It was from Victoria.

He fancies you, it said.

CHAPTER FOUR

Victoria logged on to the domestic violence helpline most days. The pictures of abused men and women were from all kinds of backgrounds, through every social class right up to the wealthy. So, she was in there somewhere. It was chilling to think that her clever, good looking husband went through the same process in his head as an abusive alcoholic with a knife in his hand. He was a worm caught inside a rose. The latest apology looked to be taking the form of an Irish thoroughbred mare called Rolling Cloud.

It was a stunning animal. Nature's finest engineering. When she watched it move, it could move her to tears. Victoria had no idea how many thousands of pounds it cost and would continue to cost, she only knew that it was extravagant, and out of context with her life. She'd shown a passing interest in riding again, and this was the result. If she refused the gift, she refused him. If she refused him, he might just feel less in control.

It was becoming more of a problem, the possession and the physical knocks.

It had started a long, long time ago; she just hadn't noticed it as anything abusive. She'd thought he was a bit overprotective that was all, and jealous sometimes. But then gradually over the years, the control had tightened and developed into something more sinister. When Richard and Emily went off to university, it had stepped up a gear. Max thought the horse would keep her nicely occupied in a predominantly female environment, and it was a massive status symbol to boot. For Victoria, it wasn't enough, this aimless life of indulgence paid for by Max. Everything was paid for and provided for by Max, and therefore it belonged to him. She wanted to know who she was; she wanted to find something which identified her as Victoria.

She looked at the website for The Lakeside. It looked impressive, the changes Daniel had made to that horrible, old fashioned hotel. He was advertising for staff now... chef, breakfast cook, kitchen help, cleaners and outside catering for events.

Respond via e-mail only.

Daniel had loved her Welsh fusion food. It had been so gratifying to have someone show commercial interest in something she'd created. Lots of Max's big clients were old generation Welsh, some of them from foodie backgrounds, so it never failed. She'd got the idea from a local food fair and adapted it for parties, made everything bite-sized. Miniature Welsh lamb pies with wild bilberry sauce, local goat's cheese rarebit, Welsh mead pate on lava bread, Bara brith ice cream.

Her finger hovered over *reply*.

Would that tiny action be the start of something she'd regret, or would it open up something exciting and challenging? Did Max even have to know? He'd had his own secrets from her. Victoria knew he'd had affairs, discreet little liaisons throughout their marriage and at the time Victoria had turned a blind eye, put the family first. What she was contemplating wasn't in the same league.

Well then, maybe it was time the worm turned. Max had his fun and his freedom. It was her turn now. She hit the reply icon and watched the computer send its little envelope spinning round the world.

*

Lunch was at The King George in Conwy, with Charlie Summers' ex-wife and a couple of the other wives in their circle. Victoria parked next to Karen Summers', Mercedes soft top. Charlie's ex had evolved into a shallow, materialistic woman and as far as Victoria was concerned, Charlie was well shot of his ex. She'd had lovers on the side for years and screwed Charlie for everything he had. At least they'd never had children. Charlie was lovely; she hoped he hit it off with Linda.

They ordered their low fat meals and a bottle of Zinfandel. The conversation was all the same superficial nonsense and Victoria found herself zoning out.

'You're quiet today, Vic. Good party at yours the other night.'

'Yes, Max enjoyed it.'

'Who was that guy with the falling over blonde? The one who's bought that hotel?'

'Dan Woods.'

'He's cute. Where do you know him from?'

'School.'

'*Gorgeous* eyes. Like those terribly expensive dark chocolate almonds from Michel Cluizel.'

'He's just got married.'

'So? I *like*,' and they all laughed.

Victoria went home and checked her e-mail... nothing. The disappointment was pathetic. Almost like the time she'd been fifteen, when he'd asked her out and she'd said no... pathetic.

It wasn't until the following morning, after Max had left for the office, when Victoria flipped up the lid on her laptop; there was the familiar red flash, new e-mail. You have one un-read message. He'd replied just before midnight.

"Are you serious? I hope so. Come and talk to me.

Bring pie."

Victoria laughed out loud and replied in the affirmative, then spent the morning costing out her recipes and making a full size version of the lamb pie. She felt euphoric, and that was pathetic as well when she thought about it.

She deliberated over what to wear, then just pulled on a pair of denims with a white shirt, leather boots and a sparkly scarf. She grabbed her leather jacket and set off for The Lakeside, the pie in a basket on the passenger seat of her little car. It was a warm March day and although the trees were still struggling to acknowledge spring, there were daffodils and crocuses on the grass verges along the valley road. There was a new sign indicating the turn for the hotel.

The Lakeside looked even better up close. It was such a stunning location, that Victoria stopped the car for a moment to drink it all in and listen to the birds, the sound of the wind in the fir trees and the sunlight touching the water. Everything was coming to life again, but it was infused with peace. She hoped it was all symbolic.

She parked next to Daniel's car and found her way into the reception. For a long moment she was distracted by the incredible chandelier; and the extension over the lake. Daniel's son Troy, whom she recognised from the wedding, directed her to where Daniel was interviewing. He was on the decked area, head bent over paperwork, with a pot of coffee. He looked up when he heard her approach and smiled. 'Have you brought it?'

Victoria carefully lifted the cloth-covered pie out of her basket and slid it onto the table.

Daniel reverently lifted the cloth to look at it.

'*Wow*. A big one, you've got the job.'

She laughed, and he indicated she take a seat, poured her some coffee, then changed his mind and disappeared into the kitchen. He returned with two plates, a knife, some glasses and a bottle of red wine. He began to cut into the pie.

'This is the best food I've seen all day,' he said, 'and I've seen quite a lot. What do you want to know about the job?' he said, pouring her a glass of Shiraz.

'First, I want to know how you've done this amazing transformation!'

'Do you like it?'

'More, much more than like,' she said, sipping her wine. 'Though I don't know what I'm supposed to ask you, I've not had a job interview for about twenty-five years.'

'Okay. I'll tell you what's bothering me about you.'

'Oh. Go on.'

'You don't need the money.'

Victoria took another gulp of wine, wondering how much to tell him. 'Well no, but I do need the work. I *want* to work. I won't let you down, if that's what you're thinking.'

'What about hubby?' Daniel said, leaning back in his chair. 'How does Max feel about you slaving away in a hot kitchen for me? You see, I can't imagine he'd be over the moon about that.'

Victoria shifted uncomfortably; he was more astute than she'd bargained for. 'No, I don't imagine he would,' she faltered. 'Look, Daniel I won't lie to you. I haven't told him; not yet.'

'Ah.' A pause while he considered this with a charismatic, knowing smile and Victoria felt her face flush with heat. He was flirting with her! She broke the contact and looked across the calm water, suddenly feeling fifteen again and tongue tied.

'Okay. If you reckon it's worth the risk, then so do I,' he said, back to being business-like.

She gulped her wine, 'I'd love to be a part of this, Daniel, I really would.'

'Good answer. You're better at interviews than you thought.' He clinked his glass against hers. 'Congratulations. You are the official catering manager for The Lakeside,' he said, then glanced at his laptop. 'Okay down to business. First date I've got for you is a press party, Easter. Be about fifty covers, and it would be nice if you could be here and mingle and chat up some of the guests, drum up some business. I know you're good at that, I've seen you in action. Is any of that going to be a problem for you?' he said, settling his dark eyes on her again, this time with no smile.

'No, tell me what food you want.'

'No. That's your job now.'

Later, at home, Victoria swayed between elation and a feeling of dread. Max was home late but still wanted to hear about her day. Then he wanted sex. It wasn't making love; it was sex, but at least that meant it didn't last too long. He wasn't too gentle or caring these days, but she was getting good at faking and zoning out. It didn't upset her anymore, her mechanism for dealing with it was that Max had a mental illness and the best form of self-protection was to be calm and compliant.

His older brother had bullied him, she knew that much. As a theory for understanding Max, it still seemed too disconnected with herself, and so long ago it was off the scale. But who knows what lay dormant in the brain and how it reformed and manifested itself over the years? It had been the right decision to let Daniel in on her deception. She knew she couldn't keep it to herself for very long, but she would need to plan when to tell him, and for a while it was oddly comforting, to own a slice of life she didn't share with Max.

Escapism!

The Lakeside was going to be so special. Daniel had shown her all of it. It was classy, simple and beautifully finished but that was his trade after all.

'So, what made a builder want to be an hotelier?' she'd said.

'I wanted to come home to the hills.'

She'd laughed, then realised he was mostly serious. 'Really?'

'I've got something to prove, to myself as much as anyone else.'

Victoria had nodded, understanding.

*

The following week, Daniel rang her about a food safety hygiene certificate.

'Have you got one?'

'Em... no, sorry.'

'I need you to have one for the records. It's just a day course that's all. There's nothing local till next month, can you get to Manchester next Tuesday?'

'Sure.'

'Great. I'll e-mail the details. You can meet up with Tina; she can be an alibi for you.'

'What's Tina doing there?'

'Huh. Dunno really. She's at the flat, packing clothes and stuff as far as I know. Maybe you could pop round?'

Victoria told Max she was having lunch with Tina, followed by late night shopping in the Trafford Centre. Hopefully it wasn't too far from the actual truth, although actually she'd been unable to get hold of Tina. Daniel and Tina had an even weirder relationship than Max and her.

She was at the college in just over an hour. The course was quite intense but there was a two hour break in the middle, before more of the same, and then a test of understanding. A lot of it was common sense but some of the commercial legislation, and the names of the different kinds of food poisoning were tricky to remember. Victoria knew she should have revised her notes at lunch time. However, Daniel and Tina's flat was literally just a minute's walk away and she'd love a coffee and a sandwich with her old friend; then she could tell Daniel everything was fine. Victoria set off at a brisk walk, it wasn't far and she didn't want to lose her precious parking place.

Didsbury was a nice leafy suburban area, with a lot of period properties divided into student lets because of the close proximity to the university. Apparently the Didsbury flat had been their joint home for years, on and off, in typical Daniel and Tina style. Daniel told her they intended to rent the flat out, if he could get Tina to give it up; but she'd been dragging her heels, still wanting a bolt hole close to the shops and the life they'd had before. Victoria had asked Daniel a bit about the life they'd had before, and even the bare bones of it sounded like a work of fiction.

Apparently, he'd also owned a large house and a half share in a construction company. When the partner of the company suddenly suffered a fatal coronary, Daniel had un-expectedly found himself sole proprietor and the recipient of a lump sum of capital as well. Seeing an opportunity to make a life change and a lot of money, he'd sold both house and company before the property market bombed. And bought a falling down hotel in North Wales instead, and a Porsche.

It made her smile, thinking about Daniel. He was so different to Max. Max was all old money, the family firm of accountants going back several generations. She hated the stuffy snobbery which went with it, as if anything new or someone from a different background did not hold the same worth. Max's idea of a hard day's work these days was playing a round of golf without upsetting anyone.

Victoria neared the address Daniel had given her. As she was standing in the street, working out which one was number 22a, something made Victoria glance round, just in time to see Tina get into the passenger seat of a white van. She almost shouted out, but realised how futile that would be. The van spluttered off down the road. Victoria stared after it for a moment before beginning the trek back again.

It was a long afternoon, and the subject matter was much tougher. She'd not had much time to revise the first lot of notes never mind have lunch, and then she wasn't really concentrating, more deliberating over what to tell Daniel, if anything. After all, it didn't amount to much anyway.

By some miracle Victoria passed the written test and scraped through the verbal. Elated, she called Daniel's mobile. The line was awful and his voice kept fading away.

'Victoria? Can you hear me, hang on...can you hear me? Did you see Tina?'

'No, not really.'

'How do you mean?'

'Just missed her, she got into a van with someone.'

A beat passed. 'A *white* van? Was there a pizza on the roof? And did it say Fernando's in red and green down the side?'

'Er... possibly, it was white anyway.'

'*Fuck.*'

He disconnected and Victoria looked at the phone in disbelief then switched it off and threw it in her bag. A pizza on the roof? She drove to the Trafford centre and spent a few hundred pounds of Max's money on dinner, a handbag and a lot of silk underwear. When she finally reached home, the car headlights picked up the glow in the dark meerkat sat up in the camellias. Max had put it straight into the red-cross sack, but Victoria had rescued it.

'Good day?' Max said affably.

'Yes, good thanks, you?' she said, piling her bags onto the kitchen table. 'Tired now though, it was a long day, walked miles.'

'And Tina? Managed to stay sober did she?'

'It was fine; like I said, a nice day.'

'Good, good. What did she buy? Tina?'

Victoria grabbed a bottle of wine out of the cooler, anything to keep her hands busy.

'Let me guess,' Max said, following her round the kitchen. 'Buy one get ten free from Matalan? Mmm? Or, was it something red and racy from La Senza?'

Victoria poured the wine. 'What if it was? Why are you so interested?'

'Oh I'm *very* interested. I'm an accountant. I'm interested in things that don't add up.'

She watched Max go into the hall and turn on the telephone answer machine. After a bleeping noise and the date and time, Tina's voice came out of the tinny speaker. 'Hiya! It's Tina! Vic, look I'm sorry I've been out of touch, I've gone and lost my bloody mobile with all my numbers in. I remembered I had your landline from years ago; it was still in the flat in an old address book can you believe. Anyway, I didn't want you to think I'm ignoring you or anything. Catch up soon yeah?'

The machine reset itself and then there was a dead silence.

'Well?'

'Okay I didn't go with Tina.'

'So you lied?'

'I changed my mind, I wanted to be alone.'

'Because? Victoria?'

'Because... I was going to surprise you! Come to your office in the new underwear at lunch, but I ran out of time.'

'Really? Well let's not waste any more of it. Why don't you put it on now, and we can balance the books?'

Victoria went heavily up the stairs, dropping the glossy bags everywhere, clutching the bottle of wine. Once in the bedroom, she swallowed a full glass of ice cold Sancerre, as if it were anaesthetic, followed by another.

*

In the morning, Max brought her breakfast in bed. He'd made scrambled eggs and smoked salmon, as if they were on holiday, or she was ill. She wasn't ill, but it was a form of sickness. She was in a loveless marriage with a bully; there was no dressing it up with complicated psychological terms. Her insides were sore and bruised, and she had a hangover but that was the least of her problems. She drank the orange juice and coffee, then lay back down again. Her husband even pecked her on the cheek, as if it were all normal. When she heard Max reverse off the drive, she ran herself a bath and took the maximum dose of Ibuprofen.

When Victoria finally switched on her mobile there was a text from Daniel. 'Sorry, sorry I hung up, love, bit stressed.' According to all the latter day feminists, calling everyone 'love' was meant to be a little patronising, but Daniel said it as a genuine term of endearment; the fact he'd bothered to put the word in a text though, filled her eyes with tears. Daniel wasn't patronising in the least. It was just that word, *love.*

Victoria texted back then deleted both messages and lay back down again. She should get dressed, but even that was too much effort and she mostly spent the day looking at the television, but not watching or hearing it.

Max performed true to form, and came home full of remorse, he was a textbook abuser. She heard him climb the stairs and then he looked round the bedroom door, like a naughty child.

'Hi,' he said. His face was slack, eyes cast down.

'Go on, say it. *Sorry.* No flowers this time? No present?'

He came and sat wordlessly on the bed and Victoria held her arms out, where there were two weals of bruises developing on the insides of her forearms. 'See that? You did that, Max. You did that on the inside as well. I feel all used up, and my body is like a husk, like I've had my insides dragged out and thrown on the trash. What does all that say to you?'

He had the grace to look sickened at that, or maybe it was just the words she chose, her lack of tears or emotion. She'd never cried in front of him, and she never would. She'd had tears from him before though, and it was surreal and strange, like when his mother had died.

His voice was so low she could barely hear him. 'I don't know what to say.'

'I do. *Stay away from me.*'

'I'll get help.'

She made a derisory noise and he put his head in his hands. He'd done that before as well.

'Victoria I... just don't leave me, I couldn't stand that. Think about the children.'

'Me think about the children? That's all I've ever done, but they don't need me now.'

'Please, don't leave me Victoria. I'm *begging* you...'

'Doesn't go with your slick image does it? Be all over the papers. The details would be juicy, Maxwell Morgan, respected businessman, even stood for the local council once, and now *divorced* for raping his wife. Imagine your father's horror. Imagine how the will would change, eh Max?'

'*Rape?*'

'I asked you to *stop* Max. That makes it rape, in my book.'

He looked beaten, swallowed up at the hands of his own dysfunctional psyche.

'Please, Victoria I'll do anything...'

She swung her legs slowly out of bed, pulled on her dressing gown, went over to the window and leant on the wide sill for support. The garden was just visible in the dusk. She thought about his words, about her unspoken power.

'Anything? I just want my own life,' she said.

*

A few weeks later, and the Easter weather grew steadily more unpredictable. One minute there were clouds gathering and a sudden wind would send the surface of the lake into folds of silk, and then there would be a rainbow cutting through the silhouette of crags behind the hotel and diving into the water, spilling its pot of gold. Sometimes, after a token rush of rain, the sun would come out and sear everything with a spell of intense heat.

When the sun did come out it was all very pretty, there was no denying that. For Tina however, the shadowy depths of the water in the lake and the towering scale of the mountains somehow made her feel out-manoeuvred and swallowed by the forces of nature. She'd never even thought about the forces of nature before, let alone become obsessed by how life-changing it could be; isolating in every sense.

Not wanting to drive again didn't help, but Tina didn't want to think about that. Maybe she was still spooked by the accident. Weird thing was, no matter how hard she tried, the actual point of impact and the few seconds leading up to it, remained a blank. As did the embarrassing episode at Max's birthday party; she had no recollection of actually falling over. It had taken her several days to feel right again after that. Although Daniel had been sweet about the car accident, he was deeply irritated about the way she'd shown him up in front of Max and Victoria, and all their snotty friends.

'I reckon some idiot must have spiked my drinks, Dan.'

'Don't be stupid. They don't have idiots as friends!'

He was right, but it was easier to blame something or someone else for how she felt and what had happened. Although Tina was beginning to tire of her own confusing mix of dread and denial so she could hardly expect Daniel to take her seriously.

'Maybe I'm allergic to the countryside, hey babes?'

'Huh... what? Bit late to find that out,' he said, tapping

something into his phone. He'd stopped listening to her. It was the day prior to the launch, and he was preoccupied. The launch party was all Daniel could think about. And that was another thing, no matter how hard she tried, Tina just couldn't find the same energy and enthusiasm as everyone else.

Even Victoria had arrived at The Lakeside just after eight that morning, in a brown velvet tracksuit with her hair twisted into a glamorous knot on top of her head. With her huge doe eyes and slender limbs she looked like a prize gazelle. Even worse, Daniel's mother had also arrived and declared herself Victoria's sous chef for the day. Tina had hung around; interested to see how *that* would work out, but to her surprise Victoria seemed to find an instant rapport with Marian. Tina had never got on with Dan's mother in that way, she always seemed so disapproving somehow, but on hearing her laugh with Victoria, it felt like a snub and left her feeling childishly jealous. The one time in her life she just might have turned to Marian rather than her own already burdened mother, was quickly pushed aside.

Tina steered clear, she didn't trust herself round the knives and not from a fantasy viewpoint either but she needed to *do* something; even if it was only cleaning up after Master Chef and her accomplice. As the morning wore on, Victoria began to irritate Tina. She'd imagined they could have gossipy coffee breaks all the time, but Victoria was incredibly serious and focused, as if their friendship was a poor second to being the catering manager.

And then Bluebell had made an appearance, looking for breakfast. For a twenty year old, Daniel's daughter knew a lot about the darker ways of the world and yet had no idea how to feed herself properly. Marian had set about showing her how to make smoothies in the blender, secretly in her element. The resultant mess was handed to Tina to wash up, but not before she'd dropped the jug on the tiled floor and splattered every surface with a dark pink stain.

Then it was Troy, looking for reject pies.

'Troy, you *really* need to make a decision about cleaners,' Daniel said, following him in and plonking a big box of mop heads in his arms, then piling cleaning fluid, scrubbing brushes and toilet rolls on top. Troy's head was just visible. 'Yeah, I can't decide between the blonde or the brunette, or the polish twins.'

'You better be joking.'

'Why can't our Mandy be a cleaner?' Tina said to Daniel.

'No friends or family, *we agreed*.'

Tina wiped the kitchen sink for the third time. She couldn't remember that particular conversation. 'So who's Victoria, and Bluebell and Marian?'

'Mum is temporary and comes free. Victoria is self-employed.'

Marian rolled her eyes at Victoria. 'Charming, I didn't know that.'

'And what does Bluebell do?' Tina said, her eyes fixed on the taps.

'She's just here, that's all. She came back to me and she's *not using*. Why can't you just accept that for now? Look, just leave Blue out of it!'

'Stop it you two! You're worse than any children,' Marian said, but looked mostly at Tina.

Fuming, Tina flung the wet cloth at Daniel's head and went outside.

Presently, Victoria joined her with a tray.

They sat at one of the new tables, a mixture of weathered wood and steel, with big candles inside weighted hurricane lamps. Victoria poured the coffee.

'She's split us up before you know? *Bluebell*,' Tina said, knowing Victoria probably didn't want to hear about it but she didn't have the mental energy to keep it all contained any more. She lit a cigarette and threw the packet down. 'Just wish she'd go back to her bloody drama queen of a mother.'

'Split you up?'

'Yeah... Daniel gave up a year of his life to get her off heroin, practically locked her up. The only trouble was he was locked up with her. She nearly died and it almost broke Dan. Bloody Marian played the supporting role as usual.'

'Hell of a thing for a parent to go through.'

'Oh everyone loved him for it, but he left me and Troy to go and save her.'

'Tina, you've got to put all that behind you.'

'I know. I thought I had. Troy was fifteen, he needed his father,' she said, mystified where all the soul searching had come from, but then it had been so easy to forget it all, away from everyone in Manchester. 'Troy and I need him now.'

'And Daniel needs you,' Victoria said airily.

God she even sounded like Marian now.

Towards the end of the afternoon, Tina lay on the bank with Daniel by the lake shore, where there was a small gravel beach and a huddle of broken boats and canoes. For a while, it had been good to escape down by the water, just the two of them, but it hadn't lasted long; everyone else slowly appeared and threw themselves down on the parched grass. All except Victoria, who was still slaving away in the kitchen with a manic sort of urgency. What was all that about, was she hoping for a gold star from Marian?

Marian reclined nearby in an old sun chair she'd found in the boot of her car, reading the paper, spectacles on top of her head. Troy and Elle were messing about with the boats, trying to determine if any of them were trustworthy in the water, and Bluebell was rolling tobacco, sat on a rock like an elf, with Cupcake, the Chihuahua. Bear was digging up rocks from the bottom of the lake then bringing them to shore and making an important pile. Daniel said Bear was showing the Chihuahua what real dogs did, and Bluebell gave him a rare, private smile.

'Does that dog have no legs?' Tina snapped. 'Why do you carry it all the time?'

'So you won't kick her.'

Daniel picked up Tina's hand and held it across his chest and the firm warmth of his touch dispelled the tension, and she felt a sudden overwhelming rush of love for him, her gorgeous husband. He didn't deserve to have a moaning old bitch as a wife. He deserved the very best did Daniel. Tina breathed deeply, threaded her fingers through his and closed her eyes against the sun, and he kissed the back of her hand. She hoped no one saw the tears escape the corner of her eyes and run into her ears, because then she'd have to explain them. And what on earth would she say?

In the hazy background, she could hear the manic splashing and snorting of the dog in the water, then the push and slide of the gravel as the boats were manhandled, and Troy's voice as he showed off to the girls. Shouts, laughter, arguments and family stuff. It brought back memories of family holidays and happy times but now they were Mr and Mrs Woods, proprietors of The Lakeside Hotel. It seemed daft to Tina that despite all the money, they would all be working round the clock again.

The sun went behind a cloud, and everyone moaned. Bear shook himself and the water went everywhere. Enjoying the effect, he did it again before settling down to dig a hole; soil flying everywhere. Tina prodded Daniel to make him move but he just grunted.

'Babes, are you asleep? How can you be asleep?'

Marian said, 'He's been working sixteen hour days, that's why he's asleep.'

Tina shot her a black look. Here we go, she thought. Daniel, although he'd heard the exchange, took an age to come round. 'What did you say that for?' he said to his mother, rubbing his face. He did look tired, and he had about three days of stubble.

'Daniel, you're exhausted!'

'How's that Tina's fault?'

'I know why Dad's tired,' Troy said, grinning, 'he's all shagged out.'

Bluebell just twitched the corners of her mouth. Marian looked at him with huge disapproval, folded up her newspaper and snapped her chair shut. Daniel pulled his sweater back on then lay back down again, and Tina walked back to the hotel with a tiny measure of comfort. Troy had got the famous Marian look for a change, and Daniel had stood up for her.

*

It was dusk by the time Victoria had finished in the kitchen. She'd wanted to do as much prep as possible in order to leave her time free on the actual launch day so she could mingle with the guests. She'd had an amazing day, despite all the petty arguments. It was just so good to be part of it all.

The Lakeside was looking like a fully functional hotel, although they were only running on a skeleton staff till the bookings increased. As a result, Daniel was wearing so many hats he sometimes forgot who he was or what he was doing, on top of which he was interrupted every few minutes by the phone, or their son. Troy was in much the same position as his father, one minute learning to plumb in taps, the next interviewing cleaners, but mostly in Troy mode at half speed and needing plenty of instruction.

He was very like his mother, but Troy certainly didn't hold the same bitterness over his half-sister. When Victoria had heard her plucking a guitar, singing old Coldplay songs, she had to stop what she was doing, almost stop breathing so she could savour every refrain. She caught Troy doing the same thing when he was sweeping up outside.

'Hey, that's my sister,' he said, grinning at Victoria.

Then there was that bitter little conversation with Tina over coffee. Honestly, Tina had no idea how lucky she was. *No idea.* She came across to Victoria's car when she was closing the boot.

'So, this is it,' Tina said. 'Our big day tomorrow, if we all make it through the night without killing each other.' She looked across the expanse of water in the dusk. 'Sorry I've been a moody cow. Sometimes, I want to run away and be a kid again. Just Dan and me.'

'Everyone is tired, that's all.'

'Yeah, I know,' she said, looking down at her feet. 'Daniel wants us to dress up, in black or white. Please pick the white, then I can be black. It suits my mood and hides all my fat.'

'Okay I pick white. You look great in black, I don't.'

When Victoria set off down the lake road, the sun was dying quickly, exposing the hard black ridge of Cefn Cyfarwydd. Daniel was still there, lying on the cold grass, his arm still across his face. Everyone had disappeared except the dog. Bear was still busily digging his hole, so deep now that he pivoted round the circumference.

Daniel knew the sound of Victoria's car, and he lifted his hand in a desultory wave. She almost did the same but quickly realised he wouldn't be able to see her. When she reached the end of the lake and looked in her rear view mirror, he still hadn't moved, but Bear had flopped down at last, his big head on his master's legs.

Victoria's self-employed.

Victoria had thought about that quite a lot, whether it was a throwaway comment on Daniel's behalf didn't really matter. It had planted a seed. She would only be called on to cater for The Lakeside on the occasions they had events. There was nothing stopping her throwing the net a bit wider, only Max maybe, but she could become independent, she wouldn't need Max.

She was home before him. Their relationship had become disturbingly quiet, but that was the pattern. There was no physical affection or terms of endearment, they didn't laugh, they didn't smile, but at least there was no sex. They even had separate bedrooms. She'd healed physically, but the mental scars were far worse.

Victoria thought about Dan and Tina. They were always fighting, verbally anyway, but the cohesion between them was far stronger than it appeared. Just that afternoon, Victoria had disturbed them both, going through the wrong door, looking for fresh linen. They were lying on the bed fully clothed, in each other's arms, just talking. Tina had her hands round Daniel's face. They were unaware of Victoria. It was painfully intimate, more so than if they'd been making love. She tried to remember if Max and herself had ever done anything like that, but she couldn't remember.

She'd gone through all their family photographs, trying to see where it had begun to erode. The early years had been good, but then when the children were small and Victoria was tired and preoccupied, the infidelities had started. When she'd first met Max she was a bit in awe of his older, more experienced man image, and she'd never been a femme fatale in the bedroom so in a perverse way, it was easy to turn a blind eye.

At first, his more subtle control had been attractive, but when Victoria thought about the forced sex Max had put her through, she felt a rise of nausea. It haunted her. She should have gone to the police, but at the time the thought of relating it all, having someone examine her for evidence, was just too awful to contemplate. And how did that work exactly, if they were married?

She thought she could handle it.

And now, it was too late.

Max knew it was too late as well. The cycle was starting

to build again. He hated her working at the hotel. He hated Daniel. He hated a lot of things. Victoria made his favourite supper, a homemade fish pie and opened a bottle of Sauvignon Blanc to go with it. She didn't know why she tried to please him, to balance out the hate was one theory, and it only needed a tiny shred of hope to keep hanging on, but it was painful, hanging on by your fingertips.

They ate in silence.

'Have you been to work today?' he said eventually.

'Yes.'

'What did you do?'

'Cook... I enjoyed it.'

'You can cook here.'

'I still do, Max.'

Victoria cleared the remains of their meal, switched the dishwasher on, then went upstairs and took out the white dress, still in its sheath from the dry cleaners. He came and stood behind her.

'What are you doing?'

'The dress? It's for tomorrow, for the launch.'

'I don't think so.'

'What...?' Victoria said, her heart hammering.

'I bought that dress.'

'Yes... but you didn't buy *me*. I was never for sale.'

His anger at her words was almost tangible, she could taste it, smell it.

Victoria made to dive across the bed to the door, but Max was faster.

He grabbed her ankle and she fell awkwardly, hitting the side of her face against the solid oak headboard. For a moment she was stunned by the pain of it. Victoria somehow found the strength to grab the brass bedside clock and hurl it towards Max. It fell several feet wide of the mark. She listened to it thud against the door and roll to a halt on the deep pile carpet.

He laughed. Slowly, he dragged her back towards him by her ankle.

Her shirt began to ruck up, exposing her midriff and most of her bra. The blood from the cut on her head left a dark stain on the cream throw. She could feel panic rise in her throat as she clutched the bed linen, a futile act, as all it did was slide with her.

Neither of them heard footsteps running up the stairs and then Emily was there, her beautiful grown up little girl, her arms full of Easter eggs, her heart full of love. 'Surprise...'

'Emily! Oh Emily,' Victoria said, almost crying with relief and buried her face in the soft goose-down of the bed, trying to hide the panic in her eyes and her voice, but it was too late. Emily stood at the bedroom door, slowly taking it all in; the strange scene her parents were engaged in and the gash on her mother's head. There were a hundred questions poised there, but it all took just a few seconds to distill.

'Oh my God! Mum...? *What's going on?*'

Max dropped Victoria's ankle like a stone, then staggered back against the wall. Emily ran to her mother, helped her off the bed and into the bathroom, all the time glancing back towards her father, but Max remained motionless and un-seeing, unable to make eye contact with either of them. He slid down the wall and sat on the floor, disturbing in itself as it was so out of character.

Emily tried to bathe the cut on her mother's head, but she was trembling and kept dropping the cotton wool. Victoria took it from her, and looked at her in the mirror above the basin. 'I need you to help me pack some things,' she said, as evenly as possible.

'Where will we go? It's late.'

'The hotel.'

Emily nodded. 'What's wrong with Dad? Has he hurt you? Is he ill, is that it?'

'I don't know, yes maybe.'

Victoria had no clear cut answer for her, not really. She struggled to hide the feelings she had suffocated for many months. It was about protection again, but not her own this time, she could fool herself but Emily altered the axis of her thoughts entirely, and her daughter wasn't a child, she could work out the missing gaps, and then the floodgates would open.

Together they stuffed things into bags, going through drawers and cupboards with not much thought. Victoria, holding a wad of dressing against her head, snatched the white dress off the wardrobe door.

Max was still on the floor, hugging his knees.

'I *hate you*,' she said, but this time there were tears streaming down her face.

'I hate me too.'

CHAPTER FIVE

It was early, only about ten, but Daniel lay in bed and tried to relax. During the day he'd fallen asleep on the grass and in an upright chair, but it wasn't happening in bed.

He could hear owls.

'Can you hear that, Tee?'

'Are they real, Dan? It sounds spooky. Everything's spooky round here at night, shadows and stuff.'

After a few moments, he could hear a car approaching. He got out of bed and peered through the slats on the blind. 'You won't believe this.'

'What, it's not the bears is it?'

'Kind of... who do you know drives a pink BM?'

Tina wailed and put her head under the pillow. 'Mia? Noooo, get rid of her, Dan!'

Bluebell's mother Miriam Woods, with the same surname as himself, a pure coincidence also a D-list celebrity soap star. One night stand twenty-two years ago. One millisecond of drunken cocaine sex and Bluebell happened. He'd done the DNA.

Ironic then, that it had taken a year and a half for Tina to become pregnant with Troy. At first Daniel had thought he was on to a good thing, Tina wanted sex every spare minute of the day. Most of the time it was funny, part of their persona as a couple. They were looking for beds for the flat once, in a huge multi-storied furniture warehouse, with just a handful of disinterested staff on the ground floor. On the top floor Tina found a wardrobe so big she could climb inside. Giggling, she'd dragged Daniel in as well, closed the door and started to strip off. They still laughed about it now. They even pulled off the right level of nonchalance as they walked out past the dumb assistants.

Daniel had said later, 'If you are with child after the wardrobe sex, will we have to call the baby after its conceived location? You know, like celebs do?'

'Like you did with Bluebell?' Tina said, spoiling the moment. 'Not quite as romantic, The Great Northern Furniture Warehouse, is it?'

The locations became more exotic, based on baby names, and for a while it was quite challenging. They made love at Florence Nightingale Heritage Centre, in a borrowed flat on Penny Lane, and more daringly, Benny's For Beds.

With every month she didn't fall pregnant, Tina was devastated, for a while blaming the abortion she had when she was fifteen. Then the spontaneity went out of it, and it all turned into a military operation with no smoking or drinking. She checked her temperature, checked her ovary production and anything else that could be monitored, like a scientific experiment. There was even a graph and a thermometer by the bed.

After a much shorter time than he could have imagined, Daniel was begging for a day off.

When it did actually happen, Tina was as sick as a dog for nine months and because she was a high risk pregnancy attracting dozens of scans, they soon knew she was expecting a boy. Tina said she felt he'd been conceived when they were on holiday in Turkey.

'*Turkey* Woods... you *have* to be joking.'

Tina endured a two day labour with every complication known to man, she really went through the mill, and she made sure Daniel went with her. She told him to go, told him to stay. During contractions she screamed at him like a wild animal, '*Why can't you just fuck off?*'

However, she shared the gas and air with him, and laughed hysterically when he fell headlong into the midwife's trolley. Then the tears would turn to sobbing, clutching at his clothes, begging for it all to stop. But Daniel only cried when his son was born. Troy William Woods.

William had been his father's name.

Troy was a legendary city in Turkey.

Mia Woods had had a planned Caesarean somewhere in America.

She didn't even cancel her manicurist.

Daniel pulled his jeans and shirt back on and made his way down to reception in bare feet. He had to unlock everything and switch all the alarms off. Mia shoved two large leather holdalls at him and smiled her big white showbiz smile. She was blonde again, with a short sharp bob. She wore leather trousers with a fur jacket and six inch heels. From some angles she looked about twenty, but from other angles she looked about forty, enhanced with some very good plastic surgery. Her eyes were just a bit too good, mouth slightly too full, breasts too high.

'Dan. Long time no see.'

'Why are you here?'

'It's a hotel, isn't it?' she said, looking around. 'Very bijou.'

'Why are you here... to see Bluebell?'

'Fitting in, is she?'

'Don't mess her up, please.'

'Why would I mess her up, Dan? I've got some time off, thought I'd see how my daughter is. She tells me you've got a press party tomorrow. You know how I love the press,' she said, looking through her oversized handbag. 'I could make a few calls if you like, raise the profile for you?' She looked up at him with intense green eyes, challenging. 'Or lower it, you choose. Why are you so pissed off?'

'You haven't said anything to make me smile yet.'

She laughed and threw a credit card on the desk. 'I'll take a room with a view.'

Daniel dropped both her bags unceremoniously to the floor and went through the key card system. 'Room two, view of the car park.'

'Perfect.'

Daniel was just about to lock up again when Bear started barking and Victoria's blue Mazda pulled in. It parked haphazardly, and stopped abruptly as if the driver had released the clutch too soon. Daniel walked down the front steps. 'Vic?'

Victoria got out of the passenger seat. She was holding a blood-soaked bandage to her head, and the white dress was over her arm. Her daughter got out of the driver's side, fumbled with the keys.

'Victoria? What the hell's happened?'

Daniel went across the car park and took the luggage from them, hardly noticing the gravel digging into his bare feet.

'Can you help my mum?' Emily said, almost sobbing.

'Emily! Stop being so dramatic. I'm all right,' she said to Daniel, but her eyes said something different. 'It was an accident, looks worse than it is.'

'An accident?'

There was a tangible beat of silence before Emily said, 'Tell him the truth, it was Dad! They've had a fight. He's been hurting her!'

'What sort of fight?' Daniel said to them both, but he already knew the answer to that. 'Have you called the police?'

'Can we not do this now?' she said, her eyes flicking to her daughter.

Daniel collected up their things and they followed him up the steps. Mia had been watching and she pulled the doors open for them, full of curiosity. 'Trade picking up already?'

'Are you still here?'

They all watched her climb the stairs and Daniel went to find another key card. He sent Emily up with their cases and the dress while he led Victoria into the kitchen, so he could look at her head under the bright lights. 'A fraction deeper and that would need stitches. What's going on here? What sort of animal does that to his wife?' he said, then found an almost empty bottle of cognac and drained it into a large glass. 'You need to call the police.'

'I don't want to,' she said, accepting the glass from him but setting it down again.

'You don't *want* to? So... where is he, Mad Max?'

'Home.'

'*Home?* He needs locking up,' he said, throwing the empty bottle into the recycling bin, then kicking it. The noise of smashing glass made her jump.

'I'm sorry,' Daniel said and caught hold of her. Victoria flopped against him like a rag doll and he just about held her up, 'Sorry.' Her eyes closed and she relaxed against him but only for half a minute. She followed him wearily up the stairs to room six, where she hovered just inside the door. They could hear Emily running the bath.

Daniel said, 'You know where everything is? You know where I am.'

'Dan...'

'He won't get to you here. I'll set Cupcake loose.'

A tiny smile and a nod, then she closed the door, and locked it.

'Night, love,' he said to the door.

Tina wanted to know where he'd been for over an hour? With Mia? By the time he'd related it all, Daniel was thoroughly wound up again. Tina, her hand clamped over her mouth and her eyes wide with shock, wanted to go to Victoria. And she wanted *him* to evict Mia. He managed to talk her out of both ideas and firmly turned the light off.

Presently, all he could hear were the owls.

*

Something woke him; it could have been the massive crashing sound in the bathroom. At first, he thought all the glass shelving had collapsed, and in a dream he was telling Troy to use the correct fixings. Then when he saw Tina wasn't lying next to him, and he heard her pattering about in the kitchen running the taps. Daniel turned over on to his stomach and put the pillow over his head. Ten past six in the morning, it was almost fully light. The owls had gone to bed and the day birds were up and about.

A few more minutes and he was fully awake. 'Tina? What are you doing?'

She appeared at the door in her dressing gown, with a glass of water, shaking a packet of tablets. 'Needed some painkillers, sorry babe did I wake you?'

'No. I'm still fast asleep.' Cursing, Daniel went to use the bathroom, took in the chaos and noted that the shelves were exactly where he'd left them, but the contents of the medicine box were everywhere.

'Painkillers?' he said, finding her in the kitchen, filling the kettle.

'Just a funny pain that's all.'

'A funny pain, so does it make you laugh? Hey I had a phone call from your auntie Brenda, thanking us for some vintage champers. I thought she was teetotal?'

'Do you want a coffee?' she said, busying herself with the filter machine, eyes everywhere except on him. He caught hold of her hand. 'I don't want a coffee, I want you.'

'You've got me, you married me, remember?' She disentangled herself from his grip and went to the fridge for milk. She spilt some of it, missing the cup entirely.

'Yeah I remember. It was so recent we're still supposed to be in the honeymoon period.'

'I'm not in the mood, Dan.'

'Why?' he said, and took the mug from her. She sat at the little table by the window and Daniel seated himself opposite, hating this gulf between them. It was getting wider. They'd had times like this before; in fact they'd had so many ups and downs in their relationship Daniel had lost count.

Tina kept him guessing. He used to think it kept their relationship alive, but this time he was genuinely stumped, and tired. Maybe it was because they were married and grown up now.

Maybe he *was* just tired.

'What's going on, Tee?' he said, 'Talk to me. We need to be fighting from the same corner, especially today.'

'So it's still all about the hotel?'

'No, but today is kind of important.'

She looked down into her cup as if she was about to say something then changed her mind and grasped his hand across the table. 'You're right, I'm sorry.'

'You've not been yourself since you crashed the car.'

'It's too powerful, it scares me.'

'You loved driving it before,' Daniel said, puzzled by her wan smile. She looked defeated, a word not normally in Tina's hemisphere, but when he thought about it, she hadn't driven the Porsche since. Maybe the accident really had spooked her.

'I'll buy you a little car, one that won't crash or go over the speed limit.'

She almost laughed, and he glimpsed the Tina he loved. 'All right,' she said. 'But don't spend a lot of money, Dan. Get something cheap.' Her eyes were sparkling, but they might have been sad or happy tears he couldn't be sure. He couldn't be sure of anything… that was the problem.

Daniel stood under the shower for a long time; trying to banish the feeling he'd been slightly duped. Somehow he had a feeling the car was only a tiny part of something much, much bigger.

By the time he'd dressed, Tina was back in bed, tucked up in the duvet so he couldn't get to her. Daniel knelt at the side of the bed and looked at her sideways, 'Tee, you would tell me if there was something wrong, wouldn't you?'

'Dan, just let me rest,' she said, turning over to face the wall, 'Then I'll be on form for tonight.'

Defeated, Daniel closed the door quietly behind him and went downstairs, opening up, checking e-mails. He thought it was a stupid thing to say, that, 'You would tell me if there was something wrong?' People say that when they don't want a proper answer. Suddenly, gripped with the thought that both his hosts might be out of action, he rang his mother. He had to brief Marian on Victoria's problem, and she was predictably shocked.

'Daniel, you can't expect her to work!'

'I know! That's why I'm talking to you now.'

'And what's wrong with Tina?'

'Can you bring something black or white to wear?' he said, aware he was avoiding a proper answer.

'White? Daniel, no one wears white at my age! Not at any age, unless they've got a figure like Victoria,' she said, then after some thinking time; 'I've got a black trouser suit I wear for funerals.'

He looked at the ceiling. 'Fine… bring that.'

The florist arrived and spent a long time arranging lilies and greenery everywhere. She kept asking him things he couldn't answer and he could have done with Tina to help with the artistry. Victoria's daughter helped carry most of it. At least Troy and Elle were sorting out the bar, chilling the champagne and lining up glasses. Even Tony and Tristan were going the extra mile, rolling out a red carpet and threading lights through miniature trees at the entrance. Bear had had a wash and brush up and sported a spotted black and white neckerchief.

Bluebell came to find him.

'Do you want me to sing?' she said, and Daniel was touched, but it was a bit late in the day to start organising anything. Neither did he like Bluebell to feel it was constantly expected of her.

'I could do something acoustic,' she said, reading his mind. She had his almond eyes but they were green, and she had Mia's mouth, pre enhancement.

'I thought you'd be with your mother.'

'Mia? I didn't know she was here.'

'Room two.'

He watched her trail heavily up the stairs, and felt an overwhelming love for her, his wild child, lumbered with a father who had another family and a silly, self-centred woman she didn't even call mother any more. At least Mia had stayed out of the way, but then she only really came out at night.

'Blue?' he said, and she stopped on the galleried landing and looked down. 'I'd like you to sing, all right?'

'I thought... Sarah Brightman?'

Daniel frowned, wasn't she a classical soprano? 'Fantastic.'

He went to fetch a coffee from the kitchen and was astonished to find Victoria in there. She was in tracksuit bottoms, a baggy white t-shirt and there was a big blue catering plaster on her forehead. Busy stirring sauce on the hob, and making notes, she didn't notice him at first.

'Vic? What are you doing?'

She looked up, a spoon in her mouth and a blob of something purple and sticky on her nose. 'Bilberry sauce, for tonight. I promise I won't look like this. I can wear my hair loose, it covers the hole in my head, I checked.'

'No I mean... I didn't think...'

'I said I wouldn't let you down and I meant it,' she went on and gave him a schoolmarms' look. 'Now get out of here, you're in my way.'

Daniel got out of her way, and although he didn't like to admit it, he was hugely relieved.

Later in the morning, the local editorial guy from Daily Wales turned up for a brief interview and to take some daytime shots of the finished hotel. He wanted a picture of Daniel and Victoria holding hands on the decking, and Daniel had to explain that Victoria was not his wife. His wife wasn't available.

As late as he dared leave it, Daniel trailed back upstairs to see how the land lay. Tina was still in bed. There was bright sunlight outside so he snatched the blinds open and the cord came off in his hand. Cursing, he made himself a sandwich, dropping the knife three times onto the tiled floor, and slinging the cheese to the back of the fridge. He knew he was being childish creating a load of noise but he couldn't stop. The food processor was next; Christ knows why they had one of those. Maximum high speed blend; the coffee bean grinder was louder when it was on a coarse setting, it smelt good. When he looked in the bedroom the duvet was shaking. Tina was shaking with laughter. 'Dan, I know what you're doing.' Her head peered out, 'Come here you man child.'

He stood at the side of the bed and she caught his hand. 'Come here *properly*.'

'Yeah?'

Daniel discarded his clothes and she watched his every move with a funny little smile. When she kissed him it was like the first time, how could that be after all the years they'd had?

'I'm really cross with you,' he said, kissing her throat, her breasts. She was so gorgeous, his wife. She folded her legs round him, and she pulled him closer, kissed him harder and wanted him deeper. It was different, the love making. How could that be after all the years they'd had? Maybe it was *because* of all the years they'd had. Maybe they *were* grown up, and he hadn't noticed.

Afterwards, Daniel said sleepily into her neck, 'Like I was saying, I'm really cross with you.'

After a long moment she whispered into his hair, 'I know, I know you are.'

*

The guests were due to arrive around eight. Some of them were scary. Victoria was stressed about The Welsh Food Board. Daniel was stressed about everyone else; there was a lot of influential people, The Tourist Board, local Hotel Association and the New Business for Wales Group, whoever they were. Then there was the local press, and one national paper that'd shown a passing interest in his story. It had taken a lot of planning and persuasion to get all the right people in the right place at the same time.

His mother arrived an hour early, and she looked tired. He needed to do something about that. 'You look better,' she said, kissing his face. 'Right, what do you want me to do?'

'Report to the catering manager, she's in the engine room.'

Marian looked at him askance, and Daniel followed her to the kitchen. Tina was on his heels, nagging him about getting changed. His mother threw her arms around Victoria and it struck Daniel that maybe Victoria had wanted to keep her personal problems private but she didn't seem too fazed, more humbled by the support.

'I had to tell her, she would have guessed, she's got special powers,' Daniel said, while his mother had her head in the linen cupboard.

'No, it's fine,' Victoria said, sorting out the plates. She hadn't changed yet either; she was sweaty and her hair was coming loose. She looked strained and vulnerable.

'Have you spoken to Max?'

'No, I don't want to.'

'Do you think he'll turn up here?'

Tina said, 'If he does, Dan will easily take him out, won't you Dan?' She moved over to put an arm across Victoria's shoulders. 'Stay as long as you like. Don't worry about Max, Dan will sort him out.'

Marian's head shot up. 'No, he will *not*,' she said, tying on an apron over her funeral outfit. 'Daniel *won't* be sorting anything out with more violence!'

'Marian! Stop jumping down my throat! I was just being supportive.'

'Who to? Violence is the last thing Victoria wants, and if you want to be supportive, why don't you *help*?' she said, pushing a pile of serviettes at her. Tina let them all fall to the floor then stormed out of the kitchen.

Daniel followed her. She was in the bar, measuring out a big glass of Chardonnay.

'Tee, you look amazing.' She did look great, in a tight black dress with an impressive cleavage. She'd done her Marilyn hair and make-up. 'Go easy on the booze, yeah?' he said, mopping up the spillage with a towel.

'Tell your mother to stay out of my way! And why is she all dressed up? *I'm* front of house!'

'Tina, calm down. I asked her along as back-up.'

'Then tell her she's *back of house!*'

'No, I won't.'

Mia was in reception, more or less naked in a tiny animal print wrap and kitten heels. Troy was hiding behind the desk, pretending to be busy with some cables on the floor.

'Ah! Daniel,' Mia said. 'There's a problem with the shower. The knob's too stiff to turn on. I've never had that trouble before... could you take a look?'

'No but Troy will.'

'All right,' she said, peering over the desk. 'He's cute. Come on Roy. Bring your tools.'

Troy rose slowly to his feet, staring at Mia as if he was in a severe narcotic state.

'Troy? Earth to Troy?' Daniel said then took a call on his mobile. It was Tony, positioned at the top of the lake, to say that the first cars were due to arrive in ten minutes. Daniel dived upstairs and into the shower, suddenly nervous. This was it. Oddly, it gave him a certain measure of confidence that Tina had tidied up, pulled out his suit and ironed a shirt. As he fumbled with the buttons, he looked across at the lake and there was a bird of prey hovering above the bracken, like some prophetic omen. Bear was down there, trying to scrape off his cravat in the water.

On the landing Troy emerged from room two, still in a dream.

'Dad,' he said sagely, 'She might be my half-sister's mother, but she's some hot woman.'

'Did you fix the shower? Troy?'

'What? Oh yeah no problem. Tested it and everything.'

Daniel looked deep into his eyes but Troy just stared back vacantly.

The evening got started. At first, it was exactly as Daniel had envisaged, the hotel and the setting spoke for itself, the Moet & Chandon got everyone in the mood, and everyone wanted to talk to him and shake his hand. It wasn't quite warm enough to throw open all the doors, but when the lights came up and the candles were lit it looked stylish, without being stuffy and there was a nice hum of appreciation.

Mia made an entrance as if it were her party, and Daniel

watched her seek out Troy at the bar, flirting with him and falling out of her pink glittery dress, showing him how to make champagne cocktails the same shade as her lipstick. The photographer from Alright! recognised her immediately.

'Hey you're Stacey Steel in Lovers and Wives. Are you really doing I'm a Celeb this year?'

'Yes, and *yes!* You're on the money, mister. Get the man a drink, Roy!'

Other than being distracted by Mia and Troy, Tina seemed to be her usual bubbly self and Victoria was the perfect foil, cool and sophisticated in her white silk. She looked different, with her dark hair tumbled about her face and Daniel kept looking across to her. She caught his eye and smiled. After a while he could feel Tina's eyes boring into his back like two knives.

The food created quite a stir. In minutes the Welsh Food Board had him cornered.

'Do you have a chef?'

'No, not yet, I'm still looking. I might have to poach someone.'

They laughed. 'Okay, so who's done your catering?'

Daniel introduced Victoria and left her to it. She was more than capable of selling herself.

He had to do a speech. Daniel kept it all simple, thanked everyone for coming etc.; he talked about Victoria first and said a little about it being a family business, mentioned Tina and Marian, Troy and Elle. A thought occurred to him then that Tina's family hadn't even seen the hotel.

He needed to do something about that.

He introduced Bluebell, and she looked out of place in her white lace dress and torn black leggings, big boots and strange backcombed hair with purple braids. The audience was from a different world, but she didn't seem worried and sat on a barstool in front of the glass doors, tuning her guitar. To say it was an intimate gig, was a bit of an understatement, there was nowhere to hide. Daniel felt so nervous for her, his teeth were practically chattering. He prayed to God that her nonchalance was pure adolescent bravery, and not bolstered by some artificial substance.

When the expectant clapping had died down Mia said, 'It's not just about your family Daniel, she's my daughter too.' Several guests turned to look at her, and she threw a triumphant smile at Tina. Daniel caught hold of his wife's hand, 'Don't let her get to you.'

'Have you seen her with Troy? *Have you?*'

'I don't think he's complaining.'

'The bitch told me I needed liposuction!'

'Look, can you not work anything out? Just stay away from her!'

Tina snatched her hand away from his and folded her arms.

Bluebell introduced her song; Symphony, in a different key, with just an acoustic guitar. After a moment, Daniel scanned the room, aware that even the wine merchant, who was in his seventies, was captivated. Within minutes, Bluebell had everyone's attention. She seemed too young to have all that knowledge in her soul. She was like the Mona Lisa, with a voice.

Daniel looked across to Victoria and she had a tear trickling down her face. The fact she made no attempt to wipe it away, made her look slightly abandoned, sexual. It caught his attention more than it should. She was normally so contained, especially so in the white dress.

When the song ended, everyone rose to their feet and applauded, but Bluebell just stood there, bemused by the reaction and not knowing what to do next. Mia did, and she went to put her arms around Bluebell, basking in her daughter's glory, telling her about some meeting she had planned with Alpha Music in a voice loud enough for Daniel to hear. He downed his drink.

Victoria had disappeared, but Daniel found her in reception, wiping her eyes. She smiled through her smudged make-up, blotting her face with a tissue.

'Sorry it just really got to me, the words.'

'Yeah... I know.'

'She's really talented, Dan. Long time since anyone made me cry over a song.'

'I worry about her. I worry she'll get exploited. She'll go with Mia. There's nothing for her here.'

'Of *course* there is, there's you.'

'She's way too old to hang out with her dad. I'm kidding myself.'

'You underestimate yourself maybe.'

'Yeah?'

'Dan, if she goes; she'll come back.'

Elle interrupted them, her face like thunder, 'Daniel you'd better come, there's something going off and it might be me.'

Daniel walked through the milling guests to the decking where Mia was conducting her own photo shoot, some of them featuring Troy and not all of them tasteful. Tina was watching with clenched fists. Some of the party had moved outside, the smokers, and the ones insulated by drink and not feeling the chill air. Mia was in her element, the guy with the camera taking dozens of pictures.

'Look mate,' Daniel said to him quietly, 'It's not the Mia Woods' show, call it a day.'

'Aw come on, Dan,' Mia said, 'be like old times, get Blue over as well, we can do a family picture.'

The next few seconds were crazy. Tina seemed to come from nowhere, threw a perfectly aimed punch at Mia, who was caught completely off guard, lost her balance and went over the low glass balustrade with a yelp. Everyone was frozen in time, waiting for the splash, but it was more of a soft muddy slopping sound. Bear swam across, sliding silently into the water.

Tina leant over, 'What was that Mia?' she said, cupping her ear, 'I'm a celebrity get me out of here? Go on, *say it!* Oh watch out, here come the crocodiles!'

Daniel clamped her arms down, 'What the hell do you think you're doing? If I can hold it together why can't you? Go upstairs and *calm down.*'

'Don't you dare patronise me, Daniel Woods.'

The press guy carried on shooting, hardly able to believe his luck. Daniel put his hand over the lens. 'Like I said, *mate*, call it a day.'

Mia stood up then, gasping and covered in weeds and dripping sludge. Tony and Troy climbed over the glass wall and helped her back over, reassuring her that Bear wasn't some monster of the deep. Troy said, 'Stop screaming, it's only a dog.'

'Oh yes, it's a dog all right,' Tony said, to no one in particular.

Then Marian was there, fussing with towels, and Tristan was showing everyone out.

The party was over.

When he was pulling the sliding doors across the decking, Daniel took a last look across the indigo water and spotted a figure skulking down by the boats, just the lighted tip of a cigarette glowing in the dark. Max? He sent Tony a strongly worded text and double locked the doors with a definitive clunk. If that violent twisted bully came anywhere near Victoria he'd get something he hadn't bargained for in the way of retribution. The man was an animal.

Daniel went to the bar and poured himself a large single malt. Tony found him halfway through a second. 'Well? Tony?'

'It was Jones. Smashed.'

'*Barry Jones* was out there?'

'No worries boss, he was escorted off the premises.'

Daniel dived up the stairs, needing to expend some pent up aggravation. Victoria was on the landing fumbling with her key card and he almost ran into her.

'Dan? You're in a hurry!'

When he explained why, Daniel suddenly felt foolish; running about checking up on Blue as if she were about five. He had to trust her, had to. He took a measured breath and pressed his hands against the wall on either side of Victoria. She was wearing open Grecian sandals, and he found himself studying her tiny, child-like feet rather than be face to face with her facial injury.

'Actually,' he said, 'I'm wound up. I'm wound up because I thought it was Max out there.'

'Oh Dan!'

She seemed slightly flustered by his admission and ducked under his arm, then suddenly smiled and went to kiss his face, but one of them must have moved ever so slightly. Her lips brushed his, and she kissed the side of his mouth.

'Night,' she whispered, and slipped inside her room.

'Night, love.'

After a few seconds of looking at the door, or maybe resting his head on it, he became aware of Tina's perfume.

'Oh, *nice*,' she said.

He turned and looked at her properly, taking in her change of clothes, the bags. He felt borderline drunk, so it took a minute. 'What are you doing? Tell me this isn't what I think it is?'

'You want it spelling out? I've had *enough*, Dan! I've had enough of Blue and *Mia*. And don't get me started on *Marian*!' she snarled, struggling to keep hold of numerous cases and holdalls.

Daniel took them all from her and practically threw them back across the landing. 'I'll tell you what I've had enough of shall I? Drama queens!'

He watched her energetically gather everything up again,

spilling shoes and bottles, stuffing Coco Chanel into her handbag. 'You, and Marian, and Victoria have got it all sewn up here, you don't need me. I don't even want to live here!' she went on, her voice beginning to waver, and she looked at him tearfully, weighed down with all her belongings. She had about four scarves round her neck and some shoes all tied together.

'You don't need me and I'm no use to you. I can't be the person you want me to be.'

'You're talking rubbish as usual. Of course I need you!'

He tried to hold her hand gently. She made a half-hearted attempt at shoving him out of the way, and struggled down the first step, then carried on bumping her case down, her handbag spilling open again. Daniel hung over the bannister, starting to feel disorientated. It had been a long day with not much sleep and too much to drink.

'So where are you going? Oh don't tell me. *Pizza boy?*'

She stopped at this and looked up at him. 'What?'

'You heard. You were *seen.*'

'By who, you?'

'Not exactly. Victoria.'

'Victoria! How come she never said? At the restaurant, at the flat? Come on, Dan where?'

'So you're not denying it?'

'Are you both spying on me is that it?'

When he didn't respond, she went out of the door with a determined march. Daniel followed her out into the car park, picking up her scarf.

'*Fuck off,* Dan!' she said, dragging the trolley case so hard one of the wheels buckled. 'Get back to your good night kiss. She'll be waiting for you!'

He ran in front of her and held her shoulders. 'Stop it! Tina you can't do this running away all the time, we're married now.'

'Yes I can! And getting hitched was your idea!'

He looked at her, astonished. 'How can you say that? It was all part of it; the wedding, the hotel and the new start, you *know* it was,' he said, feeling his heart plummet with the realisation of what was happening. 'It was our dream.'

'No, Daniel,' she said wearily, 'all this...it was all *your* dream, not mine.'

A taxi came and she threw all the bags in the boot, and he stupidly helped her with the broken case. She slid into the passenger seat, slammed the door and stared ahead, and the taxi started to pull away.

'So you're leaving me, just like that?' he shouted through the window, 'but I *love you*, Tina *please...*'

Daniel stared after her until the taxi had reached the end of the lake, feeling cold and sober but knowing he'd had too much to drink to chase after it. When he looked up, Mia was staring through the window, drying her hair.

Other than the owls, it was silent.

CHAPTER SIX

It sounded like a couple of lawnmowers on full throttle. Nightfall was the worst, when they used the estate as a speed circuit. The scooters were presumably in place of the dog and the trampoline.

Linda sent Daniel a jokey text about it eventually, and he'd replied, 'Tell Mike to put sugar in the engine. Why won't he answer his phone? Tell him to come out for a pint.' When she showed the text to Mike, he'd just tutted. He was in the spare room now, a small progression from the sofa. Their relationship had progressed at much the same pace, a change of physical living space, but not much else. He tutted a lot, and sighed.

'I can't say sorry any more times,' he'd said to her.

'If you said it from now till eternity it wouldn't make any difference, Mike.'

'What do you want me to do?'

'I don't know, stop saying it and try feeling and showing it.'

'You won't let me!'

It must have been after midnight when the scooters spluttered and stopped. Then it was loud shouting and slamming of doors, followed by rap music. The hammering got louder, and she heard Mike pad downstairs. At first she thought he was finally going to let rip with next door, but she heard voices in the hall, a woman. Linda sat bolt upright, grabbed her dressing gown and peered over the stairs.

It was Tina. She was quite distressed and surrounded by bags and cases. When she saw Linda, she burst into tears. Mike rolled his eyes and went to fill the kettle.

'I've left Dan,' Tina said, sobbing into Linda's shoulder.

Mike said, 'Again? Is this a permanent arrangement or just for this week?'

'Can I stay in your spare room tonight? There are no trains.'

Mike put two mugs of tea on the table. 'I'm not sleeping on that sofa,' he said to Linda.

'No, it's all right you can move back in with me.'

'Really?' he said, brightening. 'I'll go and change the bed, for Tina.'

Linda watched him go purposefully up the stairs and felt, what exactly? She heard him pulling everything out of the airing cupboard, knowing he'd never find the right size sheets and the pillowcases that matched, but resisted the urge to help. A grown man should be able to find something in a cupboard, shouldn't he?

'So, what's happened?' she said gently to Tina.

'Dan's thinking *dirty dog* with Victoria in that white dress.'

A beat passed. 'There's got to be more than that.'

'Oh there is,' Tina said, lighting a cigarette and taking a big gulp of tea. 'Victoria, is thinking *dirty bitch* with Dan, and she's been spying on me. Can you believe that?'

'Em... you've lost me now.'

Mike shouted down. 'Lin? There's no more stuff for this bed!'

'*Try again!*' she yelled, keeping her eyes on Tina. 'So they're just flirting?'

'And that bloody dog Mia is there, and she's thinking, *dirty bitch* with Troy.'

'No... really?'

'Really, and Bluebell let that legless bitch pee in my hair drier. And as for his bloody mother!'

'Bitch?'

'It's like a bloody coven,' she said, taking a long pull on her cigarette. 'They all think I'm lazy and useless, and Dan is cross with me.' Linda sipped her tea and pulled her dressing gown tighter, and waited. There was more, she could sense it.

'And I hate living there.'

'Because?'

'It's not Manchester, or Chester or London, is it? I *love* London. Instead I'm *stuck* in the middle of nowhere with a load of bitches and a hot dog. *I've tried,*' she wailed, 'I've tried for Dan.'

'But you can drive to Chester in less than an hour, where's the problem?'

'I can't drive any more, since that accident.'

'Because?'

Mike thumped the floor and his voice was all muffled. 'Any chance of calling it a day, Lin?'

They both carried all the bags upstairs. Mike had put Tom's ancient Star Wars cover on the bed, with the duvet filling stuffed in the wrong way so it was lumpy and the pillow cases were pink and chintzy. Tina smiled. 'Wow, that's amazing; an eclectic mix of nostalgia.'

'Your standards are way too low,' Linda said, and hugged her goodnight, then went slowly across the landing with a sense of... what exactly? She couldn't work it out.

'Great timing,' she said to Mike, noticing that he'd assumed the right hand side of the bed and re set the alarm clock.

'Yeah well we've both got work in the morning, she can lie in bed with Luke Skywalker.'

'I'm worried about her.'

'Lin, how many years have they been like this? Since they

were both about fourteen! It's on, it's off; it drives you insane. Tina thrives on it.'

'You don't like her much, do you?'

'Dan has run after Tina, and baled her out, *all her life.*'

'I know. That's love. Even when the relationship is off he's been there for her.'

'They're constantly on self-destruct,' he said, then sighed. 'Let's concentrate on us, shall we?' He held her hand, and kissed it. It should have been a tender moment but it wasn't anything in particular. Maybe indifference was just as destructive, only slower.

Destruction... big, heavy word, war-like, with wrecking ball dimensions.

Violence was destructive.

Linda had heard about Max and Victoria. Sadly, her instincts had been along the right lines, all that training and information about abuse had been in her head somewhere.

There was no way back from that, surely?

Affairs were destructive.

Linda had seen the girl, Armenka. She didn't look seventeen; she looked at least ten years older than that, all blonde with slavic cheekbones. Her English was good, with the occasional misinterpreted word and a strange accent. Despite her awful life in Poland, she was assertive and predatory, but able to display enormous vulnerability when required.

It had only lasted a few months, and then Mike had come to his senses. Or maybe it was Armenka who'd come to her senses when she worked out that Mike had no money. He had continued to pay the mortgage on their house and all the related bills. At first Linda had thought he was being reasonable, but now, her train of thought jumped down a different avenue. Maybe he'd looked at it as a foot in the door, a way back to cosy middle-aged suburbia. He'd told Linda that he'd finished it, but what if Armenka had called time, chewed him up and spat him out, moved on to her next victim? She'd never know the truth of that; Blondie was long gone with her false documents and identity.

Linda felt her eyes well up in the dark, and she had to fumble in the box of tissues by the bed. 'Lin, we can get through this, I promise you,' Mike said, and held her close. For the first time in months, she reciprocated. Maybe they could. Despite what Mike thought, she hoped Daniel and Tina could as well, but when she knocked on the door of the spare room in the morning, Tina had gone. An hour later, a huge bunch of flowers arrived. The card just said, 'Thanks for being a friend, love Tina.'

*

A couple of weekends later, and her first free one for ages, Mike had arranged to go to a football match. At first, Linda was a bit put out; they were supposed to be trying to be a couple again. They were trying to date each other, trying to pretend it was all new instead of tired and worn out, but if they were trying to get back to normal, she had to accept that the football matches were part of normal. She stuffed his dirty overalls into the washing machine, pushed the hoover round the sitting room and cleaned the bathroom. She even dusted their wedding photograph, then picked it up and studied Mike. Tall, long-limbed with mid brown hair, worn too long then. His mid brown eyes were staring back, reliable looking and with an arm firmly around her waist. Daniel and Tina were in the background, standing apart as if they'd had a row. Strangely, she felt more upset by Daniel and Tina than the cracks in her own marriage.

Linda got into her car and headed onto the A55 towards Manchester. The traffic was light but when she got to Didsbury She found herself crawling along in a queue, and there was only a tight space to park. It was full of memories and nostalgia, being at Daniel and Tina's flat. The four of them had had a lot of good times there, in the seventies and eighties, when life had been simple, although they hadn't realised it. Victoria had been off the scene by then, at university.

She'd spoken to Victoria just a couple of days previous. Daniel wanted to invite herself and Mike to a dinner at The Lakeside. He was road testing chefs. Linda said yes, what a lovely idea. Hopefully Mike would make an effort with Daniel.

She was surprised to learn Victoria was living at the hotel. 'To be honest it's working out better than I imagined and I feel safe here. Oh God,' she groaned, 'how awful does that sound? I'm afraid of my husband. I can't go back to the house, I just can't. I don't know what to do, see a solicitor I suppose, find somewhere to rent.'

'Oh. I'm sorry, Vic, what a mess. Have you seen Max?'

'No, he's sent me an email full of remorse and a list of appointments he's made with different counsellors.'

'Does that make a difference?'

'I hope it will, for him.'

Linda wondered how to drop the burning question into the conversation.

'Do you know what's going on with Dan and Tina?'

'No idea really. Tina's got her phone off and Dan's just morose.'

'Vic... be honest with me. Are you and Dan getting flirty? You know what's he's like, and let's face it, you are very vulnerable at the moment.'

A beat passed, and she sighed heavily, 'Lin, I'm in the middle of a horrible break-up.'

'Oh I know; I'm sorry. It's just that Tina's been here and well, she's got a problem with everyone at the moment, even Marian! I thought Dan's mum was okay?'

'She is; she's lovely. Bit protective of her one and only, you know the way it is.'

'Is Mia still there?'

'No, she and Bluebell are in London,' she said. 'So… how are you and Mike?'

'Oh you know; muddy waters. I feel as though I'm swimming against the tide,' Linda said, then suddenly realised how true that was.

'I know what you mean. Thank God for this job, it's keeping me sane.'

'Is there a dress code? For dinner next Friday?'

'Yes, strictly casual.'

Strictly casual; funny term. Linda could apply it to all their relationships at the moment, all three marriages hanging by a thread, and yet the reasons were far from casual.

*

When Tina heard the doorbell, she was dozing. She would have ignored it had she not recognised the fact that Linda Williams was also yelling through the letterbox. She pulled her dressing gown on and stood hesitating on the landing. She looked and felt a mess. Being awake half the night looking up all kinds of medical websites hadn't helped. It hadn't helped at all. She didn't understand half the words and had to keep stopping to Google them; and then Troy was on the phone every five minutes.

Daniel had turned up at the flat the previous day, but Tina had slid the interior bolt across, so his keys didn't work. After shouting and thumping at the door, he finally went away. Some minutes later he'd returned and pushed a white teddy bear through the letterbox, as if they were about twelve. It was that moment though, when the toy fell to the floor in the hall and she heard his car roar away, that Tina thought she was maybe poised on the brink of making the biggest mistake of her life.

The doorbell went again, more insistent.

'Lin... is that you?'

'Who do you think? Let me in!'

They talked about nothing in particular at first, and it was awkward.

Linda followed her through to the kitchen, admiring the little extension with the glass roof and the sun terrace. Linda said she wasn't surprised the flat was kind of special. If you were married to a builder, you would expect it to be, wouldn't you?

'But I'm not married to a builder any more am I? I'm married to an hotelier, a businessman.'

'You're married to *Dan,* that's what's important,' Linda said, 'Tina, stop hedging round the big issue all the time. Look at you; still in your dressing gown in the middle of the afternoon!'

'Dan's changed; he's no fun anymore, and I'm tired.'

Linda took hold of her hands then, took a deep breath and gave Tina a little speech; something about her professional hat as a carer, how it carried the strictest code of confidentiality. Tina nodded, understanding. This was it, she was finally cornered.

'Right,' Linda said, squeezing her hands. 'I think you should see a doctor.'

'I knew you were going to say that. I've been on the internet...there's this site where you list all your symptoms...'

'I *know*, but you should see a doctor, go through all the tests.'

There was a moment suspended in silence whilst they both looked at each other.

'Lin, I'm so scared,' Tina whispered, her eyes swelling with tears. 'I'm scared and depressed and confused.'

'I know you are,' Linda said gently, her eyes not leaving

Tina's face. 'Talk to me.'

Tina talked then, and when she started she found she couldn't stop, but everything came out in a torrent of jumbled facts and figures, fears and failures. She had to acknowledge then how she'd struggled for months really, at first not wanting to upset Daniel's fast-tracked plans for the wedding, and the hotel. It had all been easier to disguise when they were living apart. Back at the flat she still called home, back working the odd shift for Fernando, she'd hoped to find that old sense of security, but despite all her earlier fight and indignation, she now felt locked in defeatism.

'I know I've been in denial,' she said, 'blaming everything and everyone else one minute, thinking it will all just go away the next. I suppose deep down, I've always known it would just get worse and I would have to face it someday.'

'I understand all that, but why can't you talk to Dan?' Linda said carefully, 'He's going to jump to the wrong conclusion.'

'I think he's already done that,' she said with a smile, but it didn't reach her eyes, 'You know the speed he goes at everything. Just thinking about keeping up with him exhausts me.'

Linda sighed with frustration. 'But Dan needs to know; you're not being fair to him! Also, you're going to need his support. He did say in sickness and health, I heard him.'

Tina looked at the ceiling so she could keep all the tears in her eyes.

'That's just it,' she said, 'I'm *always* needing him.'

'There's nothing wrong with that! It's how you both work. He *wants* you to need him.'

'Not to this degree!' she snapped and hot tears began to spill down her face. 'I'm going to be a burden; he's better off without me.'

Linda got to her feet, 'You don't *know* that, now *you're* jumping to too many conclusions!'

'Am I? Are you wearing that hat? Or has it slipped down over your eyes?'

'You're making decisions *for him*,' Linda said, trying another route, but Tina agreed and maintained it was because she loved him. 'Yes, yes... and if I decide I want to let him go at the end of this, that's because I love him as well.'

Linda turned her back, and looked through the window.

After a while Tina said, 'Lin, I need to do this bit on my own. The facts, the tests, the coming to terms with it. And I'm not ready to talk to Dan and Troy, not yet. I couldn't cope with them in bits, as well as myself. You're a carer, don't you understand that? If you don't understand it then, *please*, just respect it's how I want to do it, okay?'

Linda said yes, she understood, but it broke her heart.

'Lin, if you tell *anyone* about this I'll never speak to you again, I mean it.'

*

Mike had been texting and calling her phone all afternoon. Linda finally responded once she was sat in her car outside the flat. He sounded worried. 'Where the hell are you?'

'At Dan and Tina's flat.'

'What... in Didsbury? Have you been crying? Lin, *stay out* of their relationship. This stuff gets all messy.'

'I know, I know. Just something I had to do, niggling away at me.'

Linda drove home, forcing herself to stay focused on the road but her mind kept drifting onto Tina. Was she selfless, or just stupid? Everyone thought she was weak and needy, unable to get through life without Daniel. Maybe it was actually the other way around. Maybe she'd just tell Daniel what the score was and to hell with it; but then she knew when it came to it, she would never forget that imploring look on Tina's face.

It was messy, Mike was right about that, but it was too late not to be involved.

At home, the football results were blaring out in the sitting room, so loud that Mike was unaware she'd even walked through the door. Under normal circumstances, pre-Armenka, she would have laughed, crept up behind him. Instead, Linda crept up the stairs to the bathroom and splashed lots of water on her face. When she looked in the mirror, her eyes were swollen. Holding a cold flannel across her head, Linda went to lie on the bed, feeling sick. All she could see when she closed her eyes was Tina, dancing in the club they used to go to, miming to Blondie. Some guy thought she was actually Debbie Harry and kept pestering her, till eventually Daniel knocked him out and they were all barred.

Presently, she became aware of Mike.

'Even when they love each other, they still get it all wrong,' Linda said, wondering where that kind of measure left her and Mike. He sat down on the edge of the bed and passed her a cup of tea. 'Is this about who I think it is?' Linda nodded.

'He's better off without her,' Mike said gently.

'Oh God... Tina said that.'

'Well then; at last!'

'You don't understand.'

'I don't *want* to.'

*

On Friday night, Linda pulled out the top from Monsoon.

'I haven't seen that before, is it new?' Mike said.

'Tina bought it me for Christmas.'

'Splashing the cash.'

'Is that why you're ignoring Daniel? Because of the

money?'

'No. Can we not do this?' he said, wandering about the bedroom in his boxers, looking for something to wear. Linda threw a pair of denims and a shirt at him and he held them in a crumpled embrace. 'Look, I feel an idiot okay?'

'Oh.' Surprised at his admission, Linda applied lipstick, wondering what other gems of wisdom the evening would unearth.

They both fell silent at the sight of The Lakeside. It was further enhanced by the late April sun disappearing into the cold water and leaving a hazy blush behind the outline of crags. Bear ran to do meet and greet, and proudly brought them through the entrance.

'Isn't that next door's dog?' Mike said, frowning at it from different angles.

'No. Nothing like.'

There was a huge table set in the eating area, laid for six. The pre-lit backdrop of the lake and the ambiance of the room lifted Linda's spirits. It was ages since she'd enjoyed an evening so intimate and special. Daniel kissed her hello and she couldn't resist hugging him just a bit closer, enjoying the way he quickly reciprocated, but he'd always been very affectionate and tactile.

Her reasons were not entirely selfish. It was almost as if by holding him close she could transmit her feelings about Tina without actually saying the words, but Daniel couldn't see her face or read her mind and took her hugs and kisses as their usual playful nonsense.

'Lin stop being naughty,' he said, giving her a funny little warning look.

'That goes for you as well,' she said, this time without the joke and poked him in the ribs but he just smiled at her, and pressed a cold glass of Chardonnay into her hands. Mike had elected to drive so she gulped it down, intending to make the most of her evening.

Victoria came over and touched her glass against Linda's. 'To us... new beginnings.'

'And absent friends?'

Victoria just nodded and put her glass down. 'Right! It's like the final of Master-Chef,' she said, and handed out cards and pencils for marking the different courses. She looked very shabby chic in washed out denims and a lace and silk shirt, revealing just a hint of cleavage.

Linda heard Mike say, '*Bloody hell,* she looks a bit different out of uniform.'

She didn't catch Daniel's reply, but then the third couple arrived, and Linda was distracted by an overdressed blonde.

She was followed by Charlie Summers.

At first Linda didn't recognise him in dressed down denim.

Bloody hell, Linda thought, he looks a bit different strictly casual. She peered at the small letters across his t-shirt. Sex, drugs and sausage roll.

'Lin! Good to see you again,' he said, pecking her on the cheek. She introduced Mike.

The blonde was Charlie's date, Angela. She called herself Charlie's angel and once at the table, very happily positioned herself between Daniel and Charlie. A thorn between two roses, she said, and Linda had to turn away so she didn't laugh openly at Daniel's expression.

They were to try three different starters, then three mains and three deserts. 'I hope you're hungry,' Daniel said, I'm getting a bit jaded with it all. I'm starting to crave beans on toast.'

'Don't tell me you didn't enjoy our shortlisting process?' Victoria said.

Daniel shot her a private smile and mouthed something that looked like, 'Course I did.'

Troy served the first course. He was flustered and kept

dropping cutlery.

'Where's Elle?' Daniel said, 'Do you want a hand?'

'Oh she's not feeling well, it's okay I can manage.'

Charlie looked up from his olive and rocket salad. 'Nothing serious?'

'Dunno. It's all like, *complicated*.'

Daniel frowned but Charlie said something about his bag being on standby in his car, 'I seem to be in demand at parties these days,' he said, catching Linda's eye.

Angela touched his arm, 'You're always on call, darling; have a night off.'

The main courses arrived. Rabbit in Rioja with saffron mash, organic chicken as a modern roast, and a simple local trout. Daniel and Mike were talking about cars and football, but Victoria was miraculously included in the discussion about her Mazda. When Angela went to the powder room, Charlie leaned discreetly across the table.

'Where's your friend, Tina is it?'

Linda nodded, spearing a chargrilled mushroom, 'I'd like to talk to you, in private.'

'Okay later,' he said quietly, filling her wine glass and then his own.

They were interrupted by Troy. 'Are you seriously a doctor?' he said to Charlie.

'Yes. Problem?'

'You don't look like one.'

'I'll get my bag, shall I? You're welcome to check if my stethoscope's the real thing.'

Angela slid back into her seat and smiled at everyone, 'Oh I can vouch for that,' she said.

During coffee, everyone fragmented into little groups and Linda moved up a place, so she could chat with Victoria.

'So, how's it going with Mike?'

'It feels like one step forward, two back,' Linda said, looking across to the bar. Mike was staring into his pint whilst Daniel had a serious looking conversation with him.

'I'm sorry if Charlie being here makes it a bit awkward.'

'No, not at all. I mean, it's not as if we were seeing each other or anything.'

'He asked about you after the party.'

'Really?' she said, feeling her face flush. 'Well, looks like I'm still married, and he's got a girlfriend. I always thought Charlie was out of my league, but I am incredibly flattered.'

'He doesn't think he's out of your league,' Victoria said with a little frown, then lowered her voice. 'Charlie hasn't come from a privileged background you know, that was all Karen his ex-wife. He's had a struggle to get where he is, professionally I mean. I was at Uni with him, he lived on fish fingers and rode a bicycle everywhere,' she went on, 'Actually, I think he still does, now that Karen's had her claws in him and left him with the national debt.'

Linda refilled her glass, not quite knowing what to do with the information. She'd rather he was a total cad. 'And what about you?' she said to Victoria, noticing close up how tired and red her eyes were and she looked even thinner. She'd always been slender but her waist looked tinier than ever and she had hollows along her collarbone. No wedding ring.

'Me? Oh Max and I have reached the end of the line. You know I don't think I've loved him for a long time; it's been an easy decision. I don't think I even respect him anymore.'

Daniel called Victoria away, something to do with looking at everyone's score cards. Within seconds, they were involved in an intense discussion with a lot of eye contact. Angela began to help Mike with some champagne and then Charlie suddenly came and took the chair next to Linda. He sat on it back to front and hung his head over the back.

'You wanted to talk to me about Tina?' he said. Linda became aware of the Armani first, then his mesmerising green eyes. Both attributes did quite a lot for his bedside manner but nothing to focus her thoughts. Linda found herself looking across to the bar, at Daniel and Victoria, and Charlie followed her line of sight.

'We can always do this another time,' he said, 'but you look anxious.'

Linda nodded, 'I made a promise to Tina, but it's so tough keeping secrets for friends.'

'Mmm tricky, I do sympathise on that one, but I am utterly trustworthy, if you need to discuss a case, off the record and all that.'

Reassured by his manner, Linda found him easy to talk to. He was a good listener and alternated his gaze between her eyes and his glass of Merlot, which he sipped very slowly. Eventually he said, 'Lin, you did absolutely the right thing in going to see your friend. It's perfectly understandable, her wanting to hide away for a while. For some people it's part of the condition.'

'No one else see's it.'

'No one else has been trained to see it.'

'Ah, that's Tina's sense of humour,' Linda said, 'We used to do it all the time when we were at parties. I was an air hostess, Tina's favourite was a backing singer for Diana Ross and Daniel was always a stuntman.'

'Sorry? You've lost me now.'

'I have a confession. I'm not a nurse. I'm just a carer for the council, massive difference.'

'Oh I see!' he laughed a little. 'Not much difference actually. From what I've just heard, you have a wealth of knowledge, and understanding,' he said, and it took Linda a few seconds to realise he was serious. 'Have you thought about making the leap into nursing?'

'No. Well, no. I've no qualifications or anything.'

'You'd get a grant, as a mature student. Think about it.'

'All I do is *think*,' Linda said, watching Mike talk to Victoria. He seemed to look more animated and attractive, and she was surprised how much it needled. Charlie put a hand over hers and said something about his ex-wife's affairs, about there being no magic formula to erase the past. 'I have a confession as well,' he said gravely, 'I was always a sex therapist.'

Daniel called them over to the bar and passed round flutes of champagne.

'Okay the results are, chef B is the clear winner.'

'Did he make that amazing, cholesterol laden chocolate thing?' Charlie said, and Angela linked his arm and squeezed it, 'Charlie loves nursery pudding don't you darling?'

Daniel said, 'Same guy also did the trout, and the olive salad.'

'Oh perfectly balanced then,' Charlie said, 'I feel positively virtuous.'

During the discussion of who liked what, Troy appeared, and meekly accepted a glass of bubbly.

'Is Elle all right? Troy?' Daniel said.

Troy looked like a rabbit caught in the headlights. 'Dad, you know that problem I warned you about at Christmas?'

'If you mean the air conditioning, that's all sorted.'

'No, no,' he said patiently. 'You know how you were really, *really* stressed at Christmas?'

'Why do I get the feeling I'm not going to like this?'

'And you know how you've been getting steadily *more* stressed?'

'Troy!'

'Well that's why I haven't said anything before.'

Daniel looked at Charlie, then back to Troy. 'Okay. You're *really* stressing me out now.'

'You're going to be a granddad.'

There was a moment of contemplative silence as everyone digested the announcement. Daniel opened another bottle of bubbly, and they celebrated news of the baby.

Mike laughed about it on the way home. 'Did you see

Dan's face?'

Linda said, 'Tina should have been there.'

'Huh. *Tina.* I said to Dan not to go chasing after her this time.'

'After what you said to me about not getting involved?' Linda said, 'And what makes you such an expert?' She sighed and stared through the windscreen. 'So, what did Dan say?'

'Nothing. What's the score with that doctor, you were an age talking to him.'

'Nothing.'

Linda thought about Daniel being a granddad. It was the next phase of life. When it happened for herself and Mike she couldn't help wondering if it would be another, messed up spoilt family occasion that should be happy and shared, like Christmas should have been. The repercussions of Mike's affair just went on and on, like dropping a big stone into deep water and watching the ripples expand. The sad thing was, he thought because it was over, that was the end of it.

*

The following evening, Mike made dinner. It was something he always used to do on Saturdays, experiment. The food at the hotel had kick-started his enthusiasm. The kitchen was like a landfill site. He was wearing a plastic apron and watching Jamie Oliver on his laptop explain how to make a simple pasta sauce. The only simple part was the production of mess. Everything was covered in tomato juice and pulp, and there was something burning in the bottom of the oven.

Later, Linda tried to eat the pasta but it wasn't quite right and there was far too much of it. Mike had hung the weekly overall wash on the line outside, and she could see the legs flapping in the wind, still grimy and covered with years of grease and oil. Linda used to like the fact he had such a manual job, like Daniel. The difference was, Daniel scrubbed up really well in non-work mode, and he always smelt faintly sensual. Subtle… that was the word.

Mike didn't really scrub up in the same way.

He didn't do subtle. He was a what you see is what you get kind of man, and she used to admire the honesty of that, but he'd blown apart the essence of it with the affair. Mike didn't do what he said on his tin any more.

He'd made an effort, setting the table and turning off the football results. The problem for Linda was her goalposts had changed position. She studied her husband across the table, aware that the sex issue was getting ever closer. The trouble was Mike had dragged it down so many levels with Armenka. She'd likely been a whore in the bedroom. Mike had got used to quantity, rather than quality. For Mike it was just Saturday night, football, beer and bed night. It was all Linda's fault, she'd moved him into her bed, and then turned her back on him. Although what used to work between them; now seemed lacking in imagination and finesse.

In a weird way, Linda could almost envy Victoria because she seemed so certain in her mind, but emotional hurt was never as black and white as anything physical, it had so many shades of light and dark, so many layers of fact and fiction.

Linda decided she felt distinctly grey.

She put her cutlery down. 'Sorry, not very hungry.'

Mike refilled her wine glass. 'This isn't working is it?'

'Do you mean it's not working as an aphrodisiac?'

He laughed, 'I don't think even Jamie Oliver can do that with a lump of pasta from SuperPrice. Well, maybe if he'd cooked it.'

'Do you think Jamie Oliver prefers Armani or Givenchy?'

Mike took a few moments to consider, drank his beer.

'Okay, where's this going, Lin?'

In the end, the words just fell out of her mouth, as subtle as a vat of crude oil.

'I don't want to sleep with you.'

Later, Linda heard him dragging everything out of the airing cupboard and making up the spare bed again. She'd told him it was too soon; but maybe it was too late.

She listened to the scooters begin their nightly vigil, and allowed herself to think more thoroughly about Charlie Summers, about everything he'd said and everything he'd done.

His mobile number was stored in her phone as Charlotte.

He'd told her to ring him anytime, about anything.

CHAPTER SEVEN

It had taken weeks for Victoria to find the courage to tell Max she wanted a divorce. The time away from him had distilled everything in her mind, and brought about the inevitable moment when she had to face him. Daniel wouldn't let her go alone to the house.

'I think you should maybe go to his office, and I think maybe Tony should wait in the car.'

'Max won't do anything, I know how he works,' she said, but in truth Victoria thought it was an incredibly good idea. It was odd having Daniel look out for her, but she noticed he did the same for most women in his circle. It was a bit old fashioned but Victoria liked it, she liked it a lot. It was poles apart from the way Max operated with women. Max used mind games then resorted to physical force. Daniel was something of a stereotypical protector, but soft as putty on the inside. Victoria had seen him cuddling the dog, talking gobbledegook to it and kissing the top of its head.

For a gay man with a lot of camp ways, Tony was a big, imposing kind of guy. He drove her to Max's plush office in Llandudno, then folded his arms and leant against the car with a mean face, chewing a cigarette. She felt like a celebrity with her own personal bouncer, but she had to admit, it made her feel recklessly brave to know he was waiting just outside.

Max was with a client, but his secretary chatted away to Victoria as if nothing was wrong, fetching coffee and Vogue magazine, if anything a little overly concerned, Victoria thought.

When she eventually got to see Max, he jumped to his feet and pulled out a chair for her. 'I'm so glad to see you. You've no idea how I've missed you, are you feeling better?'

'What? Max, please don't. I'm here on business.'

'Business? I take care of that. You don't need to worry about money, I haven't stopped your allowance and I never will. *You're my wife.*'

'I don't *want* to be your wife. I want a divorce.'

Her words seemed to stop the world. Max contemplated her with a curious expression. She placed her solicitor's card on his desk and moistened her lips, 'If you agree, we can site irreconcilable differences?'

He laughed, almost scornfully. 'And if I don't? If I don't fall in with your plan?'

'Then I'll have no option but to disclose the full facts to my solicitor, the police and the press.'

'There's nothing to tell! I'll deny everything you say.'

'No matter, it will still cause a horrible smear, and don't forget Emily saw it with her own eyes, so don't hide behind the children. That's too low, even for you.'

'You *think* you've got it all worked out,' he said, and leant back in his chair. 'Emily saw nothing, I've spoken to her.'

'You've spoken to Emily about it?'

'Yes, and she agrees you have been acting very strange, not yourself at all.'

'Max *please*! This is not going to work. I've had a lot of time to think things through,' she said, willing herself to speak clearly and calmly, 'I'm trying to offer you a dignified way out.'

'I'll show you a dignified way out,' he said, then crossed behind her and opened the door.

Victoria zipped up her handbag and left without another word. Tony took one look at her face and started the car. 'Pub?' he said hopefully. 'Boss said to take you to the pub next.'

She almost smiled. 'Not yet. Drive me to Capelulo. There's some stuff I want.'

It was a warm May day, the trees were heavy with blossom and birdsong. The garden at home looked magnificent, quite clearly the gardener was still employed. Tony followed her through the house, exclaiming at the beautiful paintings and objets d'art. He watched Victoria pick up some of them, then put them all back. She wanted none of it. It was worthless. It all formed part of her beautiful prison and why would she want a reminder of it?

Upstairs, she pulled out all the suitcases she could find and filled them with her clothes and personal effects. Tony loaded everything into the car, then at the last minute Victoria dashed back into the kitchen for her set of Le Cruset saucepans and collection of cookery books, and somehow slotted them into every available space.

'Pub now?' Tony said, his chin resting on the top of Faster Pasta, and this time she nodded. At the end of the drive she made him stop again, whilst she rescued the meerkat out of the camellias. Tony looked at her with admiration.

Back at The Lakeside, Daniel was laying flagstones along the edge of the car park and lifting huge planters into place. He came over to her car and looked blankly at all the stuff crammed up against the windows.

'Well?' he said, 'Did he agree?'

'No. He tried to imply that I was Lady Gaga.'

He didn't smile at her joke, wiped the sweat off his brow on his arm and watched Tony carry her cases inside. 'I'm not that surprised, are you?'

'No. I was kidding myself, wasn't I?'

He held her eyes for a fraction, then frowned at the

meerkat sat up in her lap. 'Where did that come from?'

'You gave it to Max for his birthday, don't you remember?'

'Did I?' He took it from her with a quizzical expression and placed it in the middle of the architectural planting. It looked faintly ridiculous but it made her smile. Daniel said, 'Not much to show for twenty-five years of marriage is it? Full custody of the meerkat and a set of pans.'

'It's more about what I *don't* want, at the moment.'

He made a small nod of understanding, and went back to shovelling top soil.

Victoria watched him for a moment, then went to her room, overflowing with clothes and bags. She'd taken one of the staff rooms. It was tiny compared to the suite overlooking the lake, but the hotel was getting busy and she was beginning to feel she'd overstayed her welcome, although Daniel had continued to be supportive, relying on her to fill part of Tina's role.

'I couldn't have done a lot of this without you,' he'd said after the press party, but Victoria could have said the exact same words to Daniel. The weekend of the party had been a turning point for Victoria. Leaving Max had been dramatic enough, but the press party had been a blessing with the distraction it created, and it went a long way to confirming to Victoria that she'd done absolutely the right thing.

Tina leaving Daniel had been something of a shock, for everyone. The following day Daniel had been utterly despondent. Victoria had come across him on his phone a couple of times obviously talking to Tina, and obviously not getting anywhere. He'd spent a long time standing on the decking staring at the water. He'd not spoken much and as far as she knew, not eaten anything all day, which was not like Daniel at all.

A couple of days later, Victoria overheard an argument in the kitchen.

Marian had been fuming, banging pots and pans, loading the dishwasher.

'How many homes have you made for her over the years, Daniel? You work yourself into the ground to make a nice life for her and this is what she does, every time! I suppose she'll want a divorce. I can see it now; it would ruin you and make them all millionaires wouldn't it? Her, and her family. Then they can drink and smoke it all away!'

'She wouldn't do that.'

'No?'

He'd burst out of the kitchen at this point and Victoria quickly bowed her head, busy with the computer on reception. Marian had followed on his heels, and caught Daniel before he went outside. She flung her arms round him, her eyes teary, 'I'm so sorry, I shouldn't have said that. I'm sorry, darling.'

Daniel hung his head over her shoulder for a moment, 'Forget it,' he said, suddenly disentangling himself and marching to his car. They watched him speed off down the lake road and Victoria passed Marian a tissue.

'I'm worried sick about him.'

'He'll be fine,' Victoria said, squeezing Marian's arm.

Privately, she thought Tina was quite mad.

The immediate problem was that they were seriously short staffed without Tina, and now Elle had time off without warning. Elle said to Victoria, 'Who was that doctor friend of yours?'

'Charlie? What of him?'

'I would hate him to be my regular doctor, having to go for examinations.'

'How do you mean?'

'Well he's quite fit, for an older guy. And he's *funny*. Told me I was probably short of iron but not to lick the toolbox. Don't tell Troy he's really insecure.'

Victoria laughed and almost sent Linda a text about it,

then deleted it. She was trying to re-build her relationship with Mike, although they didn't look like a couple any more. Daniel had told her that Mike didn't know what to do. Daniel didn't know what to do either, except work. Victoria had never known anyone work so hard, and it was mostly hard physical labour during the day; he was landscaping some of the outside areas, and then in the evening he'd be running from the reception to the restaurant and the bar, covering everyone's breaks, sorting out problems and chatting to guests.

The new chef was young, intense and quite brilliant, but no one was allowed in the kitchen if he was on a shift. He had a thick-skinned assistant called Anton whom he shouted at quite a lot, but the waiting on staff were terrified of him. Daniel had to constantly intervene. Troy had more or less taken over the bar so that meant Victoria and Marian picked up the slack on reception and front of house. Although it was seven days a week without a break for Daniel.

One weekday, a hot day towards the end of May, Marian insisted he took the day off away from the hotel. 'Go out somewhere!' she said, making a shooing motion. 'Go on, it's quiet here.'

'Go where?'

'Anywhere! Go for a walk. Take a picnic.'

'A *picnic*? On my own?'

Marian's response was to coax Victoria along with him.

Victoria made the picnic and Tony loaned her a rucksack to put it all in. Daniel's contribution was to pinch a bottle of Amarone from the bar. 'That's not sensible on a hot day,' Victoria said, looking at the label. A powerful Italian red, *sixteen percent proof.*

'Yes, it is. White would get too warm wouldn't it? Anyway, I don't feel like being sensible. I'm sick of sensible.'

'Oh okay.'

They took the track from the back of the hotel, a wide

grassy expanse of lush pasture, until it began to rise steeply and wind up the flanks of Clogwyn Mannod. Within half an hour Victoria was shouting at Daniel to wait. He laughed at her. 'Come on, you're only carrying a lipstick and a bottle of wine. I've got a sweating Italian cheese and six loaves in this bag.'

'Plus a lot of water. One of us has to be sensible.'

He waited for her, helped her over a stream and across some rocks. An hour later, they reached the summit of Crimpiau and Victoria collapsed on the grass. Back within signal range, Daniel's mobile sprang to life with texts and calls, mostly Troy. Daniel paced about, trying to establish a clear line. 'Troy, you need to grow a backbone. What can I do about Elle if she's feeling sick? Tell chef to calm down. Then *stay out of his way.*'

Victoria said, 'He's only eighteen, give him a break.'

'You think I'm too hard on him?'

'Sometimes.'

He looked at her with mild exasperation, then sat down and kicked his shoes off. 'He's gone and thrown chef's ginger root in the bin.'

'Oh dear, easy mistake.'

She took a long drink of water, and piled her hair on top of her head. There was a welcome shiver of cool air filtering through the heat haze, even though it made the distant peaks look fuzzy. 'Do you know the names of all those mountains?'

'Collectively, it's Snowdonia,' Daniel said. He was flat out on the grass, his white pork pie hat over his face. 'The big one is Snowdon. What more do you need to know?'

'Stop being so crotchety, *Granddad.*'

Victoria looked at his denim clad legs and her eye travelled up to his torso. He had a naturally toned body, as if the muscles were there by circumstance and not design, and that made him all the more attractive, his lack of vanity.

She forced herself to look back at the view, then assembled lunch and poured out some wine, cut hunks of olive bread and mozzarella.

'I think bread and cheese and wine, is quite possibly the most divine creation.'

'Unless you're talking processed, and that stuff from the Spar shop that Mandy drinks in pint pots.'

'Well, *obviously* not.'

They talked about the new chef, and the new lives they seemed to have inherited without partners. Daniel said nothing about Tina. Victoria was a lot more talkative. 'If I stay away from Max for two years I can divorce him on the basis of separation, can't I?'

'How the hell should I know?' Daniel said, and lay back down. 'You know what; I'm tired of thinking about broken relationships. I don't understand mine anymore, I don't even know if it's broken and I sure as *hell* don't get yours.'

Slightly stung by his manner, Victoria lay down but turned her back to Daniel because the sun was in her eyes. After a few moments, she felt him move next to her and place his hand on the hollow of her waist.

'Sorry, love, I didn't mean to take it out on you.'

Victoria froze at the feeling of him being so close.

'Vic? Are you not talking to me now?' He began to gently kiss the nape of her neck. Victoria closed her eyes and almost stopped breathing, trapped in a floating paralysis, the kind that begged to be paused in time. She didn't want him to stop.

But of course he did, and sighed heavily, 'Okay, shouldn't have done that either.'

Victoria stared at the ground for long seconds, then turned over. Daniel was lying on his back, one arm over his forehead and his eyes were closed against the sun. When Victoria leant over him, her shadow made him open his eyes.

'Now what are you doing?' he said quietly, 'Victoria?'

She put her mouth on his, hardly recognising herself. She had a fleeting image of Karen Summers, and those types of women who just took what they wanted, but if she closed her eyes, she could zone out everything she didn't want, exactly as she'd done with Max. Only this was a reverse process. A master class in making Tina and the rest of the world disappear. It was easy.

After the tiniest hesitation, Daniel began to respond to her kiss, and in doing so, pulled her across his body. The feeling of being wrapped in his arms after years of perfumed pain with Max, felt almost too intense to analyse. It could wait.

She opened her mouth to his, and his hands travelled up to her hair, pulled it all loose. Daniel slid his hands under her shirt and she mirrored everything he did, luxuriating in the feel of his body against hers. She thrilled in the fact he wasn't Max, but Daniel was so unthreatening, the way he just lay beneath her, holding her and kissing her. And the pretty grass was studded with alpine flowers, and when he turned her so she moved beneath him, the high clouds were running like snow in a pale summer sky.

Safe and intoxicating like a dream.

Gradually she became aware he was saying her name, and it was like being slowly woken up. Daniel carefully grabbed her hands and kissed them, 'Stop it,' he whispered, and the moment was gone, he was gone. They both lay back down, inches apart but it felt like miles.

'I'd forgotten what it was like, just to have someone hold me like that.'

When he made no reply, Victoria lifted her head to look at him, and she was shocked by how serious he looked. It was just a kiss, a stolen, forbidden kiss, wasn't it?

The rest of it was safe in her head.

Daniel continued to stare at the sky for long moments,

then he picked up her hand and his humility made Victoria swallow over a lump in her throat and feel a pressure building behind her eyes. Max had stolen her senses, mixed them all up. She didn't know what was right any more, only that she craved what she couldn't have. Maybe it was that simple after all.

Hours later, or so it felt, Victoria woke with her head resting on Daniel. He was in a deep sleep, with one leg propped up, and she must have slept as well because it felt late; the sun was sinking and the air was dramatically cool after the heat of the day. Victoria shivered, pulled on Daniel's sweatshirt and the sleeves dangled past her hands. It smelt of him; a mixture of his skin, fabric conditioner and a male fragrance, something old and faded. A pair of red kites hovered some way down the slopes and there was distant bleating of lambs calling for ewes and the drone of some farm machinery or a wood cutter. Daniel hadn't moved. It was strange, seeing him so still. He normally made her feel lazy... even when she was running around.

She tickled his face with a long strand of grass. He took an age to come round, and he was predictably grumpy. 'What's in that *bloody* wine? I've got a stinking headache.'

'Alcohol.'

He made her laugh, the way he stomped about, stuffing things back into the rucksack and switching his phone back on. It immediately began trilling and buzzing. He turned the wine bottle upside down and smiled at her. 'Look at that, it's burning the grass! I dreamt something really weird, could be scarred for life.'

'Sure it was a dream?'

'Pretty sure, I was pregnant with puppies.'

Back at the hotel it was bordering on pandemonium, most of it good pandemonium in that it was busy with lots of people wanting to eat out on the decking, including Charlie and Angela with another couple Victoria didn't know. Bear was swimming in the lake, and Troy had a young noisy audience at the bar, watching him as he was throwing cocktail bottles and shakers around, and occasionally dropping them. Marian told Victoria she had two e-mails and a telephone message in the diary, and as soon as she'd changed could she take over because she was dead on her feet?

Victoria showered, changed and hurried back down to reception. Daniel was drinking water out of a bottle and talking to some Americans about the trout in the lake and how he'd designed the structure of the building. Elle was trying to clear tables but she looked so pale that Daniel took over from her and sent her to lie down.

Victoria watched him for a moment, serving Bara brith ice cream and coffee, still in his Levi's with the back pocket falling off. No one cared; everyone wanted a piece of him.

She made herself look at her messages.

There had been a call from her parents, asking her to call at the house. An e-mail enquiring about food for a wedding in September, from the daughter of The Welsh Tourist Board guy who'd grilled her at the press party. It made her heart leap. Victoria responded instantly, suggesting a meeting. There was also a mountain of information about properties to rent in the area from a local agent. She scanned through some of them, and the prospect excited her.

Both e-mails were life-changing.

Daniel brought her a coffee. 'Chef said do you want some goat's cheese thing with beetroot salad? I can't stand the stuff.'

'Lovely. Look at this,' she said, and watched his face as he looked at the screen. He smiled at the first one, then frowned and shook his head at all the pretty cottages.

Victoria said, '*What?*'

Daniel pulled up another chair and went through them one by one. 'Too isolated, too isolated, and er... *way too isolated.*'

'You're being totally negative! I can't live in a staff room forever. I want to start a business.'

'I know. But what's the best thing about living here?'

'What do you mean?' she whispered, searching his eyes.

'Vic, you're married to a psycho. Do you really think being in an isolated cottage down the valley by yourself with no mobile signal is a good idea?'

She considered his words. 'Well no, but I need to move out.'

He considered *her* words. 'All right, but let me come with you and look at the options. Oh, and by the way, you can't start a business in a rented property.'

Deflated, Victoria took her goat's cheese salad to her room, declining Charlie's offer of a place at their table. He was right though. Daniel was right. She needed to come out of her dream world and throw away the tinted spectacles.

A couple of days later, Daniel drove Victoria around her shortlisted properties. They now included a Victorian flat in town with a security entry system, another flat on the river within a gated complex; and an isolated cottage down the valley with a stream running through the garden, and a magnificent wisteria clinging to the rotting window frames.

Victoria fell in love with the cottage but was mostly petulant about the flats. They were fusty and old fashioned, but half the price. Daniel thought both the flats were okay, and suggested she took a small industrial unit as well, once the catering had got to a commercial level, and her spirits fell a little further. Victoria had imagined herself in a big country kitchen with herbs growing in pots, eggs in baskets and bunches of dried lavender.

'The trouble is, you're not used to slumming it, are you?' Daniel said, inspecting her glum face.

'I don't need to *slum it.*'

'Thing is though, the money hubby's making available to

you out of the goodness of his heart could dry up at any time.'

'I have other funds. I can pay in advance, the whole year if need be.'

'Then what?'

'I'll have my own income with the catering, and my divorce settlement will be through.'

'Huh... you really do need a reality check. You've not even started proceedings yet. That property of yours could take years to sell, and that's if he plays ball.'

Victoria stared out of the passenger window of Daniel's car. Predictably, he drove slightly too fast and had a penchant for rock music. She didn't mind either, no point in driving a Porsche like a granddad was there? She increased the volume on the Kings of Leon.

'I didn't have you down as a rock chick or are you trying to shut me up?'

'Both.'

Victoria made another appointment to look at the flats, by herself. Daniel noticed she'd torn up the cottage details and grinned at her.

'You've no romance,' she said.

'Oh *I* have. The key is, to remember there's none in business, or divorce.'

Keeping his words in mind, she made another phone call to her solicitor. On the day of the appointment, Daniel was manhandling bags of ornamental grit into the planters. She told him she was going to get a reality check. Face the world.

'So, are you going to involve the police?'

'What's the point, now? It's his word against mine.'

'Emily was a witness.'

Victoria felt a shadow cross her heart. If all their recent telephone conversations were anything to go by, she had a strong suspicion that Max had got to Emily, gradually worn her down with his calm reasoning, until she couldn't be clear about what she'd seen. But how could she make her daughter testify against her own father? And then everything would have to come out, the rape and all the other knocks and pushes. It was all grubby and horrible. It was best left buried where it was.

'Could you *honestly* put your family through all that?' she said, feeling a tense knot in her stomach at the thought of it. It made her feel sick. '*All the details of your sex life?*'

Daniel snapped his eyes on hers, and Victoria could have ripped her tongue out.

'*Sex life?*' he said slowly, and the bag of stones he was holding dropped from his hands. 'Vic, are you saying, what I think you're saying?'

Victoria took a moment to consider how to answer him, but her face gave her away. She took a deep breath, 'Okay. So now you know. Could you put your daughter through that?'

Daniel searched her face, 'No.'

'I have to be strong enough to just walk away.'

Daniel looked mutinous, and stabbed the soil with a spade. 'So he gets away with knocking you about, and worse!'

'Max hasn't got away with anything! It will live in his head forever.'

'And yours!'

'There is *nothing* I can do about that,' she said emphatically, but he wouldn't speak to her, just leant on the spade and looked at the ground, then kicked the bag of stones.

There was nothing she could do about any of it.

Except maybe fall in love.

Victoria drove along the lake road, and when she looked through her rear-view mirror, Daniel was still staring at the ground.

It was a long, difficult afternoon she'd set for herself, her reality check. The solicitor was first. She took the approach that she could no longer live with Max. No violence, no affairs. Even if the whole thing took two years, she could divorce on the grounds of separation.

Irreconcilable differences

It sounded like they'd had an argument about what car to buy. Victoria wondered how many battered women were forced into the same option. At least she had a financial cushion, having substantial funds in her name only, one of Max's tax dodges. She drove aimlessly round flats for rent and tried not to think about her beautiful home, or Wisteria House.

Daniel had stood in the overgrown garden, poked the rotten wood on the window frames and almost pushed over a wobbly gate at the side of the property, just by touching it.

'I'd be a nervous wreck if you lived here,' he'd said, and his words went through her head over and over. Towards the end of the afternoon, as Victoria was driving over to the industrial estate to look at the units, a call from the lettings agent confirmed that the river flat had received an offer. Victoria turned around and headed back to their office in town and went through the paperwork for the villa, before her options ran out. So that was that. She was officially the new tenant of flat 5 Mostyn Villas, officially separated from Max, officially single.

Officially scared.

Victoria drove to her parents' bungalow in Deganwy, with the intention of telling them everything; but as soon as she walked through the door, it became clear that Max had already been to see them and offered his considered opinion regarding her state of mind.

Victoria took a deep breath and attempted to unburden herself. Surely once they'd seen how upset and passionate she was, they'd stand by her? She needed their support. Her father was very quiet, disappointed in her. Her mother was full of questions.

'Max said you were *working,* in a hotel.'

'The Lakeside. I've been staying there, and working, yes. Do you remember Dan and Tina?' she said, 'Well it's theirs. Why don't you come and see it?'

Her mother looked as if she'd suggested a trip to the moon, and went into the kitchen. Victoria followed her and found three cups and saucers. They made coffee, her mother cut slices of carrot cake, but their conversation was stilted and difficult. Trying to explain how Max had controlled and bullied her was protracted enough without the addition of anything sexual. They didn't want to hear it, not really. Her mother kept picking odd words out of her conversation and repeating them as if she had no comprehension of what they meant.

'*Hurt* you? How? A *divorce,* but *why?* I don't understand. Max has been a *wonderful* husband and father! He's so worried about you, isn't he, Edward?' she said, looking at her husband's set face for reassurance, but her father continued to suck his pipe.

Victoria placed her coffee cup down. 'Have you not listened to anything I've said?'

'Well yes, but Max did say you were a bit...' she glanced back at her husband. 'How shall I put it?'

'Delusional,' her father barked over his pipe.

'Well he *would.*'

Victoria looked at both their faces, and felt like bursting into tears. She left the room, closed the front door behind her, and practically ran to her car.

It was a typical British summer evening at the beginning of June, cool and bright, everything a shade of green. The sun flickered through the trees, faster and brighter as she drove along the valley road, past sad empty Wisteria House, and Victoria fumbled in the glove compartment for her Ray Bans. She drowned out the engine noise and the trilling of her mobile phone with Sarah Brightman and put her foot down. Daniel wasn't the only one who drove over the speed limit.

By the time she reached the top of the lake though, Victoria stopped the car and allowed herself the indulgence of crying, until she was almost sick. She'd held it together for so long, but now the floodgates had burst open. She'd been naive, hiding herself away at the hotel, wasting time in a cocoon of make believe. Maybe Max was partially right, but it was how she'd lived for years. Her desperation to protect everyone and hide the ugliness of it had backfired. There was nothing to show for that clever facade. Nothing to show for her marriage apart from her grown up children and goodness knows what they thought of her.

When Victoria looked at her phone, there were two missed calls, both from Daniel. Oh Daniel... no one else cared about her. Victoria climbed back into her car and tried to compose herself before she got to the car park.

He was on the reception desk, and studied her with a guarded expression.

'You've been ages... you all right? Got another enquiry for you.'

'Great, that's great,' she managed to say, then had to drag her sunglasses off because she couldn't see properly out of the glare of the sun. Daniel said nothing, simply came out from behind the desk, put his arms around her. Victoria practically collapsed against him. Several guests walked through reception but Daniel didn't let go of her, and she sobbed into his shoulder until his white shirt was covered with her make-up. The telephone began ringing and eventually switched to automatic answer.

'We can't stand here all night like this,' Victoria said, although with her head against him and her eyes closed, it was quite possibly the best feeling in the world. Daniel reached across the desk, grabbed a box of tissues, and Victoria plucked a few out.

'Max has got to everyone. My own parents don't believe me, Dan,' she managed to say. Her voice broke down to be almost incoherent, 'You've no idea how much that hurts.'

'I believe you.'

'I know,' she said, wiping beneath her eyes. 'I've just had a horrible day.'

'Tell me about it over some dinner.'

'I've no appetite.'

'Let's get drunk then.'

'Is that a good idea after last time?'

'We can make some rules, like no Amarone. And we have to stay seated, in a public place.'

She laughed but she was close to tears at the same time. Daniel said, 'Meet me on the table no one ever reserves, and we'll choose what leftovers we want.'

'You sure know how to impress a girl.'

Once in her room, she splashed her eyes with cold water. Daniel's sweatshirt was still on her bed from the day they'd walked up the mountain. She unfolded it and spread the arms out, then lay face down on it.

Fantasy was so much easier than real life.

CHAPTER EIGHT

Daniel was jolted awake. Someone called his name and touched his shoulder.

'Mr Woods? Sorry to have kept you waiting. Mr Benny will see you now.'

When he came round, Daniel discovered he was in the dentist's waiting room and everyone was staring at him. He must have fallen asleep. He had a crick in his neck and he'd quite possibly been dribbling. It was hardly surprising considering he'd been awake half the night with excruciating toothache. He'd never known pain like it, like a million electrodes bouncing on the nerve endings. If anyone touched his face he might possibly kill them.

Mr Benny; he sounded like a jolly kids' character. They only called him that because no one could pronounce his real name. Mr Benny X-rayed his mouth, explaining in broken English that he had a *small* abscess. He agreed it was painful then sent him away with a prescription for painkillers and antibiotics.

He had to wait in another queue at the chemist, while some ancient pharmacist shuffled about, putting tablets into packets and helping some foreign tourists with directions to A & E. The girl on the counter took one look at Daniel, read his prescription and gave him some of the painkillers with a cup of water. When he got back to his car where he'd dumped it across the pavement, there was a parking fine on the windscreen and some idiot in a transit blocking him in.

Somehow he managed to drive back. At the hotel, it was reassuringly busy, but he couldn't cope with any of it, and just felt like sticking his head in the freezer. He texted Victoria and told her he was out of action and could she come over and keep an eye? He felt bad about that because she had enough on her plate really, having just moved into the flat. She responded in the affirmative, but of course he knew she would. If Tina was here, like she should be, none of this would have got as potentially messy.

The developing problem now was that he liked Victoria's company more than he should, never mind that she was brilliant at looking after his business. When Daniel thought about the pig she was married to, he couldn't get his head round any of it, why would anyone want to hurt her like that? He'd noticed the bruises on her arms a long time ago but didn't make the connection. It was where Max had held her down. When Daniel thought about it, it made his blood run hot. He was twice the size of Victoria, and she was so tiny, like a porcelain doll. She was beautiful. *Beautiful.*

He dragged his clothes off and got back into bed but it took another twenty minutes for the pain to die down to nagging agony instead of full on agony. A long time later, he was aware of someone in the room, but was in that horrible sickly sweaty, half asleep state of having taken a lot of painkillers on an empty stomach. He stayed face down, not wanting to move his head.

'Dan? You okay?' Victoria said, and touched his hand. He felt her hair brush against his shoulder, smelt her perfume.

Dan grunted.

She left a drink or something by the side of the bed, and then quietly closed the door behind her.

Hours later, his mobile woke him.

'Yeah?' he mumbled.

'You sound hung over.'

It was Tina. He told her about the dentist and she was panicking in seconds, talking about getting a train. Daniel turned onto his back and rolled his eyes at the ceiling. He rubbed his face. 'Tee, what's the point? By the time you get here on two trains and a taxi I'll be okay.'

'You're such a baby with pain. Remember the accident with the epilator?'

'What's that?'

'So you don't need me to come over?'

'Tee, I need you to be here permanently, so I can rent the flat. I need a restaurant manager. I can't afford to pay you a manager's salary while you live rent free over there. I need a *wife*.'

She disconnected and Daniel slung his phone across the bed. He fumbled about in the duvet to find it again. 'Tee? Sorry, I'm not thinking. I'm a bit spaced out.'

'I don't know why you're keeping my job open. I don't want it.'

'Which job? The manager job or the wife job?'

'It's all about you and the hotel again.'

He threw the phone back across the bed and clutched his jaw. Talking had woken the pain from its semi slumber. If he was a kid he'd be bawling his eyes out now. If he was a dog he'd be whimpering to be put down. Daniel pulled the pillow over his head and did a bit of both.

*

Two days later his face was just about touchable again and he started to shave, then had to abandon it as a bad job because of the swelling. He looked like the elephant man. Mike came over with Tina's birthday present. It was a pink car, a second-hand Mini. It was quite clear Mike thought he was crazy. He didn't need to ask what his mother thought. Victoria looked at it with folded arms.

'A June birthday makes Tina a Gemini. Split personality.'

'Yeah, it's split all right.'

Troy thought it was a brilliant idea. 'Hey Dad, why don't you fill it with flowers?'

'Don't be stupid.'

Daniel drove the car to the nearest florist and filled it with flowers in every shade of pink. People driving past him on the motorway sounded their horns, laughed and waved at him. Hardly surprising when he thought about it, the big romantic gesture. Was this what his relationship boiled down to? His marriage was based on a stupid drunken pact and he had no idea how to fix it. But he had to try. Before he did something *really stupid.*

At the flat he had to double park. He thumped on the door first, then realised he had a key because it was his flat. He stood in the hall and shouted. Tina came running out of the kitchen, drying her hands on a towel. At least she was still wearing her wedding ring, in fact, it looked like she was still wearing the ring he won for her out of the lucky dip machine when she was sixteen.

'Dan... what are you doing here? Oh look at your poor face.'

'Happy birthday,' he said, 'Come outside, I got you a present.'

She ran down to the car, still holding the towel. 'Oh Dan! Dan I love it!' She threw her arms around him, and for a moment everything was as he'd imagined, and she was the Tina he loved, but then she'd shown the exact same reaction when he won the ring in the lucky dip machine.

'Get in, go on, can't leave it here in the middle of the street.'

He needed to talk without her marching off, slamming doors or throwing things at him, and she couldn't do any of that in the car. She climbed in the passenger side, 'Where are we going?'

'Need some petrol, then I want us to talk.'

'It's my birthday; I don't want a heavy talk, Dan.'

He sighed, tried to stay calm, 'Tee, I can't live like this any longer. Are you happy with this, this *arrangement?*'

'That's the first time you've asked me directly about my happiness with any arrangements.'

'How can you say that? How long did we plan the hotel, the wedding?'

He had to stop to fill the car with petrol. Tina sat with her head bowed, surrounded by wilting flowers and cards. She'd found the pink teddy in the glove box and made it wave its paw at him through the window.

Daniel got back into the car, already losing his cool. *How could she say that?*

He rammed the car into gear but moved into the car wash queue by mistake. The guy behind him refused to reverse, so he banged the steering wheel instead. 'Great, now look!'

'So, wash it. Get me the super wax and dry.'

'This is all a laugh to you isn't it?'

They crawled along in the queue and Daniel put it in the wrong gear again. It was like driving a clapped out old van after the Porsche but he wasn't really concentrating, his mind was jumping gear as well.

'Tina, I deserve some answers,' he said, frowning at her white face. 'What do you do all day on your manager's salary?'

'If it's about the money, just stop paying me.'

'What are you going to live on?'

'Why should you care?'

'Of course I care, *I love you!*' He had to stop to wind the window down and pay the attendant. Daniel threw a ten pound note at him then wound the window back and for a moment they both sat and looked at the soapy windscreen.

'I don't need all that money anyway. I'm working at Fernando's part time.' Tina said, making a bouquet out of some of the roses scattered on the dashboard. The attendant waved them forward, put his hand up to indicate the front wheels had locked in, then watched fascinated as they rolled past, taking a good look at the back seat and all the foliage.

Daniel said, 'Oh great. Now we're getting to it.'

'I loved that job before you made me give it up. *Loved it.*'

'I know!' He had to shout above the noise of the car wash. Massive blue rollers buffeted the sides of the car with soap. 'I know! I know you did.'

She shouted back, 'You *say* that, but you don't really listen, you just hear what you want to hear.' She looked down at her lap, and her voice dropped. Suddenly she was all quiet and serious, and Daniel felt his insides plummet, like the first time she'd told him about her Italian lover.

'I know I'm hurting you. Dan, there is something I want to tell you.'

The rollers crushed against the windscreen then went over the top of the car.

'I knew it! You're seeing pizza boy aren't you? *Just say it!*'

'You're doing it again!' she yelled back, incensed. 'That was *years ago*! Okay if we're doing this, what about your affair with Mia? And what about that Australian girl and the kangaroo?'

'*Wallaby*. It was a wallaby. What are you talking about? We weren't together then!'

Daniel looked sullenly out of the window and drummed his fingers on the steering wheel. The car in front was full of kids looking through the back window at them, pulling faces. Like a silent movie. They glided past a huge red emergency button, like something out of Charlie and the Chocolate factory. It didn't look real but he wanted to push it. Another wash cycle started.

'Look, this is childish; I thought we were past all this.'

'I know, but you throw it back in my face all the time! We just keep going over old ground instead of going forwards.'

'There's such a lot of old ground,' Daniel said, and sighed. Maybe that was the problem, the old ground. 'Let's look at the new ground then. The bottom line is, I've bullied you into everything is that it?'

'No Dan, the bottom line is *you don't listen!*' she said, struggling with the door handle. 'Oh you know what, I've had enough.'

'What?...What are you doing? Tina! What the *fuck* are you doing? *Tina!*'

Before he had chance to grab the back of her waistband, she'd pushed the door open and got out. The rinse jets started and for a crazy second Tina just stood there with her eyes screwed up, still holding a bunch of flowers and getting drowned in gallons of cold dirty water. Her clothes were plastered to her in seconds and in the middle of all the madness, Daniel was suddenly aware of how much thinner she was. When did that happen?

Somehow, she climbed out under the blower as the car in front chugged forwards. The family who were sat in it were open-mouthed, the kids screaming with laughter. Seconds later the whole thing stopped and it was like opening the door of the washing machine or the dishwasher, mid-cycle. Silence, dripping water everywhere.

The guy in the car behind was sat covered in foam, pipping his horn and mouthing off. Daniel scrambled out onto the forecourt and Tina was there, shivering and holding a bunch of stems. He drove her back to the flat, and ran her a bath. Then they had another argument.

She remained adamant she wasn't seeing Fernando again, just working for him. She was also adamant she didn't want money off Daniel, just wanted to stay in the flat and give herself time to catch up. 'I've got stuff I need to sort out in my head.'

'What *stuff*? Pity you didn't do all that before we got married!'

'I didn't get chance!'

Since she seemed intent on ripping into him, Daniel sat and took it. It was partly the money she said, the inheritance that had changed everything, changed *him*.

'I used to love it when it was just you and me against the world. We were special.'

'We still are, can be. We could have it all.'

'I don't want it *all*. I just want *you*. You know you're turning into one of those people you used to despise? I'm not sure I want to be part of your master plan.'

He lost his temper then and marched to the train station. Tina ran after him, her hair still in a towel. 'Daniel Woods, come back I've nowhere near finished with you yet!'

'I have. *I've* finished with you,' he said, and the way her face crumpled tore his insides out, but he kept on walking, and switched his phone off. Her words had touched something raw, like the throbbing pain in his jaw.

Root canal surgery. The root of all evil.

Maybe it was evil for some people, but it was way too late to change that now, and why the hell *should* he? Daniel had thought it would make everything easier after years of struggling. It wasn't as if he'd not worked for it.

Barney Rubble would disagree.

That fat twit who'd tried to kill him since he was fifteen, real name Barry Jones. His stepfather Tomas Marshall, had been Daniel's boss for twenty-three years. They'd built up the tiny builder's yard into a thriving business. He'd been more than a boss really, stepped in a lot when Daniel's real father died and kept him on the straight and narrow. Daniel knew he was getting the business eventually, but all the other assets were a bit of a shock.

Tommy had left nothing to Barbara and Barry, but Daniel knew the reasoning behind that had a lot to do with Barry's drug problem, and Barbara's greedy desperation to have a big bank balance. Daniel had tried to do the right thing by Barbara and gifted her quite a bit of money but she still spat at him in the street. And what had Barry ever done? He'd never done a day's work in his life. He was just a small time drug dealer who'd done time inside.

The train stopped at Llandudno and Daniel found a taxi, but he got out at the top of the lake, so he could walk the final mile along the edge of the water. He wanted to see if his hotel still gave him a buzz. It did, but it was slightly tainted now by Tina's attack on him. Tommy would have been amazed, proud. He liked to think his own father would have been amazed, proud.

So why did his heart feel like lead? As if it had an abscess.

Bear came bounding over to greet him and Daniel sat with the dog at the water's edge, watching a pair of herons poke about in the marsh. After a while, he became aware of his mother. Marian struggled to get down onto the grass bank, then she sat next to him and put an arm around him and Daniel felt about ten years old, as if he knew nothing about life.

Later, in the bar, his son looked at him as if he'd screwed up the world peace talks. Troy was wearing the white pork pie hat at a jaunty angle. He slammed a glass of single malt down in front of Daniel, sucked his teeth like an old man and shook his head, 'Women eh?'

Daniel studied his face. 'All right, what's going on?'

'All's sweet with me. You?'

'You know it isn't.'

'Did you do the flowers?'

'I did the flowers.'

Troy looked him in the eye for two seconds then practically collapsed with laughter. 'You didn't?'

'Troy, it was your idea.'

'Yeah but I didn't think you'd actually like, *do it.*'

He poured another shot of single malt for Daniel, then began furiously texting. 'Oh man I can't believe you did that! Was it like, *filled* with flowers?' he said, making a circular motion with both hands. 'You drove that pink car down the A55 filled with flowers, yeah?'

'You got it.'

When the texting had stopped, Daniel tried again. Serious wasn't a word in Troy's vocabulary but Daniel knew his banter was a foil for everything else. He remembered what Victoria had said, and when he looked back at his son, it was as if Daniel was looking for the first time. He was just a kid really, and he'd heaped all this grown up stuff on him. Victoria was right; he expected everything of his son, and nothing of his daughter. Why was that?

'Troy, I'm sorry I messed up.'

'Hey, no worries Dad,' he said, still looking at his phone. 'How's Elle?'

He looked up then but his face dropped; a mixture of fear and bravado. 'Elle?' he said, as if he didn't know who Elle was. 'You know how you want me to make more decisions on my own? Right the thing is, I've had to get rid of that blonde cleaner.'

'Trouble, was she?'

'Kind of... but I got a replacement so no worries.'

*

Troy had been to see her several times, full of worried questions disguised as something else. Tina was used to it, could see that big beating heart on his sleeve a mile off. At first he tried to play the big man, all swagger and nonchalance as if he were going to give his mother the benefit of his worldly advice.

'Okay what's going on with you and Dad? What's he done? I don't like, *totally* get it.'

'Oh you know what your dad and me are like.'

'But I thought you were like, *married*? Yeah?'

Tina managed to field most of his questions, until she'd stupidly missed her mouth with a cup of tea and burnt her hand instead. Troy hadn't spoken for an age after that, but he was watching her all the time as she mopped up the tea with a box of tissues.

'Are you all right, Mum?'

'I'm fine; don't worry just a stupid accident.'

'You look, kinda white.'

'Well, I haven't got the Max Factor out yet, have I?'

He held her eyes for a second and Tina was shocked to see they were full of resentment. 'So, are you coming back or what?'

When she just sighed, Troy got to his feet and the earlier Troy was replaced by the real one. 'I really could do with you being around, that's all. Elle and me keep arguing about names and stuff. I told her Shane was like, a *dog's* name.'

Tina stood then and embraced him in a hug, surprised he didn't pull away like he usually did. Her son was all grown but still needed her on a consultancy level. Troy was taller than her now and he felt different, more filled out from lifting weights at the gym or whatever he did. It made her think of Dan and how much she longed for him, for both of them really.

'You won't be able to keep me away when the baby comes. I can't wait to be Nana Tee Tee.' It was the name Elle had dreamt up for her. 'You're too much fun to be called Grandma. I'll think of somat else,' she'd said and Tina had laughed.

It was easy to laugh down the phone.

The baby had added another complication. At first, it had filled her with an indescribable leap of painful joy in her heart. But it was quickly overshadowed by some awful nightmare where she dropped the baby on its head, followed by the awful realisation that she wouldn't actually be any help at all.

Troy had left a few minutes later, but only because Tina had told him she had several girlfriends coming round for lunch. Like she was having a busy fun time and there was nothing wrong. He didn't quite swallow it, but talk of Elle and the baby was almost too much. It had taken an iron resolve not to break down in front of him.

After the argument with Dan in the carwash on her birthday, after staggering back inside the flat with her hair still sopping wet, the futility of it all suddenly hit her. She managed to crawl onto the sofa where she lay flat, drenched in sweat. By some miracle, she had her phone to hand. Iron resolve on hold, she called Daniel, and sobbed it all out.

*

Daniel slept for twelve hours. In the morning, he could hear Mandy vacuuming outside his room, knocking all the paint off the skirting boards and wailing along to Abba. No worries. When he switched his phone back on, he had dozens of backed up messages and voice mail, mostly from Tina. For the first time in his life, he ignored her and deleted them.

There was one from Victoria.

'How's the toothache? Need me today?'

Need her? How the hell was he supposed to answer that? Whenever he closed his eyes, he could feel her lying across him, his hands threaded through her hair, her mouth on his. He texted back, 'No it's okay thanks, have a good day.'

There was one from Mike. 'Did the Barbie car do the trick? If so I might get one.'

Daniel responded with, 'No don't bother'.

He made coffee, ran a shower, stripped the bed, switched the dishwasher on, listened to the news and placed an ad for a restaurant manager. Then he ran out of distractions. He called Victoria.

'Dan? I just got your message. Everything all right?'

'Are you free today?'

'To work?'

'No. To play?'

'I guess,' she said slowly, 'what did you have in mind?'

He rubbed his eyes. 'Just some downtime; I dunno, go out for lunch somewhere?'

'I'd love to.'

Daniel ended the call and slung a paperback book up the wall, so hard it fell to pieces.

An hour later he was ringing the bell for flat 5. When Victoria came to the door he felt tongue tied, like a kid.

'Are you coming in?' she said to his blank face. 'Just need to get my bag.'

He followed her down the hall, taking in the newly decorated duck egg blue walls, and her rear view in French Connection denim and a linen shirt. She said, 'Has the swelling gone down?'

'W*hat?*'

'Your face,' she said, finding her bag and keys, pulling on a suede jacket, 'I was worried the other day, you were really poorly.' Victoria flicked her hair out of the back of her collar, and looked up at him under her eyelashes, waiting for some sort of response. 'Dan…?

'You were worried, about me?'

'Yes! I think I still am,' she said, a flicker of laughter in her eyes, a slight twitch of her lips. She'd really got herself on track since she'd moved into the flat and he had to admire her for that. She might look all fragile but he strongly suspected Victoria was a much tougher cookie on the inside.

Daniel drove for fifty miles along the dual carriageway then realised he had no idea where he was going. 'Where are we going?' Victoria said, frowning at the motorway signs.

'Vic, am I a control freak?' he said, glancing at her profile.

'No,' she said quickly. 'I lived with one of those.'

'But I made you choose the flat and you wanted Wisteria House.'

'Only in my best interests! I love the flat now. Dan, where are we going?'

'You choose.'

She laughed, 'Chester? Take a left here.'

Chester was one of Tina's favourite cities. It was easy to see why, with its smart shops hidden behind the medieval facade of the streets and all of the crooked balconies. They walked the walls, drank coffee and watched the street artists. Half the time Daniel just wanted to watch Victoria, and she kept catching him looking at her. He tried not to talk about his relationship, but it was more difficult than he'd imagined and he had to keep apologising to Victoria. She wasn't really bothered, 'Dan, how many times have I sobbed on your shoulder?' she said, and dived into Zara. He followed, and watched her hold outfits against herself, wanting his reaction.

'You've got me here under false pretences,' he said. 'I can't believe we're *shopping*.'

'Come on, help me out here and make a decision, if you *think* you're such a control freak,' she said, 'the blue sundress or this cream one?'

He looked at her with his head on one side and after a moment, pointed at the cream one. Victoria pouted and said the blue one. Daniel sat outside on an iron bench under the trees while she waited to pay, and looked through his phone, then remembered he'd deleted everything. Just as well really. Tina used to have him all over the place, his emotions on a line of elastic. If you stretched it far enough though, even elastic snapped.

After a long while he was aware of Victoria's sandals and a lot of bags drifting into focus.

'Tina?' she said, indicating his mobile.

Daniel squinted up at her and slid the phone back into his jacket. They wandered back along the mall and Victoria linked her arm through his.

'What happened?'

'With Tina? I still don't really know. There are so *many* issues. I can't solve any of them because it's either too late, or it's just, *confusing*.'

'I know that feeling.'

'The worst one was the dig about the money. I really lost it then.'

'How do you mean?'

'She reckoned I'd changed because of it,' he said, then suddenly stopped walking, *'Have I?'*

Victoria considered him for a moment and for the first time he noticed there were flecks of gold in her hazel eyes, 'I can't really answer that,' she said, struggling to hold all her shopping, 'but if I had to choose between love and rags; or riches and loneliness, I'd pick the rags every time.'

'She had both!' Daniel snapped. He sighed and pinched the bridge of his nose. 'Sorry, sorry, love.'

Victoria was still fixed on his face, her arms full of sliding glossy bags. Daniel took most of them from her, and peered through the handles, 'There's got to be more than one dress here?'

'There is. Expensive rags, the spoils of a rich control freak,' Victoria said and gave him a beautiful smile. 'Lunch?'

They headed back after tapas.

At Victoria's flat, Daniel carried her shopping through to the little sitting room. There was an awkward moment when he made to go. Since the kiss, every possible expectation of touch was heightened and over thought.

In the end, he kissed her cheek as he would have done if she were Linda or anyone else. But she didn't look or feel like Linda, or anyone else. His hand lingered on her waist, and his eyes lingered on hers just a bit too long. 'Thanks for lunch,' she said.

'Thanks for listening. Sorry I've been a pain.'

'You haven't.'

His phone rang, and rang. 'You'd better get that,' Victoria said.

It was Troy. He needed Daniel to get back so he could take Elle for a scan.

It was strange, expecting a grandchild.

He'd not had time to think about it really and how it affected them all. If he was honest, he'd not even noticed she was pregnant, Elle wore such floaty clothes. When he pulled in to the car park at the hotel, they were both getting in to Troy's battered car, a cloud of smoke coming out of the exhaust, with a save the elephant sticker hanging off the back window. It had a new dent on the boot.

'We get to know boy or girl today, if we want,' Elle said, leaning through the window.

'Keep an eye on Troy; he tends to keel over in hospitals.'

'Great, that's all I need,' she said. Daniel grinned and squeezed her hand, then watched them drive along the lake, very slowly. When did that happen, Troy being all sensible?

*

In July, the new restaurant manager started. Susan Lloyd-Jones was calm and efficient, had brilliant references and she could handle Chef. She didn't have Tina's social sparkle, but there was always going to be an un-ticked box. Victoria's daughter had taken a summer job at the hotel, waiting on, reception, anything really. Troy said she ticked all of his boxes.

'You will be there for your mum, won't you?' Daniel said to Emily, 'She feels a bit cut adrift.'

'I know. So do I. I think I've probably failed my first year. Don't tell her, please.'

It was a blisteringly hot afternoon and Daniel was drinking bottles of beer with Troy on the deck, watching Emily arrange flowers on the bar. Mandy slopped a cloth round the tables. She had a new tattoo. Whenever she bent over, her tracksuit bottoms would reveal a red thong and the words 100% Welsh lamb, was visible on her ample rump.

Troy said, 'Thing is, what I don't get, is how can Emily and Auntie Mandy be from the same *species*? Victoria's daughter is seriously *hot*. She's like, *smokin.*'

Daniel drank some beer. 'I guess it works on the same principle that you and Einstein were both educated, but the end product is totally different. One's a genius, one's a total muppet.'

His face crumpled into a scowl, '...Eh?'

'You need to have a word with Mandy. Get her a uniform or something.'

Troy propped his legs on the decking rail. 'Like, a massive bag?'

Daniel grinned and pushed his head. 'Are you looking after Elle?'

'Yeah... she's getting bigger and bigger, Dad.'

'She's pregnant, that's what it is.'

The heat continued well into the afternoon and early evening, and Daniel watched his restaurant fill to capacity. He could hear Chef yelling in the background, and the new manager telling him to stop swearing, who did he think he was Gordon Ramsay? Emily and the regular waitress were both running to and fro with plates. Troy was busy with the bar, and Elle sat on reception fanning her face with Alright!

magazine and chewing indigestion tablets like sweets. Outside, he could see Anton taking a fag break, dangling his feet in the lake, and Bear was lying in the shade, snapping at flies with his massive jaws. Tony was patrolling the car park, chatting on his mobile, laughing.

Daniel felt restless, lonely. When he looked around all he could see were couples enjoying themselves, even his staff were having a better time. When he looked at Emily, it was like looking at Victoria. Same long dark hair, same mouth and eyes. Her voice, and her low laugh were the same and it caught him out sometimes, made him turn around thinking she'd walked into the room.

Daniel called her number. 'Are you busy?'

'Not especially.'

'Have you eaten? Fancy coming over?'

'You're always feeding me! Why don't you come here?'

'There?'

He drove slowly to her flat.

When she opened the door, she was wearing the cream sundress from Zara.

'You told me you got the blue one.'

'I *did*,' she said, and laughed. 'I'm impressed you even remember.'

He followed her into the sitting room, and it was mellow and golden with the evening sun.

'I got the blue one for me, and the cream one for you.'

'For me?'

The room was very Victoria, classic and traditional. The only exception was the computer desk by the window, overflowing with paperwork and cookery books. She passed him a beer, then poured herself a glass of wine. Daniel took the glass from her and placed both drinks down on a side table. She looked at him inquiringly, but there was no hesitation when he slid his arms around her, felt the contours of her body and inhaled the perfume of her hair.

'I want to kiss you.'

Victoria looked at him for a long second, 'I'm not going to stop you.'

She closed her eyes and he kissed the side of her mouth, her eyelids. She had long, long dark eyelashes, and for a fraction of a second he just wanted to look at her like that, her eyes closed and her lips slightly parted. He put his mouth on hers, and the intensity of feeling seemed magnified, out of context.

'I want to kiss more of you,' he whispered, and he could feel her heart hammering against his. She quickly searched his eyes, slowly turned around and held her hair up and he found the zip at the top of the dress. When she stepped out of it, Daniel picked her up, and she felt almost weightless. He wondered what was going through her mind; the knowledge that she'd been so abused was a massive burden for both of them in a way, but when he tried to say it, give her a way out if he was truthful, she put a trembling finger on his lips.

Her bedroom was mahogany with snow white sheets, colourless really but for a vase of vivid peonies. A muslin curtain billowed through the open window. He could smell the sea; hear the gulls riding the breeze. Daniel laid her down on the bed and kissed her throat, her breasts; he paused for a second to look at her, and was reassured that she didn't want him to stop. He removed only some of her Italian lingerie, held her close enough to feel the length of her gorgeous body, caressed and kissed her until she was soft, and yielded to him completely.

CHAPTER NINE

Tom and his girlfriend Sarah turned up on Linda's birthday as a surprise. It was Sarah's idea. Much like herself, Linda's younger son was a home lover; steady girlfriend for years, steady job, sensible car and sensible life. It was awkward, explaining there was nowhere for them to stay because Mike was in the spare room. After that, she let Mike do all the explaining and part of her enjoyed watching him squirm. In the middle of all the strained celebrations, Linda received a phone call to say that Tina's mother had died. Tracy, the elder sister, had the job of phone calls.

'Just… going through the address book, you know.'

'What happened? She wasn't ill, was she?'

'There's got to be an autopsy.'

'And Tina?' Linda whispered. 'Is she okay?'

'What about her? She's a waste of space! Not been near since she went back to Manchester.'

Linda ended the call, couldn't get through to Tina, and Mike just proffered the usual words, as if it was someone they didn't really know. Linda could only think about Tina, and how much the stress might set her back. Not knowing what else to do, she sent flowers then called Daniel.

'You've heard the news?'

'Yeah.'

'Is that all you can say? I hope you're going to see Tina.'

'She won't answer the phone!'

'Dan, she *needs* you.'

'I *know!* I can't do anything if she won't let me.'

Later, they went out for a birthday dinner, the four of them. Linda suggested Tom and Sarah treat themselves and stay at The Lakeside for a night before driving back to London, but they couldn't really afford it and Linda felt awkward then. In the end, Mike slept on the sofa and the Star Wars cover went back on the spare bed.

It was the saddest birthday she'd ever known. Mid July, that made her a home loving, caring Cancerian. She was true to her star sign, needed someone to care for, to cherish and nurture to feel complete. Linda had thought a lot about Charlie's suggestion; to the extent that a month ago she'd gone along to the local college and checked his facts. Yes, she could enrol as a mature student with a view to a nursing career. She would need to do a year's access course at the college, followed by a university degree combined with practical experience. She could still do her current job around it all, and yes, she qualified for a grant. *A degree*, Linda Williams with a degree!

Linda filled out all the forms, then she sat on a wooden bench in the college grounds by the sea, and called Charlie. 'Lin! How lovely to hear from you. How are you?'

She smiled. 'I've done what you suggested.'

'Oh dear, that always makes me nervous. Now, when I made this suggestion was I inebriated? And have you had any side effects?'

She laughed, told him about her decision to enter nursing, and he was incredibly pleased for her. 'If you need *any* help with it, you only need pick up the phone. You might find parts of it a bit tough, but hey it's a challenge. We all need to be passionate about something in life.'

On a roll with the new Linda, she had her hair cut to jaw length and coloured a shade lighter. Mike's reaction had been mixed. He loved the hair, but the university degree was a puzzle to him. They'd argued, but half-heartedly since Linda had already signed up anyway, and intended to start in September.

The day following her birthday, when Tom and Sarah had gone, Mike dropped the bombshell. 'I'm sorry, Lin, this isn't working for me, for us,' he said, quite suddenly. When she frowned, unsure of what was coming, he said, 'Look, just divorce me for adultery and let's have done.'

She was shocked, because she'd always imagined those final words would be hers.

He said, 'I can't live like this and I'm sure you don't want to either. I'm waiting and waiting for you to either throw me out, or humiliate me with it over and over again.'

Linda found herself apologising, knowing he was right; then they'd both sat and cried over the death of their marriage. Ironically it was the best talk they'd had in months. Past the stage of blame and anger, Linda could be brutally honest with herself about their relationship, and recognised how it had become too complacent since the boys had left home. She could even see why and how an affair might happen.

Mike just said it was the biggest mistake of his life, and to stop trying to analyse it.

It boiled down to money. They would have to put the house on the market. Linda couldn't afford it alone, and Mike didn't really want it. What that would leave them with was anyone's guess, enough for a couple of miserable rooms each probably.

The following day, feeling out of sorts and needing a friend, Linda called Victoria. 'I'm in town, thought I'd call and see your flat if you're not busy? Could do with a chat actually, got some news, good and bad.'

'Oh Lin... okay. Just give me an hour, yes?'

'An *hour*? Right,' Linda said, and felt slightly knocked back. She'd dropped everything for Victoria in the past, listened to her on the phone for an age, crying over her bloody pig of a husband. She took a deep breath and tried to summon some shreds of understanding, then wandered around town in an aimless fog, just wasting time.

Fifty minutes later, Linda found the right address on the West Shore, and saw Daniel's Porsche in the same street. She rang the bell, and Victoria seemed ever so slightly distracted, but she looked different... *glowing*. Daniel was in the sitting room. He got to his feet and kissed Linda and she noticed there was a different fragrance about him. Linda knew his usual after shave so well, he always wore Givenchy; always.

'Lin, you've had your hair cut, suits you,' he said carefully. 'How are you?'

'Do you want the short answer or the longer one?' she said curtly.

'Ah... do you want me to go? I can talk to you about menus anytime,' he said to Victoria, then looked back at Linda, 'I can sense a serious man rant brewing.'

Linda said, 'Before you go, you may as well know, Mike and I have decided to call it a day.'

'Oh God, I'm sorry Lin, I wasn't being flippant,' Daniel said, and hugged her again.

It was Victoria's perfume.

'No, I know,' Linda said, 'it's all amicable, just living arrangements to sort out.'

'Divorce number three,' Victoria said.

'*Two*,' Linda corrected, 'Daniel and Tina are not getting divorced, they're still married.'

Her words floated in the air, as if no one wanted to catch them.

After a few minutes, Daniel made to leave. Victoria saw him out. They were ages in the hall, then Victoria went directly into the kitchen and busied herself with refilling the coffee machine. Linda looked through the window at the sea above the rooftops, Puffin Island shimmering in the heat. It was quiet, peaceful. She wished she could afford something like it.

'Lovely flat,' she shouted, and Victoria said something in the affirmative, 'So glad Dan made me take this place now, much easier to look after than a house, and I love the view, don't you?'

'Uh huh... nice.'

Linda wandered back down the hall, glanced through the chink at the bedroom door, glanced through at the bathroom; then doubled back and looked at the bedroom again. She nudged the Victorian door slightly with her foot and it creaked open. The bed was unmade and there was a towel and a sweatshirt on the floor, not something Victoria would wear. Not something Victoria would do, leave a towel on the floor.

'So, has Dan helped you out?' Linda said.

'He's been amazing.'

Linda retraced her steps, and Victoria brought a tray out. Her conversation featured Daniel quite a lot. Two minutes after she'd poured the coffee, and Linda was about to tell her about her decision to go back to college, Victoria's phone received a text. She smiled and coloured slightly, then took a minute to reply. 'Sorry, Lin, do carry on. Just Emily being silly; I'll switch it off.'

Linda could feel her patience and her intelligence, severely tested. After ten minutes, she made her excuses and left. She walked and walked, to discover she'd gone in a circle round the streets and was almost back at Mostyn Villas. When Linda rang the bell again, her finger seemed glued to it.

Victoria came to the door, 'Lin! Forget something?'

Linda stepped inside the hall and closed the door behind her. 'Vic, don't lie, are you and Dan having an affair?'

'Er... No.'

'*Liar*,' Linda said softly.

Victoria looked contrite but only for a second. She looked down at the mosaic tiles, then folded her arms. 'All right, so what if we are?'

'What if you are? He's *married!*' Linda struggled not to shout. 'Do you remember the wedding? Just seven months ago? How can you do this to Tina?'

'It's over with Dan and Tina.'

'And you think that's all there is to it?' Linda said, rolling her eyes up at the dusty chandelier, 'Are you completely stupid?'

Victoria shot her a haughty expression, but she looked away quickly.

Linda said, 'Dan will go back to her. He always does.'

A beat passed. Victoria looked her in the eye, and the tiny chink of doubt Linda might have seen there, had vanished. 'I love him,' Victoria said, calmly and succinctly, as if the words were a final warning, a weapon, some sort of guarantee. 'I actually don't care what you think.'

Linda didn't remember leaving the flat. Thoroughly wound up, she found a bench on the seafront and tried to compose herself. The worst part of it all was she couldn't talk to anyone about it; except Charlie. His phone was on voice mail, but of course it would be, it was surgery hours. Linda left a garbled message, then by the time she'd walked slowly back to her car, felt a bit silly over how she'd phrased it all, it was too late to retract it.

She drove over to Mike's garage. It was at the end of a row of shops, an odd little area but it was close to the beach road, and petered out into a patchwork of agricultural fields so it had an open feel. The ground floor was taken up with the tools of his trade, and then above that was the flat. They'd always intended to do it up and rent it out, but time and money was always short, and Mike didn't really have the right skills. It wasn't a flat really, not like Victoria's, or Dan and Tina's. The truth of it was closer to a couple of grotty storerooms, but if he could make a love nest there with Armenka, Linda was still prepared to consider it an option.

And it came free.

Mike was under a car, his overall clad legs sticking out at an odd angle, and the familiarity of it filled her with a little stab of nostalgia. She asked him for the keys, and he thought she was mad.

'You'll hate it; it's a dump with bad associations.'

The access was round the back, up a few horrible stone steps. The first thing which struck her as a positive was the fields of cows at the rear, the only neighbours for miles and they had no use for a flock of mopeds or a trampoline. Inside though, it was like a student bedsit, just the bare basics with a sofa bed and a miserable excuse for a kitchen and bathroom. The only window looked out over the garage forecourt. She went dismally back down and slotted the keys back in the workroom.

'Well?' Mike said, wiping his hands on an oily rag.

'It's a dump.'

'It needs money spending, that's the problem. And it needs plastering and damp proofing.'

'I know a builder,' Linda said.

'He's not going to do it for nothing, and anyway Dan's not a builder anymore.'

'I'll ask nicely.'

*

The For Sale board went up in the front garden at the end of the week. Linda sat in her car on the drive and looked at it, wondering why she didn't feel more disturbed by it. Then she reversed, and drove into town to meet Charlie. It felt strange, and slightly hypocritical if she was honest, but she reminded herself it was only lunch, not out of control sex.

Following her voice mail, Charlie had suggested dinner but Linda had panicked, 'What about Charlie's Angel?'

'Who? Oh! *Angela*. Oh I'm afraid we've parted company. She was far too high maintenance for me. Karen scarred me deeply with all that kind of carry on.'

'Oh, I don't know, Charlie.'

'If it's too soon, I *completely* understand.'

'It just feels odd, still living with Mike. I need to move on a bit.'

'Lunch? Just coffee?'

School holidays meant it was incredibly busy, made worse by the grey humid weather. Linda had to park a mile away from the bistro but she was miles early anyway. She grabbed a window seat so she could observe Charlie arriving from a distance, then reminded herself that it wasn't a date.

He arrived slightly late and breathless as if he'd been jogging. He was in dressed down mode, which she liked. It was only denims and a black canvas jacket but Charlie had a certain style about him which never looked scruffy. He pecked her on the cheek and grinned at her affably and ran a hand through his floppy hair. 'Bloody school holidays. I had to park over by the swimming pool. It looked like a reverse tsunami in there,' he said, looking at the menu.

'I'm not sure what that would look like,' Linda said, looking at Charlie rather than the menu.

'I think the wave machine was on full power,' he explained.

'Ugh I hate deep choppy water.'

'Imagine it full of small children as well, all screaming and urinating.' Charlie studied her over the top of his menu, then smiled. 'I like your hair, have you changed it?'

'I've changed lots of things.'

They ordered sandwiches and coffee. 'So, tell me about these other changes as well as the hair, and the degree.'

'Change number three.' Linda waggled her ring free left

hand. She explained how it was one of those joint, amicable decisions, but she knew it didn't show on her face.

'If I had the cure for a broken heart, I'd happily make it free on the NHS. I write far too many prescriptions for anti-depressants,' Charlie said, 'I envy you the ability to be amicable. Although Karen had two affairs, she seemed to want to punish me for allowing her to do it! I used to think it *was* actually *all* my fault. It was quite devastating at the time.'

'Like an emotional tsunami?'

He laughed, and made room for the waitress to put her tray down. 'The tide is well and truly out on that one. I've even finished paying her debts for her which she so thoughtfully left in my name, so I guess I can make some changes myself,' he said. 'How do you like your coffee?'

'Strong.'

'Me too. You've gone quiet,' he said, pouring the coffee. 'Victoria?'

Linda nodded. 'She could have *anyone*, why Dan?'

'You're wrong, actually,' Charlie said, adding a lot of sugar to his cup, 'I think I dated her maybe twice? At university... she's lovely.'

'And?... but?'

'No chemistry whatsoever. Good friends now.'

Overwhelmingly pleased with the information, Linda had a big smile trying to burst out, but managed to keep it restrained and remembered the original thread of conversation. 'I still feel angry, helpless and frustrated with it all.'

'I agree it is a particularly messy triangle,' Charlie said, cutting his beef sandwich in half.

'I don't know how much longer I can keep Tina's confidence.'

His head snapped up, and his green eyes seared through hers, 'But you *must*, if that's what she wants. There's nothing more precious than trust, as we both know to our cost.'

Linda nodded, knowing he was right, 'I feel so, so cut up about Tina.'

Charlie met her eyes with a sincere, rather serious smile, 'You know you've given more air time to your friend's dilemma, rather than bemoan your own problems. That says a lot about you as a person. That's why you'd make such a good nurse.' He covered her hand briefly with his. 'But you do need to distance yourself a bit, if you don't mind me saying.'

Linda took a deep breath and sat back in her chair, cradled her coffee and studied the man opposite. Charlie was right; she had to stop whining about Tina. 'You know, I'm really looking forward to starting this course, thanks for giving me a push.'

'I've loads of study material you can have, right back to my student days. Lots of chemistry notes, never did find the love formula.'

Linda laughed, suddenly recalling their conversation about pretend jobs, 'Does this material include the famous sex therapy manual?'

'Oh no, I never had a manual for that. That was all practical.'

They parted two hours later, and Linda felt greatly cheered by Charlie's company. She even trusted herself to speak to Daniel. He was predictably guarded when he answered his phone, but Linda kept to the details about the garage. He was a bit nonplussed really, but agreed to take a look.

Tina called. They'd spoken only briefly since her bereavement. 'Can you talk? I'm having a bad day. Mum, you know... everything really.'

'Oh Tina, of course; I've loads to tell you, actually.'

'Have you? Why don't you drive up, have a few drinks and stop over?'

'What, now?'

'Would that be all right? Will Mike be pissed off?'

Two and a half hours later, Linda was in Didsbury. She parked next to the pink Mini, which had leaves and rubbish lodged under the wheels and looked as though it hadn't moved from the curb for a long time. She'd heard all about the birthday drama in some depth, including the car wash. It was so typical of Dan and Tina, this jumping between tears and laughter.

When Tina came to the door, she looked tired and drawn. Linda had a sudden vision of Victoria, looking all lithesome and loved up, rolling around in her white Egyptian sheets with Tina's handsome husband. She wondered then, if it was such a good idea being in Tina's company and under scrutiny, and under the influence of alcohol.

The flat was full of cards and flowers. Tina said Daniel had sent fifty white roses. They sat in a huge pot in the fireplace, dropping petals. There was a card slotted through the stems, but no matter how she tilted her head, Linda couldn't read the message.

They talked about her mother first, then all the tests and the scans. It was all so slow and protracted but at least it was moving along to a full diagnosis, although the way Tina talked about it all gave Linda the impression she'd already given up on her life. Tina showed her the packets of tablets, and although she recognised them from her own clients, Linda had no clear idea what they did in the body. She wished she had Charlie's immense knowledge. Knowledge was power, power to transform, that's what he'd said. Linda gulped down some wine, and changed the subject before she started blubbing.

Tina was shocked to hear about Mike, and the house going on the market.

'Oh, Lin that's all three of us now!' Tina said, her huge eyes all sorrowful.

'That's what Vic-'

'Go on,' Tina said carefully, 'That's what Victoria said?'

'Yes, that's what Victoria said. I put her right.'

'Why? Dan and me are separated.'

Linda couldn't look at her for a moment. She'd make a lousy actress.

'Tina, I want you to tell Dan about these tests, all this medication.'

'No, I'm not ready. I've no proper results,' she said, and poured another glass of wine. 'He'll bombard me with a lot of questions I can't answer, and I've got to think of Troy and Elle, and the baby.'

She looked more closely at Linda. 'What's the matter? Okay, what's he done?' She put the bottle down and they both looked at it. 'It's okay, I can guess, you don't have to tell me.'

'How can you be so calm?' Linda said.

'Because, we're talking Dan here and because, I've kind of let it happen.'

'But it must hurt like hell, you love him to *bits,* Tina, I don't care what you say.'

'I've put you in a terrible position haven't I?'

'*Please...* tell him, Tina.'

She took a long moment to think, lit a cigarette, 'All right, I'll think about it. When I feel strong enough but only to let him go, so long as you understand that; I don't want him thinking it's a cheap trick.'

*

One evening in the middle of the following week, Linda steeled herself to meet Daniel at the garage. He was already waiting for her, in his builder's truck. For someone normally so buoyant, he seemed subdued, a bit wary Linda supposed, but he still kissed her and gave her one of his bear hugs. 'Go on, show me and then I'll say, er that's a big job, be six weeks, maybe more.'

'Don't you dare give me any builder's talk.'

Inside, she watched him look around and pull faces at everything. When he peeled some wallpaper off the wall, half the plaster came away with it, 'Are you sure about this Lin? Why don't you get Mike to move out? I can't believe he was shacked up here, with that girl.'

'It's no different to what you and Victoria are doing! You just got the sophisticated version.'

He leant on the back of the sofa, knocked the plaster off his hands, then held them up in an admission of defeat. 'Okay let's get this out of the way. I know you've had a verbal with Victoria. I'd much rather you yelled at me.'

Linda went to look through the dirty window, in case Daniel saw something in her face. She'd been dreading this conversation, terrified she'd get so angry it would all come out in a frightening torrent. 'If you must know, I'm feeling sore with both of you,' she said, and made herself stare at the rusty MOT sign swinging in the sea breeze.

'I know, I know you are,' Daniel said, then sighed, 'You will keep it quiet? Victoria's already vulnerable.'

Linda spun round, 'It makes lots of people vulnerable! You should have thought of that!' She folded her arms then and practically bit her tongue. 'Okay I *so* don't want to do this.'

He just nodded, but with a quiet resignation. 'I know you talk to Tina a lot. I did *try* you know, I ran out of steam.'

'You are going to the funeral?'

'*Course* I am.'

Linda sniffed and looked at the ceiling, trying to stop her face crumpling up. He looked at her carefully and his dark eyes were almost black, 'Do you know something I don't?'

'Dan, I've said, *I don't want to do this.*'

He searched her eyes quickly, but relented, 'Okay let's

stick to business.'

The rooms were even more dismal in the gloomy evening light. Daniel looked at the plumbing connection under the sink and the whole unit almost came away from the wall. Linda rolled her eyes but he just gave her one of his cheeky grins. He shoved it all back into place, then as an afterthought, shut the water off with a big wrench. When he pulled the carpet back and kicked at the floorboards a cloud of dust enveloped them both and there was a strong musty smell.

Linda wrinkled her nose, 'Is it bad?'

'What gave you that idea?' He poked at the loft access with a broom handle. She waited whilst he got a ladder off the truck, manhandled it up the stone steps, then rammed it through the trapdoor of the loft and went up with a huge lamp.

Linda watched him sit with his legs dangling down in dirty trainers with no laces, then he disappeared. After a while, she held the bottom of the ladder and shouted up, but his reply was all muffled and she couldn't hear him properly, just a scrambling noise, some thumps, and a lot of swearing.

He poked his head back through, 'Well, it's damp, I think there's a leak on the chimney flashing.' He slid back down. 'That's the smell. Otherwise, I reckon you could put a couple of Velux windows up there and make a proper bedroom, it's got enough height. That's your best bet. Sit and look at the cows.'

'Really? You could do all that?'

'Course I could *do it*,' he said, pretending to be all indignant, and she laughed, glad the tension had gone. 'It needs a proper kitchen and a bathroom.'

'Can't afford all that.'

'I've got some units from the original hotel, better than the stuff you've got here.'

'Costing?'

'Nothing. You can have them. Buttermilk white they are. I won't use them, but they were too good to scrap. I was going to put them in Tina's mum and dads but I think your need is greater.'

'Were you?' she said, chewing her lip, her thoughts jumping to Tina. The card Daniel had sent with the white roses had said, 'love, always.' She'd made a point of looking when Tina went to the kitchen.

Linda said, 'So, we're talking labour costs and the windows?'

'Not even that, Troy comes free. Just the Velux, I'll sort everything else,' he said, then twirled a screwdriver round like a baton, 'see if I can pick up a spiral staircase on eBay, or a posh ladder.'

'Oh God, Dan, that would be just brilliant.'

'Right, I trust you don't want to keep anything?' he said, as they locked the door and went down the steps. 'Other than the hundred head of cattle out the back?'

Linda laughed and punched his arm gently, 'No, I don't want anything but the view, and the peace.'

'I'll get Troy down here with a skip first thing, get it all cleared out.'

'That quick?'

'Why not?' he said, throwing the ladders on the truck, 'Life's too fucking short.'

Linda gave Daniel the keys, then got in her car and watched him drive along the beach road, scattering a flock of oyster catchers. 'You might be fucking right,' she said softly, to no one but herself.

Still watching the oyster catchers, Linda called Charlie. 'Look, I know it's a bit weird for a date, and I know it's short notice but will you come to a funeral with me, tomorrow afternoon?'

'Yes,' he said slowly. 'On one condition, will you come

for a weird dinner afterwards? I've got to go to a medical convention about colostomy bags and catheters, but the food afterwards is always top notch.'

CHAPTER TEN

The supermarket was chaotic. School holidays, she'd forgotten.

Victoria wandered a bit aimlessly with a basket. Sea bass, baby potatoes, some rocket and pine nuts, and maybe some cherries, just because she liked the look of them. Daniel was easy to feed, other than goat's cheese he ate anything really, in any combination or time zone. However, he was difficult to pin down, he wasn't used to someone feeding him at regular times, he'd said, and it made Victoria laugh, the way he was, the things he said.

She put a cherry in her mouth and twisted the stalk off.

The trouble with Daniel was he was just, *so compassionate.* This morning, he'd been round at Mike's garage flat with Troy, sorting out something for Linda. He'd gone back to the hotel after that and then it was Tina's mother's funeral. She had no idea how long that would take.

Victoria couldn't go to the funeral because she couldn't face Tina, or Linda, but that was the price she had to pay. Victoria had sent flowers and a card following the death of Tina's mother. Tina had tried to call her and Victoria had dropped the phone as if it were a bomb.

Daniel was concerned about Tina's father and how the sisters were going to cope with him. Victoria couldn't complain about the drain on his time, it was his thoughtfulness which had drawn her in the first instance; it was part of who he was. If there were no emergencies at the hotel, he'd promised to be back in time for a latish dinner, so Victoria had all day to think about her own projects, and prepare a meal.

She picked up some Italian blue cheese, and it took her back to the day on the mountain and the kiss. The first time they'd made love had been a frightening leap of trust for Victoria. She had a massive stumbling block in her head after years of Max. After learning to switch off, she now had to learn to switch back on.

But Daniel was her nemesis.

They'd made love just a couple of hours ago, and she could still recall the delicious sensations. She'd woken because he'd been holding her, gently kissing the nape of her neck and her shoulders, until she could bear it no longer, and she turned to face him, in a floaty, dreamlike state of being fully aroused but not fully awake.

'Morning, beautiful,' he'd whispered, kissing her eyes, her hair and her breasts. His hands moved down beyond her spine, pulling her onto his body, and the moment of connection had been beyond exquisite. She'd been unable to take another breath for long orgasmic seconds.

She opened her eyes, exhaled and slowly registered the fridges of cheese and yoghurt. A woman was trying to manoeuvre round her with a full trolley. 'Are you standing there forever?' she said, giving her a strange look, 'Hello? Did you even hear me?'

'What? *No*, no sorry. I mean, I'm not standing here forever.'

Victoria moved away, tried to gather her thoughts, tried to stop grinning so inanely. She had to stop going places in her head, but then she was so good at it. Daniel was so good at sex.

She put another cherry in her mouth.

Olive oil flavoured with lemon, some crusty bread,

tomatoes.

After they'd made love, he'd held her for a long time and Victoria loved that almost as much, both of them slightly breathless and spent; her face in his hair. She wondered how many other women Daniel had slept with. Maybe she'd just ask. Did it matter? Maybe she wouldn't.

Before Max there had been only one other partner in her life, practically virginal by modern standards she supposed. Emily was already on lover number three, which was at times disconcerting, and yet this generation seemed to be so clued up on what they wanted, needed. Victoria envied Emily her freedom and knowledge of the world, of herself. Everything was transparent. In a way, she found it irksome that Daniel wanted to keep their relationship private.

'Why? We're both adults. Our kids are all grown,' she'd said. 'We're not going behind anyone's back.'

'We are! Don't be so naive. You're going through a divorce with a nutcase and I've no idea what I'm going through,' he'd said, 'I know it starts off as grown ups spending time together but then it seems to end where we're all arguing like kids. Can you imagine the fall out if all the families want their say?'

'Does it matter?'

'Yes, I think it does,' he'd said, and Victoria had backed off. He was right, she knew he was right, and in a way the clandestine atmosphere created a better romantic frisson, that Victoria could see the appeal of it. The only downside was the insecure feeling it generated, and she had no experience of how to deal with that.

One evening Victoria had shown him the old school photographs she'd come across, jumbled up in a box of keepsakes she'd grabbed from the house. They all looked impossibly young, younger than their own children, which Daniel agreed was pretty scary.

'So, have you slept with all the girls in 3b now?' Victoria

said, and he'd laughed.

'No way! Well, not the fat ones, and *not* that one there,' he said, pointing to a tall girl stood at the back. 'She was strange. Do you remember her?'

'Uh huh, Sarah Fox-Lloyd now she's married to the director of North Wales Research; Max's biggest clients.'

'Yeah?... *and?*'

'Why do you say that?'

'You look like you know something, come on?'

'All right; I think Max had an affair with her.'

He logged the information, then looked back at the photo. 'And not you,' he said slowly, 'you wouldn't even go out anywhere with me.'

Victoria smiled at him, *so he did remember*. She looked back at the photo, 'Is that Barry Jones at the back?'

'Yeah, big freak Barney Rubble. Still wants me dead I reckon.'

'Linda said she looks after his mother.'

'And Linda, never slept with her. Have you made up with her yet? Saw her in town with Charlie the other day.'

'Don't change the subject. That still leaves about... *fifteen.*'

He grabbed the photo from her, shot her a sly look and stabbed his finger at it. 'I never slept with her...'

'*Fourteen,*' Victoria said, 'and you managed all of this whilst still seeing Tina?'

'Are you questioning my morals?' he said, grinning, 'You sound like my mother.'

*

Tina tried various combinations of sombre looking outfits, eventually selecting her black dress. It was a party dress really, and although it seemed irreverent that she should wear it for her mother's funeral, it was the only item in her wardrobe that fitted her well enough, cinched in with a wide black belt.

She'd dropped two dress sizes. Under any other circumstances this fact would have thrilled her; the realisation that it didn't actually suit her frame or her heart-shaped face was yet another blow. So there wasn't even a small payoff for everything she'd given up and been through. She couldn't even manage to look vulnerable or waif-like. Typical, but then, it dawned on Tina that she didn't really care anymore. All those years wasted on diets and expensive make-up. All those years wasted on stuff that in the grand scheme of things, just didn't matter.

The real change had taken several months to mature to a conclusion in her mind. It had nothing to do with the way some of her bones were visible, or the way her right hand sometimes wouldn't stop shaking. It had nothing to do with the way her vision blurred, or the nausea and tiredness; but it had everything to do with the way she'd dealt with it, *was* dealing with it. Alone. For the first time in her life Tina Woods had found something inside herself that had nothing to do with Daniel Woods. She could almost laugh at the unintentional double entendre.

Who knows how far this new inner strength could take her?

Driving her birthday present was still a massive deal though. She'd sat in the pink Mini several times and only managed to turn the key in the ignition. The fact that Daniel had apologised for deleting all her messages on that day had eventually filled her with enormous relief. If he really was seeing Victoria his actions there had reinstated her pride, and forced her to face up to the decision she'd made.

He'd called her about the funeral.

'Do you want me to make any arrangements? Only I don't think your dad's up to it.'

'Look, Dan, me and Mandy and Julie'll do it.'

But of course in the end her sisters couldn't be relied upon to do any of it. Mandy was a snivelling wreck and Julie was more concerned about who was going to pay for it. In the end, Tina chickened out and got Dan to do it, but through Troy. It was all sorted out in a couple of days, and Dan called her with the details. He was a bit brisk, at first.

'Where are you going to stay after the funeral? When are you driving over?'

'I'm not driving, I'll be upset and it's too far.'

'Oh. Okay, love... how about I get Tony to come for you?'

Tina had sat and looked at the ceiling and almost caused her lower lip to bleed the way she'd twisted it through her teeth. Bloody hell, it still didn't stretch to her arms and legs, this inner strength. 'Yeah, that'd be good.'

On the day of the funeral right outside the very place where she'd married Daniel; her confidence took another nose dive. She clung to Tony's arm and walked into the church, stopping only briefly to talk to her sisters, then Charlie and Linda, Troy and Marian; but her eyes were everywhere, looking across the mostly empty pews, her legs shaking with nerves. Please God don't let Victoria be here as well, they wouldn't do that, would they? It had cut like a knife, when Linda had *intimated* he was with Victoria. Tina had mentally steeled herself for the moment Dan would meet someone else...but so soon, and *Victoria?*

He was already there, holding on to her father. Mercifully alone, but then he had his hands full with the job no one wanted to do. He gave her a serious little nod with full-on eye contact. In some ways, the brief intensity of that single look was more emotive than a whole week of sobbing and wailing. It was enough that he'd arranged and paid for it all, let alone taken on the job no one else wanted; that of taking charge of her increasingly difficult father.

Throughout the short service, Tina was distracted by Daniel and her father a lot more than she should have been. Her emotions concerning her father had shocked her. She knew he was ill but she just couldn't forgive him, not yet. The autopsy said that Lily Bradshaw had died of heart failure, stress and exhaustion, probably aggravated from years of caring for an alcoholic with Alzheimer's. She'd just given up.

The parallel between herself and her own family, and the way her mother had given half her life to caring for her father, confirmed how right she'd been to go it alone. But what Tina hadn't reckoned on was how it made her feel, looking at Daniel with an arm firmly round her father's frail, but astonishingly strong and unpredictable body.

In the pub afterwards when Daniel finally held her in those very same arms; the temptation to fall apart was balanced on a knife edge. She couldn't stop the tears then but Daniel imagined it was down to the ordeal of the funeral, and almost made it all worse when he hugged her that bit tighter. After a while he looked at her more carefully, holding her at arm's length, 'Tee I'm worried about you. You been on some kind of fad diet?'

'Yeah, it's called shock,' she said, almost belligerently and pushed him away, snagging his silk tie on her lucky dip ring in the process. If she could be nasty to him then so much the better, it stopped anything getting out of control. She could thank him for everything in a text later, it was so much safer. Unfazed, Daniel steered her to the table where Troy and Marian were and went to the bar, but he kept looking back at her.

Marian put a hand over hers.

'I know everyone says it, but if there's anything we can do?'

'Dan's done it all, thanks.'

That summed it all up, Dan's done it all. Yes, only he'd

done it all with Victoria, and when the large glass of cognac came, she gulped it down and sent Daniel for another. If she wasn't driving, she may as well make the most of it.

*

Around eight, Victoria had a text from Daniel to say he'd be about half an hour. She didn't bother getting dressed after her bath, slipped on French lingerie and a robe, busied herself dressing the salad instead, and checked there was a bottle of white chilling in the fridge.

Daniel was late, but his embrace dispelled any irritation, left her wanting more. She slid her arms around him, felt the solid warmth of him beneath the thin fabric of his grey shirt. He looked tired but dazzlingly attractive in a dark suit, and as usual his skin smelt so good.

He dragged off his black tie, undid the top button of his shirt, 'I've had a bloody awful day.'

'All of it? How was the funeral?'

'*Horrible,*' he said, hugging her, burying his face in her hair, 'Really horrible. Don't want to talk about it.'

'Okay. Are you hungry?'

'Not sure, feel a bit weird.'

'Drink?'

'Yeah, alcohol,' he said, finally studying her face. He had amazing eyes; she could sink into them and pull the velvet darkness of them around her. She poured the wine, curious about his day, but knew the timing wasn't right and so just passed him the glass instead. He almost drained it, so she smiled and refilled it.

'Does this mean you're stopping here tonight?'

'Probably, is that okay? Just need to call Troy and Sue, make sure everything's all right.'

Victoria nodded, loved the way he asked her first. As if

she'd say no, *as if.* She popped the sea bass back into the fridge and ran him a bath. He emerged some time later wearing a bath towel, and threw himself down on her sofa and closed his eyes. She tried feeding him slivers of smoked salmon but he waved it away, 'I'm not a bloody sea lion.'

'Don't they just get raw fish heads and a beach ball?' Victoria said, noticing he'd almost finished two bottles of Sancerre. By the time she'd made herself a sandwich and returned to the sofa, he was engrossed in a reality series about men who unblock drains and sewers, but his eyes were becoming glazed.

Twenty minutes later he was in a dead sleep on her shoulder and his glass was tilting towards her silk cushions. He wasn't easy to rouse, but Victoria made him go to bed and resigned herself to channel hopping, then finally switched the television off. He'd left his mobile on the coffee table and it had buzzed all night with texts and voice mail. Victoria stared at the blinking phone for a full minute, then picked it up and scrolled through the messages. A few from Blue, one from Mia, Mike and Troy. *Mia?*

The most recent was from Tina.

'Sorry we didn't get to talk much. Stop worrying bout me I had a stomach bug that's all. I know today was hard. Ta for looking after Dad, for everything you done. Love you babes.'

Victoria deleted it, before switching his phone off.

If only she could delete the actual people.

*

They didn't see each other for a couple of days following the funeral. Daniel said he was tied up having to do Mandy's cleaning and cover the bar because Troy was sorting out Linda's flat, but Victoria suspected it was more because he felt low.

Anton had burned his hand and had to go to A&E and Elle was struggling with being almost eight months' pregnant in the July humidity. Victoria offered to go over but was secretly relieved when he said he had it covered. It was difficult hiding their relationship under the watchful eyes of everyone at the hotel, and anyway she really needed to concentrate on her own future.

In an attempt to be more focused, she introduced herself to all the bridal companies in the region in the hope it might generate wedding business. The funeral had triggered another avenue of thought, and she'd spent some time researching the local directors and dreaming up a more sober looking menu card, something just as stylish but more suited to a wake.

When Daniel rang, she forced herself to let it ring five times. Four days, and she was desperate to see him. It actually hurt, being away from him.

'Hi, love, are you busy?' he said, and Victoria took a beat to think, forced herself to look towards Puffin Island. It was the start of a beautiful summery evening and the sea was still sparkling with end of day sun. 'I am actually, but I suppose I could do with a break,' she said, pleased with her majestic effort at nonchalance.

'Pick you up in an hour?'

Victoria stretched and smiled, logged off her laptop, 'All right. Dress code?'

'I dunno! Whatever.'

'Just a small clue, heels, or not?'

'Er... maybe to start with?'

Daniel was early, arrived in black denims, a Hugo Boss shirt and an expensive looking leather jacket. He kissed her as if he'd been away at sea for six months, held her so tightly her feet left the ground. 'Why are you still not dressed?' he said, carrying her towards the bedroom.

'Well, *where are we going?*'

'I thought a posh dinner, followed by sex in the woods,' he said, pushing open the door with his foot, 'Winning combination.'

'Are you joking?'

'No,' he said fixing her with a stare, then released her slowly so she slid down his body, and her stomach did an involuntary flip. She'd never known anyone quite like him.

She went to fling open her wardrobe doors and frowned at the contents.

'I don't know what to wear for dinner and sex in the woods; it's a really tricky date, outfit wise.'

'Okay, I'll choose,' he said with a shrug. She watched him pull out some of her Janet Reger lingerie, and go through her clothes and shoes. She didn't know whether to shoo him out of the way, or just laugh. He laid out his preferred selection of items on the bed, and she folded her arms.

'Dan, I am not going out for dinner wearing stockings and suspenders, no knickers and Christian Louboutin heels, then staggering about in the woods.'

His face fell and he groaned, 'But you've made it sound so amazing now.'

They were late for their table at The Grapes Hotel. Daniel wanted to snoop, she knew what was behind the booking, but it was lavish and gorgeous, and she loved the table he'd reserved overlooking the estuary.

'Choose the steak; see if the sauce is as good as Chef's.'

'*No*. I want lemon sole,' she said, her eyes flicking onto his over the top of her menu. 'You have it.'

He ordered champagne and Victoria was slightly horrified when he said she'd have to drink two thirds of it. 'I'm driving. Your turn to get drunk,' he said, and caught hold of her fingers across the table, 'Sorry about the other night, slipping into a coma.'

'You'd had a tough day, that's all,' she said, watching

him closely.

'Her mum had a heart attack, did I tell you? She could have pulled through apparently, but chose not to. Tina's dad thought he was at the wedding again.'

She studied his serious face, 'Dan that's so sad. I'm so sorry.'

'Tina looked terrible, really white and she's lost too much weight. I don't know what's going on there,' he said, turning the stem of his glass round and round, 'I haven't heard from her, maybe I should go and see her.'

'Why? If you've finished it, Dan, won't she get the wrong message?'

'Huh, yeah probably. Our whole bloody life's been like that. Twenty-five years of crossed wires and mixed messages.'

She concentrated on the bubbles in her drink, 'So, what will happen to Tina's dad now?'

'I've offered to pay for him to get looked after properly,' Daniel said, then sat back and grimaced. 'Should have done it years ago, shouldn't I?'

'You can't blame yourself.'

Victoria excused herself to go to the powder room, kissed the top of his head as she went past, and he gave her a wan smile, squeezed her hand. Victoria looked at herself in the mirror, and felt utterly ashamed about deleting Tina's text message, it was childish, pointless and it had backfired. What was wrong with her? She had to get a grip, it was real life and Daniel and Tina were trying to deal with it. Her sheltered, privileged existence was an insensitive curse at times.

The food arrived and Daniel insisted on tasting hers as well.

'I enjoy it more when I know our chef is better.'

'That's too weird,' she said, but fed him a forkful off her plate, pleased he'd not wanted to dwell on the funeral and its implications, although she knew it all played on his mind but she couldn't really help. The champagne helped.

After dinner, feeling much more light-hearted, they drove along the lanes heavy with summer foliage, shouting over the nostalgia of old U2 tracks. Daniel grinned and turned off the road into Gwydyr forest, pushing the Porsche along the dirt roads.

'I can't believe you're serious about this!' Victoria said. It was only just dusk but the density of the trees made it seem darker. The sky was approaching midnight blue, all shot through with a rosy blush towards the west, where the heat of the day had died.

Daniel stopped the car, alongside an expanse of still water and produced an old tartan picnic rug, spread it on the pine needles with a flourish, then helped her out of the passenger seat.

Victoria shivered, 'So, this rug, has it seen a lot of action?'

'Doubt it. Lived in granny Woods' vintage motorbike pannier before I inherited it,' he deadpanned. Victoria narrowed her eyes, never sure if he was making things up. He flashed her a winning smile, and she still couldn't be sure. She perched on the rug, kicked off her shoes and carefully rearranged her wraparound dress, swiping at the gnats. Other than the blackbirds it was silent, and slightly eerie. Max said once she had the hair of a thousand wild blackbirds. It was many years ago, but the strangeness of it made her shiver.

Daniel put an arm around her and she leant into him, managed to resist kissing him for all of thirty seconds, managed to resist lying flat for another thirty, but then she said the rug smelled funny and it was too small and itchy. 'Be a gentleman and let me lie on you.'

'Only if you promise not to say I'm too small, or smelly and itchy.'

'Never, I promise.'

He manoeuvred himself beneath her, and he was heavenly to lie on but she still couldn't relax. 'Oh God I swear there's eyes in the trees, and my legs are being bitten.'

'Who do you imagine is watching?' Daniel said, 'I know, Casper the friendly ghost?'

'Right, *that's it.*'

Daniel laughed, 'You're such an indoor girl.'

'I resent that!' she said, snatching up her shoes, then fell over a clump of nettles, 'Okay, I'll accept that.'

'They don't make picnic rugs like they used to,' he said, shaking it out, 'I remember a time when you could lay full length and still fit a woman alongside you.'

He drove her home and she wondered if he was peeved with her, but when she broached the subject he frowned, 'What? don't be ridiculous!'

Max would have been all huffy if he'd expected something of her and she'd failed to deliver, even if it was something innocuous like collect him on time from the golf club, or remember to get the dry cleaning, let alone anything approaching sexual promise. Tonight, he would have told her she was a tease, piled on the guilt. When she thought of her marriage to Max, Victoria felt curiously removed from who she used to be. Max hadn't responded to any of her solicitor's letters, so it was easy to pretend none of her previous life existed, to embrace the changes with confidence.

Daniel was so easy-going and although she loved him for that, it sometimes made her feel humble and exposed, not emotions she was familiar with, and occasionally it caught her off guard, that unexpected unfamiliar rush of yearning. She looked out of the passenger window so he couldn't see her face.

Maybe it was just that she felt more in touch with herself, and she loved him even more for that. When they reached her flat, Victoria showed him how much, pulling him into the shower with her, then falling damp and dishevelled into bed. In the throes of making love she almost blurted it all out, but suddenly thought about Tina, and the heated exchange with Linda, then found she couldn't actually form any words and her feelings came out as frustrated, token tears.

She thought she could handle it, thought she could handle an affair with a married man in much the same way she'd handled Max, but pretend emotion with Max had been easy, and this was gut-wrenchingly real.

'What's the matter?' Daniel said, searching her face.

She swallowed it all down, 'I don't know, ignore me.'

He kissed her eyelids, kissed all the tears off her face, 'I could never do that.'

*

The last weekend in July, Victoria had secured a substantial wedding breakfast job. It had come about because the bride had cancelled the original caterers once she'd been to The Lakeside and tried Victoria's lamb pie. Daniel had told Chef to put it on the menu as a promotion for her.

The bridegroom had roots in sheep farming, so Victoria had easily sold the whole idea with her Welsh ingredients and the ease by which it could all be transported to a marquee in a field. Emily elected to help, and Daniel loaned her Carys, the Welsh beauty from Llanrwst who had a van and looked great in wellingtons, apparently. She didn't ask how he knew.

'It won't be muddy, it's going to be baking hot,' Victoria said, glad about the van though.

The girls got on well, full of mishaps at The Lakeside and gossip about all the staff, especially Troy. They talked and giggled non-stop and Victoria was lucky to get a word in.

'Are you still enjoying it at the hotel?' she asked Emily, knowing full well what the answer would be.

'Oh, Mum, it's just the best summer job I've ever had.'

'And you don't mind staying in that little staff room?'

'No, why should I? No petrol to pay for, I can have a few drinks at the end of my shift.'

The girls exchanged coy smiles.

Later, she rang Daniel and asked him if he knew what they got up to. 'How the hell should I know?'

He invited her to a staff barbecue. 'We've been booked to the rafters but I've closed for one night tomorrow, no bookings in. Everyone's totally shattered; well everyone over the age of twenty is totally shattered.'

It was still baking hot for the barbecue, humid with a rumble of very distant thunder. Dragonflies darted across the stillness of the water and smoke plumed from the fire pit by the lake shore. Tony and Tristan were in charge of food and drink. Troy and Anton had the responsibility of stopping Chef from interfering. Their solution had been to tinker with his beer.

When Victoria arrived, Chef had already passed out on the grass. Weak with laughter, Troy and Anton removed most of his clothes, dragged him into a canoe and set it on the water, where it somehow drifted into the middle of the lake.

When Daniel saw what they were doing, he made Troy swim out for it. Bear ran to and fro barking and excited by the action but distracted by the smell of seared meat, and eventually collapsed whining, confused with his duties. Emily and Carys, dressed for the occasion in tiny shorts and bikini tops, were wildly encouraging from the shore, obviously impressed with Troy's bravado, Marian much less so. 'Daniel, go and help!'

'How exactly?'

'Well, can you not get another boat?'

'Where from?'

Elle, stuck in a beach chair, couldn't care less and looked

distinctly fed up and exhausted, fanning her face with a magazine. Victoria joined her on the bench under the trees, passed her a fruit juice with lots of ice.

'Oh, thanks,' she said, 'Troy seems to have forgotten I exist.'

'Not long to go, how many weeks?'

''Bout three, can't wait,' she said, pulling a face and rubbing her belly, 'It's bouncing on my bloody bladder again.'

'I remember that with Emily,' Victoria said, watching her daughter on the shoreline, 'Strange to see her so grown up now.'

Marian brought gin and tonics over, slapped a cushion down on the seat, 'Why do men never *grow up*? Light a fire and they just can't help themselves.'

Victoria and Elle exchanged a smile.

Ten minutes later, they watched the ensuing altercation as Chef woke up in his boxers in the middle of the lake. The canoe wobbled about and Troy changed from front crawl to backstroke, then back again.

'What does Troy think he's going to do?' Elle said, picking her nails, 'It's got no oars or anything. They'll both be marooned out there,' she said, 'Have you heard from Tina?'

'No, I don't understand it,' Marian said, looking at Victoria, then back to Elle, 'Mandy isn't back at work, sorting out Dad I expect. I feel awful about all that.'

'I like Tina,' Elle said suddenly, 'I miss her.'

Marian patted her hand, 'And Troy. He needs his mother more than he lets on. And I don't know where Daniel keeps disappearing to, leaving him with the hotel and that flat of Linda's to sort out, it's too much with a baby on the way,' she went on. 'For what's it worth, I've told him what I think,' she said, then as an afterthought, 'And the funeral, that affected him as well.'

There was a short silence and Victoria kept her eyes on the lake.

'Men don't grow up because women don't let them,' Elle said sagely.

They watched Troy drag the canoe onto the shore, coughing and exhausted, and Daniel threw a towel at him. 'If he'd fallen in the water pissed, what then?'

Troy, uncharacteristically, marched off. Emily followed him with her eyes and Anton ran after him. Daniel walked up to the three women and said to Elle, 'I sometimes think Troy has his brain in his pants.'

'No, he hasn't,' Elle said, bored. 'I've looked and there wasn't one.'

'Don't worry he'll be back for food, he must be starving after that.'

'See this face, does it look worried? All I'm bothered about is I need a wee again and I can't get up out of this stupid chair.'

Daniel offered his hand and tugged her upright, and when the chair came up with her, Elle looked close to tears. Daniel rescued her from the chair till it fell to the ground, then kicked it. It rolled down into the lake, she laughed and hung on to his arm.

As darkness approached, the thunderstorm rumbled closer, and a cool current of air ruffled the surface of the lake. Sue and Marian made their excuses. Other than Elle, all the younger ones were still drinking and toasting marshmallows.

Victoria heard Daniel say to Troy, 'Don't leave Elle on her own, she's really struggling.'

'Dad, I'm just having a few drinks! Elle; she just wants to talk about her *bowels*, or baby names or breast feeding. It like, does my head in!'

'*So*? She's like; carrying your kid, *deal with it.*'

Troy wobbled off in the direction of the caravan, carrying a bottle of vodka and Emily couldn't quite hide her peevish expression. Victoria said to Daniel, 'I'm going to head off, come over later?'

'Yeah but maybe just for a while, he said, keeping his eyes on Troy's back, 'Text you when I'm on my way.'

Victoria said her goodbye's, pointlessly told Emily not to drink too much, and drove home. At the flat, she ran herself a bath, checked there was wine chilling in the fridge, and put something classical on the music system. When she checked her e-mail there was the best news ever. A substantial contract with the local council she'd chased a while ago had come good. In the bath with a glass of white wine in her hand, Victoria felt suddenly elated. She could do this; reinvent herself as a single career woman, no man required. She just needed to apply the same strength of mind and logic to her love life. She needed to have a chat with Karen Summers.

Her phone buzzed with his text, '30 min X'

When she heard the security system alert her twenty-five minutes later, Victoria automatically went to release the entrance, threw open the door to her flat, then went to get another wine glass. She heard the door close behind her and smiled to herself.

'Have they put that fire out?' she said. When Daniel made no reply, she spun round.

Max said, 'Fire? Something burning?'

For a horrible moment of utter disbelief she stood and stared at him, almost forgetting to breathe. He smiled at her, in her satin robe, two glasses in her hand. Victoria placed them down on the worktop and met his stare. 'What the *hell* do you think you're doing?'

'And you?' he said, and a long beat passed, '...What the hell do you think you're doing?'

She swallowed, willing Daniel to run up the stairs, now. *NOW.*

'*Get out,* Max.'

He pulled a chair out from the little table, sat down and

looked at her expectantly.

'Well, are you going to pour the wine?'

Victoria glanced at her phone on the table, and he followed her line of sight, then snapped up her mobile, started to look at her text messages, and Victoria looked at the ceiling and closed her eyes, willing Daniel to get there.

'Hm... Hi beautiful, pick you up in ten... Can I stop at yours tonight?' Max read evenly, 'Oh, he's on his way, that's good.'

Max placed her phone back down carefully. 'I find it quite, *infuriating* that you are happy to damage my reputation, when in fact you are quite clearly having an affair.'

'Only since we've been separated!'

'Incredibly quick, so distasteful.'

She snarled at him, 'I haven't loved you for years!'

'Oh, I wasn't thinking of just you, I was thinking of Mr Woods, and his estranged wife.'

Victoria heard Daniel press the door buzzer, and she looked at Max, terrified that he wouldn't let him in, but Max responded to the speaker in a slightly prissy voice, 'Yes, Daniel, you may enter.'

He walked into the kitchen with a bottle of wine and Victoria had never known relief like it. Daniel glanced at her, then he took in Max, and for a moment Victoria thought he might just smash the bottle over Max's head. Instead, he placed it down carefully, everything was ultra-controlled. 'What's going on?'

Max helped himself to a glass of Pouilly Fume. 'I'm here because I want to talk to *my wife*. I see she's wearing the robe *I bought her* for Christmas; the year before last, was it darling? And I'm drinking the wine that *I paid for*, in a flat *I paid for*. Perfectly reasonable, don't you think?'

Daniel narrowed his eyes. Max went to open his briefcase, and slid some big photographs across the table. They were all of Victoria and Daniel, caught in blurry, black and white embraces.

'Romantic, don't you think?' Max said, 'Quite arty in black and white, look nice *mounted* and *framed*. Your car looks well in the background.'

Daniel looked at them for a second, then swiped them all off the table. 'So you've had us followed a couple of times. What is this? Miss Marple investigates?'

'You already have enemies here, don't make one of me. One petty criminal plus one load of cash, equals one very dangerous combination.'

Daniel grabbed hold of Max's collar and slowly twisted all the fabric of his shirt. '*Is that a fucking threat?*'

Victoria felt her insides twist with the same tension.

Daniel said, 'Go on, take a swipe at me, you'll find me a *lot* more nasty than Victoria was,' he went on, almost lifting him off the chair. 'You see, *I hit back*. You could call it payback for all her *pain*. Familiar with any of that, are you?'

Max began to clutch at his throat and turn a shade of puce. Victoria caught hold of Daniel's arm, but he felt wired, like a wild animal and she knew she had no hope of restraining him. 'Dan, don't it's not a good idea,' she said, but he shrugged her off.

'All right, Woods, you're very strong,' Max said in a strangulated voice, 'but you're not playing nice.'

'*Nice*? I could *fucking kill* you,' he said, shoving him backwards so hard the chair skewered on its legs and Max almost fell, struggled to right the chair, then retched and struggled to pull his tie loose. When he went to grab the glass of wine, Daniel got there first, and threw the contents in his face.

Max didn't flinch, 'You may accuse me of physical violence, but eventually you will scar her far more emotionally. Just like that wife of yours. You will break her, Woods, not me.'

Daniel threw open the door for him, 'Are you still here?'

They both waited until they heard him leave the building.

Daniel looked at the floor before he met her eyes, 'How did he get in?'

'I thought he was you,' Victoria said, wanting to curl up in a corner.

She couldn't bear to look at the photographs, but Daniel scrutinised them, before sliding them back into the envelope. 'You know when you said there were eyes, in the trees?'

'Dan, I don't want you to go, not tonight,' Victoria said, so much for Ms Independent Career Woman.

'No, no all right,' he said, but he was preoccupied, no doubt thinking about his family, his unborn grandchild, Tina, the hotel, all of it really. Later, she heard him on his phone, talking in a low voice to Tony.

The evening didn't go as she'd planned.

It was difficult to relax, let alone sleep. The storm gathered momentum, thunder, lightning and heavy rain. Victoria lay with her eyes closed but all her senses were wide awake, and she jumped at every car door slam in the street, every window rattle. It was too humid to even lie next to each other. Daniel eventually got up, and peered through the window. 'Come and look at this, it's wild.'

She padded over to him and watched fork lightning touch the sea, then seconds later the thunder sounded like the sky was cracking open. She shivered and put her arms around him. 'Dan, what did he mean, petty criminals and cash?'

'What? Oh, I dunno, stop fretting,' he said, kissing her hair.

'Do you think though, if we just told everyone about us, he'd back off?'

A long beat passed. 'No. I need to think about it.'

Tired and subdued, Victoria got back into bed and pulled the sheet around her. It wasn't as easy as she'd thought, pretending to be Karen Summers.

CHAPTER ELEVEN

The alarm on his mobile started bleeping at five in the morning. He wanted to get back before anyone noticed he'd been missing again and anyway, he had loads to do. Somehow though in-between thinking about getting up and actually doing it, he turned over and fell back to sleep. His mobile began to ring, and ring.

Victoria grabbed it off the bedside table and held it in front of his eyes.

Troy calling.

Daniel turned onto his back and pressed accept call, 'Yeah?'

Troy said he had the hangover from hell and was likely still over the legal limit to drive. Chef and Anton were apparently dead to the world and Emily was throwing up. Daniel looked at Victoria, and she rolled her eyes.

'The baby's coming *right now!*' Troy shouted. 'Where the hell are you?'

'Troy, babies don't come that quickly. Your mum was two days in labour with you.'

'Elle says the contractions are fifteen minutes apart. That's like, serious now isn't it?'

Daniel threw the duvet off, sat on the side of the bed, the phone still cupped to his ear as Troy gabbled on. 'Water?' Daniel repeated, '...What water? Oh right.'

Victoria mouthed, shall I get dressed? Daniel yawned and nodded.

Within half an hour he was on his the way to The Lakeside. The rain was hammering down, bouncing. The river had burst its banks overnight and the tiny amount of traffic on the valley road was slowly swimming through a good few inches of water and debris.

Elle's waters had broken.

Daniel yawned, slowed down in a queue of crawling traffic. He felt as if he'd had no sleep at all, and he was pretty sure Victoria had lain awake for hours as well.

When he arrived back at the hotel, Troy was pacing about, 'Dad where the hell have you been all night?'

He felt like a kid, so he answered like one, '*Nowhere*. It's all sweet, no worries, pops.'

Victoria's car pulled into the car park, and Troy looked at Daniel with a mutinous expression, and then went back into the caravan. Daniel followed and found Elle leaning on the sink, puffing out little breaths, her mouth in an O. She seemed remarkably calm and quiet; her eyes remained focused on the pots on the drainer, and all the empty bottles.

'Elle, how you doing, love?' Daniel said, getting a lump in his throat at the sight of her.

'Ten minutes apart now,' she said, and continued panting, followed by a low howling noise. Troy looked at her as if she were possessed.

Minutes later, the ambulance pulled in, and Elle grabbed at the gas and air, clamped it over her face, then nodded and shook her head as she answered the paramedics. There was a moment of madness while Troy tried to find her hospital bag, hurriedly swapping with the bag Daniel had in his hands, at the very last minute. He watched the ambulance bounce back along the road, and threw Troy's gym kit down, then closed the caravan door behind him and sat on the sofa for a moment, thinking about Tina. He looked at his phone.

'Tee? You awake?'

'Dan? What is it what's happened? Is it the baby?'

'Yeah. Gone into labour, I think it'll be quick.'

'Oh! Little Elle.'

'Call you when I know anything.'

'All right. Dan, you okay?'

'Yeah, feel a bit choked that's all.'

'I know. Who'd have thought it, us grandparents?'

'I wasn't thinking that. I was thinking about Troy,' Daniel said, looking around the caravan. There didn't seem to be much baby stuff. He needed to do something about that. 'Troy can't even look after himself let alone Elle and a baby.'

There was a long moment of contemplative silence. 'I need to come over don't I? And I need to talk to you as well.'

'Right. *About?*'

'Not over the phone and not till the baby is home and settled. Okay?'

Daniel ended the call and sat with his head back and his eyes closed, too tired to think straight, too many issues juggling for supremacy. When he made his way over to the hotel, Emily was apologetic, sitting with a white face and a bottle of water on reception, and Victoria was slamming things about in the kitchen.

'I can't believe what Emily has just told me!' she said, when Daniel craned his head round the door.

'Uh? What?'

She slammed a pan down on the hob. 'That she is ninety percent certain she has failed her first year.'

'Oh, yeah, Elle's on her way to hospital, if you're interested.'

She turned on him, 'You knew about Emily?'

Daniel slunk into the kitchen, filled the coffee machine. 'Look, she can have a full-time job here if she stuffs up.'

Victoria made a huffing noise, 'Hotel work? But she's so

much better than that!'

He looked at her askance, and she suddenly deflated, put a hand across her eyes. 'Oh God I'm sorry I didn't mean that. What I meant to say is I'm disappointed in her.'

Daniel thought about her words for a moment, 'Look, we're both tired, so I'm just going to go upstairs and sort out some paperwork and stuff.'

She looked miserable, but Daniel didn't risk touching her, for all his luck Emily would appear right behind him and he had enough to think about for the time being.

*

The baby was born at twelve minutes past midday. Troy was incomprehensible over the phone. Daniel said, 'What's she had? Troy?'

'She's had a fucking baby!' he shouted, 'It's a *baby!*'

Daniel counted to ten, 'Boy? Or girl?'

'I think it's a girl! Yeah Dad it's a girl, are you coming down here?'

'What *now*? Elle won't want me there.'

'No but I do. I want you here,' he said, then made a strangulated sobbing noise and disconnected. Daniel stared at the phone in his hand. He called Tina and his mother, and they both cried as well.

Daniel arrived at the hospital about two hours later. He'd stopped to buy some baby things and on a whim, a pink and white rabbit the size of a small garden shed. When he was trying to get it in the hospital lift, he wondered what he'd been thinking, but a lot of student nurses smiled at him, and automatically gave him directions to maternity.

When he found the right ward, the right bed, all three of them were asleep. It could have been himself, Tina and Troy nearly nineteen years ago. Troy and Elle looked too young. Elle was flat out, her outstretched arm had a plastic wristband with her name on it, and Troy was on a chair but had fallen so far forward his head was on the bed. Daniel piled all the shopping down by the side of Elle and looked at the baby first, touched its downy head and put his finger inside its curled fist. Three weeks premature, she was more like a doll and when he saw the tiny name band on her wrist, baby Woods, Daniel had to go and stand outside and pull himself together. No one took any notice of him, standing there with his forehead pressed against a poster about an impending measles epidemic.

When he returned a few minutes later, Troy had woken up and Daniel motioned to him to follow. He was like a zombie, didn't even smile at the rabbit, none of the expected wisecracks.

'Have you eaten anything?' Daniel said to him in the corridor, and Troy just shook his head. Once in the hospital cafe, Daniel made him plough through a full English. After that, they sat outside on broken plastic chairs with plastic cups of coffee in a little courtyard. Slowly, Troy came back to life and told Daniel about the birth as if it was the first baby ever to be born. Daniel remembered feeling like that, but he also remembered feeling elated as well whereas Troy seemed a lot more traumatised, but then he was even worse than Daniel with blood and guts and hospital drama.

For Daniel, the nightmare of his father's drawn out death from pancreatic cancer and the endless vigils by his bedside with his mother, dignified to the very end and hiding her grief, would be forever embedded in his mind. Up until recently he'd refused to pick over it. Occasionally though, since Tina's mother's funeral, it had re-emerged. If he were the fanciful type he might just wonder if his father was trying to tell him something.

'I'm not ready for this. I don't know what I'm doing,' Troy said, 'I can't handle it all.'

'Too late, there's no choice now,' Daniel said, 'Come on, Troy you've got a daughter.'

He scuffed his feet around the stamped out cigarette ends. 'But I can't *be* a dad on top of everything else,' he said, his voice breaking down then, 'The hotel, all of it. You're never there anymore. Where do you keep going to?'

'What do you mean? I get it in the neck for not taking any time off, I can't win!'

Troy scowled at him, 'It's getting obvious, Dad.'

'I am allowed a life outside work.'

'You *promised* it would all be sweet with you and Mum.'

'You saw. I tried!'

'Not enough!'

Daniel stared at his son, Tina's eyes looking back at him, and felt faintly disgusted with himself that all the time he'd been with Victoria, his son was heading for a minor breakdown. He'd just chosen not to see it. Marian had warned him but he'd not taken much notice. Daniel put an arm across his son's shoulders and Troy just seemed to collapse against him. Daniel said nothing, just hugged him into his chest. He never couldn't recall his own father doing that, but why should that matter?

The outside space began to fill up with nurses on their breaks. They likely thought someone had died; the way himself and Troy were hanging on to each other.

'I'm sorry, Troy.'

'What for?' he said, wiping his eyes across his sleeve.

'All kinds of stuff. I promise you it will all be okay. Everyone will help with the baby, you can take time off, come on, you're not on your own here. Tony and Tristan can't wait to babysit,' Daniel said, holding him upright then so he could look at him eye to eye, 'We'll talk some more, when you all get home.'

Troy nodded, but it was as if he'd not really registered anything. A good while later they made their way back to

Elle. The baby was still cocooned in sleep, in the post birth way newborns sleep. It was likely the calm before the storm, but Daniel thought it best not to say anything along those lines. Elle was awake but still lying down and staring at the rabbit. 'What use is that?' she said, then considered their blotchy faces with faint scorn. 'Have you *both* been crying?'

Daniel kissed the top of her head, 'Elle, she's just gorgeous.'

She grinned slightly and clasped his hand, 'You need to seriously man-up, Granddad.'

Troy wouldn't come home with him, wanted to stay, which Daniel saw as a good sign. His son followed him down to the car park though, and Daniel said, 'It's not just about us any longer. Look after them both, won't you?'

Troy nodded, 'Be a father, you mean?'

Daniel took a moment to reflect on his words, feeling the weight of them press down somewhere uncomfortable. But then, by the time he'd driven back to the hotel, he could feel a certain measure of self-pity take hold.

He'd worked hard for the future of his family, set them up for life with the hotel and he had to admit it did irk him to feel that they were all on his case with such animosity. Even Mia was calling him all the time because Blue had gone walkabout, stormed out of their Californian apartment and disappeared. Somehow it was all his fault, even though he was in a different country.

'Has she turned up at the hotel?'

'No. Have you been putting her under pressure?'

'You mean giving her career opportunities?'

'I mean *putting her under pressure.*'

'Piss off, Dan.'

Not for the first time Daniel wondered whether he should have blown all the money, sat on his backside in the south of France and drank himself to death.

So he had a relationship with Victoria, *so what?*

Daniel knew he was talking himself round the block. Max had made everything complicated. On the other hand, there was no way he was going to drop to his knees in an admission of defeat because Max had thrown his toys out the pram. Back at the hotel, Daniel tried calling Blue but there was no reply, then as soon as he'd disconnected, a text came through.

'I'm okay, Dad.'

Victoria came running across the car park in an apron splattered with sauce. He wanted to throw his arms around her and he could see she was thinking the same, but they stood apart.

'Are they all right? The baby...?'

'Yeah, yeah fine, a little girl. Troy's had some kind of meltdown though,' Daniel said, locking his car. 'And Blue's gone AWOL. Don't know what that's about.'

'I'm sorry about before, Emily...'

Daniel nodded; he had more important stuff on his mind than Emily's exams. He walked across to the caravan and flung open the door, then sighed and surveyed the contents. Victoria followed him.

'They can't live here with a baby,' he said, stepping inside and falling over the washing basket. He noticed the locks had broken on the windows and a horrible thought ran through his mind.

'I'm going to swap living quarters with them,' he said, 'let them move into the hotel.'

Victoria folded her arms and looked around, 'You're going to swap your rooms for this?'

'Yeah, I don't need all the space, they do. They need some privacy.'

'And security? Is that it?'

'It's an added bonus.'

He saw a shadow cross her face and he went to her, crumpled her up in his arms, kissed her, and she felt as weak and tired as he did, 'I want you,' he whispered, 'go and find an empty room… text me which one.'

'You're so very naughty,' she said, 'but that's why I love you.'

Love. She'd never said that before, it just fell out of her mouth, naturally. Daniel didn't say that word enough. He watched her saunter across the car park, trying to ignore the kick it gave him, that she was Max Morgan's wife, knowing it must eat Max up inside to know she was with him, despite the danger it attracted.

*

It was still light in room three when Daniel woke. When he glanced at his watch it was just after six in the afternoon. Victoria was still asleep. He turned to face her, then traced the curve of her arm where it lay across his pillow, and moved her hair. Even in repose, she was incredibly arresting. The most beautiful woman he had ever been with, if he was honest.

Earlier, they'd talked about the more positive happenings, her new catering contract, then Troy and Elle and the baby. Victoria had been quiet when he'd mentioned Tina coming over.

'She's going to want to see the baby, help out Elle.'

Victoria had frowned, 'What about Elle's parents?'

'She hasn't got any.'

Daniel kissed the inside of her wrist, then when she stirred, kissed her mouth. 'Vic? Wake up, love, got to go sort out the bar.'

'I'll see you down there. Mine's a large one.'

'I know,' he said, grinning.

She opened one eye, 'I was referring to a gin and tonic.'

'Yeah, right.'

When she came to the bar an hour later, she slid onto a stool, stirred her drink and stabbed at the lime and ice. 'What are we going to do about Max?'

Daniel was kneeling on the floor, stocking up the small fridge with mixers, 'I don't know, not had time to think about it really,' he said, and looked up at her, 'You don't need to worry about him getting to you. You're safe in the flat.'

'So long as I don't let him in?'

'Even *if*, you let him in. It's me he wants to get to, my family, my business,' Daniel said, realising that now he'd said it out loud, subconsciously it had been on his mind for twenty four hours. 'You've nothing to worry about, nothing to lose really.'

'How can you say that?' she said, leaning over the bar slightly and lowering her voice, although there was no one around, 'I could lose *you*. What if he does something to your car, or... I don't know! I don't trust him.'

Daniel stopped stacking bottles, and looked at her for a long, silent moment. 'Maybe we should cool it for a while, just till Tina has been and gone.'

'*Why?* What difference will it make?'

He began stacking again; filling the ice machine, 'Let him think he's won for a bit. It might make him back off. To be honest, I'm going to be tied up here all the time anyway.'

Victoria looked crushed for a second, then she drained her drink and placed it down with a small decisive movement. She got down from the stool and Daniel went to grab her hand, but Sue came through with some guests, and Victoria was gone. Daniel watched her disappear through the glass doors and could have cut his tongue out but he was too tired to do anything about it. Almost simultaneously, Troy materialised, still looking shattered but marginally more pleased with himself, and Daniel suddenly decided he was more important.

He asked Daniel for nearly fifty pounds for his taxi from

the hospital. That dealt with, Troy slumped down on the same bar stool Victoria had just vacated and Daniel opened a half bottle of champagne.

'Congrats, Daddy,' Daniel said, and poured the foaming liquid into a pint pot.

'We gonna call her Lily, after Granny Bradshaw,' Troy said.

Daniel smiled. 'Call your mum and tell her, will you?'

They toasted Lily and Daniel told him about the room swap.

'You *want* to live in that caravan?' Troy said, missing the point, then missing his mouth with his drink, 'Like some sort of eccentric millionaire?'

'No, not especially, but your need is greater.'

'That's just amazing,' Troy said, 'Elle will be made *up*.'

'Now go and get some sleep before you fall over.'

'Good idea,' he said, then started walking backwards, still holding the drink and spilling it, punch drunk with tiredness and emotion. 'Hey Dad, why are you such a soft touch?'

'Same reason I yell at you. Cos I love you.'

*

Several days later, when baby Lily came out of hospital, Daniel moved into the caravan. Bear also decided to change camp from next door. He moved from Tony and Tristan's spare bunk bed, into his master's domain, then craftily worked his way up from sleeping on the floor, to lying next to Daniel on the bed. Over the course of a week, he had progressed to digging himself under the duvet, and then the ultimate prize, resting his head next to his master, on the duck down pillow. Whenever Daniel opened his eyes, Bear was staring back at him, waiting for instruction.

Back in the caravan and sharing it with a subservient

Husky, Daniel tried not to see it as a backward step. In the summer months it was fine, but there was no way he was spending winter in it, even taking into consideration the dense, snow proof coat of the dog, and the knowledge it was his for sharing. Actually given it was August, the weather was pretty miserable and the dog was very soft and cuddly. He even sat on the sofa next to Daniel and enjoyed the same films.

His mother was predictably torn, excited about the baby but unhappy about Daniel's living arrangements and his distracted state of mind. She pulled out all the cleaning stuff from under the sink in the caravan.

'I can't believe you let that big dog climb in the bed,' she said in a scolding voice.

'He loves me, what can I do?' Daniel said, more concerned with replacing the window latch and lock.

Marian tutted and poured bleach into a bucket. 'Is Tina still arriving at the end of the week? Where's she going to stay? I never know with you two. I can't see her bunking up with a Husky.'

'Blue's room I guess,' he said, throwing the screwdriver back in the box. 'You haven't heard from her have you? Blue, I mean.'

'No. I think she's given up sending me those abbreviated messages. Why can't she just make a phone call now and again?'

On the day Tina was due to arrive, Emily announced she'd officially failed her first year and didn't want to re-sit. She asked Daniel for a full-time permanent job.

'I'd be happy to employ you,' Daniel said truthfully, 'but you've got to discuss it with mum and dad first.'

She'd come back to him within minutes. 'Okay, told them both. When can I start?'

'And they were both all right about this?'

She pulled a bored face, 'Okay, Dad was a bit livid.'

'Oh great,' Daniel said, finally drawing his eyes from hers and studying all the gaps on the staff rota created by Elle, Troy and Mandy. 'Tell you what, just fill in all these gaps and it's a deal.'

She laughed, and it was her mother's low laugh. Daniel called Victoria, 'I expect that's another nail in my coffin now.'

'Not funny,' she said, then 'Has Tina arrived yet?'

'No,' he said, glancing down the lakeside road. They'd made up since their little tiff on baby Lily's birthday, but Victoria was more twitchy about Tina's visit than anyone. Marian said she was going to either ask for a divorce, or ask to come back; it was that wide open with Tina.

CHAPTER TWELVE

Tina felt surprisingly serene and calm on the drive down. How long that would last was anyone's guess, but it was a good place to start for what lay ahead. That old saying was true; about the not knowing being the part that really messed up your head, not knowing what was ahead and now that she did, there was some satisfaction in being able to explain some of it.

Of course the pills helped, and the support group.

Then there was baby Lily. She couldn't wait to see the baby. Elle had fixed up Skype for her in the flat but all that had happened so far was an image of Troy holding up different items of clothing. 'Mum? Is it like, okay to wash this, with *this*?'

She arrived at The Lakeside by taxi, wearing her River Island jeans, the ones she swore she'd never get into. Daniel was all huffy at first, wanting to know why she'd left the mini rotting away by a kerbside in Didsbury? He imagined the taxi had come from the station, but the truth of it was the taxi had come some ninety miles from Didsbury, prepaid.

Mercifully, Daniel didn't notice this fact because in the very next breath he was telling her all about the baby, wanting to be there when she saw Lily for the first time, wanting to share it all with her. This brand new part of her husband, the proud grandparent he'd become in her absence, caught

Tina out with its complicated mix of emotions. She watched him gather up all her bags and presents, and followed him inside.

In their old rooms, Troy and Elle had moved in, and it seemed strange looking at all their young mess. Troy said he was exhausted with it all and *please* don't wake the baby because he'd only just got her back to sleep, then busied himself trying to find suitable garments to add to his white wash, collecting things off the floor and carefully reading every label, like the new man he was so desperate to be.

'Elle, what do the crowns mean?'

'It means only the queen can wash em,' Elle said, exchanging a grin with Tina. 'And anything with a P on means Prat wash. That means only *you* can wash it.'

'Yeah right, I know what the P is for Elle! It stands for like... powder. Don't it?'

All chores done, the presents were gone through and for a while it was like Christmas, until Daniel sent Troy and Elle to go and get some lunch in the restaurant, and at last they were left alone with Lily.

Daniel lifted the baby from her basket. At first her arms flew out and she made a little mewing noise. 'Look, look how small she is, Tee,' he said, making a snug cocoon out of the blanket. Tina remembered him doing the same to Troy, one of Marian's little tips. This time though, it made her heart flip over watching him now with the baby, how careful he was with her. She'd not appreciated all this with Troy, but she clearly remembered Daniel doing it all, and how vile she'd been to him.

He wanted her to hold the baby. Nana Tee Tee.

'Wait. Let me sit down first,' Tina said, and settled herself in the leather chair, then held out her arms for the baby. Although she'd rehearsed how it would all go in her head, she'd wildly underestimated how it would all make her feel. Motherhood had not been the best of times for her, but this was different.

'She looks like a doll, don't she, Tee?'

Tina just nodded, her eyes on the baby.

Lily was tiny, with delicate little fingernails and a turned down rosebud mouth. It reminded Tina of her own first few difficult days with Troy, but in a way this was better. It was a bit like plucking all the joy from something without having to endure the effort to get there. The payoff was substantially higher.

'I always wanted a girl, didn't I. Do you remember, Dan?'

When she drew her eyes from Lily to look at him, there was an odd little moment of suspension, and she could swear Daniel was thinking the same. *Well you've got one now.*

Eventually, Troy and Elle returned and Tina realised that she and Daniel had sat there for nearly an hour just watching Lily, barely speaking. It wasn't that they didn't want to, more that they didn't *have* to. The sudden, cold realisation that Tina was going to change all that with what she had to say, set her heart thumping again. This was where the bubble burst, but if she didn't get it all out fairly soon she might just bottle out altogether. She waited till Daniel dumped her case in Blue's room.

'I need to talk you, Dan, alone and in private.'

'What about?'

When she didn't respond, he followed her to the caravan where he pushed open the door for her. It was small and stuffy after the hotel and it made her feel slightly panicked. The huge dog didn't help, watching her every move and sticking its nose in her best bag.

'I've got something to tell you and I want you to promise me that you'll listen, without interrupting me. *Promise me.*'

He shrugged. 'Yeah, okay.'

She swallowed over her dry throat and tried to keep her eyes focused on his face. Daniel had absolutely no idea what she was going to say, she was certain of that. She felt nervous then, weak with nerves. When she went to sit next to him, and cupped his face in her hands, he looked at her as if she had a screw loose, but she ignored that.

'I hope you're going to understand what I've got to tell you, and why I had to do it in my own way, in my own time, because it's actually taken quite a lot of courage for me to do this today.'

He almost started to say something but she placed her hand over his mouth, 'You *promised.*'

The dog started lapping water from its bowl, and it sounded too loud, too intrusive.

'Dan,' she began slowly, thinking about every word before she said it. 'Dan, I'm ninety percent sure I've got MS.'

At first, he had no idea what she was saying. She continued to stare back at him, then dropped her eyes from his, but managed to keep hold of his hands.

'It started last year,' she said to his hands, 'just, a few strange symptoms. I didn't think they were even related. Remember I kept dropping stuff? You were furious I'd spilt all those tiny screws for the alarm. Do you remember?'

'*What?*'

Tina stopped for a moment, asked him if he was okay, then she carried on talking, telling him about the blurred vision, the slurred speech, the odd pains in her joints and the sudden exhaustion. 'I didn't tell you because I didn't know, not at first.'

Daniel got to his feet and she offered him a cigarette but he waved it away and went to lean on the kitchen unit with his back to her.

'You've not said anything... Dan?'

'You told me not to!' he said, quickly rounding on her. He made a throw away gesture with one hand. 'It's you who needs to do all the talking!'

Tina nodded, took a moment to remember where she

was up to. 'At first... at first, I went through a stage of denial, so you see I couldn't even tell myself. I panicked, needed the truth, and that took time. I needed to deal with it in my own head before I gave it to anyone else to deal with. Can you understand that?'

'No! I don't. I'm your husband, why couldn't you tell me any of this?'

'I couldn't face it. And I didn't want to rain on your parade, it clashed all the time.'

'*Rain on my parade?* You thought I'd put a wedding and the hotel before your health? Do you think I'm that shallow, *honestly?*'

'I did try, a couple of times, but I bottled out. You'd be full of questions and I knew I couldn't answer them.'

'So answer them now!' he almost shouted, and she jumped when he slammed his fist onto the sink unit. The dog leapt up for a second, then hunkered down again, watching.

Tina went over it all again, ignoring the heavy feeling of panic in her chest, told him how the testing was only conclusive when she'd had two or more episodes lasting twenty-four hours and occurring a month apart. She'd had MRI scans, a lumbar puncture. Daniel wasn't listening by then, judging from his face he was completely baffled by all the medical jargon she was spouting.

'I don't know what all this means! I don't even know what MS is.'

'Multiple sclerosis. Well, in a nutshell, it's a neurological disease,' she said, and sighed, 'Okay you know those big electric cables for the lights and everything? Imagine the insulation gets damaged and it all short circuits. That's what it is.'

'I don't know what you're talking about!'

Tina raised her voice a fraction, 'It's where my immune system attacks itself. It's not curable and it will likely get to the stage where I rely on a wheelchair. There, I've *said* it now.'

Daniel looked as nauseous as she felt. She went to say something else but he put up a hand and stopped her. He made it to the small bathroom, and began to retch. After a minute or so, Tina went to the door.

'Dan? I'm sorry. I know it's a shock.'

When he came out, she led him back to the narrow little sofa and put the kettle on, and for a moment its cheerful whistle made it feel like they were having a caravan holiday. Daniel watched as she made the sugary tea, a cure all task she'd inherited from her mother. Marian might be a swaddling expert but Lily Bradshaw had known all there was to know about tea making.

Mostly to give him chance to recover, Tina began to talk about her mother and all the wasted years she'd had with her father, being his carer. How the funeral had cemented her decision.

'What decision?' Daniel said irritably, and waved the tea away.

'I know you're seeing someone else,' she said, and placed a placatory hand on his chest, 'I'm okay with it. Don't look at me like that.'

'What the *fuck* are you saying now?' he said, and the dog jumped up again.

'Dan, I'm saying...what I'm saying is I don't want you back. *I wouldn't want you* to be my carer, for years and years.' She looked away, looked anywhere but his face, while she waited for the words to sink in. 'I love you too much for that.'

When she finally made herself meet his eyes, she could only whisper, 'Don't you get it?'

'No,' he said darkly. And there was something in his face that she'd never seen before, in the lifetime she'd known him, she'd not seen that expression, didn't even know what it was.

*

Daniel continued to stare at her until Tina finally fumbled about, trying to find her bag. She hugged him, but his limbs felt wooden and unable to respond. She closed the caravan door behind her and he was left with his thoughts. They raced all over the place, until he felt breathless with it, thrown into cyberspace. It was so far removed from what he was expecting; his brain just went numb, like someone had pulled the plug.

All he really knew was that MS was something medical, and things with initials were usually serious. Of all the stunts she'd pulled on him over all the years they'd been together, this had to be the ultimate. Basically, he felt wrong-footed by her admission, and flipped open the laptop, thinking for a wild moment that Google would prove her wrong.

But it was all there, everything she'd said and more, lots more. He began to read the list of main symptoms with an almost belligerent disbelief. Pain, vertigo, fatigue, bladder and bowel problems, memory loss, muscle spasm, sexual problems...The list went on, and he slowly made all the connections in his mind, right back to Max's party and the car crash.

He closed the laptop and forced down the cold sugary tea.

When he returned to the hotel, people spoke to him but he just looked at them and climbed the stairs. Tina was asleep on top of the single bed in Blue's room, worn out with the strain of telling him. He saw all the packets of tablets next to her bottle of Coco Chanel and it all registered then, fell into a big slot in his head. On the point of touching her white blonde hair, his phone suddenly buzzed in his pocket. It was a text from Marian. *A text.* It was all grammatically correct with no abbreviation - it must have taken her twenty minutes at least - but rather than find it funny, Daniel found himself grateful it was all spelt out.

'Hello darling, don't worry, Bluebell is with me, love, Mum.'

Love, Mum. He clung to those two words, it was what you needed to hear, when major stuff went wrong. Although Tina had neither of those. She had no mum now, and not much love in her life. He could hear baby Lily screaming down the hall and felt an overwhelming need to scoop her up and tell her how much she was loved and how nothing bad would ever happen to her.

Daniel went over to the door and listened outside for a minute, then tapped.

'Elle? Can I come in?'

When there was no response, he went inside and Elle was lying in bed with the blinds drawn. Lily was yelling in her moses basket, her little blanket lifting up as she thrashed about.

'Oh, is that you Dan?' Elle said, tired and relieved.

'Sorry, did I scare you? You should keep this door locked, you know.'

'I can't *believe* she's crying again.'

Daniel picked up Lily. She was rigid with indignation but then she suddenly stopped screaming and began to grizzle on Daniel's shoulder. 'Where's Troy?'

'I think he's gone for a kip in the beer cellar, that's where he usually goes.'

Daniel picked up the baby paraphernalia with the basket and edged out the door. Elle had already turned over and pulled the duvet over her head. He took the baby and sat in reception with her, until Lily was bored with his explanation of the online tax return system, and her eyes rolled to the top of her head. Given her fragility, the attention she could provoke belied her size. He laid her back in the basket. 'Okay Lily, now stop being a drama queen.'

'Enough of them in the family already, hey?' Tina

whispered, and Daniel spun round, unaware Tina had been watching. 'Do you want to tell Troy, or shall I?'

'Troy? Don't you think he's got enough to deal with?' he said. 'I don't even want to think about it!'

'Give me the baby, go for a walk or something, please Dan.'

Daniel drove to his mother's bungalow in Deganwy. Once there, he rested his head on the steering wheel, his thoughts all over the place. He had a key for the front door, and he fumbled to find it.

When he stepped inside the hallway, he shouted out but there was no reply. He went through to the kitchen and there was the smell of cake, chocolate cake, cooling on a wire tray with an apple pie. On any other day, he would pinch a big hunk of it, but not this time. Through the window he saw his mother and his daughter, and they were digging in the garden. His mother was kneeling on a mat, poking at the earth, and Bluebell was passing her cuttings and bits of greenery. After the conversation with Tina, it all looked surreal, like something in his imagination.

Daniel banged on the window and they both looked, surprised at first, then their faces dropped when they tried to understand his expression. His mother came to him first, 'Daniel? What on earth...?'

He wanted to cry on her shoulder like Lily, aware that his mixed up twenty year old daughter was watching, but could do nothing about it. In the end emotion got the better of him and he sobbed out the story like the time he was six years old and his world had fallen to bits because he'd fallen off his bike in front of Barney Rubble.

'Daniel, MS is not life threatening,' Marian said, patting his arm, 'Come on, you're just in shock. Remember the postman's wife? She had it, walked with a stick, that's all.'

Bluebell understood that that wasn't the issue at all. She said nothing, but her eyes were locked onto Daniel's and for a second, they were both back in the nightmare of her drug withdrawal. She'd been scared of her own body, scared of showing Daniel the truth of it all in case he wouldn't love her any more. Scared of telling the full story because it made it all the more real. But then sometimes the imagined, was darker than the truth, or was it the other way around?

'Poor Tina,' Blue said quietly. 'Nobody could see it. We were all *horrible* to her.'

It stopped the conversation. The simplicity of her comprehension cut through his and Marian's complicated analysis of it all. Daniel noticed for the first time that all the black makeup had gone. His daughter looked different, fresh almost. He was pretty sure it wasn't all down to the Californian sun either.

'We didn't *know*. Now we know, we can help, if she'll let us,' his mother said to them both. Bluebell cut a slice of chocolate cake, and Daniel shared her slight smile when it collapsed in the centre. 'We've been trading secrets,' Marian said, squeezing her granddaughter's shoulder, looking for her special cake plates. 'I *know* how to text.'

'Matter of opinion,' Daniel said, then looked back at Bluebell, 'So, what happened with you and Mia?'

'I'm just not into that scene,' she shrugged. 'I want to live with you, can I?'

Daniel nodded, 'Tina's in your room.'

'I want to see her,' Blue said, picking the cake apart, 'I want to tell her stuff.'

Back at The Lakeside, the dog was waiting for him. His big Husky head filled the small caravan window and it was framed by the curtains. He looked incredibly concerned and there was a lot of smearing on the glass where he'd pressed his nose against it. He was Grandma Wolf, and she was Red Riding Hood, Blue said, carrying the cake and half the apple pie into the caravan.

Inside, the kitchen bin had been fully excavated. Blue

laughed, and it was strange to hear her laugh like that. Daniel shooed them both out in the end, Bear to pee on the ornamental shrubs, and Blue to see the baby, talk to Tina, be with her family. Her family. She included Tina in that phrase.

Victoria had been right about Blue, but they'd both been wrong about Tina. Daniel called her, and she grilled him about their meeting. He didn't lie, but he was pathetically obtuse.

'So, what did Tina want?'

'Nothing. Easier to say what she doesn't want, she doesn't want me back.'

'Okay, so...has she asked for a divorce?'

'No, didn't discuss that.'

'Did you tell her about us?'

'She knows, well she knows I'm seeing someone.'

'She *knows*? Has she got the photographs?'

'I don't know! Can we not do this?'

Victoria apologised, made him promise to see some film with her, and in some ways he was glad of the escapism. Everything was so big and emotional and complicated that sitting in a dark cinema and watching someone else's life, seemed like a good idea.

They all knew now, about Tina's condition. Troy had been broodingly quiet. Daniel had wanted Tina to be economical with the truth, but she was right when she pointed out that Troy would end up Googling it, and then the opposite would happen. It was Blue who'd astonished him the most, it was his crazy daughter who had the most intelligent things to say, could distill it all into a single clever sentence, like the singer songwriter she was.

Daniel went to collect Victoria a couple of evenings later, and she ran down to his car. She was wearing the cream sundress and carried a black linen jacket over her arm. She was tanned and full of life and when she kissed his face, he detected a new summery fragrance.

The cinema was quiet because it was the middle of August, and it wasn't raining. Most families were on the beach or at least outside somewhere.

'So, what's this film?' Daniel said. He glanced round at the advertising. 'Shark Attack Five, Terminator Ten, or Candy's Day Trip?'

'None of those.'

He followed her meekly, into the embryonic confines of screen three, and she laughed at his expression, tugged him along as if he were going to the dentist. Daniel had always imagined people who sat in dark cinemas on hot sunny afternoons to watch a French film from 1933, were a bit sad. It confirmed his suspicions. Les Miserables was miserable, and it didn't inspire him to forget anything or induce a feeling of escapism.

If he was there with Tina, they would have argued over Candy's Day Trip and The Terminator. Tina... she'd been on his mind every second of the day and night since she'd dropped her bombshell. Her condition dominated his thoughts, every little episode she'd had and how he'd reacted, where they'd been and what they were doing; it was as if his memory was on a repeat loop. He'd read everything he could find on the internet, sickened by the fact that while she'd been trying to deal with it by herself and having all the tests, he'd been spending time with another woman as if there was nothing wrong.

But then he'd feel angry that he'd been kept in the dark, angry that she'd set him up to feel like this. He swayed between wanting to shout at her, and wanting to gather her up, protect her from it all. Neither option would solve anything, sugary tea was still the only known antidote and the only scrap of comfort he was allowed to proffer. She'd made it plain she didn't want him, she loved him but she didn't want him. She was either incredibly strong and selfless, or she was full of pity and begging to be rescued. Knowing Tina, it could be a complication of all of those, or it could change on a daily basis.

Daniel woke up two hours later with a crick in his neck.

Victoria wasn't happy. If he was with Tina, she would have left him asleep, taken his wallet and got a taxi home, or gone shopping and blown all his cash. Victoria didn't sulk though, whereas Tina was an expert at that.

'Are you coming in?' she said, back at the flat. 'I've got some Parisian Noir Espresso. I know it's French but it might help you stay awake in my boring company.'

He watched her move around the kitchen, needing to talk about it all but needing to escape it almost as much. 'Sorry,' he said eventually, and she smiled. He went on to blame the funeral, the baby, the weather, Chef's tantrums. Everything really, except the big issue.

Daniel stared into his coffee until it was almost cold.

'So, did you guess who tampered with the helicopter? Or did it surprise you when the bomb went off in the Champs de Elysee, killing the shark and the French prostitute?'

'*What?*'

'Daniel, you've obviously got something on your mind,' she said, tipping the coffee down the sink. 'Either talk to me, or just go and do something about it.'

'I like the idea of the French prostitute,' he said. She gave him a curious look, but nevertheless, led him into the bedroom where she proceeded to unbutton his shirt. She slipped out of the sundress, began to kiss him. She felt buttermilk smooth, pampered and prepared. Daniel felt so slow to respond it was as if he'd drunk a bottle of scotch without being aware of the fact. Usually though, even drunk, there was a certain measure of arousal even if it was in his head in the form of French prostitutes, but there was nothing in his head, quite simply there was nothing.

'Was there really a shark in it?'

'No,' she said, a tad irritably, then gave up with him and lay flat. If anyone had told him, even a week ago that he wouldn't be able to make love to the practically naked woman lying next to him, he would have laughed in their face. His sex drive was something he took for granted. Daniel was tired of apologising, but felt compelled to.

Victoria was gracious, as in everything. 'Dan, you've just too much on your mind,' she said, slipping on her robe, 'that's all it is, it doesn't matter.'

He was still in his underwear, and he began to get dressed because even that felt wrong. He told her then, told her about Tina, and the timing seemed all wrong, but if he were honest everything coming out of his mouth seemed all wrong. At first she was silent, until he got to the part about Tina not wanting Daniel to be her carer, not wanting him full stop. He sat on the edge of the bed and concentrated on the oak floor.

'I can understand that,' Victoria said, and she seemed flooded with relief.

'That's not the whole issue.'

'I know, but Dan she's accepted it and moved on.'

She put her arms around him, and Daniel buried his face in her chest, but he couldn't think of anything to say. He must have said something, because minutes later he was in his car.

For a while, he just sat there, aware out of the corner of his eye that Victoria had glanced through the window and disturbed the curtain. She sent him a text. 'Love you.'

After a while, he started the car engine, and drove home.

*

Tina stayed for a week then announced she was going to see Linda, plus she had a few days rest in the sun with auntie

Beryl in Spain, her mother's sister. After that she had to get back for a hospital appointment. Daniel watched her pack a bag.

'Tee, what's this appointment?'

'Oh big consultant guy, can't remember his name. Something about conclusion of all the tests, fine-tuning the medication and basically confirming what I already know,' she said, throwing all the tablets into a bag, as she turned to face him. 'I'm hoping I can drive again.'

Daniel nodded; everything he wanted to say wouldn't come out of his mouth, so he caught hold of her instead. Tina relented for less than a minute and allowed him to hug her, but then she pushed gently at his chest and gave him a little warning look.

'Blue can have her room back. She talks about you a lot,' she said and resumed packing, beginning to squash shoes into a holdall. 'About the time you saved her from the jaws of hell.'

'Don't joke about that.'

She stopped and frowned. 'I *wasn't*. She's been a sweetheart, actually.'

Daniel carried her bags downstairs when the taxi came. Troy and Elle, Blue and baby Lily came to do hugs and goodbyes. Daniel walked across before the taxi pulled away, and she rolled the window down.

'Don't say anything,' she said, 'just let me go, Dan.'

So Daniel said nothing, but he leant in the window, and kissed her for long, long seconds, until she pulled his hands down from her face.

CHAPTER THIRTEEN

'So, anyway,' Charlie said, 'There I am, a red-faced student doctor trying to support this woman in the throes of giving birth, and she starts shouting at me, yelling that it hurts so much I must be trying to push the baby back in, rather than assist the natural laws of nature.'

Linda laughed, drained her glass. She had stomach ache from laughing at Charlie, or maybe it was the food. They were in his old fashioned cottage garden and they'd eaten just about the unhealthiest meal Linda could imagine. A Chinese takeout, and a huge bowl of homemade chocolate mousse. They'd also managed to consume a serious quantity of beer and wine.

'I feel quite disgusting,' Linda said, and sat back in an old striped deck chair.

'I don't,' Charlie replied with a frown, 'Hell, I must be used to it.'

'Tell me some more funny stories.'

'Could move on to the doctor-doctor jokes, there's dozens of them. Or, we could play doctors and nurses,' he said, then raised his brows, 'Or just doctors.'

'Okay,' Linda said warily. 'What does it involve?'

'Well, you lie on the bed and I have to decide what's wrong with you.'

Linda grinned at his deadpan face, watched him scrape

at the bowl of chocolate mousse. 'We've played that game before, Charlie. Only it went under a different name; sexual operation, I think.'

'I know, but I never tire of it.'

'I think, given what we've consumed, a lie down would be nice though.'

'We could practice resting heart rates, that's relaxing.'

'No, I just want you to lie down as well.'

'Well, if you put it like that, it would be terribly rude not to,' Charlie said.

Linda smiled, made her way to Charlie's bedroom. Through the window, the little garden petered out into a tumble of overgrown gorse and there was a broken gate onto the steep flank of Foel Lus.

Charlie lived in a small cottage in Dwygyfylchi. Basically it was old, quaint and dysfunctional, but it fitted his persona perfectly. It was an awful mess, a mostly clean mess she'd discovered, but overflowing with books, files and artefacts, so much so it had a slightly old romantic film quality about it, like Brideshead Revisited in miniature. Except for the bathroom, which was more of a nod to his medical student days. It had a skeleton on the back of the door wearing a blonde wig with an old stethoscope round its bony neck and a plastic banana where its private parts might be.

The small second bedroom was stuffed full of clothes, like a dressing up box.

'Karen's fault,' Charlie said of the bulging wardrobes. 'I think she presumed she could exert some sort of control, by whatever she dressed me in. You know, like a mood altering drug.'

Of his marriage, Charlie blamed the folly of youth, said he'd been dazzled by Karen's immaculate toenails and her heritage diamond collection. At the end, he claimed Karen had been only interested in his salary, and the prestige and trappings of being a doctor's wife.

Linda was always asking questions about his work, she was genuinely interested though, and Charlie seemed to enjoy having a protegee. When Charlie was on call, sometimes his mobile would ring and he'd have to leave in the middle of the night, to go and save someone's life, or take a child to hospital. Linda had to admit, the medical thing was incredibly attractive.

Even so, she was slightly startled at how she'd managed to find herself with a man like Charlie. He was intellectual, romantic, funny and confident. The first time they'd made love, it had been a slow burn of discovery rather than all out passion, but it left Linda with the feeling that there was something special developing between them. They both shared more aspirations about the foundations of life, rather than concerns about what went on on the outside.

They just seemed to click.

Linda had seen Karen Summers several times, mostly cruising along the coast road in her soft top Mercedes; and she'd seen and heard her having a loud conversation (about herself) in the smart new coffee shop in Deganwy, with a man who was obviously much younger. She was quite scary, in a theatrical overpowering sort of way and Linda felt quite ordinary in comparison.

'I like ordinary,' Charlie said, picking up on her reticence, 'I like honest and ordinary.'

His car was honest and ordinary, an old Land Rover knee deep in toffee papers and copies of The Lancet. It was equipped with the latest satellite navigation. He peered at it in his reading glasses sometimes, then would switch it off and open out an old map decorated with coffee cup rings.

Charlie was actually far more interested in the performance of his mountain bike. Linda had even seen him cycling in town, weaving between the traffic with a 'doctor on call' sign strapped to the frame. After Mike, she rather liked Charlie's disinterest in all things mechanical, and it meant he always had clean finger nails.

She felt like a different person with Charlie, he brought out something different in her, but she had to admit the new Linda was helped by her new, independent living arrangements. As promised, Troy had filled a skip with the stuff out of the garage flat, and fitted a new kitchen and bathroom. Daniel had plumbed it in, sorted out the dodgy electrics and put in a spiral staircase and a Velux window into the loft space. It was only big enough for a bed, a wardrobe and a desk but it was perfect for Linda to sit and study. Charlie had practically furnished a wall with medical books for her and the space was already taking on the atmosphere of a Parisian garret. It was better than she'd ever imagined. She had tried to pay Daniel for more than the window, but he wouldn't let her.

'I inherited a fortune, Lin,' he'd said. 'If I can't help out friends once in a while, then I'd rather just give it all away.'

'But you've spent so much time.'

'So? Same answer.'

The view through the loft window was mostly bleached sky dotted with grey gulls, fading gradually into the parched, windblown grass of late summer. Linda loved the blank canvas imagery of it. It was the clean slate she'd drawn for herself. The addition of colour would come in time, the lights and darks of life would fill it all in again.

Tina said Linda had strengthened herself from the inside out, which was a pretty deep analysis for Tina, but then she'd been reading a lot of self-help books.

'I hope I'm not becoming self-obsessed,' she'd said to Linda.

'I think you're learning who you are, all over again, same as me.'

She arrived by taxi on Friday night, dropped her bags down and sat on Linda's new sofa bed with a tired droop. She'd developed a slight limp, hardly discernible. 'I've done it Lin, I've told them all.'

Linda put an arm across her shoulders. 'How did Daniel react?'

'Predictably, angry, shocked and confused, then all emotional,' Tina said, turning her rings round and round on her fingers. 'I've totally messed his head up. And Troy was, I don't know, just destroyed really.'

Although Linda was glad to be absolved of her secret, part of her felt as if she'd underestimated the impact of it all, would rather it was all contained again. Tina looked round at the little flat and the quirky staircase.

'Has Dan done all this?'

'He has,' Linda said softly, watching her face. 'And Troy.'

She seemed to crumple at this. 'I've been really good, all calm and controlled, but now..'

'But now you're not?'

She wagged her head, bit her lip. 'I'm sorry, Lin; I promised myself I wouldn't do this to you. I thought I had it all under control.'

'Why does it upset you?'

'Because I'm married to the best man I know,' she said, 'My heart wants him, but my head and my malfunctioning body is on full reject.'

Linda gave her a glass of wine and a box of tissues, although watching Tina trying not to fall to pieces, was like looking at those awful advertisements for world disasters. If she put a hand in front of her face and waited a few seconds, it was gone. Learning to live with something so life changing and not letting it impact on those she loved, had sometimes made Linda wonder whether it was tainted with martyrdom, but now, looking at Tina trying to swallow it all down, she felt sure it wasn't.

Tina blotted her eyes, 'I had some bloody pictures sent to me, of Victoria and Daniel.'

'What kind of pictures?'

'Take a guess.'

'No, Oh God, who the hell...?'

'I know. Who would do such a thing... Max?' she said, then dropped her eyes. 'You know what? I don't care.'

Linda didn't believe her.

*

Charlie collected her the following evening. He suggested they go to The Lakeside for dinner but when he saw her reaction, tried to think of an alternative, although there was nothing with the same summer evening ambiance. Linda told him about Tina's visit, expecting him to admonish her somehow, but Charlie was not Mike. He never saw the difficult path; it was always the right path, whatever it cost. She liked that, she liked the steadfastness of it.

'Lin, you have done nothing wrong,' he said, his green eyes on hers.

Charlie drove to The Lakeside, but they had to wait for a table, so walked down to the edge of the water with drinks. It was easy to pass the time; the pony mares all had foals and allowed them to stand a few feet away as they cropped the dry grass. After twenty minutes or so, Daniel texted Charlie to say there was a table for them.

Bluebell was strumming a guitar on the decking, singing Coldplay. The atmosphere was romantic, ageless in a way, modern without being abrasive. And it was nice that everyone knew them, recognised them as a couple. Elle came to show them baby Lily, and Charlie wanted to hold her, commiserated with the difficulties of breast feeding and told her which nipple cream to buy.

'If you get fed up, there's no shame in giving her a bottle you know, formula milk is so sophisticated these days baby wouldn't know,' Charlie said, enjoying pulling faces at Lily.

'Huh, Troy doesn't know any difference either,' Elle said, taking Lily from Charlie. 'I spent hours expressing it yesterday, and he went and made milky Mars with it.'

'Sorry?'

'It's just chocolate bar melted in milk to make a drink. I know, childish and disgusting.'

'Actually, it sounds nice,' Charlie said thoughtfully. 'Does he melt it in the microwave?'

Elle looked wrong-footed, 'I'll ask him.'

When Elle had gone, he said 'I had a patient once with the most appalling nipple problems. Turned out she was breastfeeding her bloody Tibetan terriers.'

'Freaky,' Linda said, buttering a warm roll. She loved Charlie's wacky stories. 'Have you never wanted children, or puppies?'

'Oh yes,' he said, 'but Karen put a stop to all that.'

She put her knife down. 'Charlie, did your ex have no redeeming features whatsoever?'

'Er,' Charlie frowned for a moment and shrugged. 'No, I honestly can't think of any.'

He asked about Linda's sons and Charlie said he'd liked to meet them, if it wasn't too soon. Linda thought it probably was. She talked about Tom and his girlfriend in London, and then Sam. It made her realise how much she missed her more adventurous son, how this generation took world travel in their stride, as if it were as accessible as the internet. Maybe it was.

'He's in Australia, he seems to love it there,' she said, and sighed, 'he's very good at e-mail and text but I haven't seen him in months. I miss him.'

Emily brought the food to the table, and Charlie asked about Victoria.

'Oh fine, busy with this catering thing she's setting up,' Emily said, placing their cutlery down. 'She's calling it The Celtic Catering Company or something like that. Got a big posh wedding on for the daughter of the Welsh Tourist Board guy. It's here as it happens, all hands on deck,' she said, pouring their wine, then pulled a face. 'No drinking allowed, not even the night before,' she went on, then lowered her voice, 'although it's my brother's birthday as well so I'm escaping to that afterwards. His mates know how to have a good time, if you know what I mean.'

Linda watched her move round the tables and thought about Emily's mother. She should really try to make amends with Victoria, but then she'd feel disloyal to Tina.

They ate grilled goat's cheese, carpaccio of beef with horseradish, and local lamb. Charlie ordered three desserts.

'Am I being a pig? Just say. I'd rather you told me the truth, it might make me reconsider.'

'Really?'

'Well, no.'

She smiled at him, lining up his cutlery. She loved the way he brushed his hair back with his hand. It was slightly too long, a bit bohemian in a way, but it suited him. He fed her huge wobbly spoonful's of brandy mousse, summer pudding and raspberry cake with white chocolate sauce. She tried not to laugh when the spoon came towards her and Charlie made a covetous expression.

Daniel brought them coffee, then pulled a chair over to their table on the pretext of discussing the merits of Chef's new puddings. Linda showed him the three plates, which looked as if they'd already been washed. They talked about Lily and the hotel and the weather.

Eventually he said, 'Lin, have you seen Tina?'

'You know I have.'

Daniel looked at her with sad, fixed eyes. 'Come on you knew, didn't you?'

Linda inhaled, knew what was coming, 'About the MS? Yes, I knew.'

'Bloody hell, Lin!' he said suddenly, 'How many years

have we known each other?'

'All our lives,' she said, ready for the accusations. 'And I love you both, but Tina needed me more.'

'She needed me! How could you keep such a massive deal from me?' he said. 'I've got into another relationship and now it's all an uncontrollable mess!'

'Your affair is all down to you and Victoria.'

'But if I'd known!'

'If you'd known what? If you'd known your wife was ill, or if you'd known Max would turn nasty and start taking snaps?'

For a couple of seconds, Daniel looked horrified, as if it was beyond his comprehension.

'What? Tina's had the pictures?'

Charlie butted in, 'Daniel, I like you a lot but you're not being fair. Lin has been an absolute rock to Tina. She's kept her promise under exceptional circumstances,' he said firmly. 'I'm asking you not to grill her, or shout at her.'

'Sorry, you're right,' he said, 'I'm sorry if I've spoilt your evening.'

'You haven't,' said Charlie, 'but let's not forget who the victim is here.'

'I know, I'm just gutted for her,' Daniel said quietly.

'We all are,' Charlie said. 'But she needs peace and support, no stress.'

'Thing is, I don't really understand the condition.'

Charlie said, 'Well, it's complicated, individual. You know I can't discuss her case but I can talk to you generally,' he said, 'and I will. Just not tonight.'

Daniel nodded, 'Okay. I'd appreciate that.'

He scraped his chair back, and Linda watched him go despondently across the crowded restaurant. She threw her napkin down.

'Now I feel awful.'

'So does he,' Charlie said, and touched her hand, 'I'll talk to him.'

Daniel came back with two large glasses of cognac and put them wordlessly on the table. When they tried to leave an hour later, Charlie said that Daniel had waived the bill.

'No one's mentioned Victoria throughout this triangular vortex of contorted love,' Charlie said, as they drove home through the dusk of late summer. 'The problem is, they are all perfectly decent people, caught in an indecent mess.'

'Except for Max,' Linda said, looking at the shadowy trees bend into the water, 'Why is he so cruel? Why can't he accept their marriage is over?'

'You don't think Daniel will do anything stupid, do you?'

'Very possibly, yes.'

They went back to Charlie's cottage, snuggled up on the sagging sofa to watch a week's worth of Holby City, which Linda enjoyed but Charlie said it was a bit like being at work, but with much more glamorous characters, although he kept pointing out small inaccuracies and smiled at all the operations and the defibrillator. There was a trailer for a programme about I'm A Celebrity, and for a second Mia's face filled the screen, followed by a potted history of her career. Linda smiled at the bucket load of bugs poised to fall on her head.

'Tina will have the number for that on speed dial.'

'I love that program,' Charlie confessed. 'Oh I'd love to see Karen in the Australian jungle.'

'Would she eat the bugs?'

'Good heavens no! Her body was a temple. She would only swallow microscopic portions of low fat protein and organic fruit,' he said, handing Linda another glass of wine, 'Whereas mine, mine is the temple of sweet temptation,' Charlie said knowingly, as he disappeared into the little kitchen.

Linda followed him with a grin, peered round the

door. She could tell he was itching to make milky Mars, or something along the same lines, because he was going through the big cupboard he reserved for sweet stuff in the kitchen.

He gave up, closed the door dismally, 'I haven't got the right ingredients.'

'What, a chocolate bar and some milk?' Linda said with a bubble of laughter. 'Don't tell me, you haven't got any milk. I've never known anyone eat such rubbish, and you a GP! You must have worms. Why don't your teeth fall out?' she said, folding her arms.

'It's getting out of control isn't it?' he said, clutching his waist, although there was hardly anything there. 'It all started when I gave up smoking. If I ever need an operation, they'll have to cut through a layer of sponge and custard first, like they do in Holby City.'

'Yes well, I wasn't going to mention it, but going off the empty bags in your car, there's at least another layer there, made entirely of Jelly Babies.'

'I'm turning into trifle aren't I?' he said resignedly.

'I may have to present you to medical science. Worse case of sugar addiction I've ever seen.'

'What will happen to me? Tell the truth, I can take it.'

'Well, the next stage is, you may get hundreds and thousands appearing at random, all over your body and you may even grow a cherry, somewhere on top of your head.'

'Oh the shame of it!' he said, feeling through his hair dramatically.

'This has to stop, Charlie.'

'Please, feel free to be strict with me.'

'How strict?'

'Oh very, very strict, cold turkey strict.'

'Are you going to do as I say?'

Charlie nodded meekly. 'Yes nurse Williams,' he said, and allowed her to lead him upstairs. She played along with it for a while but Linda was always the first to crack, couldn't keep her face straight.

'You'd make a hopeless dominatrix,' he said, laughing at last, hugging her close.

He was an exceptional kisser, nothing was hurried with Charlie. He tasted of toothpaste and vintage cognac and chocolate, and considering his diet, was actually in pretty good shape. Linda didn't really care about any of that, she cared more about the way he made her feel, she loved being in his arms, loved him being in hers.

*

In the morning, she woke with a hangover, relieved she had no early shift to go to. Charlie's alarm call was early though. He brought her tea and toast.

'Make me feel better,' she demanded.

He chewed his lip, considered. 'I'd be late for surgery. Stay there and sleep off your excesses and come to meet me at lunchtime. I'll take you for something greasy to eat, then you'll be cured. It'll be like a miracle.'

'Grease... are you sure? What kind of doctor are you?'

'Yours,' he said, then lay on top of the bed next to her. 'You know you were talking about turkey, cold turkey?'

'Turkey? Ugh. Please don't talk about turkey.'

'It got me thinking about Christmas. You know you said your son is in Australia? Well why don't we go?'

Linda struggled to sit up, sipped some of the tea. 'Go? Are you serious?'

'Yes why not? I'm due at least three weeks leave. I'd love to meet Sam and we could have a holiday in the sun.'

'Holiday. Sun,' she said dreamily, then wrinkled her nose. 'But I can't afford it.'

'I can. Think about it, book it and I'll pay for it,' he said, and pushed her nose with his index finger as if it were a button, 'Doctor's orders.'

As he was leaving, she called him back. 'Charlie?... I feel better already.'

*

At lunchtime, Linda went to his place of work in town. It was a big, busy NHS practice with four doctors and in need of money spending on the tired decor. Charlie had texted to say he was running behind time as usual, but she took a seat in the waiting room and pretended to read a magazine. The three telephone lines on the desk never stopped ringing. Sometimes one of the staff said his name and it made her look up.

'Doctor Charlie? No, I'm sorry he's not available for three weeks. Yes he's fully booked. What about Doctor Jones? No?'

If she could pinpoint the moment she fell in love, Linda would always remember sitting there, in that sad room, just waiting. The moment Charlie appeared behind the reception desk, he changed the whole perception of the day for her, everything shifted axis, the wallpaper wasn't dreary after all, and the chairs, well they were just comfy. If she looked properly, from that day on, the world was actually multi-coloured even though Charlie was wearing a dark shirt, no tie and a black linen jacket full of creases. He was wearing his reading glasses and peering at a computer screen, telephone in hand.

'Mr Thomas? It's Charlie. Your blood test results are in, yes I do need to see you,' he said, tapping away at the keyboard. 'No, it's nothing to worry about. How's the toe doing? It's still there? Good, good!'

The conversation went on for a while, when Charlie

looked up and saw Linda hiding behind Motorcycle Magic 2006. He studied her for a moment, then met her eyes over the top of the magazine, and smiled.

And that's when she knew.

Linda Williams was officially over her marriage and in love with another man. He was a kind, clever, funny, messy sort of man who needed her as much as she needed him. When he eventually signalled he was free, she followed him to his room, watched him hide a bag of fudge under some paper, and log off his screen. On his desk, there was something floating in a jar. It had a name and a label on it. 'Very naughty, evasive gall stones,' he said, waggling his fingers, widening his eyes. 'You wouldn't believe the trouble they've caused.'

She almost laughed, but wanted to touch him more.

'Charlie, I've missed you.'

'Have you?' he said, amused at first. 'Since this morning?'

'Yes. You know you said, you have to be passionate about something in life?'

He frowned, brushed his hair back. 'I probably did.'

'Well, I'm passionate about you.'

'Oh, Lin!'

He moved into her arms and buried his hands and face in her hair. It was as if everything had been poised to come together for that very moment, it felt so right to be standing there, her head nestled into his shoulder. She hugged him back, slid her hands under his jacket and the room seemed flooded with light, a kaleidoscope of colour.

*

The following week, as she was preparing for the start of her college course, Linda showed Mike the new look flat, but he was more interested in looking at her.

'You never went to all that effort for me,' he said, admiring her summer outfit of loose trousers and floaty top. She ignored his comment, so he wandered around the kitchen units, the buttermilk bathroom and the loft space.

'He's done a good job, hasn't he?'

'Have you seen him?'

'Yeah, I had a pint with him. Tina's still pulling his strings, playing games.'

'You know nothing about it!'

'He's with someone else!' Mike said. 'Look, I really think that's it now, stop clinging on.'

'Clinging on? Like I tried to do with us, you mean?'

'And you're with someone else as well so let's just not go there!'

Linda stood back to let him out of the door, slightly astonished.

They'd had an offer on the house. It was well below the asking price but given the economic climate, their desperation to move on, and next door's new mega shed full of gym equipment, and the giant satellite dish clinging to the side, Linda had agreed to a sale. When she drove past later, on her way to Barbara Jones, she allowed herself a private smile at the For Sale board. It was fine, she felt fine about it; didn't even want any furniture out of it.

When she went past Tina's parents' house, it was empty and of course, it would be, but that didn't feel quite so fine. That felt sad, how her family had been pulled to bits.

Barbara Jones had a key safe outside her front door, and Linda knew the number by heart but on this occasion the door was wide open. Linda called out, made her way through the hall, called out again. She could hear an argument in the sitting room, Barbara's low grunt, and Barry's raised voice becoming more strident, opening drawers and slamming cupboards. The easy option would be to just leave, visit later.

Linda walked through, 'Barry! What are you doing?'

He turned to look at her, 'What's it got to do with you?'

'Everything, your mother has a heart condition, and serious asthma,' she said, glancing at Barbara, who was decidedly breathless, immobile on the sofa, and flapping her hand. Linda handed her the inhaler she used, and looked at the mess Barry had made.

He sneered at Linda, then dived up the stairs. Linda began to pick everything up, slide drawers back into the sideboard and close cupboards.

'What's he looking for?' she said to Barbara.

'Money,' she gasped, 'always money.'

Her breathing was awful, and not for the first time Linda was aware of the huge gaps in her medical experience, envied Charlie the knowledge to be able to fix it. Gradually though, once her son had gone, Barbara was stable enough to speak.

'He's fiddled with that lock on the door, keeps coming in when he feels like it.'

'Do you want me to change the code?'

'No point, he'll just smash it off. He's angry, that's what it is.'

'What about?' Linda said, rearranging her newspapers and magazines.

'His father, his grandfather and most of all his bloody stepfather, they've all let him down you see.' She struggled to stand up, leaned on her walking frame. 'All a waste of space, men.'

'Not all men surely,' Linda said, throwing the cushions back on the chairs. 'I thought you liked Piers Morgan?'

'Only to look at,' she said, 'He talks a load of bullshit. They all do.'

Linda helped her on to the stair-lift, then went ahead and began to run the bath. Barry had even trashed the bathroom cabinet. She helped Barbara undress, sat her in the bath chair, lowered her into the water, then left her to wash herself. The last shreds of dignity.

In her bedroom; he'd flung everything out of the dressing table. Linda tidied up, put fresh underwear on the bed and collected up a trail of items off the landing. The second bedroom door was wide open.

She'd not been in this room before. It smelt musty and sweaty, and there was something else, cannabis maybe. Linda went to open the window, then stood for a moment and looked at the posters on the wall. It must have been Barry's room since he was a child, everything was stuck in the 70's and 80's and it took her back. Back to their schooldays, and it was oddly fascinating to look at the yellowing faces of Status Quo and Ozzy Osbourne. There was an old television with a games console. The lack of dust and the way they'd been moved around suggested Barry still used them. They looked quite new, all conflict based war games with acts of violence counting towards a win.

'Are you all right, Barbara?' Linda shouted, picking up beer cans, adult comics and empty food wrappers off the floor. She waited till Barbara answered in the affirmative, then went to close the window. When she pushed past the gaping wardrobe door, it swung open, hanging off one hinge. On the inside of the door were dozens of newspaper cuttings decorated with cigarette burns, and she wouldn't have given them another thought, had Daniel's face not stared back, and then it was impossible to ignore.

She looked more closely, some of the pieces were about the hotel, and there was a yellowing picture of Tomas Marshall, his arm around a young, grinning Daniel. Marshall and Woods win massive contract, it said. She knew Barry had always been jealous of Daniel, but he was forty something now for goodness sake. Linda looked round at the room, at the belongings of a sad man who'd never really grown up.

It could have been a teenager's bedroom. She could hear Barbara shouting her, something about the bath water being cold.

CHAPTER FOURTEEN

It was amazing what a computer could do these days, Daniel thought... amazing! He dropped the two brown envelopes into the post box and allowed himself a smile. Max must have paid plenty for that private detective. On the other hand, Daniel had paid nothing, another bonus.

Max had commissioned all the work, Daniel had merely recycled it. It was all the rage these days, recycling. It hadn't taken much effort at all, to scan one of the pictures of himself and Victoria onto his laptop, and then with a clever bit of software he'd managed to superimpose two other faces into the frame. Sarah Fox-Lloyd looked weird, a goofy schoolgirl's head on Victoria's womanly body. And Max, well he looked like Max when he was ultra-serious, posing for a newspaper advertisement for accounting, but on Daniel's body. It looked a bit indecent really. A teenager posing with a fifty year old man in the woods, but it got the message across. The message was practice what you preach. Or, more simply, you've been *had*.

It wasn't as slick as Max's trick, but Daniel hoped that Max would see the irony, the hypocritical humour. Max would receive one at his office, and Mr Big Deal Fox-Lloyd of North Wales Research would receive one at *his* office. Questions would be asked, who, what, why? It was a shame for Mr Fox-Lloyd really, but Daniel felt it was more a shame for Tina. As far as he knew Mr Fox Lloyd didn't have MS or any other condition that got worse with stress.

Charlie Summers had not gone back on his word. He'd called Daniel and they'd had a meeting at his house. It was like talking about someone he didn't know, but Charlie kept going over the parts he didn't understand. 'She will have had a clinical diagnosis, supported by a number of tests, including an MRI scan.'

'She told me that.'

'For accuracy, she must have had two or more attacks on the central nervous system; on two or more occasions.'

'Such as?'

'Well, this is where it gets individual and complicated. It could be an optic neuritis affecting her eyesight, or numbness in a limb, but that could signal other conditions, so there needs to be evidence of similar activity at least a month later.'

Daniel nodded; he could never be a doctor, everything would scare him witless. Trust Tina to have something with a name he couldn't pronounce and a list of ifs and maybes.

'But the human body is incredibly resourceful, it's never all bad news,' Charlie said, handing Daniel a glass of scotch, 'You know that more than the average guy, after your daughter's drug addiction.'

'You know about that?'

'Lin told me. I know you went to desperate measures to pull her through.'

'This seems worse,' Daniel said, swirling the liquid in his glass.

'It can be managed you know. Life expectancy is not affected.'

'She'll be on drugs all her life though, with it steadily getting worse.'

'Well yes *maybe*, but let's just say, as you found with Bluebell, there are some things we can't write a prescription for. Some things respond to the heart and mind.'

Charlie topped up his drink and asked after baby Lily.

Baby Lily was flourishing.

The previous week, Elle had stopped breast feeding and as a *non*-lactating mother, she'd discovered a new freedom. 'First, I'm going to *stuff* my face with this yummy soft cheese,' she said to Troy, pushing a huge wedge into her mouth, then held up a bottle of Chablis and waved it in Troy's direction. 'And I'm going to drink all of this wine, while you go to the chemist for me and buy a load of feeding bottles and some milk and stuff and on the way back, get me a chicken madras.'

The last instruction was delivered in a muffled voice, through a mouthful of ripe brie.

Troy, knowing better than to protest, waited till she'd gone and read out the list to Daniel with a growing disbelief '...breast pads, nipple cream, baby milk, laxatives *again?* Plus something for *thrush?* No way am I like, looking for all this in the chemist.'

'Ah, the romance of it.'

Daniel was stringing up heart-shaped lights across the decking, for the wedding on Saturday. He found his wallet and pushed a tenner at Troy's chest, 'Get me some Viagra will you?'

'You are *joking?*'

'Just about. You can get me a pack of razors though.'

Daniel grinned and watched Troy walk dispiritedly to his car, then tested the twinkly lights, perfect, or they would be once darkness fell. Everything had to be perfect for the Welsh Tourist Board entourage, in celebration of the marriage of Tegan to Aled.

The wedding party had booked the entire hotel for the whole weekend. They even wanted Bluebell to sing along to a harpist. Though try as he might, Daniel was struggling to find the enthusiasm and excitement which seemed to have gripped everyone else. Since Tina's news he struggled to concentrate on anything, if he was honest. Victoria had understood, so far but that was because she was distracted by all the preparations. There was a lot to be gained from the success of a prestigious wedding. The Celtic Catering Company could really take off, and it certainly wouldn't do the hotel any harm to gain a good reputation as a small private wedding venue. And no one could argue The Lakeside didn't look as if it had been made for weddings in the soft September light, perfect for romantic photography.

Daniel asked Victoria if she'd heard from Max. 'No, I wasn't expecting to. Why?'

'I Just wondered if he'd mentioned any photographs.'

She studied him for a full five seconds. 'Okay what have you done?'

'Just returned to sender, that's all.'

She knew there was more to it, and Daniel cracked eventually and told her the full story. She didn't find it as funny as Daniel did and she didn't like the fact he'd taken her school photograph.

'Why did you do that?' she said, adding fresh mint to some peas, before tasting. 'He'll retaliate and then it just escalates. I've told you before, Max is best ignored.'

She'd made dinner, local pheasant with wild rice, horseradish sauce and parsnip chips. It was probably some kind of experiment judging by the state of her kitchen, but Daniel didn't mind that. It was presented like a work of art, and tasted like nothing he'd ever tasted before, and for a while, Daniel couldn't remember what they were talking about.

'Anyway, it was years ago,' Victoria said, pouring a rich cabernet sauvignon into wine glasses.

'What was?'

'His affair with goofy.'

'Still did it though, didn't he?'

She put her knife and fork down. 'And this is all because you're upset about Tina getting the pictures?'

'It's part of it... yeah,' he said, and watched her carefully. Part of him knew she was tiring with the Tina story, but he couldn't help how he felt, it dominated his thoughts and anyway, he'd supported Victoria throughout her ordeal with Max.

'I went to see your doctor friend the other night.'

'Charlie?'

'Yeah, he's okay isn't he? Seems keen on Lin.'

'What did you see him about? Oh don't tell me I can guess,' she said, and drew her eyes from his, then went to clear their empty plates. He grabbed her wrist, and pulled her onto his lap. 'I needed to know the facts, like I would for anyone I know.'

'I'm sorry,' she said quietly, 'I feel tetchy, big weekend coming up.'

Daniel inhaled the perfume of her, closed his eyes and stroked the tension out of her, began to kiss her. 'Just bear with me, please.'

She nodded and smiled, 'You look tired.'

'It's that bloody caravan bed,' he said, stretching, 'It's giving me a bad back. And the dog uses me as a cushion sometimes and his breath is not the sweetest.'

'Sleep here then,' she said, 'In fact, why don't you move in?'

It sounded simple. Maybe it was. His mother would love him to be with someone like Victoria. If Victoria was Mrs Woods, how easy his life would be. How lucky would he be to have this woman in his bed every night, to have her look after his every whim, to have her take care of him?

He'd actually already promised the caravan to Mandy. She wanted to come back to work but she'd been thrown out by the council for non-payment of rent and she was stuck in a miserable bed and breakfast which was nowhere near a bus route. Troy had come across her, sobbing on a wooden bench on the seafront in town, all her bags and belongings at her feet. Daniel felt sorry for her, no parents, an older sister she was estranged from and Tina miles away with a condition she didn't understand.

Victoria ran him a warm bath, then made him lie down and massaged his back.

'You've got a great body,' she said, 'like you belong to an expensive gym.'

Daniel grunted into the pillow, befuddled with food and drink and a proper warm bed.

'The building site. You'd never get membership, it's pretty exclusive.'

She laughed, 'Do I need a pencil behind my ear?'

'Yeah, only for concentration and a steel tape, always need that.'

The next thing he knew, it was pitch black. He folded himself round the sleeping woman beside him. She turned over and whispered, 'You were out cold.'

'What did you do to me?'

'It was just baby oil mixed with some patchouli.'

'It must be a spell. Do it again.'

'No. Dan, it's past three in the morning...'

He began to kiss her smiling mouth, and slowly, he felt her hands travel up his back behind his shoulder blades. One leg slid over his. Daniel pulled her in to his body and she began to respond. Slow uncomplicated sex in the middle of the night. Tina used to say there were only two valid reasons for waking her in the night; if someone famous had died, or it was snowing.

*

The following morning, Mandy was happily installed in the caravan and Bear was back in his bunk bed next door. He was a lot less pleased than his sister-in-law, and when Daniel moved his food bowls and his blanket, he look positively *betrayed*. His mother looked at Daniel's piled up cases in the hotel reception and pursed her lips, although it wasn't as upsetting as the dog's reaction. It was the sorrowful eyes that did it, and then the tail between the legs, no words necessary.

'It's a ridiculous situation!' Marian said, banging the stapler down on the desk. 'Now where are you going to go?'

'I'm working on it.'

'You'll have to stay with me, there's nothing else for it. I'll make up the spare room.'

'Right.'

Daniel scanned through the local agents on his laptop. He started looking at rentals, then got distracted by cheap, falling down cottages for sale down the valley, and how easily he could sort them all out. Mike and Linda's house was there, sold subject to contract. And there was a flat available in the same building as Victoria, available immediately.

A couple of phone calls later, and the problem was sorted. He called his mother first and told her. She sighed and tutted, 'Oh, all right. I still think it's a ridiculous situation.'

Victoria was even less pleased with him.

When Daniel saw her, his heart turned over and he wondered, not for the first time if he was doing the right thing. Her eyes lit up when she saw him, and he kissed her first, then explained that he was moving in to Mike's spare room for a while.

Her face fell. 'I see,' she said, but she obviously didn't see, because she turned her back to him, and resumed working at her desk.

'Vic?'

'Am I allowed to know why?' she said, calling up her e-mails. She kept her eyes on the screen but Daniel could see her reflection in the dark bits, basically upset and tearful.

'I just think... I just think it's too soon... timing's not great.'

There was a horrible silence and when he went to touch her shoulder, she blocked his hand with her arm, then resumed what she was doing.

Daniel felt a huge weight settle in his stomach. 'Do you want to discuss this or not?'

'There's nothing to discuss.'

'I'll just go,' he said softly, 'if you're busy.'

*

Much later, around midnight, Daniel arrived at Mike's, 'Sorry it's late, loads of problems at the hotel. Why does stuff break down when you really don't need the hassle?'

'Cars are the just the same, bloody inconsiderate.'

'The hot water system failed,' he said, following Mike up the stairs with his bags, 'Got that sorted then someone managed to block the wash basin in room two, water everywhere.' Daniel grinned at the Star Wars duvet set, 'Nice.'

'Do you want beer, beer or beer? I don't think there's much else in.'

'I think I'll have a beer.'

'What's that smell?'

'Baby oil mixed with patchouli.'

Mike grinned, nodded, 'Yeah? Takes me back to the eighties that does.'

'Yeah, good times.'

They flipped open cans and discussed the usual subjects. It was always sport first, football results and Formula One. Then it was how Daniel's car was running and the motor industry in general. Then it was more in-depth work and business matters. That exhausted, it became gradually more personal, and the house sale was first.

'Where are you going to go?' Daniel said, but Mike just shrugged, opened another can, 'How about you?'

Daniel talked about his idea of buying a rundown cottage for Troy, Elle and baby Lily. Troy had really stepped up to the mark over the last few weeks and Daniel felt it was time they had a proper home, and then Daniel could move back into the hotel. Problem sorted.

'I'm not just giving it to him. He can rent it off me till he's paid for it.'

'That's reasonable enough,' Mike said, and propped his legs on the coffee table. 'Lin's been pretty reasonable really.'

'She's that sort of person, grounded.'

'Yeah.'

'No chance of a recovery?'

'Nah, fucked up big style didn't I?'

'Would you go back to her if you thought there was a chance?'

'No. Tried that, it didn't work,' he said, then looked at Daniel with narrowed eyes, 'Don't tell me, please tell me you're *not* getting back with Tina?'

'Tina? She wouldn't have me back after what I've done. Anyway we're talking about you.'

'Are we?'

Daniel stood up, rubbed his hair and eyes. 'Victoria wants me to move in with her.'

'So, what you doing *here?*'

'I need some breathing space.'

'From *Victoria?* Are you *nuts?*'

Probably. He'd tried calling her but she wouldn't answer. Before he went to sleep, Daniel resorted to a text, but she didn't reply to that either and he had a mostly sleepless night, feeling anxious about the wedding arrangements. He'd given Chef the weekend off.

The day of the wedding fulfilled everyone's expectations, warm and dry with the smallest breath of wind pushing around a handful of golden leaves on the surface of the lake, floating like natures confetti. Daniel pulled in to the car park, next to Victoria's blue Mazda and he sat for a moment, wallowing in the relief.

Mandy was scrubbing bird dirt off the meerkat in the shrubs. She had a new uniform, a dark blue boiler suit, but all seemed well with her world and she even grinned at Daniel. Bear came to jump at his legs, all excitable and waggy, offering a soggy ball, throwing it at his feet over and over till master gave in and slung it halfway up Crimpiau. Forgiven.

Daniel wandered around his empire, noting with satisfaction that none of the staff were hung over and all were employed with the business in hand. Elle was sat on reception with Lily in her moses basket. Troy and Tristan were restocking the bar, Sue and Carys were laying tables. The florist was making amazing arty creations with white and cream flowers and a lot of ferns. She told him with a slightly concerned expression that Tony was scattering rose petals on the bridal bed.

There was a harp on the decking, new church candles in the lanterns and a white silken banner proclaiming the marriage of Aled to Tegan. Bluebell was in the middle of a practice session. She was laughing a lot with a skinny youth in white drainpipe jeans, who was playing a fiddle and larking about. It was strange to see her laughing so much, but it was the only thing to put a real smile on Daniel's face.

Victoria was in the kitchen with Anton and Emily, but she barely acknowledged Daniel was there, just nodded in his direction as if they hardly knew each other, and his smile faded. Emily and Anton were in high spirits, prepping food and folding napkins, and didn't notice the awkwardness.

Victoria looked efficient in her starched white uniform, dark hair swept up, dark eyes on the row of Post-it notes she'd made, dotted along the plate rack. Daniel made himself a coffee from the espresso machine and hung about, waited till Emily and Anton took plates and cutlery through to the tables.

'How are you?' he said, practically tongue tied.

She looked at him briefly, 'Fine, lots to do.'

'Can I make you a coffee?'

'Yeah, that would be good thanks.'

Daniel passed her the coffee and her hand brushed his. 'I'm sorry if I upset you,' he said and she looked at him for about two seconds.

'You're in my way, Dan.'

*

Later, Marian arrived to take care of Lily so that Elle and Troy could work through.

'I'll take her upstairs, we can sit on the balcony and watch everything going on,' his mother said with a beaming smile, 'I've got the best job today.'

The wedding party began to arrive late afternoon.

The bride wore sheer, sleek white silk, and carried blood red roses. One small bridesmaid in blood red silk, carrying a basket of white roses which looked nearly dead but no one was bothered by then. The groom, all light grey with a blood red silk square in his top pocket, had already loosened his tie. They spent some time down by the side of the lake near the broken canoes with their daring photographer perched up a tree. It looked modern and natural, the bridesmaid happily playing to the camera and making them laugh, the bride unsteady on her heels and holding on to her new husband.

Daniel was reminded of his own wedding day. The pictures were still upstairs in the box they'd arrived in. Tina had taken the only decent one to the flat, the one where Daniel was actually wearing his suit. The others looked like a cross between Ferris Bueller's Day Off and Four Weddings and a Funeral. He even had a pencil behind his ear in one of the pictures. Tina's dad was propped up in quite a few.

Considering everything that had happened since that day, it seemed another age away, and yet it was only months. Daniel looked at the wedding pictures quite a lot, not really knowing what he was looking for, the only answer they gave him was one of haste and regret. He wanted to explain all of this to Victoria but she wouldn't even look at him.

He wanted to explain to her that for the first time in his life he'd slowed down to think. To think and listen, to his own voice as well as that of his mother and Tina, Troy and anyone else who'd tried to talk to him the last few years. What Tina had done had stopped him in his tracks.

Victoria skilfully avoided him. At the end of play, she cleared away the leftover food, washed down the kitchen surfaces, mopped the floor and wrote up her notes in Chef's special diary. Then she locked the kitchen door and went to put the keys behind the reception desk.

'Emily's gone into town, for her brother's birthday,' she said, rummaging in her handbag for car keys. She said it as a statement, not inviting his reply.

'Oh, yeah she did mention something, no problem,' Daniel said, 'Vic come and have a drink with me, please.'

'No thanks I'm shattered, I'm going home,' she said, and without a backward glance she pushed her way out, through the crowd of guests milling at the door.

Around ten in the evening, a massive drumroll signalled the start of the entertainment. It was party time for friends of the bride and groom. Bluebell was guesting as lead vocal with a Welsh rock band, and the deck was alive with people dancing, laughing and drinking. The lights were twinkling, the candles were flickering, and the lake was illuminated with fireworks. There was a noisy crowd down by the water, and Daniel sent Tony to keep a discreet eye on them.

He tried calling Victoria, but she was still blanking him. Irritated and fed-up, he grabbed himself a large glass of whisky from the bar and watched everyone having a good time, but then had to remind himself that he couldn't have another, as he had to drive to Mike's, so he just sat for a while, watching Troy show off his skills with cocktail shakers, wearing the pork pie hat tipped over one eye. Cocky and back on form.

The smell was not intrusive at first. At first, everyone thought someone had knocked over a candle or it was just the fireworks. Daniel finished his drink and pushed his way back through the crowds of jostling people, towards the reception. There was a faint whisper of something acrid in the atmosphere, but there was no fire alarm, no jets of water from the sensitive, hellishly expensive system he'd been persuaded to install.

Feeling uneasy, he wandered the ground floor, noting from the signing in book that the hotel was full to capacity. Upstairs, the smell was heavier and he tried to tell himself it wasn't smoke. His phone rang. Tony.

'Boss? Problem. Something going on here, from where I'm standing looks like a small fire under the decking.'

'Can we deal with it? Or do I get everyone out?'

'Hard to say. Pass me an extinguisher over the side.'

It was easier said than done, dropping a heavy duty, bright red fire extinguisher over the side of the deck without alarming anyone. Daniel had to push past the band in full throttle. Tony was knee deep in the water, and he grabbed the equipment quickly.

'If you haven't got it under control in five, I'm getting everyone out,' Daniel shouted.

Tony disappeared in the dark undergrowth, and Bluebell took centre stage. No one noticed anything unusual, his daughter was captivating enough. The fiddle player gave her an introduction as the new voice of Seren Cymraeg, and the audience gave her a massive roar of appreciation. Daniel dove back up the stairs, still no alarm, so nothing to panic about.

Daniel panicked.

'Mum! Open the door,' he yelled, trying the handle. He could only hear the deafening roar downstairs, thumping bass and ear splitting drumrolls.

Elle was right behind him. 'What's going on? Why are you running about?'

Daniel looked at the solid oak door, waited for a gap in the bass riff then shouted again.

Elle grabbed his arm, 'What's that smell? Dan?'

'I don't know, it's probably nothing,' he said and looked at her for all of two seconds, but it was long enough for her to guess what he was thinking.

Elle screamed, 'Lily's in there!'

'I *know*, stop panicking.'

Daniel went back down the stairs, pushed roughly through the crowds again, shoved the fiddle player out of the way and stood on the decking rail. Some of the audience obviously thought it was part of the act and he attracted a few token claps and drunken jeers. He could feel his phone buzzing in his back pocket but it was probably Tony. He hoped he had the sense to call emergency services. God knows where he got the strength from but he somehow managed to hoist himself onto the complicated wooden facade and climb up the front of the building, and onto the balcony. For a few seconds he was distracted by a small fire licking around the base of the fir trees and spreading through the dry undergrowth, but it was impossible to tell how far it had got under the decking, or how much of the gable end of the building was smouldering.

The balcony doors were mercifully unlocked and he burst into the room like James Bond or some mad super hero.

His mother nearly had a heart attack.

'Daniel! ... *what?* What on *earth* are you doing?'

'Didn't you hear me shouting and banging on the door?'

She shook her head, 'No. I've just got Lily down,' she went on then followed him about with a frown, '*Daniel!*'

He picked the baby up out of her cot, and she started to grizzle, 'There's a fire, can't you smell it?'

'No.' Her hand flew to her mouth, 'Oh my God!'

When he got the door open, Elle was still there sobbing and smacking the wall. She took Lily from him and his mother looked around in horror, at the thin film of smoke drifting along the top of the ceiling.

'Why are there no alarms?' she said. 'Where is it coming from?'

'I don't know!'

Daniel took hold of her arm and propelled her outside into the car park with Elle and the baby on his heels. He unlocked his car, threw his keys on the seat.

'Stay there, Elle? Make sure you and Mum *stay there*. If there's a problem, drive *away.*'

She nodded glumly and Daniel noticed Victoria's car. She'd come back.

Troy waved at him from the hotel steps, 'Dad, what's going on? Why are you all in the car park? Some of us can smell burning.'

'Call the fire brigade, I'll get everyone out. You stay *here*. Do a head count.'

Troy shouted after him, 'Victoria's looking for you, she was in the bar.'

'Right.'

Daniel left him shouting into his phone, pacing about with one finger in his ear. There was a small stampede spilling out of the main doors, demanding to know what was going on and why was there no fire alarm? Tegan, still in her bridal finery ran down the steps with her father in his dressing gown and the little girl bridesmaid in her nightwear. Behind them, the mother of the bride was still clutching a glass of champagne in one hand, grandmother of the bride on the other arm. Mandy brought up the rear, carefully carrying a large lamb pie to safety.

It looked surreal, nearly as mad as his own wedding day.

Daniel made his way back inside and grabbed the microphone from his daughter, wondering what the hell to say. The young crowd on the decking, mostly drunk and making a lot of noise had no idea there was anything untoward happening. All the time he was speaking as slowly and calmly as he could his eyes were scanning the crowd looking for Victoria. Speech done, he told Bluebell to go to his car, but she hung about, looking or waiting for someone. A couple of idiots tried to climb over the glass wall and jump into the lake, but Sue and Tristan managed to stop the flow of lunacy.

In reception, there was a more serious build-up of smoke. Somehow it had doubled its capacity in about half a minute, rapidly filling the stairwell, growing into a darker, toxic cloud and it was billowing, rather than drifting.

The fire alarm had failed *big* time, he'd sue the bloody alarm company over this. Fuelled with anger, Daniel ran upstairs, threw open the fire escape at the end of the corridor, then started banging on all the doors. Some opened, some didn't. The best man came out of one of them, with his clothes on back to front and an inhaler clamped between his teeth.

In the middle of everyone trying to get down the stairs, Bluebell was trying to fight her way up. 'Dad, where's Cupcake? Marian had her.'

'Bluebell go outside *now*.'

'Dad, *please..*'

'She'll have run out. Go outside.'

Daniel waited till he'd seen her turn and trudge back, swept along with the flow of people, then he went down the corridor, looking in all the rooms. Anton had been and checked the staff rooms, and Daniel saw him dragging along a traumatised Carys, a bottle of cider and the bridal bouquet in her hands.

'Have you seen Victoria?' he said, but they both shook their heads.

'Place is empty, even checked the toilets. Dan come on, come outside.'

'I'm right behind you.'

Only he wasn't.

The lights went next, and suddenly it became more serious. Deadly serious. For a moment, Daniel couldn't see very much but he knew every inch of the place, and felt his way along the wall. He could feel the smoke then, feel it attack his lungs and he pulled his shirt up over his face. Someone had opened the door into the balcony room because there was a vestige of light tunnelling through the smog. He needed to shut it again and halt the path of the fire as much as possible, then get out. He needed to get out.

But it looked like someone was in there.

He saw Max first.

He was shouting with a handkerchief over his mouth, 'Why the hell did you come back?'

Victoria was holding Bluebell's little dog inside her jacket. He could just see her outline and she seemed carved in stone, rooted to the spot. When she recognised Daniel she sprang to life but Max stood in her way.

'Dan! I couldn't find you,' she said, part crying, part coughing, make-up streaming down her face. Daniel pulled Max's arm round, 'Get out of her way!'

'Why don't you get out of *my* way, get out of my face, in

fact get *out of my life,* Woods!' he said, but kept his eyes on Victoria. There was something different about him, his usual suave exterior had gone. He was more like an overwound clockwork toy, and Daniel realised he was actually rigid with fear, irrational. 'We were all right till you came along!'

'Max, get a grip. We're all going to die in here if we don't shift.'

Another voice in the room said, 'Die? That's maximum points. *Game Over.*'

Daniel couldn't see all of Victoria's face, couldn't make out her exact expression, but he knew she was looking at someone stood behind him, could sense her abject fear. She put a hand out to him, and her voice came out as a strangled whisper, 'Dan...'

He turned in time to see Barry Jones. The bulk of him filled the door frame, blocking their best means of escape. Max looked equally shocked to see him. '*You!* You brainless idiot.'

'What's the matter? It's all gone to plan,' he said, then lost interest in Max, 'Get out of here, posh boy, leave it to me.'

His hooded eyes settled on Daniel. They were dead eyes full of hate, like a shark hunting down prey. Daniel dodged out of his way but Jones was surprisingly fast on his feet for a big guy and grabbed the front of Daniel's jacket, pushed him till they both fell backwards over the coffee table. It collapsed instantly. Daniel felt the decorative marble apples beneath his back as Jones sprawled on top of him. In a superior position then on his knees, Barry grasped Daniel round the throat, and it was like twenty-five years ago. This time though there was more at stake than the 3b science project.

The next few seconds were the longest of his life, some of it even flashed before his eyes. Death by strangulation, a big pair of hands around his neck squeezing the life out of him.

Victoria screamed, 'Max, help him!'

'Why the hell should I do that?'

On the point of blacking out, Daniel heard some sort of scuffle and the pressure around his throat relaxed ever so slightly, enough for him to take a breath and bring up his knee hard between Barry's legs. He made a noise like an animal.

'You fight like a bloody girl, Woods,' he snarled, holding his crotch. Daniel could feel the broken leg of the coffee table under his hand and somehow he managed to manoeuvre it into his grip. He slashed it hard across the side of Barry's head. Slightly stunned, he closed his eyes just long enough for Daniel to scramble away; but not quite long enough. A booted foot made hard contact with his ribs and Daniel was bent double, gasping for breath, crawling across the floor, then finding the sofa and using it to stagger to his feet. His throat felt scorched, bruised. Out of the corner of his eye, Max was trying to pull Victoria away but she struggled against him.

Barry started to laugh, and there was a touch of insanity about it. He picked up the table leg and advanced towards Daniel, swiping at him as if it were a sword, driving him towards the balcony. Disorientated and dizzy, Daniel staggered backwards, skating over the marble apples. He picked one up, felt the smooth weight of it.

'Fancy a bit of free fall, eh, Woods?'

He could see the fire was just starting to curl around the bottom of the balustrades. To the left it was an abyss of burning sections of seasoned oak, and black charred trees. To the right, the wedding sash and the white table linen were still fluttering in the dark, decorated with flying fragments. The lake was glowing in the moonlight, appearing like molten liquid where it met the reflection of the fire.

'Go on, Woods. I saw you shin up it like superman,' Barry grinned, 'now, why don't you fucking *fly off it?*'

Daniel aimed the marble ball just as Barry stepped on to the balcony. There was a cracking sound, so loud it could have been wood or it could have been bone. At first, Barry fell towards him, slain like Goliath, and for a moment time seemed to stand still. Daniel couldn't tell if it was intentional that Barry went to clutch the front of his jacket as he went down, but in the seconds that followed he found himself shoved hard against the top of the handrail. Daniel struggled to release Barry's grip, but everything suddenly seemed to tilt and slide beneath him, and they were both falling, and the sensation of it went on forever.

He could hear Victoria screaming his name, or maybe it was in his imagination.

He could hear sirens. Thank God, he could hear sirens.

Then everything stopped and there was nothing, not even his imagination.

CHAPTER FIFTEEN

They were walking barefoot along the beach and it was hot and he was thirsty. They should have been at school but it was a summer day in June and Tina had made a picnic of chocolate, cigarettes and vodka. They were drunk before lunch time, making out in the sand dunes. Afterwards, because she had sand in her toes and her sandals were rubbing, Daniel gave her a piggy back over the pebbles, but he'd waded into the sea and she'd been furious because he'd dropped her. They were on holiday and it was hot, and he was still thirsty. They were in the pool and Tina looked gorgeous in her white bikini. They'd had a stupid fight about where to go for the day and ended up doing nothing very much. Tina was cross with him, but when he scooped up some water and sprayed her, she was laughing at the same time. She swam across, into his arms and just when he thought she was going to kiss him and he was forgiven, she shoved his head under the water.

He wasn't expecting it, hadn't taken a breath deep enough. The bitch was trying to drown him, just because he hadn't wanted to go to some stupid handbag factory. For a few seconds he thought his lungs would explode. He fought his way to the surface, but the water was deeper than he thought, he was drowning, couldn't find another breath...

He could hear a horrible retching sound, deep under the water because there was a gurgling sucking noise as well. Pain,

intense and then light so bright he must have finally reached
the surface. Someone was holding his hand; a woman's hand,
but not Tina's, and he would likely be in trouble over that as
well. They had amazing fights, she gave him a proper hard
time but he loved that about her. She had real passion and
fire in her.

Fire.

There was a fire in the garden, but he was still hot and thirsty
even though it was cold and dark. They were all wrapped up
and holding sparklers, writing each other's names in the black
sky. Victoria was there and she'd been crying. It made him feel
distressed, but instead of doing something about it, he walked
right into the middle of the bonfire. Some idiot had made it
on a steep slope, so instead of the ground staying level beneath
his feet, he began to fall. At the bottom he put his hands out
and the noises were there again. Maybe they were putting the
fire out.

Pain, intense light, so bright it made him screw up his
eyes. Someone was calling his name. It sounded like his father,
shouting at him to get out of bed or he'd miss the school bus.

'If I have to come up those stairs...'

But he must have come up the stairs because his face was
right there, and his arms were right there, pulling him up. Even
when he imagined he was upright there was still a sensation of
being pulled up, pulled out?

It was something to do with sons and fathers anyway. He
was watching Troy play in the garden; so happy he could burst.
Tina smiled at him, told him she was happy too. 'Do you think
we should try for another baby?'

'After what you went through?'

'I'd do it again, if you wanted me to.'

'Would you, love?' he said, and he remembered thinking
he was with the most amazing woman that ever walked the
earth.

Maybe he was being reborn. Maybe he'd died and he was

being reincarnated. After a while he realised what it was. Someone was pulling his insides out of his gullet, dragging and tugging, and the gurgling sucking noise grew louder. When he tried to take a tiny painful breath it made him retch because there was something down his throat. And then coughing, so painful it seemed to split his head open. Even breathing hurt, and there was something horrible in his mouth, something that shouldn't be there.

'Daniel, wake up.'

Wake up? He wasn't asleep, was he? His mind went on random search in the way that dreams did, picking up threads of memory and mixing it with the here and now to see if it made any better sense. He knew his mouth was open but when he went to speak nothing happened.

Daniel woke up, but quickly wished he hadn't.

Everything screamed with pain, even his eyelids, so he closed them again, but the woman holding his hand wouldn't let him drift off back to where he'd been. When he took in his surroundings, the first thing he noticed was that the walls were off white, dingy with a flowery border. It looked familiar, the border. Daisies and cornflowers on a repeat pattern, with a green fern every third daisy. He moved his head slightly and the woman holding his hand came into focus. He had no idea who she was, and although she was smiling, her eyes were concerned.

'Welcome back.'

Where from? Where the hell had he been? He hadn't been on holiday had he? Daniel remembered where he'd seen the border; it was Bangor hospital where Lily was born. *Shit.* He was in hospital. Voices, more urgent then bleeping machinery.

Someone asked him his full name and where he lived, and did he know who the Prime Minister was? Why were they asking him that? If they'd asked Tina she wouldn't have known, and she'd never have got out of there. Even when he told them who the Chancellor of the Exchequer was as well for good measure, they all just grinned. For all his political knowledge it didn't look as if it would get him a passport to freedom. He wasn't going anywhere. The nurse holding his hand told him he'd been in intensive care on a ventilator for two days. The pain was due to multiple fractures in his collar bone and right arm, three broken ribs and severe bruising to his back and throat, and one broken finger.

But they told him he was *lucky*.

Lucky he had no severe head or spinal injuries. He was allowed one visitor for five minutes. She'd waited thirty-six hours they told him, slept in the waiting room and wouldn't go home till she'd seen he was awake and breathing by himself. Presently, Tina shuffled in. She looked tear-stained and dishevelled like a tramp, with a shopping bag and a blanket trailing behind her.

'Oh, Dan, what the hell have you done?'

She gently kissed his face and hair, as she threaded her fingers through his. His arm didn't stretch very far because of the drip in it so she had to stand by the bed, 'Everyone's been worried sick. I even prayed for you.'

'Why?' His voice came out a hoarse whisper and it sounded far away, like an echo.

'*Why?* You've been in an accident. Troy called me. He didn't know what else to do.'

'Dad was here, where's he gone?'

She frowned, looked briefly at the drips and monitors, 'No, no you must have been dreaming, you're full of morphine.'

'Why? What happened?'

Tina looked at him perplexed. He could recite facts, but he couldn't make sense of anything else. He wanted to ask a lot of questions but couldn't form them in his head, let alone make them come out of his mouth but she understood that and squeezed his hand.

It made him feel incredibly vulnerable, helpless like Lily.

'Tee, I want to go home,' he said, knowing he sounded pathetic, 'Help me get out of here. I don't feel very well.'

For a moment, Tina looked overwhelmed but then bit her lip and smiled through it, like she did when Troy was little and had to have his tonsils out. 'You can't, love. Not yet.'

*

After four days of lying in a sedated trance, they moved him to the High Dependency Unit. The nurse looking after him was called Pat. She told Daniel she was fifty-six, married with three grown up children and had worked on HDU for four years. Daniel couldn't have cared less but she insisted on telling him all the facts, dragged him slowly into a conversation, although Daniel's response was mostly a grunt, or one word. She was stoic, with a sort of bland seen it all before empathy when he whimpered about the pain, and the way his body constantly retched up the debris left by the ventilator and the smoke inhalation. But on the other hand, he couldn't have coped with anything emotive, so her demeanour was clever really, although her sense of humour was mostly sarcasm directed at men.

Pat asked about his family, already knew the names of his wife, son, daughter and mother.

'How do you know all that?' Daniel mumbled.

'How do I *know*?' she said, checking his chart. 'They're on the phone day and night asking about you. Feels like I know them.'

'I don't want to see anyone.'

'What's up with you today?'

'Not slept.'

'Is that all? Got out of bed on the wrong side have we?'

'Is that meant to be fucking funny?'

'Stop swearing,' she snarled gently, 'most fellas enjoy it in here, nice lie down, nurses waiting on them hand and foot. When you get to go on the recovery ward you can watch sport all day, and then it's just like being at home really.'

She made it sound like a hotel, and Daniel could see the irony.

As soon as he could string two sentences together, the police paid a visit; a ferrety looking man and a big butch woman. Pat told them they had five minutes, but she had to stay in the room to keep an eye on his blood pressure.

They were interested in the abrasions on his throat.

'You say someone tried to strangle you?'

'Not *someone*, Barry Jones.'

They made a lot of notes, asked about the fire and the fall from the balcony. Then it struck him that Victoria was his key witness really. If she'd not come back to see him that night, Max and Barry could have stitched him up. Daniel was surprised by how stressed it made him feel, how laboured his breathing became. Pat glanced across, slipped an oxygen mask over his face and gave the police a dirty look. They hung around, expecting him to make some sort of miraculous recovery. When he suddenly started retching over the side of the bed, they sloped off.

Pat said calmly, 'Did you do that on purpose, to get rid of them?'

Daniel lay back exhausted with it all, and made a derisory noise.

'Next time, not all over the floor,' she said in his face. 'I have to clear it up.'

*

Eventually, with his agreement, visitors were allowed. Family only, one at a time, ten minutes. His mother was first. It was quite obvious she was trying to hold a tidal wave of emotion behind a brisk wall of uninteresting facts. Troy, Elle and the baby, and Bluebell were all staying in the bungalow with her but Daniel couldn't even pretend to be interested in any of it. There were so many questions in his head, but even the energy required to put them all into coherent words, was beyond him. She'd brought him some pyjamas and a dressing gown and various sundry items.

'By the time I can get those on, I'm out of here,' Daniel said. His voice sounded like he'd been smoking fifty fags a day and licking the ashtrays as well.

'Don't be silly! What are you going to do? Catch a bus, dragging a drip stand behind you?'

'If I have to.'

He was relieved when her time was up, which kind of shocked him.

Then as Marian was leaving, Victoria tried to enter the room, held the door open with her hand and foot. Daniel knew she was there, knew her voice. She confessed to not being family and there followed a quiet confrontation with Pat, until Daniel called her name and she was allowed five minutes.

Victoria didn't look as if she belonged in the hospital even as a visitor. There was a freshness about her in her vibrant clothes, her clean glossy hair and her quick step. Her vitality made Daniel yearn for the loss of his own. Close up though, even her clever make-up couldn't hide the fact she'd been crying for days. There were dark circles under her red eyes, and she burst into tears again as soon as she saw Daniel.

'Dan, Oh God I thought you were going to die!' she said dramatically through a handful of tissues, and Daniel could sense Pat stiffening with concern, glancing up from her notes.

Daniel said, 'Come on, love, I'm okay.'

'That's the *dumbest,* most *stupidest* thing you've ever, *ever* said.'

'I'm not dead, come here,' he said, and she kissed him carefully on the mouth.

Slowly, in-between wiping her eyes, she began to tell him about her ordeal with Max and the police. How they'd both been taken in for hard core questioning after just one night in hospital. Apparently everything was all over the papers but Daniel couldn't have cared less about any of it. She took his disinterest as discomfort, and put two fingers to his lips, 'It's all right don't talk, I know it must hurt to even breathe.'

Her familiar perfume wafted over him, her hair touched his shoulder, but even that was almost too much, too potent with memories and requiring something from him he just couldn't give. It took him back to the room in her flat with the muslin curtains blowing in the sea breeze. All he could do was lie there, thinking.

When Pat looked at his face and indicated that her time was up, Victoria stopped at the door and looked back at him, mouthed that she loved him, but Daniel couldn't even smile at her, could only nod. Like some stupid dumb invalid.

*

When Pat went off duty at tea time, there was a young male nurse called Dean who was too brisk and cheerful, but he tolerated Daniel's swearing and could rattle off the sports results. Dean looked inside the bag Daniel's mother had left and grinned. 'Nice, kind of *cosy*. What you'd call high dependency PJ's.'

Daniel almost smiled, but even that was an effort.

'Too many visitors?' Dean said, catching his expression. 'Hard work most of them. Needy, they are.'

The police returned a couple of days later, the most needy of all.

'How are you today, Daniel?' the ferret said.

'Same shit as before.'

He pulled a chair over to the bedside. 'Got some bad news for you. One of your employees died on the night of the fire,' he said, glancing at his notebook. 'Mr Lovell, Tony Lovell.'

He gave Daniel a few moments to digest this, then he said, 'I'm very sorry but I'm going to have to ask you some questions. Are you okay with that?'

He must have nodded. He wasn't okay with it, not really, but he was desperate for some hard facts. His mother, Troy and Bluebell told him very little about the hotel other than the place was cordoned off and police and forensics were crawling all over the place. Everyone was being interviewed.

The police said Tony had sustained a blow to the back of the head, which wouldn't have been fatal had he not fallen face first into a few inches of water. They confirmed to Daniel that the fire was deliberate and that the alarm system had failed because it had been tampered with.

'Where's Jones?' Daniel said, closing his eyes.

'Don't worry, he's not going anywhere,' the ferrety one said, 'He's not very well either. What can you tell me about your relationships with Max and Victoria Morgan?'

Pat looked at him, 'Are you all right with this?'

'Yeah, get it over with.'

*

Mia arrived later. She demanded she see Daniel immediately because he was the father of her child, she had a plane to catch for a TV show and a taxi waiting outside.

'Tell him it's Mia *Woods.*'

Pat said in a bored voice, 'Wait *here.*'

Daniel didn't want to see her. Mia was the last person on earth anyone would want to see if they were incapacitated, and after the police interview and the news about Tony, he'd had enough for the day. When Pat smugly relayed the information, he could hear Mia kicking off outside the door, starting with the, don't you know who I am routine, right down to plain old begging. She went eventually, but not until she'd issued vague threats about written complaints. Daniel only relaxed when he heard her heels snapping back down the corridor.

He wondered what Pat must make of his visitors and the story he told to the police, all of it really. She always found something to do, checking equipment or writing notes, pretending not to listen.

'My life sounds like a cheap film,' Daniel said. 'Manslaughter, drugs, arson and an affair with a beautiful woman. I even stole a Husky and ripped up a kid's trampoline.'

'None of my business,' she said, fixing a pressure cuff to his arm, 'I just want to see you walk out of here unaided.'

'My wife has MS,' he said, 'She spent a day and a night on a waiting room bench.'

'Your wife?' Pat stopped squeezing the little pump, contemplated this information, then carried on looking at the blood pressure dial. After a while she said, 'She must think a lot of you. That waiting room is the last place on earth I'd like to spend a day and a night.'

'Will you make a phone call for me?'

'You want me to call your wife? Not sure which one that is.'

'No, call my son. I want him to go check on her.'

Troy came to see him the following day and Daniel could tell he was agitated because his arms and legs were twitchy. They went through the usual exchange of information, then Daniel said, 'Have you seen your mum, where is she?'

'Dad she's gone home, she's *shattered*. She missed that appointment with the specialist because she was camped out *here,*' Troy said, trying to hide his anger from Pat. Pat had her head down, sterilising something in the sink.

'Not my fault,' Daniel said, knowing full well it was. It popped into his head then, something Tina had said about *praying* for him. What was that about? The Tina Bradshaw he knew didn't do religion or sentiment.

'Course it's your fault!' Troy said vehemently, then lowered his voice, 'All this death and destruction *is* your fault. You and *Victoria*. I hope she was worth it. *Tony...*' His face twisted, he looked up at the ceiling for a second then suddenly went from the room.

Pat looked across to Daniel, 'Want me to go after him?'

Daniel shook his head, and she looked a bit closer, 'Sure?'

A man had lost his life because he'd had an affair. He'd had an affair with a woman who'd carried a lethal combination of conditions with her. Three months, that was all. What did it really add up to? Daniel could feel his eyes welling up, but not for himself.

'Emotional fallout's sometimes worse than the broken bones,' Pat said sagely, and looked at the drip, 'Want some more morphine?'

'Give me all of it.'

She made a harrumphing noise, 'No can do. Anyway, good looking fella like you with a sense of humour and three women on the go should soon be up and about.'

Troy came back about two hours later, threw himself down on the chair by the bed and tried to hug his father, tears streaming down his face. 'Dad, I'm sorry... *I'm sorry.*'

Pat had to stop Troy mauling him, made him sit back in the chair and rubbed his shoulder. 'Your dad can't cope with that, love. Not yet eh?'

*

After what seemed a life time but was in fact only a matter of weeks, Daniel was moved to a general ward. He was lucky, they said, he had a bed by the window. The downside was the five other occupants and the visiting system, which was open season. Anyone could come and go as they pleased, the prospect of which scared him more than the foreign doctors who spoke broken English and asked the same questions over and over.

Tristan came to see him, the day after Tony's funeral and it was a difficult protracted meeting. Not only would he miss a very loyal friend, but face to face with his grieving partner Daniel felt suffocated with guilt. Tristan said he wanted to stay on, stay in the caravan and keep an eye on everything. Mandy was still next door, and they seemed to have a strange rapport.

The only person Daniel seemed to have a rapport with was Pat. The nurses on the general ward constantly changed; some of them not very pleasant or sympathetic and the food was diabolical. Chef had brought him all kinds of stuff but he had no any appetite for anything, and spent a long time staring out of the window at the dark range of mountains. Beyond them somewhere not very far away was his hotel, falling into the lake. Troy said it wasn't that bad, mostly the front facade and the deck had taken the worst hit, and then the rest of the interior was just smoke damage.

Daniel had seen all the press coverage now.

The Doomed Crafnant Hotel fails again, was one of the headlines. Mia had managed to get her picture next to a decorative spiral of smoke, looking distraught and holding Cupcake squashed against her left boob.

Daniel said to Troy, 'Keep Bear *out* of the papers. Don't let him be interviewed. He might be recognised.'

'Bear?' Troy's face fell. 'Dad, don't freak out but I can't find him. He must have got spooked and run away. I've walked through the woods loads of times shouting him, carrying his jingle bone.'

'*Run away*?' Daniel said, horrified. 'Well keep shouting him! And take a bloody real bone. He knows the fucking difference!'

They argued about it, both knowing it was just a cover to let off steam, until the Sister in charge told them off. Troy said he didn't have the time to search for Bear, he was too busy with paperwork, the most important of which was sorting out the loss adjuster from the insurance company, and trying to get the old team up from Manchester to make the place secure before the winter. Then there was references and final pay to sort out for Chef, Sue and Anton, although none of them wanted to leave.

Sue had composed an apology from everyone with a huge bouquet for the daughter of the Welsh Food Board, and Victoria had pledged a free buffet for a future occasion. At least Aled and Tegan would have nice wedding pictures. Troy said he'd rescued Daniel and Tina's wedding album, and most of their personal effects from the rooms, although a lot of it was sopping wet.

The enormous, miserable job of what his son was doing, brought Daniel up short and he rubbed his eyes, 'Troy, I'm sorry. I don't know what I'd do without you.'

Troy licked his lips nervously. 'Is this a good time to ask if I can use some money to get a rented cottage or something? Me and Elle... Gran's like, it's driving us *nuts*.'

'Bring me the stuff to sign.'

'Nice one.'

As he was leaving, Daniel shouted him back, 'Troy! I'm so fucking proud of you,' he said, and everyone on the ward looked round.

*

Tina found the ward easily, but she hesitated, telling herself she was double checking to see if Victoria was there but according to Elle, Victoria was at some fancy food fair in Llandudno.

The majority of blame for the emotional fallout had moved around the triangle depending on Tina's mood. At first, she'd been happy to split it with Daniel but now it was all Victoria's glory, every last bit of it. It irked Tina that Victoria had seemingly got the easy deal out of all this mess. Not only did she escape the fire with nothing but a lot of sympathy, she neatly escaped Max and managed to hang on to Daniel. Even her bloody company was up for some food award.

Bitch. *Bitch.*

When she peered round the door he was all alone perched on the edge of the bed, earpieces in and staring at the floor. In the lifetime she'd known Dan, she'd never seen him look even close to vulnerable, but if she dwelled on the way it made her feel, then she might not make it down the ward.

She'd imagined, after seeing Daniel so unbearably ill in an intensive care unit, seeing him on an ordinary ward would be so much easier to bear. It wasn't. She leant back against the wall again in the corridor, and one of the nurses asked if she was all right. Thank God she hadn't brought Lily with her. At first they all thought it might give Daniel a boost, but the engineering of it was like a military operation. There was so much to carry, Tina didn't really want anyone to help her, then they couldn't park close enough to the entrance, and on and on the complications went.

Elle dropped her off in the end.

She had to be careful not to make him jump or turn too quickly, so Tina positioned herself directly in front of his face and put a hand on his shoulder. He snatched the earpieces out. 'Tee? ...I didn't know you were coming?'

Face to face, she couldn't find any words. She had plenty of stuff to tell him but something stuck in her throat and snatched her breath away. In a last ditch effort to hide it, Tina very carefully embraced him but he made the mistake of putting his good arm around her. Within seconds, she was blubbing into his neck, great shuddering gulps of tears which seemed to pour out of her like a never ending fountain. When she finally pulled away and sat next to him on the bed, she could see that at least, some of the tears were his. They talked about Lily then, because it was the only thing Tina could think of that wouldn't have them falling to pieces again but even that was touch and go. Inevitably, they got on to medical matters, and The Meadows Nursing Home. Tina had been twice, she'd wanted to forgive her father for all the bitterness in her heart over her mother's death, and although he'd listened to what she had to say, after ten minutes it became clear that her father wasn't entirely sure who she was. She said nothing of this to Daniel. 'Are they looking after him?'

'Yeah the place is nice. Thanks for all that, paying for it.'

'Tina, it's your money as well. *We're* paying for it,' he said, then 'I heard you didn't make that appointment.'

'Ah well, they'll send me another,' she said, with as much devil care less as she could muster. 'It's not a big deal. I'm fine, really.'

'You don't fool me,' he whispered, 'Not any more.'

*

Victoria bought him a new phone, with as many numbers pre-programmed into it as she could think of, except Tina's but Daniel knew that one anyway. She helped him with his dressing gown, put his good arm through a sleeve and pulled the rest of it around him, then they both sat on the edge of the bed and looked at the view. Snowdonia was starting to blush with autumn colour. In direct contrast below, the A55 was busy with rush hour traffic, car headlights streaming snail-like along the dark ribbon of road.

They didn't have much conversation, Daniel couldn't think of a thing to say to her sometimes, but he was unbearably grateful for the way she took time out of her busy schedule to just sit with him, her arm around his good shoulder, or his hand in hers. Despite the aborted wedding, the Celtic Catering Company was thriving and she had taken a commercial building on the industrial estate. Both Carys and Emily were working for her.

'I've more news,' she said, the day she brought the phone. 'Max is out on bail, pending trial for manslaughter.'

'So, where is he?'

'At his parents', in South Wales,' she said, her face shining, 'but the best part is, he's agreed to a divorce, and I'm moving back to The Old School House.'

Daniel was pleased, glad lots of positive things had come out of the ashes for her. It was what she deserved really. Somehow though, he couldn't express it as she wanted him to.

'Vic, I'm so sorry, love. I'm like this with everyone. In my head I'm shouting from the rooftops for you but in reality, I just feel numb and I can't think of the right words.'

'It's okay, I understand.'

Victoria was so gracious, even in the face of his naff dressing gown. She hugged him carefully and looked at him with unconditional love, like Bear.

The phone was a mixed blessing. He liked to listen to Lily gurgling down it, but if anyone called him when Coronation Street or Question of Sport was on, Daniel got extremely irritated. To the point where he switched it off and flung it across the bed. He knew he was getting depressed and institutionalised. Mentally he had nothing to stimulate his mind very much. Emotionally, nothing new went in or out. Physically though, something had changed, but not for the better. His persistent cough had turned distinctly sinister.

Sometimes there was blood, and the agony of it always left him gasping for breath.

'I don't like the sound of your breathing,' Doctor Williams said, 'I want you to have a bronchoscopy.'

'A what?'

'Don't worry, you'll be sedated.'

Daniel already felt fully sedated but chose not to respond. If his assumption was right, then he really didn't want a blow by blow account of the impending procedure. Having tubes forced down his swollen throat was not something he wanted to think about.

'You have mild pneumonia,' the Doctor said sagely, a couple of days later.

Daniel wished she hadn't put a medical name to it. It was just a bad cough before she came along with her stethoscopes and her oxygen masks. Didn't they think he had enough to contend with?

His collar bone and his ribs were still sore and the way he was strapped up meant he shuffled about like he was about ninety with severe arthritis, but at least he could make his own way to the bathroom. The first time he looked in the mirror and saw the tired, bearded face look back, Daniel couldn't stop staring at himself. Other than the loss of muscle tone, he looked like an undernourished arctic explorer, without the tan. Or the Husky, he missed the Husky.

*

Bluebell came to see him with the skinny fiddle player. He was called Jonathan Black, and he wanted to take Bluebell on tour with his band Seren Cymraeg, all over Europe. He said he'd look after her, and the old fashioned chivalry of that, was the first thing to swell Daniel's heart for months, and kick-start his sluggish emotions.

'I won't go if you don't want me to, Dad,' Blue said, looking at his oxygen mask with a frown. She'd brought him some music, an iPod loaded with her latest material, and all his favourite album tracks.

'Course I don't want you to go,' he said, and managed to grin at her crestfallen face, 'But I'm going to *make* you.'

'We'll be home for Christmas.'

'You'd better be,' he said, holding his girl in his arms. They were anxious to be away, and Jon clasped his hand briefly. Then they were walking backwards down the ward, Bluebell blowing him kisses. His kids were fantastic, the way they'd grown and evolved and it killed his despair, watered it down. He wanted to share that feeling. He called Tina and they talked about their little disjointed family, how much Troy had grown up.

'He's had a lot to deal with this year,' Daniel said, 'but he seems to be thriving on it.'

'Chip off the old block?' she said, and laughed. It lifted him, to hear her laugh.

Then it was all about Elle and Lily, and finally, Bluebell's tour. 'She called me,' Tina said, 'told me all about it.'

'Did she? Blue *called you?*'

'I think she's in love, Dan.'

When they ran out of safe, superficial things to talk about, Tina suddenly said, 'I gotta go babes, meeting some of the old crowd. They all send their love by the way... Dan?'

'Bye, love,' he said quietly, but he didn't move for long minutes, just looked dumbly at the handset, then stared through the window with the same blank expression, his thoughts racing one minute, stagnant the next. When he thought about it, and he'd had a lot of time to think, he could finally relate to Tina and her condition from a different angle, could understand a bit better that initial space she'd wanted. When he eventually turned around, Victoria was there. He wanted to ask how long she'd stood there, but her face told him.

'Hi,' she said, and she sounded forlorn. She dropped some books onto the bed, and put some fruit on the table. Her eyes locked on to his, and he could swear she knew what he was going to say, which made his heart race uncomfortably. He sensed her inevitability; it came off her in waves, washed over him like a cold restless sea.

'I need to talk to you.'

She helped him walk down the corridor, to a small outdoor courtyard with wooden seats around a broken stone fountain and gravel paths, sprouting weeds and dead daisies. They found a bench in the weak autumn sun and she pulled her little suede jacket tighter. She was trembling, and Daniel almost changed his mind, but he squeezed her hand and kissed it, tried to impart some humility. He'd wanted to wait till she was in a good place with the rest of her life, and he also needed to have the backbone to do it, and that had taken a long time, too long because of the accident.

'Vic, I've got to say something to you and I know you're not going to like it.'

Victoria simply closed her eyes and removed her hand from his.

'Dan please don't do this.'

'I don't think we should see each other,' he said, forcing the words out, 'I want us to finish.'

'You're just not yourself,' she began, '... after what you've been through.'

'No. No it's not that,' Daniel said quietly, 'this MS of Tina's. I've made a mistake.'

Victoria got to her feet, 'A *mistake*? Is that what I am?'

He could have explained that the feelings he had, it wasn't just lust, but it wasn't love either. It was something in-between, but God knows how that would come out of his mouth.

'I still love my wife.'

Time stood still.

For Daniel, the admission of the truth was immensely cathartic; it stripped back everything to a level that made better sense. The reasons he'd never loved anyone except Tina was probably buried too deep, and it went back years and years. The idea of exposing it all, picking over it to make a neat conclusion seemed pointless. He'd tried this route many times and failed, and so had Tina. Maybe this time though, he'd just simply failed and hit a brick wall.

'Vic? I'm so sorry,' he said to her back.

She stiffened, and her shoulders drooped. 'So, you're going back to Tina, is that it?'

'No, no it's nothing like that. I've totally messed up my marriage.'

'Because of me?'

'With rash decisions I guess, with being impulsive, and yes with you.'

'So, you've thought it all out?'

'I just want to be on my own. I wish it could be more interesting or original, but that's it.'

He hated the brutality of it, the finality, but it was honest, and that was the least she deserved. Without a backward glance, Victoria took a huge intake of breath and walked slowly back to the entrance. She slipped behind a door of frosted glass. Her blurry outline paused for a moment, then she was gone.

Daniel carried on sitting in his dressing gown in the cool air, looking at his slippers. His mother had tragic taste when it came to slippers but he stared at them until his teeth began to chatter and his broken ribs ached with the cold.

Love and hate were meant to be close, just a kiss apart.

Life and death were pretty close as well, just one breath away.

CHAPTER SIXTEEN

Marian collected him from hospital. Daniel made her stop the car outside the florists in Deganwy. There wasn't much choice, it being November, but the girl behind the counter was helpful. He wanted to write the card himself, and put it securely inside the envelope before his mother or the girl saw it.

Marian was itching to know who he was sending them to, but the hospital address gave it away. In the end he just wrote, 'Pat, sorry for all the swearing and moaning and stuff. Thanks for everything. I think you're fucking brilliant.'

He shuffled back to his mother's car and she carefully pulled the seat belt across him.

'That was a nice thing to do,' she said, 'send flowers to the nurses.'

'Just the one,' he said, then glanced at her profile. 'Not what you're thinking.'

'You don't *know* what I'm thinking.'

Daniel rolled his eyes, put his head back. Having nowhere else to go, and still needing help, he was resigned to convalesce with his mother. She couldn't wait to have him captive, feed him up and fuss round him. Daniel also had the feeling she was going to express an opinion about his love life at some stage. In the end, he'd not really wanted to leave hospital, which was strange and unexpected. The outside world, full of November rain seemed cold, dark and inhospitable.

Inside the bungalow, the central heating was on full blast.

Daniel lay across the chintz covered double bed in the guest room, and looked at the matching chintz lampshade on the ceiling. At least he had his own bathroom, and there was a portable television on top of the chest of drawers. In a way, its small containment, not requiring any effort or admiration was cocoon-like. He fell asleep fully clothed, and only woke when Marian began to briskly pull the curtains, shutting out the ridiculously overstocked, old fashioned garden, and the distant contrasting view of Conwy Castle ruins.

'Now, what shall we have for tea?'

'What is there?' Daniel said, hoping it was the correct response. His mother was a good cook, but it was proper home cooking in big quantities and his digestion was still struggling and delicate, suppressed with bland hospital food.

'I've made a cottage pie.'

'Whatever,' he said, and struggled to sit up.

'I could make something else.'

'What? I've said pie now!' Daniel sighed at her perturbed face. 'Help me get this shirt off will you, I want a shower.'

It was hard work, getting dressed and undressed all in one day. After the pneumonia, his collarbone injury had developed complications, with fractions of bone going AWOL, so it had taken longer than usual for his bones to become realigned. He had a complicated bandage which immobilised his right shoulder and prevented any sudden movement. And yet the physiotherapist had had him doing all kinds of rotating and extending with his right arm, within the limits of pain. He still had a big bag of tablets, mostly painkillers.

On top of all that, or probably because of it, Daniel had

no patience. He felt nauseous with any effort, depressed with his life and unable to cope with his mother's over emotional face. She was clearly shocked at the appearance of his torso, and struggled to understand the complexities of the support bandage.

'I don't think you should take it off, what if you slip in the shower?'

'I won't slip, there's fucking handrails *everywhere.*'

She sucked her breath in and looked at him with some of her old defiance, and Daniel knew he was on rocky ground. She turned the shower on for him, then disappeared into the kitchen and slammed a lot of pans about.

Ages later, he found her crying while she peeled carrots.

'It's just these onions.'

Daniel put his arms round her, 'Mum, come on I'm sorry.'

'No, no it's all right. It's just me being silly.'

'You're not silly,' he said resting his chin on top of her head, 'Well, sometimes you are.'

'It's just, well you nearly *died.*'

'I know, I know. But I *didn't*. I'm still here, causing you grief.'

She nodded into his chest, told him to get dry and put something on his feet. Daniel went dripping back into the bedroom but just sat on the bed in a state of inertia.

'Do you want cheese on top of the pie?' his mother shouted through to the bedroom. 'You always used to love that, cheese on top of the mash.'

Daniel wiped his eyes on the bath towel. 'Yeah, go for it.'

After a short silence she said, 'Why don't you think about booking a holiday? Get some winter sun.'

'Oh yeah like skiing maybe?'

He heard his mother make an exasperated sigh, 'Just *rest*, Daniel.'

So that meant sitting with a load of idle rich or a load of geriatric rich, somewhere in the Med, all by himself.

Mike brought his Porsche round for him and all the bags of stuff from Mike's old house. Troy had added to the collection with whatever spoils he could rescue from the hotel, including Daniel's leather jacket which stank like a smoked ham, a few pieces of clothing and the wedding album, water damaged but carefully dried.

'It's bloody great to see you, mate,' Mike said, humping all the bags and a case into his room, then handed him his car keys. They took up residence in the lounge, opened cans of lager and discussed the football results. Marian tutted at the beer, 'Is that a good idea?'

'Course. Good anaesthetic is this,' Mike said, and held the label for her to study. Marian said she was going to hang Daniel's jacket in the garage.

Mike brought Daniel up to date with Formula One, then it was the car industry and related subjects. 'Troy's been driving your car, *like* up and down the lake road, just to keep it running,' Mike said with a grin.

'Little bugger, he's not insured for that.'

'It doesn't look so bad up there you know, the hotel and everything.'

'I don't want to see it, not yet.'

Mike nodded thoughtfully. 'The house completed.'

'Yeah? So, where are you living?'

'Back at Mum and Dad's,' he said, pulling a face. 'Got some money but I don't know what to do, where to go. Might close the garage for a bit, go travelling, have a mid-life crisis.'

'If I was fit I'd come with you,' Daniel said, 'Take me months to get right though.'

'How long till you can drive?'

'Technically, twelve weeks. In reality it might be different.'

Daniel could feel his keys in his tracksuit pocket, digging

into his leg. It gave him a sense of freedom, suggested he could go anywhere, if he really wanted to, and if he knew where to go. Pat had said to him, 'The best advice I can give you is, if it hurts stop doing it.' Daniel wondered idly if that philosophy could be applied to other areas in his life.

Mike opened another can. 'I heard you dumped Victoria, was that your mid-life crisis?'

'Where did you hear that from?'

'Victoria must have told Charlie, he told Lin and Lin told me.'

'Has she told Tina?'

'Don't involve me in all that,' he said scathingly, then sighed. 'Oh okay, *probably.*' He frowned at Daniel's set face. 'Why the change of heart?'

'Victoria? It just got painful, so I stopped doing it.'

When Mike had gone he found his mother in the conservatory, Bluebell's Chihuahua on her lap, flicking through the wedding album with a soporific little smile. Daniel backtracked, lay back on the bed and thought about his conversation with Mike, more specifically about the grapevine gossip. He sent Tina a text, just saying he'd been moved from one prison to another, from high security, to an open one. Just so she'd know where he was. He watched the phone for twenty minutes, but she didn't respond.

*

A notable highlight of his recovery was accompanying his mother to the supermarket. It was full of Christmas tat and a scrawny Father Christmas collecting coins in a bucket. Daniel couldn't lift anything, and had to sit down at the checkout on the row of chairs reserved for the elderly and infirm while his mother took an age packing stuff and chatting to everyone in the queue, discussing the church flower rota and other sundry events and responsibilities she filled her life with. Daniel's progress was clearly avidly discussed, and a few of her queue buddies smiled and waved.

Linda rescued him. She appeared like a mirage, stole him away to the coffee shop and promised Marian she'd return him back home before he got overtired. Linda hugged him carefully, then made him sit down again while she went for the coffee. Daniel watched her from a distance, happy and confident with her life. She looked a bit slimmer, hair a bit lighter and shorter. Charlie was obviously good for her health and wellbeing.

'You look great,' he said when she finally sat down.

'Well thanks, but I have to return the compliment. The last few times I saw you, you were in your sick bed,' she said, stirring her latte. 'You look loads better. Have you heard about Barry Jones?'

'Only that he's been released from hospital and charged with manslaughter.'

She nodded, 'I think he broke your fall to a degree. Bitter sweet isn't it?'

Daniel stared into his espresso. 'So I've been told.'

'I don't visit Barbara anymore.'

'No?'

'She won't have me set foot in the house since I helped the police with their enquiries.'

Daniel frowned, 'How do you mean?'

He listened with macabre interest as Linda described Barry's old bedroom, the cigarette burns in the newspaper cuttings and the war games. 'Bloody hell, Lin, something else you kept to yourself.'

'Have you *still* not forgiven me, for keeping Tina's secret?'

'Yeah, course, course I have,' he said, and met her eyes. 'Have you seen her, Tina?'

'Yes,' she said, with a knowing look. 'Dan don't do this!'

'Do what?'

'Fish!'

He sat back in his plastic chair, 'Just concerned that's all, she's still my wife.'

'If you're talking about the MS she has her consultant meeting coming up.'

'When?'

'Dan,' she said patiently, 'if Tina wanted you to know, she would have told you.'

'Come on, Lin,' he said, his expression serious. Daniel could tell Linda was torn, hovering on the brink. 'I want to be there for her.'

When Linda played with the teaspoon, Daniel leant across the table. 'Lin, I *need* to know.' He watched as she drained her coffee, twisted her mouth with indecision, then fixed him with a stare. 'Okay it's this afternoon.'

Daniel got to his feet, '*Where? Come on, Lin.*'

'What are you *doing? Sit down!*'

He sat down reluctantly and she fixed him with a stare, 'What's got into you?'

But she didn't need a reply, not really. The answer was in his face, the answer had probably ripened on the grapevine, in fact the answer was already predetermined in the echelons of history.

Linda rolled her eyes, gritted her teeth. 'I could bang both your heads together!' She almost laughed and leant back in her chair. '*If* I tell you, I don't want you to go haring up there. You could just call her later, couldn't you?'

'I could.'

He got it out of her eventually, all the details. Linda drove him back to Marian's bungalow and stopped at the bottom of the drive behind Daniel's car.

'Have you driven it yet?' she said, stubbing out her cigarette.

'Round the block.'

'Dan, I know the path of true love never goes smoothly with you two, but you will be sensible won't you? I'm glad Charlie and I are off to Australia soon then I won't be in the line of fire.'

'Don't worry; it's always me in the line of fire.'

Before she could drive away, Daniel stuck his head through her wound down window.

'Say hi to Mia when you get to Australia, she's in the jungle doing I'm A Celebrity.'

'I know. Tina's run up a massive phone bill voting for her to eat the bugs.'

They exchanged a grin, then before Linda could close the window he put his hand on the top and talked through it sideways, 'Lin, have you seen Victoria?'

'No.'

'I'm thinking, she could maybe do with a friend.'

'You're priceless,' she said softly, and firmly wound the window up. Daniel gave her a nonchalant little wave, then blew a kiss as she pulled away.

He'd spoken to Victoria once since the awful break up at the hospital, but it was still too raw for her, and too confusing for him. She felt used, and Daniel blamed himself for that.

Once on the dual carriageway, Daniel put his foot down and felt the familiar thrill of driving the Porsche lift his spirits. Stevie Nicks was singing her heart out, filling the small space with her lyrical angst. His shoulder wasn't too happy but he chewed some codeine tablets and the adrenaline picked up the slack.

A year ago, Daniel had been ready to be married; a year ago he was ready to be a hotelier. A year on, he was both those things but only on paper, they weren't in his heart. No one could live like that. Pat had said the essentials of life were simple; having someone to love, having something to do, and something to look forward to. She was full of stuff like that, cheesy rubbish that made you cringe as she was saying it. Then for some unknown reason, it lodged in your brain and popped up again and had you actually believing it was all true.

His mother used to chant similar little wisdoms throughout his life, but Daniel had taken no notice. It had taken a near death experience to make him slow down and think more about his actions. More haste, less speed, that was Marian's favourite.

His mother had taken his leather jacket to the cleaners, and transferred the wedding pictures into a new album. It had surprised him, the way she'd been about the photographs, about a few things.

'Tina and I haven't always got on, but I have to say this,' she'd said holding his arms so he couldn't escape, 'You haven't been happy since the day she walked out back in Easter, the day of the launch.'

'I know.'

'There's a lot I didn't understand about her, still don't.'

'I know.'

She searched his eyes. 'Victoria wasn't right for you.'

'I *know.*'

And that was all Marian had to say on the subject. Other than Daniel was like his father. When he probed her on this, his mother said something about him needing a partner who epitomised a velvet fist in an iron glove. He wondered idly if that was Tina, it certainly didn't describe Victoria.

Daniel weaved through the slow traffic and picked up a few dirty looks. Daniel didn't care, he left them behind, watched the speedometer creep up, and turned the music up. He'd been hovering around a hundred miles an hour for about ten minutes before he picked up a police escort. The flashing lights in his rear-view mirror came first, followed by the siren noise. Daniel groaned and pulled over reluctantly. The two officers walked around the car, partly admiring it, but mostly kicking the tyres and trying to find something wrong before one of them leaned in the window.

'Where's the fire?'

Daniel ignored that with a wry grin. 'My wife is in hospital.'

'The way you were driving, will put us all in hospital. Step out the car please sir.'

One of them gave him a breathalyser test, whilst the other ran a pointless check on his number plate. The test was difficult because of the required lung capacity so he had to lift up his t-shirt and show them his injuries. It was raining and they were standing in a layby with heavy goods traffic straight off the Irish ferry zipping past, some of them sounding horns, or shouting out of the window. Most of the abuse was directed at the police, some of it at the Porsche.

They made him sit in the back of the police car. 'What's your wife's name?'

'Tina,' Daniel said, starting to feel weak and dizzy. He glanced at the clock on the dash and put his head in his hands. All he could visualise was his poorly wife, sat in the waiting room, alone and scared.

'Which hospital's she in?'

'Manchester General.'

The officers looked at each other and studied Daniel's white face. Something must have tipped the scales in his favour, or maybe since they'd seen his scars they'd presumed it was a life and death thing at Manchester General. In Daniel's head, it was.

'Here's the deal. Let's try and keep to the speed limit shall we?'

More haste, less speed.

They escorted him all the way at 69 miles per hour, then left him at the car park, which was completely full. After circling it three times, Daniel abandoned the Porsche up a steep grass verge, damaging a sapling and a no parking sign. He had no cash for the meter and he was late for Tina's appointment. Sweating with nerves and anxiety, it took him another twenty minutes to find the right room in the neurological department.

Daniel burst in, by then running on love and fresh air. Tina looked up and her mouth fell open. 'Oh my God! What the bloody hell are you doing here?'

It was a small stuffy room, and every single chair was full. Every single person turned and looked. Daniel thought he might pass out and Tina had to surrender her seat for him. It wasn't quite the heroic entrance he'd envisaged, him sat with his head between his knees. Tina fetched him a plastic cup of water and fanned him with Alright! magazine.

'What's that smell?' she said, wrinkling her nose, '...Like smoky bacon crisps?'

'It's this jacket.'

Daniel sat upright slowly and Tina threw the magazine down and folded her arms.

'Dan, why are you here?'

'I just want to be with you,' he said blankly, trying to catch hold of her hand, but she snatched it away. '*Be* with me? You've been with another woman!'

'You *made* me!'

Tina bared her teeth, like Cupcake did when she was warning Bear. 'Have you *any* idea how deranged you sound?'

The entire room fell silent with their eyes cast down, heads buried in books or playing with mobile phones. A couple of people showed a more obvious interest and actually closed up their reading matter and looked at them both expectantly. Daniel looked around the room furtively then lowered his voice. 'I don't *mean* that. What I really mean is I've come to support you, today. *Forever*, if you'll let me.'

'You're talking gibberish! You're in a worse state than me!'

'Kiss me and I'll recover.'

'Then what, do you turn into a slimy toad?'

Someone sniggered. Daniel got shakily to his feet and tried to make her sit down again but she wouldn't have it. 'Daniel, just go home. I don't want you here.'

Someone cleared their throat. 'Give him a break, love.'

Daniel was tempted to say he had one, several in fact.

When Tina's name was called, she looked around startled, but then glared at Daniel, daring him to follow her. Frustrated, Daniel stared at the grubby floor and wondered what the hell to do. He didn't feel up to driving the eighty miles or so back to North Wales. The guy next to him nudged his shoulder, his better one fortunately.

When he looked up, Tina was there again, holding out her hand to him and she looked distinctly more humble, even her lower lip was a tad twitchy. Someone voiced a sarcastic response and someone else slow clapped. Daniel was starting to feel like they were some sort of show for the NHS, developed to entertain the waiting rooms like they did for the queues in Disney World.

He scrambled to his feet and took hold of her hand, threaded his fingers through hers, then they walked wordlessly down the corridor, until they got to the door marked Mr R. Shepard, Consultant Neurologist.

Tina hesitated, 'I know what he's going to say, but I'm still freaking out inside.'

He crumpled her up in his arms and she didn't push him away. It was an awkward hold because of the strapping on his shoulder, and it was beginning to hurt, but there was a bigger ache in his heart. His wife felt so thin, even through her winter coat, and it tore him apart.

She pushed him away gently, and knocked on the door with her head bowed. It reminded Daniel of waiting outside the headmasters' room, waiting to be told off for changing the classical records in the music department to heavy metal, or necking during a serious assembly. This time though, it wasn't funny. It wasn't funny at all.

Mr R Shepard went through Tina's notes, while Daniel held her hand in his. He kept looking at her in profile, and although she remained calm and resigned on the surface, her nails were digging into his hand.

'Okay let's get the burning question out of the way,' the consultant said, looking directly at Tina, his manner professional, his face expressionless. 'I feel you have a primary progressive form of MS rather than the relapsing, remitting type.'

Daniel had no idea what he was talking about. He looked at Tina and her shoulders slumped slightly, 'So it's going to get worse?'

'I know that sounds frightening but it's not all bad news,' he said, tapping away on his keyboard. 'We found no lesions in the brain at all, just in the spinal cord, which is typical of this type.'

Tina said, 'So, I won't get massive attacks or anything really obvious?'

'No that's basically right. Your symptoms will remain subtle, and because the lesions are spinal, the problems will manifest themselves around that area, over a long period, I'm talking years.'

'Walking?'

'Uh huh.'

Daniel concentrated on the row of Christmas Cards across the windowsill, his mind all over the place, full of so many questions but scared of the answers. Tina talked about the drugs she was taking, and Mr R. Shepard listened politely and made adjustments to her prescription. 'Any questions?' he said eventually, 'Anything you want explained again, anything at all you want to ask me?'

Tina moistened her lips, 'Can I drive again?'

'I don't see why not. Just listen to your body, if you're feeling fatigue then no. You will need to inform the DVLA though,' he said, then made a point of acknowledging Daniel, 'Tina, you can manage this really well, and with the love and support you obviously have, so much the better.'

They both remained silent as they found their way out to the car park. Daniel's car had a parking fine notice flapping on the windscreen. He stuffed it in his pocket, and held the passenger door open for Tina, ignoring her mildly contemptuous expression as she clambered over the mound of muddy grass in her heels. Daniel reversed down the bank and the ornamental tree sprang upright. Tina stared straight ahead, with huge pensive eyes. 'I've had the worst year of my life,' she said.

Daniel nodded; he would have been more than happy to lose all their combined hospital drama. He leant across and kissed her cheek, 'There's still three weeks to turn it around.'

She looked as if she might cry, then put her head back and closed her eyes.

At the flat, he followed her in awkwardly, watched her make tea and sandwiches.

'I wanted to do that,' he said.

'I'm making these for *you*. Go and sit down before you fall down,' she said, giving him a little push, 'you're as white as a sheet.'

Daniel went in the sitting room and threw himself across the sofa. It felt strange being in the flat, a bit like he'd come home after living in a parallel universe or woken from a long dream. All their familiar belongings were scattered about, all the history and memories that made up the unsteady, towering layer cake of their relationship, school pictures of Troy, a new one of Lily.

Their son rang; the exasperating, funny, affectionate product of their union. He was so like his mother, not a bad bone in his body, and with some of Daniel's manual skills and enthusiasm. Basically, they'd made a comedian with a hammer. Tina chatted away to him, 'I'm all right. No, it's okay your dad's here, yes I know he shouldn't have driven all this way,' she went on, fixing Daniel with a stare.

Daniel forced himself to eat. After a while Tina said, 'What are you going to do about the hotel? Troy wants to start again but he says you've not even been near the place.'

Daniel shrugged, 'Dunno. I haven't got the mental energy, let alone anything else.'

'Let Troy do it, he's bored, Dan.'

'He's too young. He thinks he knows everything, but he doesn't.'

'Get a manager then,' Tina said, opening a packet of biscuits. 'Why can't you start again? Don't you want to be an hotelier?'

'It wasn't the same without you,' he said gruffly.

'Too late for this conversation,' she said, and looked into her mug.

'But not too late for us? Tee, what if I spent twenty percent of my time as an hotelier, and you filled in the rest?'

'What does that mean?'

'We live here again, just went to the hotel at weekends and see to Lily.'

Her head shot up when he mentioned Lily, but she gave him a dark look, 'We both know it wouldn't be like that.'

'It could be!'

'Dan, you don't know what compromise is!'

'I've just said it haven't I?'

'You'd be bored with my steady existence.'

'I like the sound of a steady existence.'

'That's only because of your injuries. When you get strong again you'll be like a pacing lion looking for the next project, filling the flat with stress and yelling down the phone.'

'I've got to do *something* with my life. That proves I haven't changed because of the money, I don't know how you can say that.'

'No okay,' Tina said and studied her nails. After a short silence she met his eyes. 'What went wrong with Victoria?'

Daniel knew this was the big one and wondered how to put it. He went boldly for the truth as usual. 'I tried to fall in love, but I couldn't, *didn't*. When you told me about the M.S, I felt cheated somehow. It all fell to bits after that.'

'I pushed you away for the best reasons.'

'Very noble of you,' Daniel said, watching her expression. She began to collect up the cups and plates, 'Are you driving home?'

'No. Can't face it.'

'Spare room?'

'I'm getting to be an expert in spare rooms,' he shouted through to the kitchen. 'Maybe that's why I feel like a permanent spare part!'

At least he got a break from the chintz. He rang his mother and told her where he was, as if he were about fourteen. Tina helped him run a bath.

Daniel watched his man parts bobbing about in some expensive bubble bath for half an hour, but he had to shout Tina again because he couldn't get out. 'Bloody hell, Dan, I can still see some bruising,' she said, and went through the bathroom cabinet looking for Ibuprofen because he hadn't thought to bring painkillers. All he'd thought about was getting to the hospital for her. Now, he just felt a burden, instead of the manly shoulder to cry on he'd so wanted to be. He wanted her to need him, just as much as he needed her, or was it all just blind hope? She hadn't been the one alone and scared in the waiting room, it was him.

Later, he lay wide awake and listened to her in the kitchen, locking the door, switching the dishwasher on. Then she came up the stairs, closed the bedroom door and for a while he could hear her pulling open the drawers in the dressing table, hanging her necklace on the mirror. The chink of light disappeared under the door and every fibre in his body was screaming for rest, but there was no way he was going to sleep. He shrugged the duvet off, padded across the landing and pushed the bedroom door open. It creaked slightly, as it had always done. 'Tee, you awake?'

She threw the bed covers back, like an invitation to a small child who'd had a nightmare. When he lay beside her, they both knew it wasn't a pretext to anything sexual. In a way, it went beyond anything quite so easily expressed or presumed.

Daniel found her hand. Eventually he said, 'I just wish you hadn't shut me out, with the MS. If I'd *known*...'

'I know, but at the time it was all mixed up with everything else, my own denial I guess. My doubts about the hotel, and then, when it got serious I wanted to give us both an escape route,' she said patiently, sadly. 'And you found one really fast, with Victoria.'

'Victoria just ended up being the scapegoat for our failings! You can't blame me for *all* the fallout.'

'I know that too,' she sighed. 'But for us to be together again I'd still have to get past Victoria in my head, do a massive U turn on everything I'd told myself.'

Daniel stared at the ceiling, determined to get all his feelings out, 'I'm sorry. I'm sorry for not listening, and I'm sorry for the mess with Victoria, I really am. The MS doesn't make *any* difference to how I feel about you. You're my wife and I *love* you.'

'It's just pity.'

'It's *not* pity!'

She seemed to ignore his emotion, remained stubbornly reflective. 'It's changed me you know, having this disease. It's made me stronger in some ways, made me face stuff and deal with it,' she said, 'I've learnt I can actually live without you, for the first time in my life.'

'But do you *want* to?' he said, feeling her love draining away like sand. 'I've learnt that I *can't*,' he said vehemently,

'I can't imagine a future without you in it.' Daniel looked at her pale shining hair fanned out on the pillow next to him. 'I'd do *anything* to fix us.'

'I'm not sure it's fixable, I reckon we've got a relapsing, remitting kind of love.'

Daniel lay listening to the heavy rain and sleet outside, but he must have slept eventually. And then when he woke in the early hours of the morning, it was to find Tina firmly entwined around him, as if she'd tried to soften all their hurts and confusion with plain body language. It was typical of her. No matter how much she'd screamed at him during the day, she could melt away any lingering anger in an instant with her laugh, or her embrace. Daniel inhaled the scent of her and fell into a deep dreamless sleep in her arms.

CHAPTER SEVENTEEN

The following afternoon, after sleeping till past midday Daniel found himself alone. There was a scrawled note from Tina, propped on the mirror. *'Sorry babes had to go to the docs and stuff. You were out cold. Don't wait for me, be ages. Drive slowly eh?'*

It ended with a standard declaration of love and a kiss, but it still felt like a snub.

Daniel drove home slowly through a miserable curtain of sleet.

So that was that.

They hadn't discussed anything practical but the thought of going through a divorce was unbearable, unthinkable. The only comfort had been in laying his soul bare, because then at least he knew he couldn't have done any more. However, the thoughts which had finally come to fruition about the hotel had at least distilled a clear path of action. He had to face the fact he wasn't fit enough to take back the role he'd had, and it was counter-productive to do nothing at all. The hotel would just fall to bits like the rest of his life, and that seemed a pointless waste, an admission of defeat, and it would take everyone else down with it, the people he cared about. Barry Jones and Max Morgan and all the sceptics would claim the biggest victory.

Instead of going back to his mother's bungalow, Daniel

carried on driving. It was real snow, closer to the mountains, and traffic slowed down through the slush on the roads, but he was in no hurry this time. He went across the bridge towards Conwy, past the castle then down the familiar valley road, past the still empty Wisteria House, and finally came to the right handed turn to The Lakeside Hotel.

Closed for refurbishment, the sign said.

Daniel steeled himself at the top of the lake and prepared himself to see the gaping charred hole the fire must surely have left, like the one inside his guts. It had destroyed not only his dreams but almost his life. He drove slowly along the lakeside, concentrating on the slippery road. The intense light and colour of the summer had gone, leaving a mostly monochrome vista of water and sky. The cold silence was strange, after the heat and noise of the wedding party. It seemed a lifetime ago, not just three and a half months. As he drew closer he could see the wooden facade of the building in more detail. It was a mess, propped up like himself with a confusion of scaffolding and flapping tarpaulin.

But he needn't have worried about the impact.

The snow had softened it all with a new blanket. The burnt trees, although damaged and black beneath their mantle still marched along the white horizon, and gave the impression of winter hibernation like all the other trees. If he was a true Celt, or just feeling fanciful, he'd maybe see some kind of parallel there.

He didn't see the dog at first. It blended into the landscape as well, like a white Husky would. Daniel almost skidded into him as he limped across the road. He stopped the car and got out as quickly as his debilitated body would let him.

'Bear!'

The dog stopped in his tracks, turned at his voice and came slowly towards him, head down, tail wagging apologetically, dragging himself along. He was in a pitiful state, thin and wet. Daniel got the picnic rug out of the boot, spread it over the passenger seat and manhandled the dog in, but the effort took everything out of him, and Daniel climbed back in the car in much the same state as the dog.

Bear hunkered down, licking his hand as Daniel rested his head on the steering wheel.

'Look at the mess we're in,' he said, stroking the dog's damp ears. 'Where you been eh?'

The dog was apathetic, its pale eyes drooping and despondent. Daniel turned the heater up and soon, the car stank of wet Husky and smoky bacon crisps. It was strangely comforting.

In Deganwy, his mother wasn't happy about the dog being in the bath, but Daniel suspected the Husky was none too keen either. Marian shampooed him with her over sixties colour enhancing lotion for naturally grey hair, then rinsed him with the shower head. Daniel couldn't do much to help, but sat lost in thought on the closed toilet seat. His mother gave him a hard time about all the driving he'd done and shot him an exasperated glance.

'I'm not going to ask, about Tina. How, why, where or what?'

'Fine... good!'

'Shall I put some conditioner on him, do you think?'

'Go on then. Make him all soft.'

When Bear was rinsed off again and towel dried, Daniel sat on the bedroom floor and finished the job with the hair drier. The dog sat quite majestically through this, his eyes half closed, as if he were having a blow wave at Vidal Sassoon. Any minute now, Daniel thought, he'd hold out his claws to be filed and polished. If Tina was here, she'd do it anyway just for a laugh.

'I expect you both want feeding now,' his mother said, mopping the bathroom floor. The dog pricked its ears. Clean and dry, Bear ate a warmed up leftover casserole, plus all the spare Chihuahua food they had. Daniel suspected he might have eaten the actual Chihuahua if Cupcake hadn't retreated into his mother's wardrobe, disgusted with the latest developments.

'I mean, I'm sure you'd say... wouldn't you? If you and Tina *were* back on,' his mother said, wringing out a cloth and throwing it in the sink. She poked her head round the bathroom door. 'You were gone a long time.'

A long waste of time, Daniel thought.

His whole life had been one long waste of time.

*

His time was gradually filled again, predominantly with a lot of mundanities. On the plus side, he was recovering physically and felt motivated enough to talk to the staff, what was left of them. Sue pounced on the manager's job with no hesitation whatsoever, and began to draw up an action plan. Order of works, advertising, recruitment and top of the list the staff Christmas party.

Daniel held a meeting in the pub to announce the rebirth of The Lakeside. Chef and Anton, Mandy and Tristan were all more than happy to be reinstated.

Troy punched the air, an inane grin on his face. 'Hey Dad, I thought of renaming the bar like, The *Phoenix*. What do you reckon?'

'I reckon you should get a round of drinks in.'

The provisional opening date was set somewhere towards the end of January. The staff Christmas party was set the day before his first wedding anniversary, but everyone seemed to have forgotten about that. It was also his forty-second birthday but no one really knew about that either, except his mother. Marian said, 'Lovely, we can have a double celebration.'

'That makes you Sagittarius,' Elle said, looking in the

back page of Alright Magazine.

Troy pulled a face, 'What's one of those?'

'An optimistic centaur with philandering ways,' Elle said, 'They fire arrows everywhere, and gallop about searching for the truth. Have you *never* seen one?'

'Yeah, course I have.'

'I don't want any fuss,' Daniel said, watching Troy Google something on his phone. Elle plonked Lily on Daniel's lap, 'Well you're gonna get it Granddad, whether you want it or not.'

Troy's face slowly dawned with realisation. 'I *know* when you're winding me up, Elle!'

'No, you so *don't*. You have to check.'

*

Victoria told herself she wasn't remotely interested in the refurbishment of The Lakeside Hotel. Even so, she found herself drawn to the article in the local press with a slightly cynical smile. Filling the espresso machine with water, she made some strong coffee. Then she took the cup and the paper into the conservatory, where she smoothed out page five onto the glass table.

She took a moment to consider that twelve months ago, she'd done the very same thing. She crossed to the French windows to look at the green, damp garden. She'd had the ancient trees cut back a little, allowing more light to flood the lawn and she'd ripped all the moss and vegetation from the statue, exposing her hopeful face and her poor chipped, stone heart to the world. This new vision of Aphrodite holding out her hands to catch the winter sun was so much braver than the old one. Her ivy blinkers gone, she was the epitome of truth laid bare.

Daniel had not once said he'd loved her. Not once. What

was that awful saying? Better to have loved and lost? Victoria turned to page five and read the feature then pushed the paper into the log maker in the formal sitting room and felt a certain measure of satisfaction in crushing all the words, ready for burning.

*

On December 15th the pub in Deganwy was full of Christmas parties, and The Lakeside party took the biggest table they had. They were all there, the old staff line up and his family, but Daniel felt distinctly subdued.

He should be feeling brighter by now, surely? He knew why he didn't. He'd not even had a two-worded text, let alone a phone call or a card from Tina. She couldn't have forgotten it was his birthday surely? Not that it mattered, not really.

The champagne went round the table and Daniel looked at all the happy faces, other than Chef and Anton who were already having a heated argument about the basting, trussing and roasting of festive poultry. Sue and Marian were in conversation about a new rota for the reception and Elle was trying to pull together the back of Mandy's glittery dress where the zip had stuck, with the aid of a huge nappy pin. Troy was cradling Lily on his lap, blowing raspberries on her tummy until Elle told him to stop because it sounded disgusting at the table.

No Victoria of course, so that meant no Emily, and Carys seemed to have deserted them for the other camp as well. It was okay, he was pleased she had support, pleased she was doing so well to the degree she didn't need the hotel passing on any work.

No Tony.

Daniel had spent a lot of time watching Tristan, knowing he was putting the smiles on for everyone else's benefit. He felt he ought to make some kind of gesture but he didn't quite know what yet. Elle forced a paper hat on Daniel's head and put a glass in his hand. He checked his messages again. Nothing.

Troy stood up and tapped the side of his glass. He had three pink balloons tied to the back of his head. Someone must have blown up the two round ones very carefully because they resembled wrinkled testicles. The sausage shaped one in the middle was overblown and bobbed up and down. Sue said it was childish so Anton popped it with the wire off the champagne cork and everyone groaned.

'Right, Dad we got a bit of a surprise for you,' Troy said, rubbing the back of his head.

'I don't like surprises,' Daniel said automatically, feeling his heart hammering. Everyone turned to look and Daniel watched the entrance, his mouth dry.

And it was a good surprise, it was.

It was Bluebell, back from tour with Jonathan skinny legs. For a while they both stole the show with their loved up effervescence. They were full of funny stories of foreign travel in a transit van across Poland, but no one minded. Welsh Star was declared The Lakeside's resident band and everyone clapped, sent up the party poppers. Then it was another round of drinks.

Food was ordered.

Daniel asked Troy who the empty seat was for at the opposite end of the table. 'Oh, I tried to get hold of Mike but he couldn't make it,' he said dismissively.

'Mike? He's gone bloody backpacking in the Med. I *told* you.'

'Did you? Dad, take a chill pill will you?'

Just after the starters, his phone rang and Daniel leapt up, without looking who it was.

'Sorry got to take this,' he said, like some big hot shot businessman.

It was Linda, calling from Australia. 'Happy Christmas birthday!' she said, 'It's early morning here so I'm sorry if this isn't a good time?'

'No, it's okay,' Daniel said, wandering outside to the car park. He needed some air, needed to take a few deep breaths. There was a pergola reserved for smokers. Daniel sat on the picnic bench and looked up at the fairy lights threaded through the ivy covered trellis.

'Got to just tell you this, Charlie and me are engaged! How mad is that?'

He agreed it was mad. His friends could call him from the other side of the world, but his wife couldn't send him a text from Manchester. They talked about the heat in Oz and the snow over Lake Crafnant.

Daniel saw the car then, reversing in a wonky line, narrowly missing Chef's restored VW. Even in the shadowy gloom of the evening, the shocking pink was impossible to miss. Tina climbed out of the passenger door, dropping her keys and then something out of her handbag. She walked towards him, his beautiful crazy wife. Her big grey astrakhan coat, the one he'd bought her last year, was draped lopsidedly over her shoulders and beneath that was the black dress she'd worn for their wedding party. Daniel got slowly to his feet, his shirt flapping in the keen sea breeze. His paper hat blew away, but he'd forgotten it was there.

'Dan?' she said, 'What are you doing out here? You must be freezing like that! I'm supposed to make an *entrance*. Troy, he's got it all planned.'

For long seconds Daniel couldn't speak. Linda was still shouting in his hand, her voice sounding very far away. Probably because she was, she was in Australia. But Tina wasn't far away any more, she was there. Right there in front of him, all dressed up for his birthday.

'Happy Birthday, babes,' she said softly, and touched the side of his face. Daniel only had to turn slightly to kiss the palm of her hand. He caught hold of her more firmly, in case she blew away like the paper hat.

'Tee, you *drove* here?'

'Yep, I did,' Tina said, looking back at the Mini as if she didn't quite believe it herself. 'Sorry I'm so late, I went really slow,' she said, and she still seemed nervous, kept flicking her eyes on and off his, then she looked up at the fairy lights, and her eyes reflected all of their sparkle, 'You know what tomorrow is?'

'I know what tomorrow is.'

'Fancy doing it all again? I mean, just saying the words, just the two of us?'

'Only if I can reinstate *obey*.'

'Not a chance,' she said, smiling. 'Dan, before we go inside, I want to say something, there's so *much* I want to say to you.'

'I don't need to hear it,' he whispered, and bent to kiss her. His wife slid her arms around him and the way she looked into his eyes, it was like being brought back to life.

THE END

Jan lives in Snowdonia, North Wales, UK.

This ancient, romantic landscape is a perfect setting for Jan's fiction, or just day-dreaming in the heather. Jan writes contemporary stories about people, with a good smattering of humour and drama, dogs and horses.

For more about Jan Ruth and her books:
visit www.janruth.com

WILD WATER

BY
JAN RUTH

Jack Redman, estate agent to the Cheshire set.
An unlikely hero, or someone to break all the rules?

Wild Water is the story of forty-something estate agent, Jack, who is stressed out not only by work, bills and the approach of Christmas but by the feeling that he and his wife Patsy are growing apart. His misgivings prove founded when he discovers Patsy is having an affair, and is pregnant.

At the same time as his marriage begins to collapse around him, he becomes reacquainted with his childhood sweetheart, Anna, whom he left for Patsy twenty-five years before. His feelings towards Anna reawaken, but will life and family conflicts conspire to keep them apart again?

CDIDNIGHT SKY

BY
JAN RUTH

Opposites attract? Laura Brown, interior designer and James Morgan-Jones, horse whisperer - and Midnight Sky, a beautiful but damaged steeplechaser.

Laura seems to have it all, glamorous job, charming boyfriend. Her sister, Maggie, struggles with money, difficult children and an unresponsive husband. She envies her sister's life, but are things as idyllic as they seem?

She might be a farmer's daughter, but Laura is doing her best to deny her roots, even deny her true feelings. Until she meets James, but James is very married, and very much in love, to a wife who died two years ago. They both have issues to face from their past, but will it bring them together, or push them apart?

Made in the USA
Charleston, SC
20 January 2014